The Ocean Callings
by
Ruby

Published by Ruby

GW00801684

An open heart truly feels life.

Insight:

'They're us and we're them. There will never be a time when the two tribes will not be drawn to one another - that is our curse, our burden and our secret.'

CHAPTER 0
The Resonation
1834

A bizarre humming filled the air and swirled about the remote Scottish village of Gardenstown - she was searching. The villagers purposely avoided discussion, glanced at each other knowingly and scurried to the safety of their grey, stone cottages. Trouble was brewing, she would have her wrath and the culprit would die - it was inevitable.

CHAPTER 1
The fluid motion.
June last year.

The waves that crisp morning peeled elegantly towards the shore. Rainbows danced amongst the salty spray. The undulating motion of the scarlet-tinged ocean drowned out her subtle call. Her love was unaware he had chosen her and that she had accepted.

Marty, wearing dark jeans and a green hoody, stood at the edge of the cliff top, gazing down at the sea with his arms folded. The smell of damp grass and seaweed wafted on the same breeze ruffling his dark, wavy hair. With a quick flick, he swept a few wispy strands behind his ear and continued to dither. Should he go in? The thought of climbing into a damp wetsuit at that time of the morning was enough to turn anyone off! Rubbing his tired eyes, he was consumed in his usual shall I or shan't I routine. After picking fluff off the arm of his hoody, he shuffled towards Bertha, his camper van, turned back and paused. Was that a woman swimming?

Out to sea an enormous set of waves rose on the horizon. The unsuspecting swimmer maintained her rhythmic crawl. Surely she would notice. The rolling waves gathered momentum as they pursued her and prepared their weighty descent.

"Bollocks!" he muttered under his breath. With a jolt, he tore down the rickety staircase, navigated the slippery cockle-crunching shoreline and broke into a sprint on the compacted sand.

The first wave towered above the girl.

"You need to come in," shouted Marty, waving frantically from the beach.

With the repetitive crawling rhythm, the swimmer did not break her routine. Instead, she continued oblivious to the rising ocean walls. With a sense of helplessness, Marty watched the wave peak, tumble and crash down. She was gone.

He waited for some indication of her location. Nothing. With a glare at the water, he gritted his teeth. Why did it always happen to him? In aggravation, he kicked off his flip-flops and waded into the shallows. The froth of the first wave roared towards him. He dived and surfaced. Sucking in a lung-full of air, he submerged intending to swim beyond the break. As he swam, he urgently searched for even a hint of her presence. There was nothing. Surfacing for another breath, a huge wave rose above him. Marty gazed up at the glistening, fluid wall and ducked back to the churn beneath. Could he see hair or seaweed? The circling ocean motion spun his athletic physique into an area of calm where a peaceful figure was suspended. With a mass of golden hair drifting in all directions and mischievous glint in her eye, she smiled. It was her!

His heart pounded as the air slowly evacuated his lungs. As he sunk, he gazed at the beautiful creature knowing he had to surface. With a strong kick, his survival instincts overrode his desire to stay. Full of curiosity, she followed him, circled and silently peered into his soul. She emitted a gentle hum that tingled through his veins. He had to surface! With an amused expression she radiated the feeling of love.

With the expression of confusion, he touched his heart.

She smiled and radiated again.

Butterflies tingled in his gut.

He was mesmerised. He desired to stay.

4

CHAPTER 2
Connection.

The ache of desperation shot through him. The instinctual throb of survival drove him as he clutched at the water and frantically struggled to the surface. With a massive gasp, he filled his lungs and Crash! The tumbling wall of water cast him into an uncontrollable spin. After a number of rotations, the bubbling froth spewed him into the breaking zone. Taking in as much air has he could, he urgently dived. Aiming at the shore, he cleared the underwater stir and arrived at calm water. Where was she? Was she even alive? What had just happened?

With the awareness of yet another set forming, he scanned the break for signs of her. What should he do? His mind constructed the limited information whilst his body bawled the need for warmth. Patches of dark red sun reflected on the green water like poppies on grass. Should he go ashore? If he went to find help, she could drown. If he didn't, she could also drown.

After four strokes to shore, he paused. Why was there no one to tell him what to do? He was only nineteen, why did things like that keep happening to him? 'It' had happened to his father only six months previously. 'It' could happen to anyone. Had 'it' just happened to her?

Marty wiped his nose, his gut 'said' find help – he had to learn to follow his gut and stop thinking all the time. "Think about not thinking?" he had asked the councillor.

"Your endless thinking is what gives you the headaches. You need to find a way to be in the moment. You can't spend twenty hours a day staring at a computer screen to avoid feeling. You need to spend time in reality," she had said.

The memory fractured as the new set of waves travelled elegantly towards him. "Bloody reality!" he muttered. He reached into a lesser wave and body surfed towards the shore. He needed to find help.

Behind the wall of water, Marty caught a glimpse of a shadow travelling at the same rate as the wave. Rotating onto his back, he attempted to gain a better look. It was gone. As he drew close to the

5

shore, the underwater girl bothered him. Why wasn't she frightened? How could she hold her breath for so long?

Consumed in analysis, Marty waded through the shallows. At first he didn't notice the subtle resonation, but the sound intensified and begged attention. He came to a halt and stood scanning the area. Something was calling but there was nothing there. Was it the beginnings of another headache? The sound penetrated his mind and pulsated in his heart. The more he searched, the more the sound circled and spiralled. Splash! In the distance, a shape broke the surface and disappeared. He stood squinting at the shifting shapes of the waves and swayed with dizziness.

The water became motionless but the resonation remained. To Marty's left, the girl rose from the ocean but only revealed her shoulders. She ventured tentatively closer, smiled in amusement but studied him seductively.

Marty was transfixed. Her rusty, wet hair contrasted with her pale, clear skin. The glowing green eyes were stunning! She looked like a pre-Raphaelite painting – like Ophelia. The bare skin and the curve of her neck hinted at nakedness. Yet her hair conveniently covered anything obvious. Still he couldn't help but gawk.

The girl gazed at him in a sensual manner with her chin down and a certain glint in her eye.

The resonation pulsated like a heartbeat.

The radiating love warmed him. He stepped forwards.

She jerked away.

"I won't hurt you," he said softly.

She remained silent but blinked; her eyelids moved sideways.

Marty fought a frown but was inquisitive.

She ventured closer and gazed into his eyes. The way she looked softened him. With the pounding hum of a heartbeat, she reached out and touched his hand. A spark of blue light travelled across the surface of his skin. A tingle of warmth travelled through his whole body and burst into his heart. With a gasp, he threw his head back and dropped to his knees in the shallows. He was helpless as the moment expanded. For the first time in a long time he could 'truly feel!'

The resonation increased, the radiation tingled and the rhythm of the ocean overwhelmed him. She had penetrated the depths of his soul. They were connected.

CHAPTER 3
Ripples

"Marty what on earth are yer doing?" called a strong Scottish accent.

Marty glanced over his shoulder, which broke the spell.

Danny, Marty's seventeen-year-old housemate, waved.

Urgently Marty turned back but the girl was gone. A ripple remained on the surface with a circle of fading blue light. *Shit!*

With a flurry of sun-streaked, strawberry-blonde hair and a smattering of freckles underlining his pale, grey eyes, Danny strapped his surfboard leash to his leg. He glanced at Marty and frowned. "What yer doing swimming in yer clothes?"

Danny, at the grand height of five foot six, was smaller than your average seventeen-year-old but made up for it in character. He was born and bred in Banff; he was shy until you knew him well but then he was the cheekiest blighter around. His random thoughts were famed, "if yer did ney chew spaghetti then how would it come out the other end?" Was one unfortunate comment that would haunt him from the age of thirteen.

"So why yer wearing yer clothes in the ocean then?" Danny asked again.

"I thought someone was drowning," Marty replied, scanning the ocean.

"I bet it was a seal," said Danny. "It's always a seal."

Marty frowned, "no it wasn't a seal."

"So what was it then?"

"Don't worry about it," Marty said with a shrug.

"Go get yer wetsuit on and we can go for a surf. That's unless yer want to surf in yer clothes." Danny's particularly cheeky grin always meant trouble. Wind-up time had most definitely arrived.

"I reckon a wetsuit would be better." Marty wringed his sodden clothes, "I'll be back in a sec," he said, turning towards the harbour wall.

Danny watched his friend faffing about, "what's bothering yer Marty?"

"Nothing."

"Is it yer dad again? Or the over-thinking thing?"

Marty shook his head.

"Have the nightmares calmed?"

Marty waded up the beach. "I'll be back in a bit..."

"You know one day you will feel better..." Danny launched onto his board. "I'll see yer out there... We can continue to avoid grown-up conversation all yer like!"

Once Marty was in his wetsuit, he launched himself onto his board and paddled out back. He sat silently watching the waves for a while but 'felt' strange. "Danny... This place... It's got a lot of legends hasn't it?"

"Aye, loads."

"Anything about people and the sea?" he asked.

"A few... Actually, most of them are about sea witches or women who used to swim out to save pirates from shipwrecks. Actually... There are loads about pirates. Why?" Danny observed his friend's peculiar expression. "What's going on?"

"Just interested. We've only been here a few weeks and I don't really know much about the place. Plus, legends are interesting," he said trailing his hand through the water.

"Oh there's plenty to learn, but I thought you were supposed to be emptying your brain - ney filling it," said Danny.

"I was told not to sit in front of a computer working. I am sure I can hear a few legends. That's hardly thinking is it?" he replied rubbing his chest.

"I thought yer were told to try and 'do' nothing Marty!"

"Have you tried doing nothing? Do you know how difficult it is?"

"Difficult for some an' easy for others... Well if yer insist we can go and see me gran at some point and she will tell yer story after story," said Danny. "Oh and she'll feed yer home-made shortbread too. Mmmm."

"Shortbread... Mmmm lush!" said Marty thoughtfully, as he traced his finger over the connection point.

Danny watched his friend, "you know, Marty – if I was yer doctor I would prescribe yer some fun. Yer need to live a little and have new experiences then yer would ney spend yer time thinking. Yer really can be quite grown up. What about just letting go?"

"Set coming," said Marty, nodding towards the rising walls of water.

"Always a distraction, Marty… Now race yer," said Danny paddling full speed.

Marty shook his head and followed – he was such a grub! Marty quickly caught up and once the wave lifted, flicked himself to standing. The pair glided up and down the wall of water, absorbed in the cool liquidity of the transparent element.

"Look… Shana and Johnny are on their way out," said Marty riding off the back of the wave.

"Marty!" Shana called eagerly, with her excitable Irish accent. Shana was tomboyish, athletic and full of spirit. She wore her raven hair high and tied back. Her sharp, blue eyes showed a distinctly astute demeanour. Her eagle-like observation scrutinised people's behaviour. She never missed a thing or commenting on it. Marty liked her brutal honesty. He always knew where he stood with her – even if it wasn't favourable. He had never had that with any other girls, especially ones who were just eighteen.

"Marty, you were out early this morning," she said, being drowned out by a wave.

"Just after some quiet time," he replied.

"Well, now yer got the whole gang. It will hardly be quiet now will it Marty? Shame about that, eh?" she said, flicking some water in his direction.

Johnny Boy, at twenty-three, was the oldest of the group. A Celtic tattoo scribed over the right side of his face drew attention away from his freckles, or maybe even joined them. He was solid, brash and for his own entertainment wore red lifeguarding trunks with long socks. No one else ever got it but that was Johnny all over. He was his own person in his self-amused world.

"Shana get your arse on a wave!" he said. "That's unless you're going to flounder about like a wee girl."

"Ach shut it Johnny! I AM a girl," she said, rolling her eyes.

"Come on Shana, you know it's about physique. I'm a hunter and you're a gatherer," he said flexing his biceps.

Shana shook her head. "Ah? Gatherer eh? I t'ink youse should be careful what yer say, kilt boy!"

"Hardy, Ha, Haaa!" he laughed flatly.

With a glance at the horizon, Shana noted the next set was on its way. Johnny seized Shana's board.

"Johnny!"

He held her there whilst grinning mischievously.

"Will you let me go? Next ones mine. Ladies first and all that!" she said, prizing herself from Johnny's grip. As she paddled, she glanced over her shoulder and gave Johnny a filthy look. Johnny trailed behind like a pet dog.

"He so fancies her," said Marty, with a raised eyebrow.

Danny was quiet as he watched her catch the wave.

With a swift paddle Johnny Boy bounced his overly bulky body onto his board and raced along the next wave pulling as many manoeuvres as he could.

With an elegant dive Shana finished her ride and was in the midst of paddling back when Johnny pulled a floater, landed it and ended his ride with a showy, backward splash.

"He's such a tart!" said Danny shaking his head. "Shana can do so much better than him!"

The pair slowly rotated their boards; a fresh set of perfectly formed waves were approaching.

"Erm… Danny, I had bit of a strange thing happen this morning," said Marty sucking his lip through his teeth.

"Aye… And?"

"Look, I thought I saw a girl drown today. She was under for ages... Then after about ten minutes she just turned up... It was so weird. And you know what? I think she was naked... What do you think?"

"Naked? She must have been cold," he said, glancing at the horizon with a twinkle in his eye.

"Danny, before the word naked there were a number of other sentences. Could you tell me what you reckon to those as well?"

"A naked women under the water for ten minutes? That's ney possible- is it?" said Danny stroking his chin.

"That's what I thought," said Marty.

10

"They normally wear something," said Danny, turning to paddle with a smirk.

Marty's eyes narrowed; his friend continued to grin as he cut into the wave.

After Marty finished his next ride, he returned out back to find Danny facing the horizon.

"Joking aside Marty. Did yer really think she was drowning?"

"Yeh. She was under for ages. It doesn't make sense and there was this weird... Sound," he said quietly.

Danny shifted on his board and studied his friend thoughtfully.

"Did she fart?"

"No!"

With a pause, Marty smirked back, "For God-sake Danny! This is serious!"

"Okay! Well then, she probably had a diving canister and that made the noise. Marty there is always an explanation. Don't start getting involved in the legends... The legends around here will drive yer mad!" he said honestly.

"I really don't know how to say this but she... Well she was different. It wasn't right. Her eyelids did weird things too," said Marty.

"Marty, mate, listen to yerself... Anyway, girl's eyes always do weird things when they fancy you. They get all wiggly and twitchy! Now I think we need to catch something an' get back to shore. We can talk then," said Danny, glancing at his watch. He gestured at the next rising wave, paddled and rode it all the way in.

For a moment, Marty dithered but labelled it 'contemplation.' He glanced at the next set and paddled; a second later, it closed out on him. He ended the pummelling by pushing from the seabed and forcing himself to the surface. For a few seconds he grappled for air before the next wave landed on him. It was always a struggle! Amongst the underwater turmoil, a female hand reached out and guided him to the shallows. That same magnetic sensation pulsated through his arm and filled his heart. That sensation liberated him!

Once Danny reached shore, he waded up the beach to join Johnny Boy and Shana who waited impatiently. "Do yer think he'll ever get any good?" asked Shana.

"He's not bad for a newby," replied Danny. "Aye, but he's got to learn to stop analysing everything and just let it happen. He thinks about everything in too much detail."

"We are talking about Marty who has been banned from anything mathematical or involving calculation for a year," said Shana cringing as Marty received yet another pounding.

"That one was particularly bad," said Danny with a pained squint.

"But not humiliating," said Shana. "Remember when I was washed up on the beach in front of a group of old women sitting on a bench, wearing white hats, stuffing ice-creams into their wrinkled, old faces. Look, it's a girl - I told you, Morag. They said in fits of laughter. That is humiliating!"

"We all have those moments," said Danny glancing at Shana in a certain way.

In the shallows, silence and serenity expanded as Marty and the girl gazed into each other catching their breath.

"Iris," she said pointing at herself.

"Marty," he replied patting his chest.

She held his hand tightly and blinked. Her eyes made the same sideways motion, "tomorrow. Here."

A resonation filled the air.

"Tomorrow?"

Iris searched the horizon; but appeared guilty.

She blinked a couple of times. Her eyelids followed the same sideways motion.

"Go now," she said reaching out to touch Marty's hair.

A second later, she submerged.

On the beach, Johnny jiggled whilst drumming on his board. Shana shot him a narked glance. It made him smile and drum louder.

"JOHNNY!"

For a moment the water calmed and the group witnessed the woman submerge.

"Is Marty with a girl?" asked Shana curiously.

"Aye. The little bugger!" said Danny with a jolt.

"Come on yer rat, spill the beans," demanded Johnny watching him for clues.

"Erm… I do ney know exactly. Just a girl!"

"What exactly do you mean by that then?" asked Shana curiously.

"Was she... Naked?" asked Johnny brightly.

"Yep. Bare as baby's backside. She could be even barer!" said Shana.

"How do you get barer than a backside?" wondered Danny. No one answered.

"Let's go and get changed. We'll be late for work and I canny say it was a naked lady that made me late!" said Johnny, preparing to walk up the beach.

Marty emerged from the ocean, picked up his board and jogged up the beach.

"Marty, whose yer friend?" Johnny said glancing over his shoulder.

"Just a swimmer… Now let's get changed," he replied walking towards the rickety old staircase.

"Well she's hot!" said Johnny giving a typical 'boys only' nod.

"What's going on, Marty?" asked Shana. The quick shrug and averted eye glance was typical Marty!

"Let's get dressed. Now I canny pee in this suit any more, I'm getting cold," said Danny, stomping through some bladder wrack.

"Nice, very nice, glad to know that there Danny," said Shana with a sigh.

"We all pee in wetsuits, Shana, even girls. They just have the added advantage of getting both sides at once. Nothing worse than having one leg warmer than the other- I say!"

"Ach, Danny!" said Shana shaking her head and following him to the stairs. Why were boys so crass?

CHAPTER 4
Crooked cottages
Bent straight lanes.

"Danny, yer smell like a rotten wellington boot!" said Johnny
covering his nose.

Danny wasn't going to deny it, so continued wrestling the wetsuit.

"I like it here," said Shana pulling on her cherry, fleece
sweater.

The group stood on the cliff top overlooking Gardenstown.

"There's something mystical about it," said Danny hopping on
one leg as he fought to remove his wetsuit boot.

Johnny raised an eyebrow as he loaded the boards on the back of his
hulky red Land Rover. "Come on, yer wee girl," he said to Danny.

Danny folded his arms and glanced at Shana who smiled
seductively at him in his towel.

"Move yer skinny wee arse, Danny! We'll be late for work,"
said Johnny noticing how he looked at her. "Get in then!"

"Let me get me pants on then!" he replied, pulling up his
underwear and clambering in.

"Get some shorts on, eh," said Johnny with a slam of the door.
With a roar of the engine, he nodded at Marty and Shana as he drove
off.

"Are you coming with me then Shana?" asked Marty.

"If that's okay now," she said watching Johnny drive away.
"It's not like we have a choice now. Plus Bertha is far more
comfortable than that hulky Land Rover. You know… I t'ink Danny
must have run here again," she said glancing down the steep hill.

"Danny's always running somewhere," Marty said
opening the camper door and gesturing for her to climb in.

"You'd think he was running away from something."

With her arms folded, Shana paused and watched Marty closely. Was
he talking about Danny or himself? "You know I like the little houses
next to the harbour. It really is quaint and reminds me of cream teas or
fish and chips," she said tipping her head to the side.

"I can see that," he said glancing over his shoulder at the cove and climbing in the van.

"That girl," said Shana sitting beside him.

"What about her?"

"You like her, don't you?" said Shana studying Marty's flushed cheeks.

"Shana, I only just met her and she seemed nice enough," he said with a shrug but unconsciously rubbing the back of his hand.

"Did yer get a tingle in yer dingle, Marty?" she asked watching Marty circling his finger over his knuckle.

With an amused glance, Marty cracked a grin, "a tingle in me dingle, Shana?"

"Yep, a dingle without a tingle keeps a man single," she said matter of factly.

With a loud bang, Bertha's engine exploded into motion.

"Yer going to have to let me sort out that connection, Marty. That bang is just not right!"

"I kind of like it. It makes me feel alive and it let's others know that I'm around," he relied.

"Marty, the fact is that noise may well give one of the oldens a coronary…"

"Okay… Now can we leave it," he said slowing for a corner.

With a fold of her arms Shana glanced at the harbour. "So you're glad to be here in Gardenstown, aren't you?"

"Yeh… It just takes getting used to. A year ago, I was going to work with dad in the city and then... Well then... We know what happened. Suddenly it all seems so ridiculous… So here I am… Somewhere completely different with no clue what I am going to do with my life…" Unconsciously he shook his head and sighed.

"Don't start t'inking again, Marty… You know me gran says that a crisis will bring a person to change. You've had the crisis so yer life has changed. When yer look back it will be for the best," she said glancing at Marty and giving him an affectionate pat.

With a loud sigh, he navigated a steep corner, "I wish that was the case. I would rather have my dad around, Shana. I was finally going to get to spend some time with him - even if it was working."

15

He glanced sadly at the empty road ahead as they navigated the desolate streets leading towards the harbour. That heart-wrenching emptiness rose up again making him turn rigid.

"I'm okay as long as I don't think about it," he repeated.

"But that is why you got the headaches, Marty; you were studying too much and not resting. Avoiding…" she said.

"I'm okay as long as I don't think about it," he repeated. The cycle was about to begin again. "My goodness Marty - quiet isn't it? The morning rush is as much as an old man on a bike and someone walking their dog!"

"Don't you reckon the houses in the village look as though thcy'vc bccn pilcd on top of cach other by a giant hand?" said Marty, glad of the subject change.

"If that's what yer see Marty, then that's what yer see," said Shana, quite obviously not seeing it.

"I am an artist…"

"Ach, Marty yer are what yer are…You see a giant hand and I see a cluster of tiny cottages all cosily snuggling up next to each other like baby owls. If we were all the same now…" she said.

Bertha came to a halt by a circular bay near the harbour. Marty attempted to gauge the size of a parking space next to the harbour edge. He paused and glanced up Straight Lane.

"Crooked Cottage on straight lane… I love it," said Shana, hugging herself. "Now you picked well there, Marty. Who would have thought we would live in a cottage with such a nuts name now. It really is brilliant and it is an individual amongst the other cottages. I like things to be unique!"

"I like the fact that Straight Lane suggests it's straight. How wrong could they be?" said Marty, tilting his head at the lane's curve.

"Now I reckon it must have been named by someone who was wasted trying to walk in a straight line. A circle would have been straighter," said Shan with a smirk.
Marty glanced at her. Not only did Shana laugh at her own jokes but also had a certain way of saying things that made absolutely no sense. She was stupidly brilliant or brilliantly stupid! Alternatively, even marvellously ridiculous!

"Now let me out before you get onto that damned harbour. I hate that bloody sheer edge!" she said. Quickly she launched herself out of the door and scrambled up the hill. Marty carefully parked with enough room to climb out of the door without landing on the beach. That ten-foot drop to his right left no room for error, only a sizeable descent.

After he had checked the hand brake three times and Bertha was definitely secure, he climbed out of the passenger side. With his hands in his pockets, he strolled up the lane to Crooked Cottage. The curtains either side of the lane twitched. *Why didn't people think they could be seen through backlit net curtains?* He stopped and waved at one particular old woman peering through the curtain at him. She looked behind and made a hobblesque run for it. Marty chuckled and fumbled for his keys. When he glanced up at the cottages, he could now see Shana's three fluffy owl chicks. Cosily nestled in the centre, Crooked cottage carried a warm, contented glow.

He turned the key in the lock and took a deep breath. He could already hear commotion.

"Get out me way, I'm a girl I need to wash!" screamed Shana, thundering down the dark wooden staircase wearing nothing but a towel. "I'm going to be late Marty. I mean it Danny, get out of me way!" shouted Shana scrabbling for the shower room and slamming the door in Danny's bemused face.

With a sip of steaming tea, Johnny Boy sat at the rosewood kitchen table in a daze wearing his red trunks and long white socks. He held the blue-striped mug with both hands and sighed. "I reckon she'll be at least a half an hour Danny," said Johnny.

While all that was going on, Marty hung his jacket on a hook made of metal hands. He quietly took off his shoes and aligned them with the wall on the dark ceramic tiled floor. Johnny watched and raised an eyebrow, "Marty, yer going to have to let go and get a bit messy now and again. Everything in lines and in order does ney stop the world being in chaos!"

"I like things in order and I like things in straight lines," he said, re-aligning his shoe.

"Ach, Marty, talking of chaos - I need to get me behind outta this cottage," he said. "Then you'll have yer peace and quiet to fanny around with putting things in order n' nice and all girly tidy! Did no one ever tell yer that real men make mess?"

Turning slowly, Marty smiled to himself, "did no one ever tell yer that women like clean-cut and tidy men?"

"Get outta me way," said Shana skidding across the tiled floor, past Danny and up the stairs.

"Have yer got pants on?" asked Johnny launching from his seat.

"Two pairs," called Shana. "Just in case!"

"Just in case what?" said Johnny glancing over at Marty who was placing toast in the silver toaster and giving it a bit of a wipe.

"Marty, there are three crumbs on the work surface over there and I saw a speck of dust on the wood burner in the corner!" said Johnny. "If you want we can paint these walls absolutely brilliant white – not just white," he said thundering up the stairs with Danny trailing close behind.

Picking up a damp cloth, Marty polished the brass taps, and wiped down the grey slate surface of the worktops. For an old cottage, it was quite a find with the oak beamed ceilings, crisp white walls, dark tiled floors and black wood-burners in most of the rooms. What made the cottage homely were the heavy crimson drapes and matching rugs with gold thread.

Just as he straightened the rug and picked out some fluff, a flurry of bodies descended upon him. Each hurried about the kitchen grabbing food, picking up bags and slamming the fridge. Why Danny was involved was a mystery, he worked at the local surf shop - a laidback joint where he hung out all day talking about surf. Johnny had ten minutes to make it to the Lifeguard hut on the main beach between Gardenstown and Banff and Shana had nine minutes to run up two hills to reach her apprenticeship at the local garage. Marty, on the other hand, had space and time. His studio was only one floor away. He had paintings to make and plenty of opportunity for procrastination. Fluff on the carpet, arrangement of paints and paintbrushes were the perfect distraction.

"Now Marty, you make some time to relax! You're always faffing around doing something. Yer need to have a break!" said Shana, as the physical tornados burst out of the front door in an indiscernible bundle. All fought playfully to get onto the lane first.

Marty breathed a sigh of relief, *space*. He wondered back up to the middle floor and paced about his digital dark room and art studio. He fiddled about for a while with the preparation of pens and paints.

After a while, he finally sat on the specifically designed chair – created for his art. For about ten minutes, the blank canvas stared at him. Should he paint straight away or draw stuff in? That already required a decision. He glanced at the computer. He had been limited to two hours in a day. A timing algorhythm was supposed to stop him. Of course, he could crack it, but he wanted to get himself better.

"Pencil it in," he muttered. "But pencil what in?" The potential was endless - so how did a person narrow it down? With a loud sigh, he just began to draw and not think. The over-thinking hadn't got him anywhere. The final result involved comfort eating and headaches.

After staring into space and mentally testing out the underwater world, he sketched enthusiastically. Every image he completed he stuck to the wall. On completion of the third sketch, he stood up and admired what he had created: a series of images of Iris under water. One image was a pose that resembled Venus de Milo. With a chew of his lip, he adjusted her legs. What did they actually look like? No matter what he did, he just could not get them right. Were they long, short, slender or defined?

With the urge to fidget, he wandered across to an old bookcase in the corner. He traced his finger across the outer covers. Candide by Voltaire, Nautical Tales and Olde World myths of Mermaids. Marty picked up the third book and flicked through. A section called Mermaids and muses - a compilation of stories caught his attention. The Little Mermaid by Hans Christian Anderson 1836, Ondine by La Motte Fouque 1811, and Mermaids, Sirens and other lures 1835. At the back of the book was a handwritten scrap of paper.

13/6/1836
'Never was I so shocked as the day that the little lady came singing at us from the water. She sang so well she mesmerised. The innocent wee creature seemed nervous and hid behind a rock. I thought she a little strange as she swam, almost bare, with breast like that of a woman. The girl, fair and pale, showed no worries of growing cold either.

Doris, my fellow seaweed gatherer, made her way for a closer glimpse. We thought it strange the wee girl not say a thing and just sing - if that is what yer call it. The eerie hum bore through my very being and swam through me mind. Something about the girl did ney feel right. Fear hindered me making a step forward. There were stories of the women of the sea and their curses. I did ney want to be part of it.

Doris was more adventurous and ventured forward for a closer look. When she saw through the water, she reacted violently. The whites of her eyes and no blood in her skin ended in collapse. The wee girl did ney like the reaction and disappeared under the water. As she departed, we, all of us, saw something strange: her legs moulded together and deformed. She swam gracefully at speed and then disappeared. I... no... I canny say... but the Devil mutates his spawn. There have been stories from the circus when they pass. They say this area provides many a spectacle.

15/6/1836

Today a body of a deformed woman washed on the beach. My Cameron caught her in a net. He was distraught, as if he had killed a human and ney a mutation. It was said by Gilbert that we were to keep this finding quiet. It was too late, for the three of us had confessed to the priest the night before. We asked to be released from the Devil. A remembering appeared in the chronicle who published the findings. I canny say who released the information of THE INCIDENT. Nevertheless, on that day, in those empty eyes, I saw my future and it ripped through the depths of my soul...

CHAPTER 5
Mermaids at Dawn.

What had he just read? Marty searched the rest of the pages for more information. There was nothing other than an excerpt from a tatty newspaper article. It was barely readable but an etched image of a mutated woman was displayed on the front page.

"That can't be all there is," he muttered. He searched the rest of the bookcase until he discovered a worn book with a tatty cover on a shelf above. 'Mermaids at Dawn'.

Bang. Bang. Bang! There was a loud knock at the kitchen door. "Not now - Christ sake!" he said aloud.

He was tempted to ignore the knock, but stomped towards the door and flung it open. A portly man stood on the doorstep cradling a shotgun. Malcolm, his landlord, was rather eccentric, but visiting tenants carry a shotgun was extreme! Malcolm was in his sixties. He was a ruddy-faced, portly man who liked to hunt. His stomach flopped over his trousers, which were secured by a sturdy leather belt. The head of a pheasant belt buckle pressed into his podge.

"Erm... Is there something I can help you with?" said Marty stepping away from the shotgun.

"Just came for a look around?" he said polishing the gun proudly with his sleeve. "We're goin' shootin'- over by Eden. You been there yet?"

"No I haven't been yet. Err-sorry? Erm, Malcolm... Could you put the gun down?"

"Nope. She does ney leave me side. So if yer wondering... I thought I would drop by after your first week in Crooked Cottage. Or should I say Cram Tay," he said.

"Cram Tay?" asked Marty

"Means crooked cottage in our dialect, Cram Tay of Gamrae. So..."

"The cottage is... really good," replied Marty politely.

"Well, I had best come in and see," said Malcolm pushing past Marty before he could refuse. With a definite trudge, Malcolm stomped up the stairs to the studio.

"Well- it seems you can," said Marty under his breath.

"Are yer making any money from yer art yet Marty?" asked Malcolm stomping into the studio and studying the sketches with a wheeze. "What are these?"

"Just sketches." Marty shifted awkwardly and chewed his lip.

"No this? Is it masking tape?" He said fingering the sticky tape on the wall.

"Yeh, masking tape."

"Will it hurt the walls?" asked Malcolm.

"No, masking tape definitely won't hurt stone walls," said Marty reassuringly.

"A word of advice, Marty," he said peering at the images. "Nice landscapes are what yer need to be drawing and painting. Ach, why not draw heather or fishing boats? It sells in the towns. Them tourists buy - raw and stark. I would ney bother drawing the people of the sea," said Malcolm. "It won't sell and will only draw unwanted attention."

Marty folded his arms. A man wielding a shotgun was hardly the one to advise him what to draw!

"I'm just sketching, it's just ideas. What do you mean by the people of the sea anyway?"

Malcolm flinched and averted Marty's gaze, "they're good sketches, all right. You have a real talent there young man."

"So, is there some kind of legend?" asked Marty curiously. Malcolm fiddled nervously with his shotgun, "heard something as a child - but nothing special. They say it was a dolphin anyway. They sing see. Or the seals... It's always a seal. Right...I have animals to shoot," said Malcolm waving his gun.

"Malcolm, I have to be honest, I don't get why you're here. Is there something you wanted to tell me or visited me for?"

"Just curious as to what you've done to the house. Any strange noises?" he asked glancing at the landing.

"No... Why?"

"It gets a bit creaky here. Sometimes a little noisy. She must like you, then," he said.

"Who?" asked Marty.

"Oh, no one - it's nothing. If it's quiet there's no point disturbing it," he replied.

"Malcolm?"

"Nothin' happenin' at all on the middle floor?"

"Not that I'm aware of. Like what?" he said growing aggravated.

"You know the house chooses the people. It won't just let anyone in. Many have been driven away in the first two days. You've lasted a week with ney problem. That's good. The people who have lived here have lived difficult lives. They have feelings. Each person leaves a print on the house. There are layers in this house. That be why some sensitive sorts leave. You must have some blood in yer somewhere," said Malcolm convincing himself.

"Right..."

Malcolm carried a flush and appeared to be searching for the nearest exit. "What I will say is this house has lots of imprints. There has been tragedy here," he whispered. "Right, Marty I need to shoot me gun. Another time maybe? Oh, before I forget - I'll be leaving for me hols real soon," he said and sighed. "Oh... And I'm sorry to hear about yer father."

"How do you know?" asked Marty in surprise.

"We're in a village. When a story is caught on the wind, it knocks on all doors or enters the letterbox. There's nothing we do ney find out. Oh and a word of advice - do not say anything in the bakery or store because everyone will find out within the hour," said Malcolm smugly.

"Well, how come I've heard nothing?"

"Ach, Marty, that's how village life works - we talk about yer - not to yer," he said with a grin. "For now, you're an outsider. You must prove yourself to be trustworthy and ney a mere passer-by. In twenty years or thereabouts you may become an honorary local," he said with a slappable smugness.

In twenty years' time? "Now that is a long time to take to prove anything Malcolm. Who knows what will happen?"

"You know looking at that wonky nose of yours - I think there's clan blood in you somewhere. I feel it, the house feels it and she's being nice now. If anything disturbs her, there'll be change. So keep yerself good Marty and do ney piss her off!"

Marty coughed to conceal a laugh.

"As they say in the village only a few have left, but most return. Others are caught on a wave and brought home. It travels in the bloodline you know. The desire to be at the origin," said Malcolm, studying Marty and stroking his chin.

Marty remained silent, Malcolm not only liked the sound of his own voice – but he was insane!

"You've been chosen by this house. Enjoy it. Now I hope it lasts. As they say in America-have a nice day!" Consumed in thought he strode down the stairs and skidded in his oversized wellington boots, grabbed the railing and bashed himself in the face with the shotgun. "Draw some countryside it'll sell," he said dramatically. He then strode out of the house, nodded and closed the door behind him.

Marty stood at the top of the stairs looking bemused. Shaking his head, he returned to the studio. Something was bothering him.

CHAPTER 6
The visitation.

The word eccentric only went part of the way of describing Malcolm, but Marty had other things on his mind. The collection of worn books stood neatly in order of height on the bookshelf. Marty craned his neck whilst skimming his finger along the withered titles. "Ah there you are."

The particular leather-bound book that had caught his attention was tatty and layered in dust. It smelled darker than the other books, as if tobacco had been caught amongst the pages. When he turned to the first chapter, a tingling sensation travelled up his neck. That book was special.

Mermaids at Dawn
Summer 1836

The air was humid that clammy afternoon. It always was in Gardenstown during the warm season. A subtle mist laid on the calm surface of the sea and a gentle resonation spiralled through the air. Underwater a shoal of silver fish swam twisting and turning. The first fish turned, the others followed; so simple, so automatic and so graceful.

Amongst the dark green depths light shone in beams from the surface. The shoal pulsed through the luminous shards and sparkled like silver dust. The glitter explosion re-formed, sensing danger when a dark shadow darted past. She was ravenous.

With a sudden burst the shadow attacked. The shoal scattered. The creature cut through the chaos and snatched the slowest fish. Blood clouded the water as she feasted. Once she was satisfied, drifting alone and bloody, the dead fish had what appeared to be a human bite ripped from its middle.

Amongst the depths, the creature glided towards the beach. When she surfaced she inhaled the crisp aroma of seaweed coating the grey shingle. On that hostile shore three women in bulky dresses battled against the fierce wind gathering the kale crop. One particular gatherer caught her attention. She watched her reap the green harvest from behind a barnacle-encrusted rock. That was when the resonation began.

The crop collection ceased, the gatherers stood up and wiped their hands on their green stained aprons. In silence, they glanced at each other. The eerie sound circled, testing their response. What did she want?

"There," said Megan, pointing wildly at a rock just beyond the shallows. Her tight red curls framed her wide curious eyes.

"I want no association with this, this creature! You know what they say..." said Mawd, the wiry spinster, stumbling backwards.

Doris, the most buxom of the three, dragged Mawd back. "No matter where you go she'll call yer."

Silence.

The resonation intensified.

"Doris, let me go!" Mawd weakly struggled.

"She's here for a reason Mawd. Yer know we must stay together otherwise she'll take one of us to our death," said Doris. Her crimson headscarf perfectly framed the frown lines of her weathered face. Crouching down she scraped back the escapee strands of brittle, grey hair. What had made the creature seek them out?

"She's really watching us," said Megan, who was all of twenty-three years old and luminous with fascination. Her mass of curly auburn hair kept lifting in the wind and her haunting grey eyes peered into the very soul of the creature. The intense sound filled Megan's mind and in that second she became entranced.

Slap! Doris broke Megan's spell, "do ney let her take yer Megan! Yer easy prey 'cause yer sensitive!" Megan jolted; she had fallen into a trance so easily.

Doris stepped into the shallows, blocking Megan and peered directly at the creature.

The creature identified Doris's vulnerabilities and smiled mysteriously. The resonation increased, no one could resist the sound if she chose to emit fully.

"Go no closer Doris! Stop! She could be with the Devil. I no want burning for talking to this Demon. Doris stop, for the love of God!" cried Mawd desperately.

"What are yey me love? So wee and so sweet?" asked Doris, growing increasing inquisitive. "What are yey doin' in so colder water?" she said softly. The creature's eyes were like mirrors, after the creature blinked, Doris was provided with her first vision.

Mawd turned and scurried up the beach. At a safe distance, she shifted awkwardly with her arms folded. The creature had selected her victim and there was no way Mawd was going to be associated.

Megan stood close to the water's edge. The creature appeared so beautiful, so innocent and pure. She could kill in a second if she wished, yet she had spared her. Was she testing her? Something in Meg's stomach was ill at ease. She would see her again; the glimpse combined with the sound had revealed that.

The tone of the resonation shifted, the sound became deeper and the static sensation moved down their bodies to a position below their ribs.

"She's testing us!" With her bulky dress floating behind her, Doris came to a standstill and clutched her stomach. The blood retreated from her skin; she began to shake violently and stared into the creature's reflective eyes. The creature held her gaze and intensified the sound some more. Tears tumbled down Doris's cheeks as the creature invaded her mind with images she had denied.

A scream so tremendous rose from Doris's core as she collapsed onto all fours and lost control. For a minute, she convulsed, retched and cried.

"Stop! Stop for the love of God! Have mercy! We do ney wish to hurt yer!" cried Mawd rushing forwards.

The sudden motion broke the sound. The creature released Doris, turned to face Megan and held her gaze. Dark images that she had denied stampeded through Meg's mind. She covered her heart with her hands but only saw mental shadows.

The resonation intensified.

Megan's nose bloodied.

"Stop! I beg yer!" Meg finally cried. The tone of her voice was enough to reveal the depth of her pain.

With a mysterious smile, the creature submerged and was gone. Silence.

Once the ripples ceased, Mawd waded into the water and held Doris who trembled and sobbed.

"What? What was it? Tell me Doris…" demanded Mawd.

On the shore, Doris collapsed in a heap and curled into the position of a baby. When the emotion calmed, she rolled onto her back and her limbs went limp.

"Are yer alive?" asked Megan softly.

"I am more than alive. I have been cleansed. Mawd, Megan, the child before us. Well, she could see into my heart and my mind," said Doris croakily.

"I tell yer she's a demon," said Mawd holding Doris.

"Ney, she's ney demon. She is beyond us, she sees into us and all that we hide."

The pair were silent.

"Is she a witch?"

"Ney, she is something we canny know and she came with a warning… Tragedy is coming. One of her kind has been scorned," said Doris.

"So what made yer scream?" asked Megan curiously.

"She revealed the darkness in my heart and it hurts to know the truth of what I deny in me," said Doris, her lip trembling. "The girl is pure and well I am tainted by the human sorrows. When you gaze into the mirror of purity you witness your own darkness," said Doris softly.

"Someone needs to know of this visitation. If tragedy is coming then someone needs to know," said Megan.

"We should keep it quiet, between us. We could be burned for association," said Mawd fearfully.

"We should report it to our priest. He will know what to do," Megan crossed herself. "He'll no let us burn."

Slowly pushing herself to standing, Doris shook her head and studied Mawd.

"I ney want anyone to know 'bout this. Nevertheless, if it has to be spoken of - I want the priest to do the talking. I am not one of three witches. There'll be no fire on this body," she said emphatically.

"Not like those other poor souls who burned for bearing knowledge of the creatures," said Mawd.

The three women remained silent. The potential consequences of association could result in death. "I wonder if my Cameron has ever seen such a creature in the ocean," said Megan gazing out to sea. "Aye, I have no doubt. He is the perfect lure," said Doris flatly.

As one of the pages moved past Marty's thumb, a separate page fell out. It was an old family sketch drawn in pen and ink. The image contained a pregnant woman holding a five-year-old child's hand, her husband and two older boys. Scrawled on the back:

1837 - The family.
Two months to go until the bairn arrives. How I long for a girl.

CHAPTER 7
Secrets and their purpose.

Why did secrets turn up when a person was supposed to be concentrating on other things? Marty sat at his writing desk in the corner of the room and switched on his laptop. Once he had loaded up the internet, he searched for MERMAIDS and Scotland. There were numerous sightings, although, Gardenstown and Banff had their own listings.
Click.
'The true information about sightings disappeared. It is rumoured that there was more than one sighting. When investigated, the sightings were denied - or covered up.'
 Marty let out a deflated sigh.
'Humans and Mermaids,' was the next listing.
Click.
     "It is said in legend that the two tribes cannot mix. Although, there are stories of women who fell for Mermen and Mermaid for men. Stories travelled with the Freak Circus popular in the mid to late 1800's. There was a webbed child kept in a water tank. She was rumoured to be the combination of mermaid and human. When removed from the tank she withered and disappeared. Again nothing has been proven or correctly recorded."
     Marty hit the print button.
Thud!
Marty jolted.
     Shana slammed the front door, clomped into the kitchen and kicked off her shoes. Stomp! Stomp! Stomp! She made her way up the stairs and thundered into the Studio.
     "Geese I'm pissed off! What is it with old men who know nothing about cars? Telling me, ME it's the fan belt when obviously the distributor -e'diots the lot of them," she said continuing her stomp. Marty sat back in his chair and watched Shana pace in a circle muttering.
     Once she had calmed she launched herself onto the worn, leather chair. Hoooooof!
Marty said nothing.

"What?" demanded Shana.

"Oh no Shana – I'm not falling for that! You're trying to draw me into an argument."

"No I'm not Marty. Now what makes you say that anyway?"

"Shana that would be the bait... So Shana, just chill or go somewhere else. If you're that angry go and jump up and down in the lane," said Marty.

"Aah, you're so rude! You know me too well!" she said folding her arms.

Marty sat silently watching Shana fidget.

"Oh Marty... They just make me so angry! They think they know it all..."

"You are there to learn. Now let it go... It's just a job."

Shana's shoulders dropped, "Ah yer right. God I hate it when you're right and all knowing... And all smug! Still it makes me angry... I was right yer know but they wouldn't admit it now would they?" Shana fidgeted again. "Well, what have you been doing with yourself then Marty?"

He pointed at the sketches on the wall. They were gone. Looking confused, he picked up the printout and handed it to her. She read the pages and screwed her face up. "Marty, now why you readin' that crap?"

"It's just research," he replied.

"Research for what?"

"The sketches," he said pointing at a neat pile in the middle of the room.

"You'll be needing a model then... You need to draw from life and not the computer," she said posing.

"May do," said Marty, distracted.

"Oh good," she blurted.

"I don't get it. You want to model?" replied Marty with a look of surprise.

She nodded, "it would be fun."

"But Shana, don't take this the wrong way... but...you're more of a Tomboy – let's be honest you're not a girly girl are you?"

Shana flushed red, "Marty, it's hard when you're a girl amongst boys. You know I was brought up with all me brothers and there have never been girls in me family. Is it any wonder?"

31

"I just find it a conundrum. You dress like a guy, act like a guy but really you are quite a pretty girl."

Shana fiddled with her necklace, tilted her chin and studied Marty. "Why thank you. It's difficult Marty. Girls' clothes aren't practical. I could never fix a car in a dress now could I?"

Marty smirked, "no Shana, but that's not the point. Girls generally don't fix cars."

Shana's eyes clouded, "ah you're so sexist! Anyway… That's the problem Marty… How does a girl do everything? I'm not one for wearing little clothing, sticking me boobs out and strutting around in high heels. So how does a girl look pretty and be active?"

Marty shrugged.

"You know sometimes I want to be girly but I just don't know how. So thank you Marty for pointing that out," she said sinking back into the armchair and folding her arms.

"Don't get all moody about it."

"It's not that Marty. Something else is on me mind," she said.

"Danny?" he asked.

"Oh how did you know that? Is it that obvious? Has he said anything?" she said, pulling her legs to her chest.

"Yep it's obvious – and yes, he has a thing for you too. I assume you wanted to know that," he said walking over and poking her in the ribs.

She sat up, gave a little clap and grinned to herself. "Well the problem now is… He's shy and I'm a good girl."

"Well, it will never happen then. Unless one of you makes a move," he said watching Shana's reaction.

Shana smiled to herself, "I think I want him to hunt me. That will give him 'man' power. No use hunting the man. It stops him feeling like a man," she said.

Marty rolled his eyes; Shana was too impatient to wait. He glanced out of the window and smiled, "You know what - I'm going to go for a walk."

"Well it's a beautiful evening Marty. Make sure you take a camera and a jacket."

"You sound like my mother," he said, with a smirk.

"Someone has to." Shana shrugged. "You know what?"

"No Shana I don't."

"We should all go for a barbeque in the bay tonight," she said thoughtfully. "Now that would be fun!"

"Yeh... I like it. Can you text the others and we'll go when I get back."

He turned past Shana, made his way to his desk in the corner and picked up the book Mermaids at Dawn. As he walked past Shana, he ruffled her hair. "Shana make it obvious for Danny, so he knows you like him. Girls can make it very difficult for guys and blokes hate rejection!"

Shana smiled and followed him to the kitchen, "okay, I'll get a t-shirt with I fancy you Danny written on it. Is that obvious enough?" Marty smiled, "a sandwich-board might be better because he'll probably miss the obvious," he said walking to the cottage door.

"Just kiss him when he comes home!" he said glancing at Shana and closing the door.

"Ach Marty!" she said throwing a wet cloth.

CHAPTER 8
Discovery

If people had evolved in the sea then why did no one know about it?
Marty strolled along the cliff top and admired the evening light. The
sun glowed red and illuminated the orange clouds on the horizon. He
set his digital camera in anticipation for the perfect picture moment.
Climbing onto a large, curvaceous rock, he opened Mermaid's at
Dawn. The book was a little crunchy where the remains of squashed
spider sat amongst the first pages. Before its death, that spider had
kindly woven a web throughout the entire book and appeared to link
the pages. Marty examined the remains of the spider, produced a pen
from his pocket and scraped the small carcass off the page. He then
wiped the remains on the grass. After checking the pen for remnants,
he reminded himself never to put that particular pen in his mouth...

Mermaids at Dawn
Chapter 2

Later that evening, after struggling up the hill, the three frightened
women stood reluctantly outside St. John's church.
"You go-" said Megan
"No you go-" said Doris
"You're the oldest Doris - so you take the lead..." said Mawd,
shoving her towards the carved, wooden door. As the door opened, an
elongated urrrrchhh echoed through the still interior.
Unenthusiastically, the women forced themselves to seek the priest's
reassurance. Each clung to each other's clothing as they crept into the
tiny church. Silence.
The church was warm inside. It smelt like incense and damp
stone. Numerous butter-coloured candles flickered vibrantly in
clusters. The golden glow revealed the distinct contrast of the dark
shadows cast by the distorted wax forms. Evenly spaced, vacant pews,
led towards the elevated altar where Jesus gazed down.
The group shuffled forwards.
The kindly middle-aged priest, Father Driscoll MacDuff,

entered the chapel from a side door. "I thought I heard something," he said softly and paused.

The silence and fidgeting amongst the women was telling. What's more, their eyes glistened. All but one appeared consumed by emotion: Megan looked empty, secretive and awkward.

"I'm sorry father!" said Mawd bursting into tears and sinking to her knees with her head bowed...

"Ladies, for what do I owe such a display of emotion?"

"We do ney want to burn Father. We, all of us, have seen a creature from the deep with bright eyes," Megan desperately blurted.

"You'll be the death of us Megan!" said Doris striking Megan's cheek. Smack!

Father Macduff was silent in consideration. "And did you have any physical contact with the creature?"

They shook their heads and glanced at each other.

Father Macduff paced towards the altar. With his hands behind his back, he sighed. "So they are returning. Change is coming." He glanced up at the cross and shook his head. "Ladies the visitation was for a reason."

"Father?" asked Doris curiously.

"A message from the others... You will not burn for this. Although we must keep it quiet, we do ney want the villagers to panic," he said turning to gauge each of the women's reactions.

Megan gazed at the priest, "what was the message father?"

"Someone has wronged them, which means there will be repercussions. Now keep the sighting amongst yourselves. Behind closed doors - yer hear?" said Father Macduff sternly.

The women nodded and stared at the floor.

"But shouldn't it be remembered father?" asked Megan.

Father Macduff pondered, what was the best course of action? "Ladies, you should return home. It is late. Now I suggest you forget you ever saw the creature and carry on with your lives as normal. I will instigate the appropriate action."

The group nodded and turned towards the door. Father Macduff watched Megan curiously, there was something...

The watching sensation travelled across Megan's back, so she glanced back.

Her mother had burned eighteen years earlier. Father Macduff wondered whether the girl knew the true cause of her mother's death. Was it a coincidence that Megan had witnessed the creature?

The sturdy grandfather clock in the corner made a series of chimes at ten o'clock. Megan sat in front of the fire and gazed out of the cottage window onto Straight Lane. The situation was unfair! How could creatures exist but no one was allowed to discuss them openly? Megan hated secrets. Her family was full of them. That was why she married as soon as she could, when she was just fifteen. She had taken on Cameron's four boys and had lost one of her own. Unfortunately, the bairn had suffered a cot death the year before. "You are cursed for marrying the widower of a witch," the villagers had taunted. It was true, Cameron's wife burned for witchery only seven years before. In the meantime, Megan's adopted family were at sea catching their livelihood. They could be away for days or even weeks, it all depended on the crop of the sea.

Megan wrung her hands and sighed. The village was full of secrets. She hated the village and its controlling ways. Thoughts clouded her mind until they formed a storm. Something had to change!

Mermaids at Dawn
Chapter 3

That niggling feeling in his gut bothered Father Driscoll Macduff as he sat in his study lit by a glow of candles. The heavy smell of dark wood and incense filled the room as he sketched. The scratching noise made by the quill on the thick parchment paper cut through the atmosphere. After a couple of attempts he paused, the image had to be as clear as possible; that way the church would know what they were dealing with. He gazed at the creature and felt his stomach knot. "With such beauty and purity why do you always bring a trail of death?" he whispered.

The piercing cold night air instantly seized Father Macduff's breath and turned it to steam. Wearing his long black overcoat, he left the church and glanced at bright stars in the clear night sky. The moon was bright when he mounted his bay horse. She nervously panted, sensing something in the Father's motion. The hastening of hoofs marked their entrance into a rhythmic canter. He intended to warn the nearby villages of Rosehearty and Banff.

On a hill overlooking Banff, his old friend answered the door wearing his nightclothes and a tired frown. Father Cullen carried an atmosphere of concern as he invited the sorrowful-looking Father Macduff inside his study. The interior of the cottage was stone with dark, wooden shelves full of dusty leather-bound books and candelabra with a multitude of candles. The pair took their seats by an open fire with only luminous coals remaining.

"So why visit so late?" asked Father Cullen.
Father Macduff unfurled the sketch and passed it to his friend. "She has visited us."

"Be prepared for death then," said Father Cullen sadly. "I wondered whether they would break the agreement. No doubt, the Resonance has begun. We must inform the others. Aye... and advise the gravediggers to start digging. Death will be inevitable," he said with a sigh. "In the meantime, I will inform the elders of the sighting and the agreement. We do ney want those outsiders finding out our secrets. Do we now?" he said as an afterthought.

That night news spread amongst the churches. Each priest visited one another carrying the message. Death was imminent!

Marty turned the page but a subtle resonation circled through the air. For a short while, he silently listened. It wasn't the same sound as Iris had made; but it was similar and coming from the base of the cliff.

He dropped to his knees and crawled amongst the dewy moss. At the base of the cliff, he noticed three women gathering seaweed in the shallows. They had organic looking sacks where they piled handfuls of seaweed. All the while, a subtle but contented hum swirled through the air.

Crawling on his front, Marty followed a track down the cliff. As he did so, he dislodged some debris. For a moment, he held his breath and strained to keep his composure.
The women didn't notice.

Once he had arrived at the base of the cliff, he sidestepped towards a rock. It barely covered him. At the same time, the lead women turned and motioned to the others.

Marty slithered through long grass and carefully prepared his camera for use. He peered through the viewfinder and... Click. Silence. Click. Could they hear? What was he doing? Click, click, and click.

The singing calmed and Marty laid low. He paused for a moment, was he mad? He was photographing three semi-naked women in the water. Did that make him a peeping Tom?

One woman splashed without using her hands. The others giggled.

With a frown, he peered at the back of his camera. He had two pictures left on his memory card and not enough time to delete. He watched in silence, another resonation came from far out to sea. As it drew closer, its intensity increased. The women emanated a response but chatted to each other in a different language, possibly an old Scottish language but one he couldn't understand. It sounded like an old Scottish language. Some of the locals spoke in a dialect called Doric, was that what it was? Their expressions revealed gossip, which ceased when a man surfaced and gestured towards the horizon. The group followed his lead and silently submerged.

To follow the group's trajectory, Marty tracked them using his zoom. The first woman surfaced and dived. A dark shape skimmed surface of the water. The other two women followed. Click. Click. With an astounded silence, Marty stared at the camera's display. He had just witnessed something he could not define. No matter how much he zoomed in – it was not clear. He needed to see the image on a full-size screen, his computer screen. Maybe then, he could figure it out.

CHAPTER 9
Apparition

Had he captured it? The sun descended below the horizon and the sky turned purple as Marty urgently scrambled in the direction of Crooked Cottage clutching his camera. Running at full speed through the town, Marty startled a man on a bike and a woman walking a dog. The dog barked with the excitement as Marty hurtled past.

"Good evening," called Marty.

"Ach, nice to see yer keepin' fit there Marty from Cram Tay - isn't it?" said the dog walker.

The dog yapped again.

"Doughnut, it's just a runner - now there's no need for fuss is there?"

Doughnut wagged her tail, licked her lips and with a mad look in her eye panted with excitement.

Marty had only a steep hill to negotiate before he reached the cottage. He jumped two fences that lead to the back warren. Aromas of barbecues, baking and smoke wafted from the cobbled cottage yards. The neighbours heard something, paused for a moment, but continued chatting whilst Marty dashed past.

With a loud thud, Marty burst through the front door, darted across the kitchen and climbed the stairs two at a time. On the landing, he disappeared into his digital darkroom without a word.

"What went on there?" asked Johnny glancing at Shana who was sprawled on the sofa. Danny sat in the armchair opposite him, in prime position in front of the fire.

The pair shrugged and continued to sip their instant hot chocolates.

"Maybe he needs a pee-," said Johnny Boy stirring his tea thoughtfully.

"Since when has Marty peed in the digital darkroom?" asked Danny.

"Who knows what he does in there? Anything's possible," said Johnny Boy flatly.

"Are yer serious now?" asked Shana studying Johnny Boy's face.

Johnny stood up and gestured for Shana to follow.

"Leave him Johnny, he'll tell us what's going on when he's good n' ready," said Danny.

"Ach-I'm not bloody waiting... He could be all night! So... Since when has Marty ever ran up the stairs?" asked Johnny.

"Ach, you're so impatient ," said Danny with a huff.

Shana stood up, gazed at Danny and smiled seductively. She took a step closer, leant forward and examined his necklace. It was a silver circle containing a runic sign resembling a seven with a dot. "Nice, I never noticed it before... what does it mean?" she asked gazing into his eyes.

"All the villagers have them, even Johnny Boy. They are... part of our history," answered Danny with a blush.

"Are yer coming or what?" demanded Johnny signalling for Shana to follow.

On the landing, the pair placed their ears against the digital darkroom wall and listened. A closed door meant keep out! Marty had made that very clear on the first day.

Inside the digital darkroom Marty downloaded his memory card. It was a crisp, white room full of orb style lighting and white or transparent equipment. It was clean, pristine and in perfect order.

"You got some dirty pictures Marty?" called Johnny.

"Marty you perve!" said Shana joining the taunt.

Danny sat silently, goose-bumps rose on his neck. Something felt odd - the atmosphere was static. As a distraction, Danny studied the nineteen thirties bed and breakfast style wallpaper with three ornamental flying pigs. After deciding it was hideous, he reached for his surf magazine, but it was gone. He glanced around; it was nowhere to be found.

"Did any of youse guys move my magazine?" called Danny knowing how Johnny loved to hide things.

With her head against the wall, Shana stared accusingly at Johnny.

"I did ney do anything - all right?"

"No. Danny you were the last in the room," called Shana.

"Oh," replied Danny searching the room and noticing that it

40

was on top of a bookshelf. "How on earth did it get there?" He jumped, grabbed the magazine and returned to his seat.

A cutting from a newspaper floated past and landed on the floor with some grey fluff attached. After wiping the paper off, he read the headline. 'Freak of Nature!' The article carried an etching of a small, deformed child submerged in a circus tank.

Inside the digital darkroom, Marty stood up and knocked some rulers from his desk.

"Marty what are yer doing?" shouted Johnny.

"Ah leave him to it – he will tell us what he's up to when he's ready," said Shana losing interest.

Johnny turned to face the wall again. "Come on, we haven't seen you that excited since... In fact Marty, I've nort ever seen you that excited before. You're not having a wank are yer?"

Sitting at his computer, Marty opened up the digital file and zoomed in. He smugly sat back in his chair, the digital darkroom was his territory and they could wait. He was allowed a maximum of two hours a day on the computer and only had only forty minutes remaining.

"For Christ sake... Will you tell us what the excitement's about Marty?" Johnny insisted. "If you don't I'll break something... Right here and you can explain that to the landlord!"

Marty considered Malcolm's strangeness and the potential repercussions...

"I have a picture of a rare bird. I don't know if I got it or not - all right?"

"Is that all?" shouted Johnny.

"Now there's a let-down," said Shana folding her arms.

Shana started to walk away but Johnny grabbed her arm. "Marty I don't believe you. You'd never get that excited about a bird. Not one with feathers. It must be something more..." he said with a wink.

"You're right Johnny."

"I told you," whispered Johnny.

"I think I saw it's nest," said Marty smirking.

"ACH! You're turning into a twitcher!" said Johnny with a small stamp. "You're losing it Marty. One-minute yer talking to yourself and the next yer photographing birds. Next you'll be stamp

41

collecting!"

"Yeh, I'm a philatelist. I have an album and I want to start. I have some rare ones on order. Oh and coins are good too Johnny... You might want to start collecting with me."

Shana and Johnny Boy said nothing. Instead, they glanced at each other in a disturbed manner.

"What's a philatelist?" Johnny finally whispered.

Shana shrugged, she then gestured for Johnny to follow her to the art studio to show him Marty's canvas.

"Have you noticed Marty seems to be a bit- well..."

"Loopy?" Johnny replied.

"I wasn't going to say that exactly. I just think he is having a hard time dealing with his dad," she said admiring the canvas.

"You mean he's having a breakdown?"

"I think he's going through a phase. He's just finding ways to process what happened... but keeps distracting himself," she said in her best psychoanalytical tone.

"How is he distracting?"

"The naked girl in the sea works..." she said.

"Well that's the best distraction a man could have." Johnny stared at the canvas; he didn't like emotional stuff - that was for girls.

"That's her you know."

Johnny peered closer and smirked. "Hmm, she's hot - but her boobs aren't big enough!" he said sifting through Marty's toolbox.

"Johnny, what are you doing?"

Johnny grinned mischievously as he took a pencil and drew additional bosoms.

"They can go from a B cup to an E. That will teach him!"

Johnny stood back and nodded. He appeared pleased with himself.

"See Marty isn't the only artist around here!"

"You wanker Johnny! That is wrong drawing on someone else's sketches. Boundaries Johnny! Anyway, if those are the shape of women's breasts then I am definitely a man... Johnny they look like bananas for God sake," she said, folding her arms.

"Nothing that a good uplift bra won't sort out... Anyway we'd better get out of here otherwise we'll be in trouble!"

When the pair returned to the front room they found Danny sitting in silence, staring at the wall.

42

"Danny? What's wrong with yer? Why are you acting all weird now?" asked Shana.

The atmosphere in the room felt electric.

"Danny?" Shana said a little louder.

Danny did not reply. He trembled with glazed eyes fixed on one solitary spot on the wall.

"Bloody attention seeker," said Johnny Boy. "Come on mate yer scaring Shana here."

Danny clasped the article and stared into space.

With a side-glance, Johnny looked to Shana for direction.

Nothing.

He followed Danny's gaze to a point on the wall where his Surf magazine was stuck.

"I think this may have something to do with it. Danny did that … make you go weird?" said Shana noticing the article in Danny's hand.

The pair crouched down and studied the picture of the girl in the tank.

"Freak of Nature. Is this the future? Will our children develop webbed feet? This woman was born of a human. So how was this creature ever conceived? There have been numerous reports of mutated creatures luring our women to the sea, to their deaths. How are we going to stop this phenomenon? How can we stop these freaks of nature ruling the earth?" read Shana.

"Well, that's a load of bollocks! I bet it's from one of those weird aliens rule the earth magazines," said Johnny in his most dismissive tone. "When was it written anyway?"

Shana searched the page for the date. "1837."

"Wo!" said Johnny pulling the magazine off the wall and laying it on Danny's lap.

"I think Marty should see this," said Shana smoothing out the article.

On the way back to the digital darkroom, the pair glanced back at Danny. The magazine had returned to its original position in the corner but Danny hadn't moved. Johnny glanced at Danny questioningly and noticed tears trickling down his cheeks. Every so often he trembled.

Inside the rather bright darkroom Marty zoomed in on one of the images using the program's magnify glass. "Yes! I…"

"Marty there's something that you need to see," called Shana impatiently.

"I'm just coming," shouted Marty fumbling about for paper to make a printout. Once he had clicked print, he made his way to the entrance of the darkroom.

"Danny found this," said Shana thrusting the article at him.

"Danny's acting real weird Marty. I've never seen him like it before. Not even when he got his head jammed in the wok stand. Or when he knocked himself out when he jumped too high on that trampet."

"Something must have taken place in the 1830's?" said Marty reflectively as he handed the article back to Shana.

"Is that all you can say? Aren't you even going to take a look at him?" asked Shana.

"Danny is responsible for himself and it's just an article," he said dismissively.

"You're not taking this seriously now are you? There really is something wrong with him. You have to see him now Marty. I've never seen him like this – really!"

"But I only have thirty minutes left with the computer… He's probably been smoking banana skins or tomato skins knowing him…"

"No - he's given that up," said Shana. "Now come on just have a look," she said dragging Marty by the sleeve.

When the three of them returned to the front room, they found the fire ablaze and Danny was now sitting facing the fire. As warm as the fire was, Danny shivered with his hair standing on end.

"Are yer having a breakdown or something, Danny?" asked Johnny in his most concerned tone.

With a shake of the head Danny gestured towards the corner. Johnny followed his gaze, retrieved the magazine and placed it on Danny's lap. He stared at the magazine, remained silent and trembled. The group pulled their chairs close to the now raging fire.

"What's wrong there Danny? You can tell us we're your friends," said Shana taking hold of Danny's hand.

Danny glanced towards the magazine. The group followed his gaze.

"What? What the bloody hell's so exciting about that

44

magazine?" Johnny demanded.

Silence. The magazine flew past Johnny's face and landed back in its original position, on the wall.

"Shit!" shouted Johnny.

Shana and Marty instinctively forced their chairs backwards.

Silence.

Panting.

"Shit… What the-" said Johnny shaking his head.

"I think we should leave the room," said Shana.

Marty shook his head. "No! We live here. We need to demonstrate that we're not scared."

"So you think there's something here then?" asked Shana.

"So we're haunted? Great! Hooray we're haunted, maybe we can do a we're haunted dance, that will scare whatever it is!" gestured Johnny as he moved erratically about the room flapping his arms.

"Malcolm said something about the house today," said Marty. "It has some kind of imprints on it."

Johnny continued waving arms in the haunted dance. He resembled a bulky ballet dancer. "Who the hell's Malcolm when he's at home?" asked Johnny mid-bounce.

"That would be our landlord Johnny," said Marty. "You know… The one I pay to live here. Malcolm's a normal kind of fellow - came round today with a shot gun."

"And that can be considered normal?" asked Johnny, catching his breath.

"What did he say?" wondered Shana.

"Just about the fact this house has carried tragedy. Not really much else," he said. "Oh and this cottage has carried all manner of story. The good thing is the house apparently likes us. We made it through a week."

"Whoopee," shouted Johnny as he leapt into the air. "Yep, it's really showing that it likes us."

"It seems that we woke something up today. We need to find out the history of the house," said Shana thoughtfully.

"Can't wait-" says Johnny kicking his leg in the air. "Probably was owned by someone mental!"

Unexpectedly the fire erupted.

"Be careful what you say there Johnny," said Shana flinching.

"Oh I have to be careful of something that's not alive? Sorry I forgot that!" called Johnny mid-pirouette. "Who makes these rules anyway Shana? The ghost should be scared of us. We're alive - it's dead!" said Johnny with his own special logic.

"What's going on?" asked Shana studying Danny.

Danny shook his head with his lips tightly sealed.

"I'm going to take him to his room," said Shana gently helping Danny up.

Once in Danny's room Shana guided Danny to the bed and sat stroking his hair. "Don't be afraid there Danny," she said in a comforting voice. "Whatever it is, she's just trying to get attention like a small child crying."

"I wasn't scared until I saw her with…"

"With what?" Shana demanded.

Danny fell silent, shook his head sadly as his lip trembled.

In the front room, Johnny plonked down on an armchair. "I'm nort scared you know Marty…"

"I know. Anyway… It's just something in an old house. It happens all the time," Marty replied.

"I'll hit it. That's what I'll do," said Johnny gesturing. You can't hit a ghost- you prick!" said Marty.

"Why not?" said Johnny folding his arms.

"Err, maybe because it's not solid?"

"Right, I'll hoover it up!"

"Johnny really… Hoovering a ghost? Where did you get that idea from?"

"Scooby Doo… They did, they hoovered the ghost. It got rid of it too and scrappy…"

"Johnny, Scooby Doo isn't a point of reference to use with a spectre," said Marty.

"Well, what do we do then?" he said.

"It hasn't hurt anyone, has it?" said Marty.

"Well... No… Not yet…"

"And it's not definite anyway," said Marty pushing himself to standing. "Well, I think I'll go and print then. I have twenty-five minutes left."

46

"I'm coming too," said Johnny desperately.

"I thought you weren't scared," said Marty with a smirk.

"I'm not! I like birds, all kinds of birds - a lot," he said.

"Marty don't tell anyone, it's my secret," said Johnny winking.

The old pipes creaked with the motion of water in the corner of the room. Johnny jumped up and looked around.

"Go to your room you giant woose!" said Marty.

"But if I'm alone, she can get me," he replied.

"It seems she's only on this floor and won't go upstairs," said Marty.

"How do you know that for sure?" asked Johnny.

Marty didn't know that for sure. "For such a big man... Don't worry about it," said Marty. "Right I'm going to print alone, notice the alone, by myself thing? Anyway, there's not enough room for two of us. As much as I would love to hear all your bird stories," he replied.

"I'm going to find Shana. She can keep me company." Johnny trudged out of the room. "Anyway, we're going to the cove tonight so we'll be out."

He climbed the stairs to Shana's room. It was empty. He stood anticipating the worst...

"No... Don't let it be Danny." Slowly Johnny Boy turned towards Danny's room. He didn't knock but barged in. Shana and Danny kissed passionately on the bed. The pair didn't notice.

"I see... Yer wet fart! Get scared and kiss the girl," he said not knowing where to place his hands.

The pair looked up, startled.

"Could you keep me company too Shana? I'm scared," Johnny said in a high-pitched voice. "You sneaky shit Danny! It's all a set up to get laid!"

"Excuse me! I am here!" said Shana sharply.

Johnny was not impressed and stormed out knocking ornaments and lamps on the way.

"What an arse!" she said glancing at Danny. "Where were we?"

Next door, Johnny stomped into his room, launched himself onto his bed and stared at the ceiling. "I am a fanny magnet- yep Johnny Boy is a fanny magnet- yes I am. Effortlessly and easily I attract a nympho!" he repeated. He had read positive affirmation made things happen in a person's life.

CHAPTER 10
Ice

The atmosphere in the darkroom chilled. The temperature dropped and water droplets froze in the air. Marty remained oblivious, he was too preoccupied with enhancing the images on the screen. Something was going on with the village. They had to be hiding something! Marty hit print and waited. Line by line Marty watched the image take shape. With a final buzz, the picture dropped onto the printer's paper tray.

Marty directed his adjustable lamp towards the image and sat back in his chair. He sipped a glass of water, peered closely and sucked his lip. A mutated shape remained on the surface of the ocean where the three women dived. Marty glanced at the second image. The second woman had the same disfigurement. He thoughtfully took another sip and frowned. Ice had formed on the surface. "Weird!" He arranged the images next to each other and smiled to himself. "I could make millions!"

Ice crackled in the glass, his breath froze and goose-pimples prickled his neck. A pale blue flame emerged from the images. Marty lunged forwards and stamped them out. A ball of blue flame manifested in the air, within the fire stood a woman with red curls dressed in black.

He froze to the spot. She stared him in the eye and reached out for him. Marty stepped backwards and knocked the glass. Water splashed across the floor. She was gone.

The water crystallised into ice, "you're still here aren't you?" he said, his voice taught. His computer screen lit up. "Shit!" He glanced at the door, "It happened when I said I could make Millions…" Carefully he sidestepped the ice as he backed towards the door. "So whatever you are, you don't want this getting out do you?"

The computer screen flickered. "You're something to do with them, aren't you?"

Silence.

The small hairs bristled on the back of Marty's neck. A cool breeze caressed his cheek but there was nothing there.

"You don't want to hurt me, do you? If that was your intention, you would have attacked by now. I know you're trying to tell me something - but what?"

The computer screen flashed again. Marty took a step forwards.

"Just write what you need to tell me... Then I will know," whispered Marty.

No response.

"Are you intending to harm us?"

Marty focused on the screen. The sound of cracking filled the air as ice crystallised and cool air wafted about him.

"Do you want us here?" he said a little louder. The pool of water melted, re-structured and cracked into an abstract form. The cool air ruffled his eyelashes. She was standing directly in front him. His stomach flipped, he had to leave!

"I understand this is secret. Do you want me to show these images to anyone?"

Ice appeared in the air and tinkled to the ground. A shudder ran down his spine. Her cold breath panted in his face. Marty's eyes remained fixed on the screen. "Are you connected with the creatures?"

His heart pounded. A frozen pair of hands appeared in the air and glided towards the computer.

"Are you - are you - one of them?" he croaked.

The computer screen flashed.

NO appeared.

"Oh God!" Marty's heart thumped. He took two steps backwards. "But you are protecting them... Who are you protecting them from?"

There was no flash on the screen – just silence. He frowned as he took another step towards the door. "Is something going to happen with them, concerning me?"

On the landing Johnny stood at the top of the stairs fidgeting. Was Marty still in the darkroom? In a slump of boredom he plodded down the stairs towards the darkroom and put his ear to the wall. Who was Marty talking to?

Inside the darkroom the frosty draft swirled and intensified.

49

"That article - it's you- isn't it- answer me-!"

No reaction.

"Answer me... I don't get it! Who are you trying to protect?" The computer flashed on. The chilled air spiralled. Marty's heart pounded. "Who are you protecting?"

'YOU' it wrote. 'DEATH WILL COME!'

A wave of nausea washed through him. His solar plexus knotted and a deep, dark sound rose within him. Whatever was in that room had touched his soul! He had to go. He launched himself towards the door but a blue flame rose, the water melted and droplets suspended in his path. The wall of ice revealed a woman consumed in flames.

"You are here for a reason!" said a cold rasping voice. "You can stop the killing! You can stop the pattern!"

Marty smashed through the ice with his arms protecting his face. He skidded and slid in the direction of the door, grabbed the handle, forced it down and catapulted himself into the corridor.

Smack! Johnny was standing directly in his path and the pair crashed to the floor. Laying on his side, Marty clutched his chest and panted.

"What was all that about Marty? And who were yer talking to?"

"Not now okay? Myself," said Marty.

"You were talking to IT, weren't you?"

Marty remained silent.

"Don't deny it - will you? I heard yer clear as day," said Johnny "and I think I heard her too."

Marty shook his head and clutched his chest.

"That's too weird, that's just too fricken' weird! Yer hear?" said Johnny. "You were having a conversation with a ghost. That's madness Marty, nothing more, nothing less - mad!"

Johnny Boy clambered to his feet and went to walk away but paused.

"Johnny what can I say? It's just weird!"

"More than weird! We need this sorted... We will get the priest in. In the meantime, we all need a break from the house. Let's get our arses to the cove," said Johnny trying to lighten the atmosphere. "Get some stuff, we'll have a fire - it'll be nice and safe there. Then we can talk Marty. There will nort be any ghosts ear-wiggin."

"Johnny can we change the subject? Actually, where are Danny and Shana?"

"Sucking each other's faces off," said Johnny in a certain tone. "Finally!"

"You knew? You bloody knew and did ney tell me? I almost made an arse of myself Marty!"

"Yeh, it was obvious. I worked it out today," said Marty honestly.

"Just my luck," said Johnny folding his arms. "An attractive girl with a brain, a sense of humour who can surf... How often do you get those?"

"Shana is unique," said Marty.

"Yeh, she's not like the others-."

"Well..."

"I know I've lost out this time but you know I'm a fanny magnet Marty," he said.

Marty cracked a smile; he had such a way with words!

"I'm just saying it how it is. And I AM a magnet. Who can help that? It's just the better ones are at the top of the tree and need chasing. That is why I wear the speedos Marty. Like bees to a honey pot," said Johnny with a sigh. "You should get some Marty- they work, I promise!"

Marty gazed at his friend, he was not willing to wear small red trunks to meet women whether it worked or not.

"Johnny what are we going to do about the 'entity' then?" Johnny shrugged "I think avoidance is the best tactic and talking about totty is the best distraction I can think of."

Marty studied his friend, at some point a person had to confront the truth. The truth was an entity had told him he was there for a reason and that reason would stop death. How could he tell his friend that?

CHAPTER 11
Answers with more questions...

Marty sat on his bed and sighed. He pulled out the book and traced his fingers over the cover. "Do you have the answers?" he whispered. "Is this your secret?"

Mermaids at Dawn
Chapter 4

Megan laid on her bed brewing. She had to visit Father Macduff.

In the darkness she hiked back to the church and entered cautiously. Inside, candles flickered and the pools of wax had grown increasingly deformed. Incense filled the empty atmosphere.

"Father?" she called glancing about.

No reply. Cautiously she crept through the church and tapped on Father Macduff's heavy study door. One candle remained alight and illuminated a sketch on the table. She gently picked it up and peered the image with a frown. How did he know what the creature looked like? Megan pursed her lips and made a decision. She thrust the image into her dark, woollen, overcoat and hurriedly spun to leave. Her coat flared and whipped through the air forcing another piece of paper to sweep onto her path. It was too dark to read but she guessed it was a written account of the women's experiences for the church records. Her eyes darted about searching for any onlooker. There was none, she rolled the paper and slipped it into her overcoat. Things were going to change!

Mermaids at Dawn
Chapter 5

Megan scrambled through the heather and gorse outside the church. Her mare waited in a nearby field. The cracking of twigs combined with Meg's urgency revealed a journey was imminent. With a run and a jump, she lept onto the mare and galloped bareback to

Aberdeen. During that journey, Megan had doubts. As much as she wanted to sell the story, as much as she needed the money, should she betray the village? Megan's mind ran riot as she galloped through the brisk, night air. They had burned her mother hadn't they? How would they know it was her anyway? Megan wasn't sure whether she had made the right decision but continued her journey unaware of the consequences to follow.

After riding for hours, Megan dismounted her horse outside the Aberdeen Chronicle. She patted the creature and took a moment to compose herself. In the darkness, she gazed at an ominous stone building and fought the urge to leave.

A pungent smell of ink and oil filled the vast printing room when she quietly entered by the back door. She arrived in a subtly illuminated printing hall where the main brightness came from the office area. Urgently she made her way up some ornate, metal spiral stairs and knocked on the office door. An old man greeted her and eyed her with suspicion. "I have something which would be news-worthy," she said producing the parchment.

The printer observed the girl curiously and read the article. When he was finished, he raised an eyebrow and nodded. He gestured for her to follow him over to a safe and counted out some coins.

"That will be your fee. Now do you want to witness what you created?" said the printer studying her response.

Megan watched his movements closely with an expression of interest. He gestured for her to follow him out of the office and down to the presses. In silence, Megan watched the printer make an arrangement of individual text blocks to create the page. A metal plate had an etching transferred on it to finalise the article.

"When you've finished I wish to see the article." She stood with her arms folded and a certain 'air' about her.

"Aye," said the printer peering at the image of the woman of the sea. "A truly beautiful creature." The printer, a master at his craft, turned his attention back to the metal plate and carefully etched. He gently wiped the engraving with a cloth. Accompanying each exacting detail was the subtle scratching noises of metal on metal. The result was the perfect image of the creature, ready for press.

Megan stood next to the printer watching, it was many years since she had witnessed such a process with her father. The article creation was enthralling - each individual letter placed carefully in perfect order set about the etching. The printer nodded in the direction of the press and gestured for Megan to follow. "Have a glance over the proof," he said watching Megan nervously chewing her nails.

"Nobody knows you're here, do they now lass?" said the printer innocently.

"My husband knows. He's waiting outside. He is with the horse. He hates people outside the village - so I say yer had best be getting on with this article before he comes in and beats yer for detaining his wife!" said Megan curtly.

The printer smiled, the woman before him was strong and immoral; he liked that. She was probably from the witching clans.

He carefully rolled the papers and handed them back. "I suggest yer take this back to where it was found. That way there'll be ney implications," he said with a wink. The printer passed her a copy of the article. "I suggest yer keep it where ney one will find it."

The printing press jerked into motion when the printer released a lever. The article fell repetitiously out of the press and into the holding tray ready for the morning. The cause would create a terrible effect.

When Megan arrived back in Gardenstown, the sun was already on the horizon. She stealthily ventured back into the church and glanced about to see if the priest was about. He was nowhere to be seen. She scurried towards the study with her overcoat drifting behind her. Carefully Megan returned the picture and article to its exact positioning. As she turned to leave she stood before the statue of Jesus. "If creatures exist and God has created them- then people should know. If I have done wrong I will accept full responsibility." Megan felt a shiver run down her spine, a knowing feeling washed over her. Something terrible was going to happen.

The following morning, in the crowded streets of Aberdeen, newspapers flew from the stands. The curious townspeople devoured the story. It was beyond their comprehension.

That same day in Gardenstown, washed up on the shore, a creature laid motionless in a fisherman's net. In foetal position, she only revealed the back of her torso clearly. Rigid with death, her bright blue eyes shone wide but deserted.

"Who brought this disaster on the village?" called a frail old woman, waving her arthritic finger accusingly.

Megan wrestled from the back of the crowd to see what the commotion was. When she saw the sight, she gasped and covered her mouth. She searched the crowd for Doris and Mawd who stared sadly at the creature.

The ruddy fisherman, Cameron, Megan's husband, stood over the girl. He wrung his hands in repetition while his sons stood away, trying to disassociate themselves.

"She swam into me net," said Cameron. "I heard the sound and then it... stopped. What's to be done?"

Silence.

Megan gazed at the creature, had her betrayal caused its death? For a split-second, Megan gazed into the vacant eyes of the girl and glimpsed a vision. Her heart pulsated, the vision revealed a curse within her family and history repeating itself. Tears welled up in her eyes and trickled down her cheek. The creature would seek her revenge. There would be death!

A smart, red-bearded man from the local council stepped forward. "We do ney want outsiders coming up here looking for truth. Keep it to yerselves, yer hear? Make a myth within thee family but never say it be true. Keep it among us and only us. If we see others no one is to tell," Gilbert paused "Just say it be a seal – it's always a seal."

"Yer think there's more Gilbert?" asked Cameron, with a look of bewilderment.

"Where there's one there's three," Gilbert replied. "That's the law of nature."

There was nodding amongst the gathering.

"Do you all understand?" Gilbert reiterated. "We must nort be affected by this... This monster of creation."

"We're cursed," whispered a small girl, grasping Megan's skirt. "Me ma said that by touching sea creatures you will become one."

Megan hadn't had contact.

The little girl pulled Megan down to her level. "The resonance is

55

coming. It will find the betrayer and drown them. That is what me ma told me in the story."

Megan studied the girl. Was the resonance coming for her?

The residents of the village shifted anxiously. The air carried a chill as they watched 'the' mist form a wall on the horizon. It was going to descend upon them. The villagers anticipated the consequences. The resonance had begun her search. Death was inevitable.

Mermaids at Dawn

Chapter 6

The villagers had already begun to disperse when Father Macduff arrived on horseback. "How has this come to pass?" he asked. His agitated horse frothed at the mouth as he fought to control her.

"Father a erm... A creature has erm... arrived on the beach. What can we do father?" said Gilbert as he strode over.

Father Macduff sighed, "let's move her to ancient crypt until the burial."

"Can such a creature be placed in the graveyard father?" blurted Megan

"Ney, young Megan, we will bury her under the oak. We do ney know whether she carries a soul." Father Macduff gazed at the incoming mist with a look of resounding sadness. He glanced amongst the weathered faces; at least one of them had caused it. He knew there was no escape because the resonance penetrated the mind and the soul. Death would seek and find its victim.

The rest of the pages were torn out. "Bloody hell!" Marty turned the book over searching for an author or something but there was nothing. He had to find out what happened!

CHAPTER 12

Sausage combustion!

Why do newly- formed couples have such a talent for rubbing singletons' noses in it? The evening air carried the smell of bonfires and cut grass. The group strolled towards the cove in the half-light with Johnny Boy plodding ahead. He carried the atmosphere of a toddler after a tantrum. Danny and Shana held hands and beamed at each other (a little too smugly for Johnny's liking!) Every so often, he glanced back with the look of a man who had received a ball kicking!

Marty was caught in no-man's land between the two factions. He walked with his hands in his pockets, ahead of the two lovers but slow enough not to catch up with Johnny and his mood. Marty was more absorbed in piecing together everything he had experienced.

As the group neared the cliff top, they slowed down. The ground was moist with dew and bracken crunched beneath their feet. Using the available moonlight, the group followed a rocky path down to the cove. A sheltered nook with an overhang beneath the cliff made the perfect place to sit and set up camp, even if the air carried the aroma of rotting seaweed. While the two lovers canoodled, Marty kept busy picking up dried sticks for the fire. When his arm was full he dumped his small bundle on the pebbles beside the snoggers and noticed that Johnny had also busied himself with gathering more driftwood. Together their collection was enough to create a decent sized fire.

Danny and Shana were oblivious to the mountain of wood that was accumulating and sat on a washed up log gazing at each other. Every so often, they caressed each other's faces. Johnny caught Marty's attention and made a vomiting gesture. Marty raised an eyebrow; he wasn't going to get involved!

Once the wood was gathered, Johnny Boy being Johnny arranged a perfect pyramid-like structure from the branches. A few insects understood their lives were in mortal danger and clambered away at speed. Johnny flicked the few remaining creatures to safety before squirting lighter fluid on the stack.

"Is that a good idea Johnny?" asked Marty before he could stop him.

The air was still in that moment. Danny snuggled up to Shana and glanced at Johnny. He shrugged, lit the match and... Voom! A blue and yellow flame wound from the newly lit match back to Johnny's hand. In that second, Johnny reflexed and launched the canister into the air. Bang! The lighter fluid erupted into flames. He bolted in the opposite direction before the fire rained onto the beach. Marty dived for cover while Shana and Danny fell backwards off the log.

For a second the group were silent, scattered patches of combusted lighter fluid burned on the beach. Johnny checked himself for burns and shuffled guiltily back to the fire.

"Would yer mind singeing me eyebrows there Johnny!" said Shana sharply.

"Shana don't get your thong on back to front!" said Johnny defensively.

Shana frowned at the thought of it, "don't you mean knickers in a twist?'

"Nope! Anyway, it was an accident," he said.

Marty stamped out the remaining lighter fluid flames and took a seat on a boulder. "I had a tutor once... In the sixties he was making a barbeque and squirted lighter fluid on it," said Marty thoughtfully.

"And your point is..." asked Johnny flatly, "no doubt there is some moral of the story on its way..."

"Well, he shot the lighter fluid with such force that it went past the barbecue and set fire to a tent with two people inside."

Johnny folded his arms and huffed, as he suspected!

"What happened to them?" asked Shana.

"Second-degree burns," Marty replied.

"Oh," said Shana. "So where did that come from then Marty?"

"It reminded me of when I accidentally set fire to the college. I did that with lighter fluid too."

"You never mentioned that before," said Danny helping Shana back on the log.

"Not really something that I'm proud of Danny."

Johnny smirked to himself.

"So... Go on," said Shana curiously.

"Well, I was doing this picture of a phoenix... To make a

firebird I put fire in a birdcage to represent it. That was why I used lighter fluid and-"

"And?" asked Johnny.

"Well, I wasn't aware that the room had no ventilation when I set fire to the cage. And..."

"And?"

"Well, the whole thing caught fire. You know how you learn to cover things on fire – you know - to get rid of the oxygen. Blah di blah," said Marty. "Well I did that."

"Amazing!" said Johnny sarcastically.

"Yeh... Unfortunately I did it with a six foot roll of flammable carpet!" said Marty glaring at Johnny.

"Bloody hell!" said Shana.

"Exactly-"

"So what happened?" asked Danny.

"Well, I was caught in an inferno when the whole thing combusted," said Marty making explosive noises and waving his arms.

"So where were the fire extinguishers?" asked Johnny.

"They were there... It was just... Well, they were black in a black studio. Luckily, my mate Dave came in at the right moment. He screamed and ran upstairs to the tutors shouting 'Marty's on fire.' The tutors came quickly but by the time they arrived, I had it under control. Well that was until they came in..."

"I don't get you," said Shana.

"Well... I used CO2, which worked for a few minutes, but as they rushed in they brought in a gust of fresh oxygen. The whole thing ignited... My head tutor screamed while I went back to putting out the fire. When the flames finally died down we threw the remainder of the carpet outside and used water canisters to drown it."

"So get to the point," said Johnny Boy.

"That tutor never forgave me. He was off with stress for two weeks," said Marty. "I passed the course though but was banned from using fire... He told me about his lighter-fluid incident. Somehow being here re-ignited the memory," said Marty with a grin.

The others cringed.

"Well, that's part of why I was going to work with dad in London. The photographic tutor was off most of the year. When he

59

was there, he called me into his office and asked me to take nice pictures of landscapes - how offensive is that?" said Marty.

"And it keeps bloody happening! Nice bloody pictures of landscapes – it's so done!"

"Who else told you to photograph landscapes Marty?" asked Shana

"Malcolm – the landlord! He said it while he was holding a shotgun too!"

Shana glanced at Danny and smirked. "A man… carrying a shotgun… told you to photograph nice landscapes… now how often do you hear that?"

Johnny grew bored of the story and prepared dinner. The group watched him produce various wrapped foods from his rucksack. He stabbed the potatoes with obvious frustration then wrapped everything in foil.

Danny kissed Shana.

"You two can cook your own or you'll get nothing!" said Johnny waving a string of sausages aggressively.

"Okay, so what are we cooking then?" asked Danny.

"Marshmallows?" said Shana trying to lighten the atmosphere.

"No. Sausages and burgers. Wrap them in the foil. Do some potatoes and chuck them on the bottom," said Johnny in a military tone. "And Danny get some beers sorted!"

"You want me to march too?"

Johnny didn't respond, but Shana saluted.

Marty stood up and wondered towards the sea. The lapping rhythm combined with the reflection of the moon was entrancing.

"Marty get your arse over here! I'm not your friggin' wife," called Johnny.

"I think he has PMT," said Shana.

"Shut it Shana!"

"Now Johnny you talk to me like that again and those sausages will be shoved where the sun doesn't shine!"

Marty casually walked from the water's edge. "Johnny would you chill out! This is meant to be fun!"

Johnny huffed and glanced back at him. "Sorry mate… I just like to get things in order…"

"Are the Speedos riding high Johnny?" said Marty crouching

close to the fire.

Johnny Boy's face cracked, he was being an arse!

"I really like it here... I think a person could really feel at peace," said Marty trying to change the subject.

"Sausages are ready!"

"So Johnny... What do you want out of life?" asked Shana.

Johnny's eyes flickered, he thought about men's magazines, Sundays, fur-lined slippers. He glanced about to make sure no one had read his mind about the slippers... He then took a deep breath and responded "Dun-no..."

"You must want something," said Marty.

It was a loaded question. If he wanted a rabbit, the analysis would be that really his inner child was a soft furry animal that ate grass. "A Ferrari would be nice. Ah yes," he said imagining it. "With a gorgeous model next to me," Johnny nodded and smiled a quirky smile.

"Why are you so bloody materialistic Johnny?" demanded Shana.

"A gorgeous model is real Shana!" said Johnny bluntly.

"Danny what do you want?" she asked rubbing his knee.

"Contentment," said Danny with a smug grin. He had read the answer in one of Shana's magazines.

"Eat your sausage you smug shit!" said Johnny glaring at Danny.

"What's wrong with contentment?" asked Danny with a straight face.

"It's not a Ferrari is it....? Danny!" Johnny Boy glowered.

After wrapping numerous sausages in foil, Marty looked up. "I sense tension."

"Leave it," said Johnny as he grabbed a bap and dropped a burger on the shingle. He quickly wiped it down, covered it in tomato sauce and thrust it at Marty. "Eat yer burger!"

Marty eyed the creation like an alien birth. While Johnny was concentrating on his next monstrosity, Marty threw the creation over his shoulder and pretended to mop his mouth with a tissue. Shana and Danny concealed their laughter and watched Johnny concentrate on his next creation.

"So Shana what do you want?" asked Marty.

"To be accepted and to feel safe," said Shana honestly.

"You friggin' girl. Next you'll say you want babies," said Johnny.

"That's natural, I'm a woman," she replied.

Johnny dropped a sausage in the fire. It exploded and expelled fat onto his hand.

"That's why we're here Johnny - to reproduce!" said Shana defensively.

"Really?" said Johnny mistaking her meaning. He smiled obligingly.

"Oh for goodness sake Johnny! I don't mean that's why we're here in the cove. I mean that's why we are alive!"

"So why are you a mechanic then?" he taunted.

"Because me dad taught me... And..."

Splash!

The group glanced over at the ocean. Something was out there watching.

CHAPTER 13
Butterflies crashing.

A loud splash followed by a series of small ripples captured the group's attention. A deep hum filled the air. The group scanned the ocean for the source of the eerie emanation. The resonation was a deeper tone than before – it was more masculine. Each of the group held their stomachs, the sound 'felt' like butterflies crashing into walls.

The resonation intensified. Johnny covered his ears but the sound penetrated the inside of his brain.

Splash!

It faded into the darkness.

Silence.

"What was that?" asked Johnny nervously devouring a burger.

"Just a splash," said Marty turning his attention to the contents of some foil.

"Now that was more than just a bloody splash Marty, and you know it!" said Shana studying him.

"Ghosts can't leave the house can they?" asked Johnny nervously.

Marty prodded a slightly burnt veggie sausage. "Don't know."

Splash! Splash!

The deep vibration circled once more. The group glanced at each other. Should they run? They all became quiet, trying to locate the source of the sound. Splash!

"It's by the rocks," said Shana curiously. "I have to see…"

"No, don't. I don't want any of us getting hurt," Johnny said urgently. "It's probably just a seal. Just leave it alone," he said with a quick glance at Danny.

Shana broke into a jog. There was no way that splash was just a seal!

"Shit! Be careful!" shouted Johnny.

"Ah, Johnny, you sound like me dad! If it's just a seal… Then there's nothing to be scared of is there now?"

"Danny if she's your girlfriend then go after her… It's dangerous round here… You know that!" Johnny noticed Marty studying him. "Danny go!"

63

Danny broke into a sprint and chased Shana towards the rocks. As he approached, Shana climbed onto the spit of rock and gazed into the ocean. The moon shimmered on the surface and Shana admired her pale, lucid reflection. Beneath the surface, a dark shape disturbed the water. Shana inhaled quickly and gasped, it was definitely not a seal! She followed the shape as it surfaced and submerged rhythmically until it unexpectedly dived. "What the?" she whispered when a figure leapt from the depths.

"Shana," said Danny touching her arm.

"Shit Danny - you scared me!" she said with a jump and a scream. She followed the creature's trajectory and pointed over towards the cove. "Look over there - something keeps jumping out of the water."

Two more sizeable figures leapt and dived in the distance.

"What do you think they are?" asked Danny.

"They kind of look human in this light don't they?"

"You know one time I smoked too much banana… And we were convinced that a stick was a snake. Then we were convinced we saw-" said Danny interrupted by three shapes leaping from the sparkling reflection of the moon. The resonance intensified and Shana was entranced.

"That's beautiful," she said holding her heart.

"How is that beautiful?" asked Danny with a frown. "It sounds like a deep hum!"

"It just is." A look of longing appeared on Shana's face, she was entranced.

"I think we need the others over here." Danny launched himself off the rocks and onto the sand. "Don't get too close Shana and definitely don't touch them!"

The deep resonation circled just beyond the spit of rock. Carefully she tiptoed to the edge but skidded on the damp bladder wrack. Once balanced, she found a good position hovering on the edge. "What on earth are you?"

"Johnny, Marty, come quick, over here," said Danny sprinting back to the fire. "You have to see this!"

"Not more weird shit Danny?" said Johnny with a loud sigh. Marty and Johnny glanced over at Shana's moonlit silhouette.

64

"I guess we should at least take a look," said Marty.

"Not interested," said Johnny. "I'll keep the fire burning."

Caught in her thoughts, Shana was engrossed in finding the source of the resonation and crouched on the edge of the rocks. She squinted to see beyond the reflection of the water. There was something down there and that something was peering back at her. There was a sudden motion and Shana jolted; a moment later, she tumbled into the cold darkness. Splosh!

Pitch-black.

The water was bitter, filled with seaweed and resembled tar. For a moment, she glimpsed the source of the resonance but rapidly descended into unconsciousness.

"Quick!" screamed Marty.

The men bolted towards the spit of rock.

Shana was gone!

Underwater beams of moonlight pierced the darkness. It was cold and peaceful where Shana was suspended. As the air evacuated Shana's lungs, the resonation deepened and circled. Whatever the resonance was, it seemed to be holding back.

Contact! A tingle like static travelled over her lips.

On the rocks Marty, Danny and Johnny Boy searched frantically. Shana was nowhere to be seen.

"Shana?" shouted Marty. "Where is she? Where did she go?"

Danny searched on his knees, just above the water. Johnny rested on his belly trying to see through the watery film.

Nothing.

"Right… I'm going in," he said undressing.

"I can't see her anywhere though. She must be at the bottom. I'll go in," said Danny.

"No I should go in - I'm the lifeguard!" said Johnny.

There was a large splash followed by three more sloshes nearing the beach. The group turned. Was it Shana? A shape carrying a limp figure emerged from the surface and dived. That silhouette appeared wrapped in a figure which darkness concealed. It had to be Shana didn't it?

"It's bloody eating her!" screamed Johnny sprinting towards the creatures. "What the hell are these freaks?" Johnny waded into the water and prepared to fight.

Underwater Shana returned to partial consciousness. Her head throbbed as she became aware that she was cold, wet and restricted. Something held her in its arms and that something was filling her lungs with air. Instinctively she struggled but 'it' was too strong. Feeling helpless, she began to sob. The resonation changed tone; whatever it was sensed how she felt. They were connected! Its intentions were pure and she perceived it could 'feel' into the depths of her soul. The resonation was different; she knew she was safe because whatever the resonance was, it made her feel loved. The different tonal vibrations revealed that other 'creatures' were close by. With her lungs filled with air, her supply pulled away and gazed into her heart. With a kind blink, its eyelids moved from the outer edges of its eye. Behind the creature, the moon was enveloped in a halo made up of rainbows. In the beauty of the moment, she was witnessing the universe from the other side.

The resonance gently guided her to the shallows. It took both of her hands, gazed into her eyes and into her heart. The connection tingled up her spine and through her whole body. Subtly it resonated, submerged and disappeared. Something profound had just taken place. Her heart was beating with a new feeling, a feeling that was clean and pure.

CHAPTER 14
Comprehending truth.

After wrapping Shana in Danny's jacket, the group returned to sitting around the fire just staring. No one could fully comprehend what they had just seen. Now, whilst staring into the flames, the reality dawned on them: something with a human form and intelligence was living out in the ocean. Did the village know?

Shana gazed into the flames and relived the experience. She remembered in detail how with final exhalation came the sensation of a static tingle running up her arm and down her spine. As she thought about the connection, she remembered how a second tingle moved over her lips and had gently a supplied her with air.

All the while, Danny stared into the fire with his mind completely blank. He enjoyed the sensation of the fire burning his eyeballs. At the same time, Johnny packed and re-packed his nap sack. Marty considered the story, the sounds and what he, himself had experienced. How could they exist and no one know?

"So, what will we do about this then?" said Shana, breaking the awkwardness.

"What do you think we should do?" asked Marty.

"Well, shouldn't we tell someone?" Shana replied thoughtfully.

"I think we should keep it to ourselves," said Danny, resisting the urge to blink.

"Who would believe us anyway?" Johnny slammed his backpack down. "Marty talks to ghosts, and yep Shana here, snogs sea creatures! Lardy dardy dar! Let's get straitjackets and direct us all to the nearest loop-home! If anyone listened to you they'd think you deserve to be sectioned and I do ney like straitjackets, not even for magic tricks - get me?"

Johnny stood up and cracked his back. "Hello my name is Johnny and I see fish people... And ghosts. Oh let's put me on one of those morning programmes...People can phone in and recount their experiences of when their sardine sang to them from a salad!" With an erratic wave, he came to a standstill. "This is ridiculous? Yer hear? I say we keep it quiet!"

Shana and Marty watched in amazement. They had never really seen their friend so passionate about anything apart from small swimming trunks and women. Danny didn't pay too much attention anti-blinkism was his 'new thing'. The heat continued to dry his eyes balls. Blink. Blink. Damn!

"Look, I hear what you're saying Johnny," said Shana calmly. Tucking his shirt in, he stood before the group with the light of the fire flickered all over him. "It's just bloody odd! Don't you think?"

"Maybe we should keep this quiet until we know more," said Shana glancing at the others for their approval.

"I think we should make a visit to me gran. She has an idea of these things," said Danny with his eyes remaining fixed on the fire.

"I don't want much to do with this, it worries me," said Johnny sincerely. "It could really affect my chances of promotion. I don't want the other lifeguards thinking I am some kind of fish-friendly-fanatic! In my opinion, this is all too weird... Just nort normal fish and ghosts... Ghosts and fish... And Ghosty, if yer can hear me yer can keep yer dead arse away from me yer hear?"

A solitary sausage burst out of its skin and spat sizzling fat onto Johnny's calf. "You said they canny physically hurt you!"

"Maybe you're the exception with the sausage ghost," said Marty maintaining a straight face.

Johnny picked up his backpack. "I do ney want to talk about this crap anymore! I'll see yer back at the cottage." With a definite stride, he headed in the direction of Crooked Cottage.

Danny, Marty and Shana dowsed the fire and shuffled amongst the awkward silence.

"What do yer want to do about this then Marty?" asked Shana thoughtfully.

"I think we need to find out more before we talk to anyone." Danny glanced out to sea, "there is definitely something out there... I reckon me gran will be able to tell us the truth... We really do need to go and see her."

"Shana are you okay?" asked Marty patting her arm.

"You know I think I have to take a bit of time to process what happened... I think I'm still in shock. When I know what I feel about it I think I will be able to talk about it."

The group slowly wondered back to the cottage via Straight

Lane. A few men with their arms slung about each other's shoulders zigzagged in the direction of the harbour. They were probably naming a street together.

CHAPTER 15
The early morning call...

It was five o'clock in the morning when the sun penetrated the crack in Danny's curtain. Curled up next to Danny, Shana laid with a beam of light shining directly in her eyes. Her arms were numb with sleep. She flopped them over the side of the bed and grimaced with the prickling sensation of pins and needles.

With a glance over her shoulder, Shana peered at Danny. She hadn't woken him had she? Shana shook her head, thirty bagpipers and a bugler probably wouldn't cause him to stir! She had learned recently that only the smell of food woke him. Whether awake or asleep, whenever anyone had food, he would start squawking like a hungry chick.

Shana took a deep breath and listened. The sound was still there. It had been present all night and had wound through her repetitive dreams. 'He' was calling.

Shana crept to the bathroom and filled a glass with water. She cleaned her teeth and checked to see whether Danny had noticed her absence. Nothing! He laid at the centre of the bed in a starfish pose. As much as he hogged the bed, he did look incredibly cute while he slept.

In the neighbouring room, wrapped in his blue duvet, Marty maintained a tight foetal position. He resisted opening his eyes, rolled over, and covered his ears with the pillow. Nothing blocked out the sound – somehow she had penetrated his skull with the calling. The problem was the more she called the more he yearned.

With the ring of the alarm, Marty reluctantly plodded across the room, grabbed some clothes and cleaned his teeth at the same time.

"Ah!" screamed Marty when he noticed Shana lurking on the landing. "Bloody hell Shana! Bring on a heart attack why don't you?" Shana smirked mischievously.

"Marie used to do that too."

"What, get up in the morning?"

"No - hide outside the toilet and jump out," said Marty remembering his malicious sister.

"Now I hardly jumped out Marty!" She noticed his puffy eyes.

"Well, whatever you did Shana - it scared the living shit out of me!"

"What rather than the dead shit?"

"Shana it's too early for banter. I need to get me head in order."

He plodded into the bathroom and spat out the remaining toothpaste. A few seconds later, Marty leant out of the bathroom, "so why are you up so early?"

"Probably the shock of what happened. Plus I couldn't really sleep. How did you sleep now Marty?"

Marty shook his head, "not very well."

The pair studied each other.

"Did you hear anything unusual?" Shana asked curiously.

Marty sucked his lip through his teeth, "what do you mean, unusual?"

"Well, not normal," she said.

"Shana I know the actual meaning of the word unusual but can you get to the point?"

"Marty, I heard the sound. I feel like something is calling me, but the noise isn't coming in through my ears… It's kind of in me head."

Marty scratched his nose, "what does it sound like?"

"That sound they made last night," said Shana shifting awkwardly and folding her arms.

"What do you think it is?" he asked.

"I don't really know Marty… It isn't like anything I ever experienced before," she replied.

In silence, Marty paced. "I would say it was shock, but I have something similar going on…"

Shana attempted to decipher Marty's expression, what did he mean?

Marty glanced at his watch, "you want to go for a surf?"

Shana nodded but held back, "Marty do you think it's 'safe' to go in the water?"

"I think whatever they are, they're fine," he said with a definite nod.

The pair quietly descended the stairs and left the cottage by the side door. In the shed, Marty obligingly brought out both surfboards. Shana hated spiders and since the shed was full of cobwebs, spiders were likely to be lurking. Shana checked her board for the eight-legged creatures, hoisted the strap of the board-bag onto her shoulder and the pair strolled down to harbour.

"Marty do you mind if I get in up the road? That drop still gives me the shivers…."

"No worries, but Shana I'm used to driving it now," said Marty.

"I wouldn't care if Bertha could fly… I still don't like that drop and would rather stay away."

Marty gestured for Shana's board, placed it on top of his and slid the van door shut with a slam.

"What's the time Marty?" asked Shana.

"Five fifteen, we had best get a shimmy on," he said climbing into the driver's seat.

"I'll meet you up the road. Now you be careful Marty… You're tired and those brakes are not the best. None of that boy racing - slowly you hear?" she said breaking into a jog.

Marty turned the key in the ignition and Brrr Bang! The sound of a dynamite detonation made Shana glance over her shoulder and smile. Seagulls launched into the air screeching and pelted Shana with the contents of their intestines.

After a ten-point turn, Marty drew level with Shana.

"I'm sure the locals enjoyed the detonation there Marty, and look the buggers hit me with last night's dinner!" said Shana wiping her shoulder with a tissue.

"It's lucky," Marty laughed.

"How is it lucky to be shat on by a bird at five in the morning?" Marty shrugged and drove towards the surf. "They were lucky they hit a moving target!"

"You know Marty…. You really should let me have a look at the engine. It sounds like you have a blockage," said Shana.

"She's fine Shana…"

"No Marty, she's not fine! Now I know how precious you are about people touching 'your' van but sometimes we have to allow these things to happen to get her into a better state. Blockage denial will only result in a big explosion and you know that!"

Marty sucked his lip.

Shana unconsciously shook her head; he was avoiding things again!

"So… Are we going to Aberdour again?" she said breaking the awkward silence.

Marty nodded.

"Which side? Fort side or cave side?"

"I reckon the same place as yesterday, by the fort," he replied. Shana gave a knowing look. "Yer think she'll be there?" Marty blushed and sucked his lip again.

"Love is in the air, everywhere I..." sang Shana.

"Come off it Shana... I met the girl once. If she's there she's there and we are going for a surf..."

"Okay... Tetchy! Anyway, it looks like it could be good - the wind's offshore again," she said glancing out of the window.

Back at Crooked Cottage, Danny woke with a jolt. He glanced around; Shana was gone. He wrapped himself in his duvet and walked sleepily across the landing. Marty's bedroom door was open. Danny yawned, stretched and almost dropped the duvet. In his half-asleep state, he made his way down to the kitchen.

When Danny arrived on the middle floor, he paused. Something was racing towards him. It sounded like the wind. "In our blood stands the curse- take heed," said a rasping voice blowing a gust of cold air in his face.

Fear rigidly gripped Danny's body. Frozen droplets appeared in the air and the landing window made a cracking noise as ice crept across the surface of the pane. Danny stepped backwards into the entrance of the digital darkroom.

"You can't escape. It's in the blood... It will happen to you as it did to me. Death is coming... You have a choice to make."

Danny closed the door to the darkroom and panted. What was it? Was he dreaming? Why hadn't 'it' followed him inside? Silently he took a seat by the computer and stared at the door. Would she follow? He sat for a short time waiting. Nothing. He glanced at the waste-paper basket beside the computer and pulled out some burned prints. He frowned as he examined them and noticed the deformation on the surface of the water. A jolt of realisation shot through him. Maybe the stories his gran had told him as a wee nipper carried truth. If that was the case, then were the stories about witches, the rituals and the pirates also true? With the scratch of the cheek, Danny turned to the computer and tapped a key. Password? Danny smiled and typed 'SURF'. The images flashed up on screen. Had Marty manipulated them or were they actually real? The happenings of the previous night flashed through his mind.

"Never live in the crooked cottage Danny, 'cause crooked things go on there…" he muttered. That was what his gran had said. "Strange things happen and that is why no local chooses to live in that house. It will just take one thing to wake her… And when she is woken… The cycle will begin again…" What had woken her? He picked up one of the printouts, rolled it up and took it to his room. He had a few things to work out.

Over at Aberdour, Marty and Shana were suited up in their wetsuits and ready with their surfboards. For a moment, the pair stood in silence admiring the beauty of the scene before them. The surf was perfect, forming large, clean walls and flowing elegantly towards the shore. With a knowing glance, the pair jogged into the sea and launched themselves. The race to paddle out back was on and this time Shana had the advantage. When the pair arrived at their destination, they rested and watched the sun illuminate the clouds with a golden glow and a series of rainbows. It was beautiful.

Both turned their boards and prepared to catch the incoming set. When it was close, they paddled and caught waves simultaneously. They were so engrossed in catching the wave that neither had noticed four shapes swimming towards them. What's more, the roar of the surf drowned out the 'sound'.

Shana and Marty rode off their waves simultaneously. There were patches of mist forming and the air felt static. "Do you think there's a storm coming?" asked Shana paddling close.

Marty shook his head, "the sky is clear – but I get what you mean."

"I guess we should accept that this is Scotland and they have ten seasons in a day."

"But there aren't ten seasons Shana."

"Exactly!"

Marty studied Shana but said nothing. Whatever went on in her head was a phenomenon.

The pair rested for a while and sat on their boards. The water around them was disturbed and the sound intensified. Shana glanced at Marty. "What do we do?"

"Just stay calm and if anything happens catch a wave."

Shana nodded but paddled closer to Marty. "I think it's better if we stay close together."

The resonation sounded and four 'creatures' surfaced. Amongst the group were two male and two female, including Iris.

For a moment, there was an awkward silence. The 'creature' that had saved Shana was beside Iris. Shana recognised his song and blushed. With a gentle smile, he admired Shana's female form in the way that a truly masculine man studies a woman. She sensed his intentions and grew increasingly crimson. "Marty what do we do?" Iris swam to Marty and placed her hand on his knee. "You here... Good!" she said with a gentle smile.

Marty nodded. "Erm... How do I ask this? Erm what are you?"

"We live sea, no land," she replied.

Shana glanced at Marty. "How come you're the only one who speaks English? In fact how come you speak English at all?"

"Please speak slow." Iris glanced at the others, "I learn from fishman in village. Keep secret please."

Marty nodded and glanced at Shana who accepted.

"I should ney tell you. Secret..." she said nervously.

"Why not?" asked Shana.

"These secrets should ney be discussed. Yer nort of village. Yer outsiders. No necklace," said Iris trailing off.

"So why do you speak to us then?"

Iris played with the water, "you in sea too. You young. Ney youngens in village. They leave; they no like secret. The olduns keep to themselves and away..." she said sadly.

The man who had saved Shana tapped Iris on the shoulder and gestured at Shana.

"El gey," he said.

"You pretty," said Iris translating. She watched Shana's pupil's dilating. "You like too!"

"Erm..." said Shana tidying her hair. "What is that language?"

"Local call Doric," said Iris.

"And what is the 'sound' you make?"

Iris smiled, "it is 'our' water speak. You like him? He need know."

Shana was silent. The creature was beautiful; he made her light up and increase her blush.

"Yer then," said Iris making a small clap.

The man of the sea smiled and Shana's stomach flipped. Shana further arranged her hair and instinctively licked her lips.

Marty watched; he'd never seen Shana so... Feminine! Her masculine armour of survival had crumbled. Underneath the 'act', she was feminine. He had never seen her that way before.

The man of the sea gestured to the beach. Some tourist surfers arrived and erratically attempted to paddle out back.

"We go... We will call," said Iris as the group submerged and disappeared.

Shana sighed and glanced at Marty guiltily. The special moment had been broken.

"I think it's time to go in," she said sadly. "Let's catch a few waves before those e-diots arrive."

"Shana we will see them again... We have a connection..."

"I'm gonna catch this wave Marty," said Shana paddling.

As Shana pushed herself to standing on the wave, Marty noticed something about her had shifted – had she fallen in love?

On the beach, the pair changed separately. Their thoughts absorbed them. Once Marty was dressed, he silently gazed towards the ocean. He could still hear Iris. How was that possible?

Shana walked to the van fastening her belt. "Just ask me Marty. I know you're brooding over something. Your shoulders raise and you have a contorted expression."

"I don't want to interfere, but what about Danny?" he asked with concern.

"I'm not going out with him Marty. I just slept in his bed once. It can just be friends," she said defensively.

"It's just... He's quite sensitive. It might be better to sort that out sooner rather than later. I couldn't bear it if you kept him hanging and I do not want to be stuck in the middle or get blamed!"

Shana sighed and arranged a patch of grass with her foot. "I will sort it out. I just have to work out how I feel about it Marty. The reality is I'm attracted to a 'man' who lives in the sea. Talk about Mr unobtainable. How is there a future in that?"

"Shana you can't help who you fall in love with," he said sincerely.

"Are you telling me or yourself?"

He didn't know. Was he talking to himself?

"Now Marty, let me have a bit of time and I will then take my action. You know me Marty, when I know what to do – I do it. Other people have a tendency to dither…" she said with a certain look that was clearly directed at him. "Although I should quote me aunt – when true love finds you take it with both hands. Love is the most important thing in life and it enables you to give. Now keep that to yourself. I don't want people thinking I'm all wafty!"

"I would never think you were wafty Shana, and sometimes you just need to surrender and let go. When you know what you want - let life do the work for you…" said Marty with an affectionate pat.

"Marty of the wisdom kind. Now would yer take yer own advice or would you think, re-think and think again," said Shana with a mocking smile. "Maybe yer just need to feel it and go with it. Get out of that brain of yours!"

With a fold of the arms, Marty accepted what she was saying.

"If you had the opportunity for true love and 'felt' it would you take it?" she asked watching his reaction closely.

"I think so…"

"T'inking is not feeling now is it Marty? Yer need to break the habit."

With a loud exhalation, Marty shook his head, 'feeling' was alien to him and now he felt for a woman whose existence was also alien to him.

"I know what you're 'thinking' Marty… From my point of view, he was gorgeous but it's not just that… I was so connected to him. I feel his presence and he feels so clean and unmessed up. Plus he has an air of mystery about him - a certain je-ne-se-quoi. Oh God… Why?" she said lifting her hands to the heavens.

"Forbidden fruit…" said Marty with a grin.

"Fruit of the sea! Anyway, look who's talking… I sense a little tingle on yer dingle Marty again…" said Shana re-directing the discussion.

Shana was right.

"Do you want to get in the van," said Marty glancing towards the ocean. Was it possible to truly love? Or was it just another illusion?

Shana watched and crossed her arms. "Marty… I know what's going on!" she said climbing into the van. "Try to feel and not analyse."

Marty turned the key in the ignition. Brrr Bang!
Some of the surfing tourists fell off their boards. The pair laughed and drove in the direction of Gardenstown. On the way, they drove past Malcolm who was cheerfully whistling whilst polishing his shotgun.

CHAPTER 16
Dazed, confused and the ancient art of egg laying.

Back at the cottage, Danny stood staring out of the kitchen window. "I wonder how many chickens are laying eggs at this precise moment?" he said before biting into an apple. "Probably quite a few." Strangely, he felt relief. When the apparition evaporated, she had left a message for him on the computer screen. Something about what she had said had calmed him. The family line had followed a pattern throughout their history. He now knew he had a destiny to fulfil and a pattern to break. What's more, his gran had the answers. As weird as it all was, there was something special about what was taking place. He would keep it to himself though.

From the window, he watched Marty pull in just before the harbour and waited for Shana to jump out. As soon as he finished his apple, he rushed down Straight Lane. When he reached Shana, he rotated her, put his arm around her waist and route-marched her back down to the harbour.

The pair perched on a wall and watched Marty navigate the thin harbour road.

"There's hardly any distance at all," said Shana cringing.

"Actually…" said Danny, letting go of Shana and running up to Bertha. Excitedly he rapped on the window.

Marty stopped mid-manoeuvre and wound down the window.

"What is it Danny?"

"Marty I called me gran. She's invited us up to her cottage. You want to go now Marty?" he asked. "Then you don't have to park… And it's Saturday… Think about the shortbread Marty."

Marty considered the drive, the shortbread and the adventure. It would be a good distraction and may reveal answers.

"Come on… You want to Marty - I know you do. Me granny's so cool… You'll love her and she knows stuff," said Danny enthusiastically.

"Where does she live?" asked Marty.

"Up by Drichen. You know… By the stone circle. They used to

make sacrifices up there," he replied.

"What is it with this place?"

"It's all part of our long, lurid history," replied Danny.

"So are you ready to go now then Danny?"

Danny nodded enthusiastically, "I just need to grab a few things. I'll be real quick."

Shana watched Danny turn and run past. "Shana we're going to me grans... Get in the van."

Shana's mouth tightened. "Danny would yer ask me rather than bloody tell me!"

"Nope!" said Danny with a cheeky grin.

Shana stomped up the harbour road to her climbing in place and watched Marty turn Bertha round.

Whilst Marty was mid-turn, Danny jogged down the road with a rucksack and climbed in the front seat. "Shana looks a bit moody. What did you say to her Marty?"

"She was fine just now Danny," he replied.

Danny glanced at Shana, what was it with girls?

Shana climbed in the back, pulled her legs into her chest and looked out of the window without saying a word.

"You know how to get there Danny?" asked Marty glancing at Shana in the rear-view mirror.

"We can go via Memsie. The woods where three witches were supposed to have lived. They all mysteriously disappeared. I can tell you more about that later," he said glancing over at Shana, who appeared to have a rancid smell under her nose.

Marty recognised Danny's gestures were edgy. What was he covering?

"So what's happening? Does someone actually want to tell me? Or maybe they could ask me..." said Shana in cutting tone.

"We're going to see Danny's Gran. First we'll travel by some sacrificial stones and then up to a place where three witches disappeared..."

"We should also make a sacrifice then..." said Shana nodding towards Danny.

Marty glanced at Danny. "Danny, mate... I think you might have done something to annoy her... I suggest you work out what it is and say sorry..."

Danny frowned. He hadn't done anything wrong had he?

"Look, a burial mound," said Marty pointing at a brown sign after fifteen minutes of driving. The group followed the road and stopped by a pyramidal pile of white stones.
"Is that it? That's the burial mound?" said Shana scratching her cheek.
"Some say the mound will make you fertile if you lay your hand on it. Others say that if you touch it you'll release the spirit of a witch," said Danny in his best 'lecturing' voice.
"It's a pile of stones there Danny. That's all! I could make better myself with a few pebbles from the shore!" said Shana.
"Leave it alone – it could be dangerous," said Danny.
"Danny! Now it's just a pile of stones!"
"Remember what happened last night… Did you think 'they' could exist before? Now I suggest you do ney belittle what you do ney know about Shana!" said Danny.
Shana huffed and folded her arms again. He was really getting up her nose!
"Oh, and I would ney be playing with the witches neither," he said seriously.
Noticing the 'atmosphere,' Marty drove in the direction of Drichen, he wasn't going to get involved.
"So is that a burial mound too Danny?" she asked pointing out every pile of stones on the journey. On that particular road there happened to be a lot of building work taking place.
"Ach, stop taking the piss, will yer?"
Shana smirked to herself, "oh look, there's another – they must be burying people in the walls Danny."
Sometimes Shana was a complete spack!

CHAPTER 17

Cottages, shortbread and insane grannys!

On the side of a steep hill, surrounded by a few twisted trees, a grey brick cottage stood solemnly alone. The only brightness in the barren landscape was the warm purple glow of heather. As the camper drew close, Marty noticed a small stream flowed beside the cottage and a curved, wooden bridge crossed it.

"How old is your granny Danny?" asked Shana.

"In her eighties," he said proudly.

"She's a little isolated. Don't you think?"

"She likes it that way Shana. She moved out here when her husband drowned. The sea reminded her too much of him. Anyway when you meet her you'll ney think she's older than fifty," said Danny proudly.

"But still… She's far away from everything and everyone."

"Wait until you meet her Shana. She's not like normal old ladies... She has more energy than you and me put together. My folks do her shopping and she visits them in Fraserburgh all the time," he said. "She's perfectly fine! – You'll see."

"So what actually happened to your grandfather Danny? I don't want to do a Marty special and put my foot in it."

"He died years ago with my uncle in a fisher tragedy," Danny replied.

"Only my father survived, otherwise I would ney be here today. My uncle and gramps sunk because they wore too heavier boots. My father threw off his boots and swam to some floating wood. He lay unconscious for days. Then you know what's strange? He was washed up on the cove in Gardenstown. He said angels carried him. He never mentions anything about it though. He kept the happenings to himself for forty years and always says he has selective amnesia."

"That's mad!" said Shana

"What a story," said Marty. "So were your grandfather and uncle lost altogether?"

"Well my Granny says they had the two golden hoops in their ears. It was lucky 'cause me father did ney. The hoops, for the fishers, are there to console them. You can be hooked and carried straight to heaven rather than be lost at sea. For a fisher there's nothing worse than your body being lost and never found."

"It's a comforting belief," said Marty.

"That's lovely and so sad. So your granny has lived alone for forty years?" asked Shana.

"Yep. She's a bit of a hermit. Some of the locals think she's involved in weird stuff because she's so young in herself. I reckon it's the family genetics and of course the locals love to make stories…"

"How does she deal with that?" asked Marty.

"She calls them daft. She says her diet keeps her young and her exercise keeps her fit. That's all there is to it."

The camper pulled up outside the cottage and an old lady, who looked remarkably energetic, came bounding to the door. She wore a tartan tracksuit, a pink hairnet (filled with curlers) and had bright blue eye-shadow. The sheer volume of hair the old dear had for her age was astounding. With a cheeky look and a mischievous twinkle in her eye, she waved them over.

"Well are you just goin' to sit and stare at me or are yer going to move yer rears into me cottage?" she asked.

Shana smirked.

Granny trotted over to Danny and ruffled his hair, "hello there Danny. Who are yer wee friends then?"

"Shana and Marty," he said patting each of them.

"What kind o' names are those? Nothing biblical in either, eh?"

"Shana means small but wise."

"Is that so?" said Granny peering at her. "Well, yer daft cookies are yer going to stand outside all day? Maybe we could talk through the window if that's the way you'll have it," she said. "Danny, how did you come by these people? They're outsiders aren't they?"

"I moved in with them Granny. I told you I moved to Crooked Cottage," said Danny with a nod.

"Now, why did yer do such a foolish thing after all the warnings?" asked Granny signalling for the group to follow.

"I'm sure yer did ney mention it before… Aye though… Lasted a week so far. Seems the old lady's being good ta yer."

With a curious glance, Marty noticed Shana was intrigued too.

"Come in. Take yer dirty shoes off and leave them on the outer step eh. I'll tell yer more over shortbread and tea. Excuse the state of the room. It's only me here. It serves no purpose to waste yer life a polishing and a dustin' twice daily - does it now?"

Marty and Shana glanced about the rustic room filled with tartan covers and sheeps' hides.

"It looks clean to me," said Shana inhaling the aroma of freshly baked shortbread.

"Aye, it would. Yer brought up in modern times where people think things are clean when they're not. But yer canny help the way you were brought up, can you? Shana is it? Now let me have a look at yer," said Granny taking Shana's shoulders with both hands. "Young lady you need some weight on those boncs! You're not much in the way of food for a wild beast, are yer? You look like a pipe cleaner!"

Marty covered his mouth and glanced at Danny who was also sniggering.

"Yer not one of those vegetable people, are yer?"

"A vegetarian?" said Shana.

"Aye, thought so. No meat on yer! You need to eat meat yer hear? How else will you survive a winter, yer daft wee girl?"

"But I'm… not.." Shana tried to argue.

Granny appeared to have selective hearing. "Come over here. Come and see me in me prime - before the bus hit me." With a strong tug, Granny dragged Shana over to the wall.

"You were very pretty," she said studying the picture. "How did you get hit by a bus when there can't be that many around here?"

"Shana being hit by a bus is just a way of saying me age caught up with me," she said peering at her as though she was an imbecile. Danny hid his mouth with his hand and purposely avoided being picked on.

"You're a nice wee girl. Now can you turn a heel of a sock?" asked Granny curiously.

"No, but I can fix a car," Shana said proudly.

"And what purpose does that serve? What yer doin' a man's job for? You're a beautiful girl. Bit skinny and a bit flat on top but why waste your femininity on oil and grime? Of course, I am glad to see you do ney display yourself as they do in those magazines. Breasts are to feed babies and not men's play things. Don't you agree… Aye?" said Granny not waiting for Shana's response.

Danny coughed as he laughed.

"Did yer ney warn them of me Danny?" said Granny watching his reaction.

"Nope," said Danny with a smirk.

"Right, you can all come into my special room with the fire and the skins. It's cosy in there. Take a seat and I'll make us tea and serve shortbread," she said turning toward the kitchen.

"Now you're nort saying much there young Marty. Has the cat got yer tongue?" she asked.

"I'm just watching Mrs..."

"I'm nort no misses. Call me Nelly. That's me name and that's all we can say 'bout that!"

"Okay, Nelly," said Marty quietly.

Shana appeared pleased the attention had shifted from her and went to sit down.

"Owe noo. I've ney finished with yer yet," said Nelly. "I need to show yer me man and seek yer approval." On the wall was a series of pictures of Nelly's family including her mother, brothers and sons.

"Sad it is. They've all departed in one way or another apart from Danny's father. Some went to Iceland and married. The others were taken by the sea. So sad it was but I still see them in me mind. They hover around now and again," she said trailing her hand through the air.

Shana glanced up at the decorated oak beams on the ceiling. "How old's the cottage Nelly?"

"No idea. Could be hundreds I suppose dear... Oh, and before I forget, here's the language book for yers. Danny said something about you being interested in old languages," she said reaching into her embroidered handbag. "Now I must mention... I know there's something afoot. Yer living in Crooked Cottage and yer want to learn the old languages, Doric or Gaelic?" she asked.

"I think it's Gaelic," said Shana. "But I would like to see both."

"I see...I will warn yer now - that house is a test me bairn," Nelly sighed. "For yer to last a week is something ney usually possible. There must be blood in yer or yer would have been driven away... Unless... Unless nothing. I'll check yer clan lines," she said and prepared the tea. "Is there blood in yer veins?" she said randomly, grabbed Shana's wrist and slapped it. "So it must be known, fate's playing a game with yer kiddies. Be careful now."

Marty glanced at Shana with a puzzled look and Shana shrugged.

"I think I need to tell yer a wee story me granny told me... This'll clear things up a little. Oh, before we start, take a shortbread. You're too skinny yerself Marty. Yer need some meat on yer if yer going to be a man... Wet farts canny survive in the wind!"

Shana smirked and watched Marty frown at the thought of such an image. Nelly offered the biscuits and poured tea from her blue, floral teapot.

"I love shortbread," announced Shana.

"How can yer love shortbread, ya daft bugger?" said Nelly eyeing her. "What kind a kiddies would yer have, eh? To love is to love a person. It is what you can give and whether they are worthy... You need to love shrewdly for sharing love with too many is self-destructive. If yer love shortbread then surely the kiddies would be shortbread boys n' girls - eh? And yer do ney want those eaten with tea!"

Shana blushed. What did Nelly know?

"You know that Gardenstown is no ordinary place. People visit and people pass by. Though the families stay the same." Nelly filled the third cup and paused.

"Are they inbred?" Danny butted in.

"Ach noo... Ach maybe. I'm sure there's a few- but it's not spoken of. Now Danny why ask such a question?" Nelly passed the teacups to each of them and gestured at the shortbread.

"Because I'm young and naïve," he replied with a cute smile.

"You interrupt again and I'll give yer a hiding! Get me?" Nelly prepared to bite into her shortbread and smiled.

Danny's lip protruded playfully.

"The families here have histories," said Nelly pausing. "Now your Crooked Cottage has had families live there. Many have prospered and moved to bigger dwellings. Others have had more than their fair share of tragedy." With a deep breath, she considered the best way to share what she knew.

"The ghost known as Megan has been there many a year in Crooked Cottage. Or should I say Cram Tay of Gamrae? She has a fixation with baby girls. She perished because of her own child."

"How?" asked Marty.

"I told yers not to butt in. I lose me trail of thought. I'm old yer know… Anyway, no one knows exactly but apparently there are answers in the cottage."

Shana glanced at Danny and Marty. What was in the cottage?

"Her tragedy left a dark mark on the interior. There is many a slippery patch on a person's doorstep. We all have them, don't we? Even me, yes me," said Nelly leaning forward to stoke the fire.

Shana gnawed at her nails.

With a swish of the poker, Nelly pointed the smouldering tip at Shana who bit her hand.

"Would yer stop chewing yer fingers? You'll chew your nails, then yer hand. What's to stop yer chewing yer arm right off! Yer daft lass!"

"So what is it with the house?" asked Shana sitting on her hands.

"The house has a special line passing through it. One side good and the other bad. Those who are good become greater. The bad often become depressed, sometimes suicidal. They have been known to be called to the water. Mark my words, any bad thoughts will bring trouble," she said waving the poker.

"They hears the thoughts."

Nelly scratched her head under her curlers, "It's all just stories though."

Shana and Marty exchanged glances; stories carried truth.

"If yer have any trouble say… Fey me Fey. Yey ger way o fash me lasho si dubh ochd," repeated Nelly.

"What does it mean Nelly?" Marty sat forwards in his seat.

"Mystical influence keep away or there'll be trouble in a dark hollow grave," she translated and stirred her tea. She watched the tea leaves form patterns in the remaining brown liquid.

"Shana you have an interesting time ahead. And Marty, you're ney as innocent as yer appear," she said studying him.

Marty smiled mysteriously and sipped his tea.

"There's reason for everything," said Nelly. "You'll see as it unfolds and you will only understand your role in the end. Oh, and Marty a decision made gives yer power. No decision hands power to others. It might be worth remembering that because yer canny resent someone who makes the decision on yer behalf because you handed over the power of that decision."

"Marty what time is it? We shouldn't stay too long..." said Shana.

"Now, the reason that I'm alone is so that I can practice me yoga and my healing arts," said Nelly purposely distracting.

"Me husband would have me cooking for him every day otherwise."

"What about the water-folk?" blurted Danny.

"You mean the sea folk? What of them?" Nelly replied uneasily. "You know you need to be concentrating on reality there young Danny. There are things we should ney talk of. Rcal people and real things should be concentrated on. Getting involved in myths and legends leads people onto unstable ground. I say keep away. It does ney concern you and nor do you want it to," said Nelly protectively.

"I think we've seen some," said Danny.

Shana kicked him and glared.

"Oh noo. You be careful. Don't speak of this to anyone, yer hear? Have any of you touched them?" she asked in a concerned tone. Shana and Marty looked guiltily towards the floor.

"They have yer then. You'll be hearing them call all the time. They'll plague yer 'cause they want yer," she said sorrowfully and shook her head.

"I have ney heard a thing," said Danny.

"You've had no physical contact then - have yer now?" she said.

Danny shrugged.

"That'll be why Meg's in motion then - clear as day. She's setting you up. Be careful. It's the bloody secret rearing its ugly head," she said gazing into the flames.

Marty fidgeted and picked the skin off his palm. "Nelly please can you tell us what you know. I need to know what I'm involved in and what they actually are."

"You of all people Shana. I had hopes for you too. I liked you instantly miss," said Nelly with a sigh.

"It was an accident," said Shana. "I fell in the water and he gave me air..."

"There are no accidents Shana. Yer might look like a pipe

88

cleaner but yer were both involved. The unconscious makes things happen which you are not conscious of... Yer both drew it in! Yer hearts made a call and they answered... Now yer just have to take some responsibility for yer life..." said Nelly wisely. "Now many years ago there were sightings - this is true. Then some from the village saw them more and more. This meant they were coming to shore and searching. Friendly as they are - they carry a curse."

"A curse? But they seem really nice," said Shana in surprise.

"They're mesmerising, beautiful creatures who don't age. We at the church never knew if they carried a soul."

"The church knows about them?" asked Shana.

"The church always knows secrets," said Nelly with a nod. A curler fell loose and dangled by her ear. "Now keep this to yerselves... If it gets out there'll be trouble. This whole area is a mystical place and many of the stories originate from truth. The circles in stone are what marks the solstice, showing how time is gathered for them."

"What, the stones on the hill?" asked Shana.

"No, not Drichen area. The ones under the water - the Mari-merma-menhirs," said Nelly as though Shana was being an imbecile again. "There's a myth about those stones too."

"Why are stones associated with this?" asked Marty.

"Timings?" wondered Shana aloud.

Nelly nodded, "aye, the timings."

"There's a saying that during the solstice sea creatures grow legs. They apparently gather the ones they want and take them to the sea. We have heard tales from the fishers who have seen a circle of stones out to sea. It is said to be able to turn human to fish too."

"But it doesn't make sense...If they can walk then why don't they do it all the time?" asked Marty.

"It's only for a certain time of year, for around sixty days, if I remember right," said Nelly chewing her lip. "In that time they have to make an absolute sacrifice and experience tremendous pain."

"Why?"

"Why is anything Marty?" asked Nelly.

"So where do they come from?" asked Shana noticing the clock on the mantelpiece.

"So many questions... At some point in evolution a choice was

89

offered. They chose the sea," answered Nelly. "There's a myth about a water god who became angry when a dolphin and a man fell in love and had a child. As punishment, the water God separated them, but for sixty days a year, she could transform and walk ashore to find her true love. The curse also made the people of the sea live eternally."

"But one was killed and washed up," said Marty.

Granny frowned, how had he found that out? "She was ney killed... They can voluntarily choose to pass, or should I say move on..."

"So they commit suicide?" asked Marty in a confused tone.

"No – they simply will themselves to the next world. The one between death and life," said Granny shaking her head emphatically. "Then they're not really dead and their essence remains. There was one creature that willed herself to pass and they say she is buried under the oak near the cemetery. When storms roll in and sea spray touches the old oak, it comes to life and sings. That was the beginning of the curse," Nelly sighed and shook her head sadly. "Now I'm tired. This is the most conversation I've had in two years. There's more to this story though but I will have to tell yer another time."

"What's their wrath?" wondered Danny ignoring Granny's tiredness.

Shana slapped his knee, "yer Granny's tired Danny."

"They sing that haunting song, young Danny. The resonance," she replied with a yawn. "Imagine a chorus of sound so hypnotising and so haunting, that it draws people to the water. Of course they drown..."

"How does the calling haunt you?" asked Shana.

"The sound penetrates your mind and hypnotises you. It then tugs at your core and draws you to the ocean. The rare few, who have survived, moved away from the sea because the resonance can only reach a certain distance. Just so you know... There has to be cause for one of the water folk to take revenge. It usually comes down to jealousy or threat."

"Blimey," said Marty.

"More shortcake anyone?"

Danny took two.

"Right, I've told yer what you need to know for now. Please be careful me wee bairn."

Nelly reached out and grasped Marty's cheek. With the special 'old person cheek-flesh-grab', she left him with two red imprints on the left side of his face.

"Do yer knit Shana?" Nelly asked.

"We must leave Nelly, we've taken up too much of your time," she said avoiding the question.

"Do yer?" insisted Nelly. "Or handy crafts?"

Shana shook her head.

Nelly sighed and propped herself on a cushion. "You young girls spend yer time trying to be like men. Then the men miss their role. Shana if yer want to find a decent man... I advise yer to knit. That's what impresses them. None of this car rubbish! Knitting's the answer... Although one time I knitted a jumper with two sleeves on one side. It did ney impress no one. But- see knitting's the way!"

Shana frowned, how did that make knitting the way?

Danny made his way over to Nelly and gave her a hug. "Thank you for looking after us."

Shana glanced at Marty and rolled her eyes.

"Visit whenever you're passing okay?" said Nelly holding Danny's hands as he pulled her to standing. "You're always welcome."

"Will yer be okay Granny?" asked Danny breaking her trail of thought.

"I've a new Yoga and Pilates DVD to get through. Will yer looky here Shana?" said Granny dragging Shana over to the television.

"Are you really okay up here alone?" Shana asked with concern.

Granny motioned to the large picture of her dancing with her husband. "Aye... But I talk to him 'till I'm blue in the face. When the weather's fine, I distil me herbs for healing. And before you say a thing I would ney be burned at the stake for what I make. Some heal and some protect. Now yer best get on yer way before I tell yer too much." Nelly gestured at a picture of a woman with her leg behind her neck on the cover of her yoga DVD. "I plan on doing that by ninety."

"Well, I surely hope you can," said Shana wondering whether she could ever do that.

"Mind over matter. Age over ageless, I say- don't yer think Shana?"

Shana nodded and made her way to the door.

Nelly watched from the front step as the group climbed into the van. Brrr Bang!

With a mysterious smile, she waved. "Life will be turning interesting now that Meg is in motion."

CHAPTER 18
Guardian cows!

Shana, Marty and Danny waved until Nelly and her solitary cottage became just a speck in the distance. Shana sat quietly reading one of the language books and glanced up at Danny.

"That's one amazing woman there Danny."

"That's me Granny," he said with a broad smile.

As Marty drove, the camper shook and shunted sideways. "The wind has picked up," he said glancing at the sky.

"Look Danny - a burial mound," said Shana pointing at a pile of stones.

"Will yer shut up with that Shana! It's not funny anymore."

"Ah, but how funny was it when yer granny was calling me a pipe cleaner?" she said jabbing him in the ribs.

"You know what? I feel we know a little more but it doesn't completely add up," said Marty steering against another gust. "We just need to find out what's bothering Megan."

"She's out for me," blurted Danny.

"Okay... And?" Shana asked curiously.

"Oh something happened this morning with... you know... Megan," said Danny.

"What happened?" asked Marty glancing in his rear-view mirror and steering into the wind.

"She blew in my face, froze some stuff and... said something," he replied with a sigh.

"She seems to be picking on you the most. Maybe she fancies you," Shana said in jest.

"Ach, shut up!"

Marty sucked his lip as he thought... Megan was definitely up to something.

Further down the road, Shana spotted a brown sign that pointed to a stone circle. "There's a burial mound... I mean a stone circle, that way...Over there," she said pointing.

Danny was just about to react but paused, "Marty slow down! There's a Victorian bridge down there. You can park there and then we can go for a bit of a stroll. I haven't been up here since I was a kid."

Marty followed the road to a blue, ornate Victorian bridge and pulled in. "I've not really seen any of this area before. Shall we go and have a look at the stones then?"

"Definitely!" said Shana with a clap.

"Oh just so you know... When we were kids, they told us to never enter the circle," said Danny mysteriously.

"Oh here we go..." said Shana folding her arms. "And why's that now – because a witch'll eat yer brain?"

"Because we'd be whisked away to another time," Danny replied.

"And why would that happen in a stone circle?" asked Shana with a roll of her eyes.

"'cause it's a ley line. Line crosses line – it's the energy of time and space," said Danny in a certain tone.

"Of course everyone knows that..." she replied sarcastically.

Danny climbed out of the van, "we were told all kinds of things like that when we were kids. I just assumed that everyone was told the same story. Obviously I was wrong."

"If I'd been told stuff like that I would be mad!" said Marty.

With a slam of the van door, the group studied the trampled footpath leading up to the stone circle. Shana glanced at the others, "it has a strange atmosphere. It feels like static," she said rubbing the top of her head. "Do you think there's a storm brewing?"

Marty shrugged, "the clouds lift at the end. Doesn't that mean a change of weather coming?"

Shana looked at the sky and pursed her lips, "that's a cool thing to know. Where did you learn that?"

"It must be from a surf magazine," he said thoughtfully.

"Have yer got yer camera Marty?" asked Danny.

Marty rummaged in his jacket pocket and pulled out his little digital camera.

"What about yer big camera? You never know what you'll find round here," said Danny.

Danny was right. Marty turned and jogged back to the camper while the Shana and Danny trudged up the muddy hill.

"I think you can use a cowpat as more of a discus," said Shana just as Marty arrived.

"I reckon a welly boot would go further," said Danny thoughtfully.

Marty frowned. "I think I walked in on one of 'those' conversations at the wrong time."

"Which can you throw further? A cowpat or a wellington boot?" asked Shana jumping from the fence.

"A welly – it won't break in the air," he said thoughtfully.

"See," said Danny sticking his tongue out at Shana.

She huffed and folded her arms, "I thought you would have supported me with the cowpat theory Marty!"

Marty smirked, what could he say?

The wind steadily increased as the group trekked the muddy path to the stone circle. At one point Shana's hair stood vertically as if a large vacuum cleaner hovered about her head. As they climbed, the hill became progressively steep and hoof prints made the mud uneven.

"I wonder why when yer get close to somewhere it looks like a herd of cows has been brought in especially to make the path more difficult to walk on," said Danny glancing ahead.

"The same thing happens in Ireland," said Shana vacantly.

Marty glanced at the pair. He couldn't hear a thing.

"It's like those crop circles. I am sure someone trains cows to formation dance," Danny said.

"Anything is possible when it comes to the unknown. Especially in places like this Danny," said Shana. "Now if the unknown was known then it wouldn't be unknown anymore!"

There was a weighted silence as the two boys tried to fathom the last comment. It was brilliantly stupid as usual!

"Now how are we supposed to get to the stones when the herd of cows are blocking our path?" she said pointing.

Marty fiddled with his camera and pointed it at the sky. Numerous randomly shaped clouds carried crepuscular rays that illuminated the stones. "It looks like the rays are pointing to the circle."

"See," said Danny knowingly, "it is a mystical place. Even the clouds can tell you that!"

"Smell that?" said Shana inhaling deeply.

"Yep," said Danny as though the fragrant aroma of herbs and lavender wasn't anything unusual.

"Well, what is it?" asked Marty curiously.

"Well they have rituals up here. The smell is used to purify," he said making an overly large breath. With a loud cough, Danny frowned.

"What Danny?" asked Shana.

"The pleasant aroma has been replaced with bloody cow's arse and methane imbued intestine!" he replied.

Shana glanced at Marty and giggled.

"These circles are supposed to have guardians," Danny said climbing onto a stile.

"Of course they do Danny," said Marty waiting for Danny to climb down.

"They're supposed to be hoofed beasts," said Danny holding out his hand to help Shana.

Squelch! Shana unwittingly jumped onto a cowpat, which combusted on impact.

"Shana!" Danny said with a look of annoyance when the remnants sprayed his leg.

The herd of cows stopped eating and lifted their heads. With a menacing stare, they bunched together.

"Those your guardians there Danny?" said Shana dragging her shoes over the long grass.

Marty climbed onto the style and paused.

"What's wrong with yer there Marty? Now why are you holding back? Scared of a few milk producers?" asked Shana.

"I just don't like cows much. When I was younger, a bull chased me. The only way dad and I could escape was by jumping a fence into another field. There was a bull in that field too," he said studying the herd.

"So what did yer do?" asked Danny with a smirk.

"We jumped over another fence, startled a horse and I got kicked in the head."

"Oh that's so typically you Marty! So did it knock some sense into you?" said Shana with a grin.

"Nope – concussion." Marty climbed down from the style and gave Shana a sharp glance. He then nodded towards the cows.

"They're coming to eat you Shana!"

The herd were curious and clomped towards the group. With a sudden crouch, Shana frowned. "Danny they don't have udders."

"Oh," said Danny "they must be male then."

"Now I worked that out meself there Danny. Something hanging down gave that away!"

"They'll be meat stock then… Anyway if you run at them they'll move," said Danny studying the herd.

Shana eyed them doubtfully and glanced at Danny. "Well go on then." Shana gestured for the boys to run at them.

"We should all go together," said Marty.

"I can't believe I am having a face-off with a herd of cows!" said Shana.

"A dance off would have been more interesting," said Danny imagining the scene.

Had he really just said that? Shana glanced incredulously at Danny who was of course gazing into space.

"You start then Danny," said Shana nudging him.

Danny pointed at a cow "yo!" he said making drum beat and breaking into his best dancing. "If it makes them go away then why not?"

One cow lifted up its tail and…

"Look what yer did Danny! It thinks yer a crap dancer!" Marty smiled at Shana and Danny. "You two are nuts! Danny made a cow crap when it saw his dancing. That is amazing! I L…O…V…E… it!"

"Marty we are bloody nuts but I prefer to call it unique! And I say we run and jump the fence surrounding the circle. The cows aren't going to jump now are they? So they won't be bothering us anymore. Go!" said Shana launching into a sprint and darting between a gap in the herd. She then jumped the fence and stood on the other side looking smug. "I win!" she said with a celebratory dance.

One of the herd mooed.

Danny and Marty followed her lead but jumped the fence.

"There's something weird about this place Danny. I can feel it in the pit of me stomach," said Marty.

"Too much shortbread," Danny replied. Marty rubbed the back of his head. Static energy filled the air. Every time they neared the stones, the tingling sensation increased. Marty glanced up at the sky. The clouds weren't storm clouds. "I wonder if this is how the underwater stones are set out."

"I reckon they'd be larger and more spread out," said Danny rubbing his solar plexus.

"What makes you say that?" asked Marty.

"It's just how I image it," said Danny tapping his brow.

"What an amazing thing to be able to see." Marty continued to rub the top of his tingling head.

"Would yer look at that?" said Shana pointing at a circular building in the distance. "Look, a circular tower and over there… It looks like a derelict manor house."

"We have to go there," said Marty enthusiastically.

"But we only just got here. Surely we should enjoy this first!"

"Is no one going to walk into the circle," asked Danny.

"I daren't. It feels too weird," said Shana.

"I don't get how they work," said Marty studying the stone formation.

"Well," said Danny adopting his 'lecturing voice.' "They are a circle…"

"Noticed that," interrupted Shana.

"Shana let me finish…"

Shana raised an eyebrow.

"They follow the sun's phases and apparently it isn't only the summer solstice that affects them. The winter solstice is supposed to light up the circle too," he said gauging their reaction.

"So what does that mean?" asked Marty thoroughly confused.

"I don't really know. I guess those are the times of change and mark the longest and shortest days. Good for crops I suppose," he replied. "Look there are signs engraved on the stones. They must mean something… And that there is the altar stone for the sacrifice." Danny motioned to a large stone, which lay on its side.

"Why a sacrifice?" asked Shana curiously.

"You give something to receive something. It doesn't have to be animals. There are other ways to sacrifice. Consider the harvest festival: you give thanks and give something to receive something. Well that's what me gran always said."

"It kinda makes sense," said Shana glancing at Marty who was lying on the ground. He was searching for an interesting angle to capture the stones and the sky.

"Right I'm going in," said Danny. Danny walked to the edge of the circle and placed his foot over the boundary. A gust of wind knocked him onto his behind.

"Looks like yer not meant to go in there Danny," said Shana smugly.

"I think only certain people who are invited in are supposed to go in. I read that somewhere," said Marty checking to see whether he had caught Danny mid-motion. "Danny I got you flying." He made his way over to Danny, crouched and showed him the back of the camera.

"Anyway, I think we need to get over to that manor," said Marty offering his hand to help him up. "What do you reckon - follow the road with Bertha or walk the track over there?"

"That way is shorter and we can go on foot," said Shana.

"Let's do the fields," said Danny brushing himself down. Marty shuffled in both directions, both would work but he had to decide.

Between the manor and the stones, the herd of cows formed a wall. "They're blocking us - look..." said Marty.

"They know what we're up to," said Shana.

"Let's go down that ridge," said Marty pointing towards a ditch. The remains of an old railway track stuck out of the ground. The twisted, metal formation rose high above their heads.

"There was a railway here then, right by the circle," said Marty trying to figure out why it was there. "I wonder why it's gone to ruin? It's as if they were just ripped up randomly."

"The cows probably got annoyed and..."

"Oh look what I've found. There are gun pellets here," said Shana urgently. "Are we on private land?"

"Probably," said Marty noticing the cow formation closing in.

"You know what? Maybe we should drive," said Shana glancing from the pellets to the cows.

"We're about to be herded by a herd," said Marty.

"That's not possible," said Shana glancing at the herd. "I take it back. They're definitely herding us."

"Don't run. Just take long strides backwards," said Marty slowly walking in reverse.

"Go!" shouted Shana.

Marty continued to walk backwards and glanced behind him. The

other two were sprinting. The cows reacted and gave chase.
With a rapid rotation, Marty turned and bolted.

The pounding hoofs were gaining ground. Running at full speed, he headed towards a gate and jumped. On his way over, he caught his foot and landed face down in mud. Splat!

There was a silence as Danny and Shana squinted as they pulled pained expressions. When Marty looked up Shana attempted to hide her amusement as she recovered and Danny hid his mouth with his hand.

"Nice face-pack there Marty!" said Shana.

"Thanks…I thought we were going to walk backwards."

"Now see we never actually agreed on that there Marty," said Shana. "And I am sorry to leave you to the mercy of the cows, but we sacrificed you to make our escape. And our escape is what we received. See I understand what sacrifice means now! So thank you," she said with a coy smile. "Now Marty you have benefited from the sacrifice."

"How?"

"Well under that mud pack you will have beautiful skin!"
Danny admired Shana, she wasn't just brilliant – she could justify everything and could always find a positive – even in shit!

"Let's get Bertha and go over there," said Marty scraping the mud off his face.

Back at the Victorian bridge, the three of them climbed into the camper and they set off towards the derelict manor.

Brrr Bang! Went Bertha when Marty turned the key in the ignition. The cows bolted.

"That will teach them!" said Marty vindictively.

"That was fun," said Shana thoughtfully.

"It depends how you define fun Shana." Mud remained on Marty's face even though he had wiped it numerous times with a tissue.

"Fun is defined as fun. Now you look caught up in your thoughts there Danny. What are you thinking about," she asked.

"Just about what me Granny was saying. It's all a little weird, don't you think?" he said.

"What do you mean?" asked Shana.

"Well I was warned not to live in Crooked Cottage but the series of events lead me there. Maybe I should have stayed away."

"Why didn't you take the advice?" wondered Marty.

"I'm young so I don't take advice," said Danny.

"Ahhhh - that rule."

Danny glanced out at the cows as they drove past. "You know what? I have the feeling that we are all here for a reason... I just can't work out what it would be."

Silence.

CHAPTER 19

Mud, sludge and Manors.

"There's no way we're getting through that mud Marty!" said Shana pessimistically.

"We will, don't you worry. We'll get there because this camper drives like a tank," said Marty confidently.

Shana shook her head at the sludgy track before them and gave Marty a certain look that he understood: Bertha did not stand a chance!

With a loud sigh, Marty gave in and parked outside a nearby farm.

"Maybe we should ask if we can go and see the manor Danny," suggested Marty nodding towards the farm.

"Good idea. I do ney want to be shot just 'cause I'm being nosy," said Danny in agreement.

"I need a pee," said Shana brightly.

"Maybe we could use you as a decoy."

"I don't want me bare ass shot, not even as a decoy," said Shana frowning.

"You could be our sacrifice," said Marty with a grin.

"Shut up!" said Shana.

"Why should I shut up Shana?" Marty replied argumentatively.

"Because I say so," said Shana.

"And what kind of argument is that Shana?"

"My argument!" she replied. "The best argument you will find – a woman's logic now!"

"I wonder if sheep get cold heads. All that wool on their body and not much on their heads…" said Danny watching sheep in a nearby field.

Shana and Marty followed Danny's gaze and frowned.

"What?" said Danny.

"Get out," said Marty gesturing towards the farmhouse. "Find out if we can go on the land."

"I need to 'go' on some land soon Danny – please hurry!" said Shana desperately.

"Why is it always me?" he said sulking.

"It never is. It's normally me. Now be away with yer!" she said flicking her hand.

Danny climbed out of the van and stomped up to the farm gate. As soon as he entered, two dogs ambushed him.

"What makes him think like that?" asked Marty studying the nearest sheep. It chewed some grass and gazed vacantly back. "They probably do get cold heads and ears - what do you reckon Shana?"

"Actually, I think all sheep should be given ear muffs for the winter," she replied watching Danny who was shaking off one of the dogs hanging from his sleeve.

"That's an idea..."

"I think they should use their wool to make scarves and hats and possibly even toilet paper," she suggested.

"You are joking aren't you Shana?" said Marty with a frown.

"Course I am... Look there, dogs are mauling our Danny and the farmer is carrying a shotgun. This journey is getting more and more exciting!"

"Do you think we should help him?"

"I don't know..." said Shana watching the smaller dog wrap its paws around Danny's calf.

"Nah... We don't want to undermine him..." said Marty watching the small dog hump Danny's leg. "Look at that little one go!"

Shana frowned and tipped her head to the side. "Why do you think that one dog wants to eat him and the other dog wants to make love to him?"

"Probably the mixed signals he gives off," replied Marty noticing the farmer's wife standing in the cottage doorway. She stood with her arms folded wearing baking wear. With one dog humping his leg, Danny gestured towards the manor house and appeared to be asking permission to enter. The farmer's wife nodded, and extracted both of the dogs from Danny's appendages. With an apologetic smile, she gestured for Danny to follow her into her kitchen. After five minutes, Danny emerged, wiped his face and climbed back into Bertha.

"Well?" asked Marty.

"That woman makes the best wee cake I ever tasted. Don't tell me gran that though!" he said triumphantly.

"Yer didn't think to invite us did yer Danny?" asked Shana.

"Nope!"

"Why not?" asked Marty.

"Well, yer did ney stop me being ravished by Archibald or Sausage - the dogs. Fierce hounds!"

"Who calls a dog Sausage?" asked Marty dumbfounded.

"I could have used their loo - Danny," said Shana jiggling.

"It's yer own fault Shana. Yer did ney come to me rescue did yer? Archi was the most aggressive and sausage humped me," said Danny shaking his head sadly. "I feel violated!"

"So errr…Can we go in?" asked Marty.

"Yep."

"What are we waiting for then?" asked Shana crossing and re-crossing her legs.

"You're waitin' for me to tell you what it is," said Danny who was purposely stalling. Would Shana wet herself?

"Okay… Go on then Danny," said Shana urgently. "Make it quick!"

"Well, it turns out it was a Manor," said Danny. "It was home to the Drichen family. Oh, and guess what? That old railway went right up to the doorstep. As for that round building up there - it's a Druid temple. They still practice rituals at the circle whenever the time is right. Summer, winter and equinoxes," said Danny folding his arms knowingly.

"Why's it derelict then? Wasn't Queen Victoria around in the late eighteen hundreds? So surely it should have been turned into some kind of historical point of interest with a roof." Shana wrinkled her nose and studied the manor.

"Well, I asked that very question," said Danny stroking his chin. "Apparently if you take the roof off a house you do ney pay tax on it."

"Ah, that makes sense. That's why there are so many derelict castles," said Marty.

"Can we go now?" said Shana impatiently leaping from Bertha and startling a pheasant.

"Daft animals those," said Danny. "Seem to have a death wish."

While Shana searched for a secluded location, Danny grabbed a twig, stuck it in a cowpat and chased her. Shana was caught off-guard and screamed. "Danny would you put the pat down and give me some privacy?"

The pat cracked and fell to the ground. Danny appeared disappointed and sighed while Shana ran ahead.

"Do you reckon anyone has ever been killed by a cowpat?" asked Danny.

"What like a kind of Chinese star? Ninja pats?" Marty replied thoughtfully as he caught up.

"Whichever way... It would be a horrible way to go...You would never live it down!"

Marty studied his friend and shook his head. "You would be dead – so you would not live it down. You're on a roll Danny. I'd say you're spouting crap today." With that, Marty climbed a wooden gate, flicked his leg and fell flat on his face in the mud again.

"And you're eating crap today there Marty," said Danny just as Shana emerged from behind some foliage looking relieved. Shana stood with her hands on her hips, "now how did you manage that Marty? Twice in one day! You're being quite clumsy aren't you?"

"A natural talent," muttered Marty. He wiped himself down, and then negotiated the boggy area in front of him with a stomp! Danny and Shana leapt the gate like acrobats and caught up with Marty. He broke through some bracken and emerged in front of the manor. "Blimey!"

An enormous, five-story, derelict manor towered above them. Marty lifted his camera and photographed. Click! "This is amazing!" Trees grew inside the rooms with orange and blue fishing nets interwoven amongst their branches.

Danny stood silently. Had he been there before? It felt familiar...

"Let's go inside," said Shana.

"Do you reckon it's safe," said Marty studying moss-covered bricks that had fallen in piles.

"Probably not, but how else are you going to get pictures Marty?"

Shana walked around the side of the manor and climbed through a window. "Look at this... Amazing..."

"Shana be careful. It could fall away at any point," said Marty anxiously.

Danny followed Shana and glanced around. "You know what? I'm definitely having a de-ja-vous. It's of a dream though."

"What happens in the dream?" asked Shana standing at the doorway that led into a cobalt-blue corridor full of trees, which smelled like dry leaves.

"It's about someone who ran away from the sea. I was watching them in my dream. They took the nets with them."

"And?" asked Shana.

"That's it," said Danny.

"Well that was interesting," said Marty sarcastically. as he climbed through the window.

"There's more to it Marty. I just need to remember. I was about six years old when I dreamt it! Actually it might be something me great-granny told me," he said scratching his cheek.

Gold leaf shimmered on the blue wallpaper covering the walls of a neighbouring room. "This must have been a library or something," said Shana studying the burnt remains of a gold-embossed book. Danny nodded consumed in thought. At the end of the corridor, he stumbled upon a broken-down stairwell. Burnt beams poked through fishing nets and shattered stairs descended to a lower corridor. Danny sat down and stared into space. Fragmented stories assembled in his mind. He frowned and glanced at the nets. The story of a woman who swam out to sea in storms was bothering him. Stories of pirates, witches and cannibals consumed his thoughts.

"Is everything okay Danny?" asked Shana.

"I'm trying to remember the stories me granny used to tell but I keep remembering nightmares."

"And?" asked Shana.

"In the dreams I used to walk down a dark corridor. A woman kept calling to me. I could never really see her face because she concealed it with her long hair. There were nets hanging all around her."

"So what did she say?"

"The water's driving me mad. It's calling me and you'll remember this one day. Never forget young Danny," she said. "Then she disappeared into a fire."

"That's weird..." said Shana with a sudden inhalation.

Startled pigeons flew towards the sky. Crack! Shana grabbed her chest and glanced behind her. Danny was gone.

"Danny?" she called.

A haze of dust remained.

"Marty help," called Shana. "Danny's disappeared!"

CHAPTER 20

Hidden nooks.

"I'm down here," called Danny.
Shana noticed the hole in the floorboards and crouched down. "Danny are you all right?"
"I'm okay. I landed on something soft," he replied just as Marty ran over.
"Nothing's broken. I'm intact but it's weird down here. I just need my eyes to adjust," he said.
"Danny I think you should get back up here as soon as you can. This place is unstable." Deep cracks in the walls and the fresh piles of rubble revealed the depth of deterioration. "I think we all need to get out before something happens…"
"I'm coming down," Shana said.
"No don't. Stay up there for the moment. I need to make sure it's safe and find a way out. I'll have a quick look round," said Danny. Silence.
"Danny?" Shana called after a few moments.
"I landed in fishing nets. Why would fishing nets be out here at the manor?"
"No idea," said Marty. "Why don't you just come back up the stairs?"
"I will in a minute… But I have just found an old door. It has a key in it – like in my dream. Shana remember how I said about the woman in the dream… She said you will remember this - it's the blood. I don't think this is coincidence. How cool – the door leads to an octagonal room. It has mad patterns on the floor! You need to see this…" he said excitely.
Crack! Marty glanced at the walls. "Shana I don't feel right about this. We need to get him out of there now. I think this whole place is an accident waiting to happen!"
"How are we going to get him out of the cellars if the floor caves in?" asked Shana
"There must be alternative routes down there," he replied walking towards the broken staircase and testing a wooden beam with

his foot. Snap!

"I think we need to go and get him," she said with a pause. The piled of fallen, mossy stones made perfect stairs. She gracefully stepped on the rocks and waved for Marty to follow. "You know what? Let's be positive. I have found a way down and we can use this route to climb out."

Marty was not so easily convinced.

"Marty this house has been standing for hundreds of years. The worry is all in our heads," she said with a quick glance over her shoulder. "You can't spend your life living in fear – now come and explore!"

In Marty's opinion, there was logic, adventure and stupidity. In this case, adventurous idiocy better described their actions. He was clumsy as he balanced on the stones and used them like steps. When he reached the basement, he glanced at the rotten beams above his head. "I think the worry is actually above our heads."

"Well, we're down here now. I say we make the best of it!" Shana replied sharply.

When Shana and Marty arrived in the octagonal room, Danny was standing in a daze staring at the patterned floor. There was something relevant about it. But what? Across the room, some bookshelves drew his attention. Were the answers there?

Remaining by the doorway, Shana inhaled the musty air and coughed, "this place feels strange. Maybe we should listen to Marty and get out of here."

"Well we're here now. We may as well have a little explore," Marty said following Danny into the room. Once at the centre Marty rotated on the spot. It was an octagonal, burgundy room with faded gold decoration. On two of the walls there were rosewood shelves containing numerous leather-bound books. On the floor, there was an ornate compass design with a Scottish flag at the centre. Marty crouched down and wiped away some dust. Why would that be there?

Danny opened one of the doors of the bookcase and skimmed through the titles. After a second, he paused and raised an eyebrow.

"What have you found?" asked Shana watching Danny inquisitively.

"The Concise Anatomy of the Sea People," said Danny in a matter of fact tone.

"What?" said Marty making his way over. "That's so odd! Why would that be?"

"Maybe we are closer to the sea than we realise," Danny said with a shrug.

Crack! The group silently looked up. The room began to tremor. Boom! Stones tumbled towards the door. Shana glanced behind her and darted into the octagonal room. As she slammed the door shut, she caught a glimpse of one of the high walls wavering.

"Quick, get to the other side of the room!" she shouted urgently.

Boooooooom! A sound resembling a detonation filled the air accompanied by repetitious shaking. The group crouched and covered their heads. The motion felt like an earthquake. Shana glanced at Danny and Marty. They all had the same realisation: they were trapped!

CHAPTER 21
Shaking walls and thinning air.

Shana watched the door expecting boulders to smash through. Danny and Marty stared at the ceiling; it shook with the impact of the falling masonry.

"How are we going to get out?" asked Shana nervously.

Another wave of pounding shook the room.

"I really don't like this…"

Marty was silent. How could they get out if the only exit was blocked and there were no windows? He glanced at his mobile - it had no signal and no one knew where they were.

Danny stared blankly at the floor, "there has to be another way… I think I've been here before."

"When?" asked Shana.

"I don't know. I just remember it for some reason. Maybe those vivid stories me great granny told me has reminded me of every detail of this room."

"Danny the reality is we're stuck in a room underground. Our only way out is blocked and we're running out of air!" Shana clasped her throat. "I feel claustrophobic!"

The shaking finally calmed and Danny stood up. In a trance-like state, he paced and muttered. "Me great gran told me the reason this room is here is because one of the gentry fell for a woman of the sea. He joined one of the pirating ships and started looting. For some reason the family had money problems. I think that's when he first saw the woman," he muttered nonsensically.

"No offence Danny, but I don't give a shit about the story! Just please get us out of here!" said Shana in desperation.

"So what happened?" asked Marty.

Danny stared at the compass and traced his foot across it. "Well, he was the youngest son of the family. He wasn't interested in the gentry; he found real people fascinating. People who survived against all the odds."

Shana crouched down, crawled towards the door and attempted to open it. She peered through a small gap to witness a pile of rubble blocking any chance of escape. With a series of deep breaths, Shana's throat constricted. She inhaled repetitiously and stared back into the room. What if they were stuck?

"There are diaries on the shelf," said Danny.

"Yeh, but how does he know the anatomy of one of 'them?'" asked Marty.

"If you remember this, you'll remember a way out," muttered Danny, returning to the bookcase and opening a diary.

"Danny if you can remember a way out I think you should do it now. I think Shana is right - the air is running out!" He glanced over at Shana. She was in a state!

Danny opened a diary and read. "Here he goes for another plunder. The people of his ship drown; yet he is saved by a woman who swims out for him," Danny paused and frowned. He gazed at the walls and appeared to be searching for something significant – a sign. "I am sure the compass has something to do with how we get out of here." He crouched down and wiped away dust from the centre of the compass. A carving of the skull and cross bones - written beneath was the name James. "There you are James… Now what are you hiding? But it's never the first one 'at no time take the first to be true Danny… I think this was his secret room. If that's the case, there'll be a way out nearby. It should lead to the sea."

"I don't get the logic?" said Marty falling into analysis.

"Just bloody get us out of here!" said Shana. "We can think in fresh air!"

"He was a pirate. He needed to be able to get in and out without being noticed," replied Danny.

Shana knelt close to the door, "I feel dizzy. The air is getting thin!"

"Danny I feel faint too. I think Shana's right… We need to hurry!" said Marty.

"My brain feels like it's being squashed too. We must be close." Danny paced in a circle and crouched over the skull and cross bones.

"I am drawn to this."

"Danny hurry," said Shana lying flat on her back.

"I'm trying to remember. Give me a chance!" Danny muttered whilst attempting to make sense of all the stories he had been told.

"If the skull is here, and the books are there… It's close to the cross…. X marks the spot Danny. Shit!" Danny glanced about the room. "Where is there a cross?"

"There are two. The flag and the cross bones," said Marty.

"I can't breathe!" cried Shana.

"It will be the most obvious – right under our noses!" said Danny tilting his head to the side.

Danny traced the lines of dust on the edges of the flag and found a subtle groove. He blew away dust from the image and discovered a square stone attached to the skull and cross bones. In the centre was a small cross. The third cross. "Everything happens in threes Danny. It's the blood," he muttered.

"I need oxygen in my blood," cried Shana. "We need to get out of here. I can see amoebas floating around me vision!"

Marty crumpled into a heap on the floor, "Danny we are going to suffocate if you don't get this sorted."

Danny inhaled and was silent as he poked two fingers in the eyes of the skull. With the other hand, he twisted the cross. "Take out thems eyes and twist 'ems bones! Clever buggers… but not clever enough!"

The motion created a clicking noise and a square door opened with dust falling from its edges. A gust of sea air rushed through and blasted him in the face.

"I found it," he said triumphantly.

Shana's eyelashes twitched as she gasped for breath. Once she was fully conscious, she crawled over. "Thank you Danny," she said kissing him on the cheek. "I've killed me brains cells… Revive, revive, revive!"

"Marty we need to take what we can so we can find out more," said Danny. "This room has been sealed for years. I wouldn't be surprised if the weight of the walls will collapse in on us."

"We'll take three things then," said Marty.

"Take the diary, the anatomy and…" said Danny.

"What should I take?" asked Shana.

The floorboards above them made a drawn-out creak. The group looked up. The rotten floorboards were warping.

"It's up to you but make it quick," said Marty urgently.

Crack! Dust fell into the room. "It's going to go!" said Marty stepping

113

into the darkness beyond the trap door.

"Shana quick!" said Danny frantically.

Shana grabbed the first book she saw and flicked through. "Bloody handy crafts!"

She shoved the book back, grabbed another. "A book of legends and the unseen. Right let's go!" she said jamming the book into her trousers and dashing towards the trap door.

Crack!

Danny followed Shana. The elongated creaking of tortured wood sounded and then boom! The group clambered down the damp stairs into complete darkness.

Bang!

Danny slammed the trapdoor closed and ran down the steps.

Pitch black! Bang! Bang! Boom!

The group groped their way down the stairs. In the darkness, they stepped into dark water.

Where were they?

CHAPTER 22

Depths, darkness and new directions.

The sound of masonry pummelling the trapdoor made it clear that there was no chance of return. The group pressed themselves against the damp, cave wall anticipating a second collapse. For a while, they stood silently breathing and waiting. Nothing.

"So…" said Shana while her eyes adjusted to the darkness. Danny shifted awkwardly.

"So… Does anyone have any clue what we should do now?" she asked.

Marty fidgeted and scratched his face. "It looks like we're in quite a warren."

"Typical! Bloody frying pan into the fire!" The rumbling of the ocean echoed through the cave system. Shana crouched down and glanced ahead, "I think we might have to swim. I can't see any proper paths."

"Look up," said Danny.

Marty and Shana glanced up. Fishing nets were suspended above their heads.

"Look over there… There's a ledge. I say we use the nets like a cargo net and get to the path on the other side. Look there are foot holes here. I'll give you a bunk-up Shana."

"Now why do I get to go first?" asked Shana.

"Well, you are the lightest," Danny replied logically.

Shana wasn't so convinced and unconsciously shook her head. "No Danny, you go first."

"I went first with the dogs… It's your go," he said definitely.

"I'll go first," said Marty. "Otherwise we'll be here all day making the decision!"

"Shit, I hope it's not high tide," said Danny with concern.

"Why?" asked Shana still slightly giddy.

"The caves are normally only accessible at low tide. Something the pirates would know, so they could hide," said Danny.

Shana shook her head in disbelief, "you really are odd!"

"Thanks. Let's get over to that path and then we'll just have to wait. It looks like the tide is at half mark. Look at the cave wall," he said pointing. "It's on its way out too – notice how it's wet above the groove," said Danny, in his 'all-knowing tone.'

Marty scaled the wall and tested the net. "It seems fine," he said swinging across to the other side. "Shana you come next."

Danny gave Shana a bunk-up and she swung across too. "I'm getting tired. I just want to go home now," she said when she landed.

Danny followed and jumped down beside them. The group traversed the footpath until they arrived at more water.

"I think we're just going to have to wait. Unless you want to swim," said Marty.

"I think it's best we wait. We don't know how far we have to swim," said Danny.

"So how long do you reckon we'll be sitting here then - in the dark?" asked Shana in a certain tone.

Danny glanced about, "I'd say we have about an hour or so ahead of us."

"I'm getting cold," Shana mumbled in a little girl's voice, huffed and folded her arms,

Danny nudged her affectionately and wrapped his arms around her. Shana nestled in and noticed Marty gave her a certain look. She purposely ignored it.

"So what triggered those memories Danny?" asked Shana.

"I remembered the full story when I saw the flag. The X marking the spot thing came up too."

"Well, if we have to wait – you may as well tell us what you remember. But please don't make it a massive monologue," said Shana. "It's not like we can get away or anything."

"Shana you're so blunt!" said Marty with a smirk.

"Well… If you don't say it as it is then you are saying how it isn't and that does not make sense now does it?"

Danny and Marty frowned, as always she was right.

"I remember the story of the gentry at the manor and their accumulating debt. The father fell ill so he tried to marry off his daughters. No one obliged, so the daughters eloped with their chosen lovers. Obviously, such rebellion caused the family more shame. The remaining son had to take drastic action and joined a pirating ship. He never revealed his background but they guessed his origin all right.

116

The way he spoke gave him away. He had a talent for pirating so it wasn't spoken of. Obviously, pirates make enemies of those they plundered including the locals. So the villagers would build fires close to treacherous coves intending to draw the pirate ships ashore. The pirates often mistook the fires for their own lanterns and would unwittingly guide their boats to smash on the rocks."

"Seems cruel," said Shana.

"Pirates were outlaws… They did a lot of things like that in that era," said Marty.

"Other times storms would form unexpectedly and blast the ships ashore. A storm caught James's ship and smashed her on the rocks near Rose-hearty. A lone woman watched from the cliff top; they said she was mad of the sea and it was a curse within her family. She'd wanted to drown herself many times but had always survived. The locals called her the sea witch. Whenever she attempted to drown, a storm would drive her from the water. Others said the devils in the sea always saved her and had sent her mad."

Shana huffed, "always women getting called witches… It's so rubbish!"

"That night she witnessed the ship smash on the rocks. She watched the poor men struggle with their lives. As much as she wanted to die, they were desperate to survive. She stripped down to her under-dress and battled the waves until she reached the wreckage. For most, she was too late because the sea had swallowed them. James was the remaining survivor. He clung to a rock in a half-conscious state. She swam with him through the waves and dragged him ashore in a nearby cove. That cove was one of the many that linked the warren to the manor. The caves were where their liaisons began. The pair had both been outcast by their respective societies. Although, James led a double life and had a private room that could be accessed by the stairway we just used to escape," said Danny.

"Did you remember that earlier, or did you just remember it?" asked Shana.

"Bits and pieces have turned up. I now remember that Grace was the sea witch's name. Over time she disclosed that she knew of the sea people and they were the ones always saved her. James became enamoured by the thought of such creatures and asked her to recount her stories. She drew their images and talked of their

117

anatomy. It was their secret."

"So what happened to her?" asked Marty.

"Everything came to a head when Grace found a sea child injured in the cove. She attempted to nurse the creature back to health. Unfortunately, the villagers discovered her with the child and brutalised it until it moved no more. The child, knowing it was in danger, willed itself to pass. As with the stories of the resonance, the storm arrived and the curse attacked those who had intended to hurt the child. In a fit of panic, Grace ran to the safety of the caves. The villagers gave chase and caught her. The villagers assumed the sea child had been born of her and burned her."

"How horrible," said Shana sadly.

"Fear," said Marty.

"The Resonance took its revenge and villager after villager were called to the sea and drowned. The sea child was reaping its revenge for Grace and its own departure. That night the manor burnt down too and James was killed in that fire. The room became a homage to him."

"How do you remember the story Danny?" asked Shana.

"Ah… My great-granny told me the 'old' stories before I went to sleep. She told the same ones over and over but she always said they were local legends. Sometimes I would dream them. Being in this place triggered them. It is like opening a mental vault," he said.

"How did you know the legends were real," said Marty.

"The stories were so vivid. The way she told them you could touch, feel and smell them," said Danny.

"They were such cruel times…" said Marty. "It simply took one person to dislike you and suggest you were a witch and that was it!"

"That's the past - this is now," said Shana extracting herself from Danny's armpit.

"It's still not right though. The woman swam out to save people and was killed because they called her a witch," said Marty. "How could someone hurt a sea child?"

"It was something they could not comprehend and they named it a Demon!" said Shana.

"Yes, but 'it' took its revenge," said Danny.

"I find this place so interesting. There's so many stories…It's such a shame aural tradition has been lost," said Marty with a loud sigh.

"People sit in front of the TV and get their stories from there instead," said Danny.

Marty nodded. "You know I was never really told anything by my family," he said tracing his fingers against the cave wall. "Honestly Danny, I'm quite jealous - you've been given so much because you were brought up in a family who cared. Mine were more concerned with making money and gaining status. I never really learned anything from them other than how to make money and spend it. As soon as I was old enough, I was packed off to boarding school, same with Marie. Of course, we used to make up our own stories but nothing like this… "

Shana patted Marty's back, "Marty you used to come to mine for the holidays. You certainly got some storytelling there. Although, Marie was never interested. God, she was such a prim git! You and I could sit in the mud, eating worms for hours, and then Marie had to ruin it. She was such a bitch, Marty. Sorry to be nasty about your sister- but it's true!"

Marty sighed; Marie and Shana were always in conflict. They were both stubborn and both always wanted to be the best. "I used to love coming over to visit."

"My family told loads of stories. As soon as you gave me uncle one drink he wouldn't shut up!" said Shana tugging at Marty's jumper, "I think we should work out how deep it is. Maybe we can walk."

Marty smiled, noticed some drift wood and measured the depth. "I reckon that is knee height - we can wade. If it gets difficult we can sit on the side and wait."

The group rolled up their trousers and slid in. As they waded the water became shallower. At the end of the dark caves, a beam of light broke through a crack in the over-hanging. The squawk of sea gulls filled the air.

"I think we're nearly there," said Shana optimistically.

"This place is a warren. It is all inter-linked. I bet if we went exploring around here we'd find loads of different systems. We might even find treasure," said Danny.

Marty stopped and looked back. "This place is immense. I

wouldn't like my chances alone here."

"It's easy each tunnel has a different colour cutting at the edge," said Danny pointing.

"I wonder where they come out," Marty said aloud.

"We should come back when it is low tide and find out," replied Danny.

Shana folded her arms, she couldn't think of anything worse. She noticed a crack in the rocks waded as fast as she could towards it. "I think we're there," she called back into the tunnel making a multitude of echoes.

CHAPTER 23
White horses and triangles.

There were some steps carved into the rocks just about where Shana was standing. She hoisted herself up onto them and disappeared.

"I can see where we are-" Shana shouted triumphantly. "We're in a cove about a kilometre from the house and over there's a white horse carved into the side of a hill."

Danny and Marty jogged to the crack in the rock and climbed up.

"Danny, it's weird how your great-gran told you that story. It was as if she had the foresight that something like this would happen someday," said Shana perched on a boulder waiting.

"Well, you know how kids play and end up in weird situations... Also she used to go on about how we were all unconsciously attracted to our origins."

"Are you saying this place is your origin Danny?" asked Marty in a puzzled tone.

"Aye, could be something to do with me ancestry I reckon. Me family has been here for centuries," said Danny with a shrug.

"Actually, me great-great-granny used to work here before it burned down. I'm sure she was as a servant to the gentry. I'll have to ask me gran."

The group ambled up the hill and walked towards the remains of the manor. The walls had completely caved in. Marty took some pictures and shook his head. "The timing for that collapse was immaculate."

The farmer, who owned the land, ran over accompanied by Archibald and Sausage. "Are yer okay?" he asked. "I did ney realise it was that unstable. I would never have allowed you in if I'd known."

"We're fine. We found a way out through the tunnels and caves to the cove," said Marty.

"Come on Marty, we did almost die though - didn't we?" said Shana dramatically.

"You were lucky. That could have been a real tragedy," said the farmer. "It is probably for the best though. This place has been cursed since it was built; what with the stones, the temple and the white horse all forming a triangle," he said gesturing up the hill.

"There seems to be loads of tunnels here. Where do they come out?" asked Danny curiously.

"Well, apparently... But I canny be sure now... But see over there, the pile of stones... That's where one of the tunnels comes out. The other is over on that hill by the pile of stones. Ancient burial my... It's a marking," said the farmer. "Apparently they made up all those witching stories to keep the gentry out. They had rituals by them to cover up their real use," said the farmer.

"Makes sense," said Marty.

"People appearing and disappearing..." said the farmer. "Shape shifters are just people who turn up out of hole then disappear back down a tunnel. Clever buggers," said the farmer shaking his head.

"I knew it. I knew it - I did yer know!" said Danny.

Shana stared at Danny and sighed, "we get you... You obviously knew it."

"I knew it you know..." said Danny with a cheeky grin.

"I just use the area for grazing now. For some reason the grass is more fertile in this area. Probably all the decomposing bodies buried beneath it," he said. "Do you want a cup of tea?" asked the farmer out of politeness.

"Why are there bodies here then?" asked Danny.

"Well, the burial mounds are areas where people are buried. It's just that the mounds are not with the bodies," said the farmer.

Marty, Shana and Danny glanced at the areas where the grass was fertile and realised the farmer was onto something. "Look at the patches of green grass. About six foot long, a body's-width wide and evenly spaced," he said pointing.

"I think I want to go home. I don't like that idea at all," said Shana screwing up her nose.

"Well, come by anytime. It's always nice to have visitors," he said.

"Thanks," said Danny watching Sausage eye Marty's leg as a potential mate. If he kept the farmer talking long enough, Marty may have a new leg friend!

CHAPTER 24
Lost, loss and losing.

Shana was the last to climb into the camper. "Everyone is so nice and friendly up here," she said making herself comfortable. "The farmer was so cute in his little wellies."

Danny raised an eyebrow.

"Not like that Danny! He's a bit old for me," she replied.

"So I don't have a navigator then?" said Marty noticing the pair were snuggled up in the back.

"Ach Marty it's easy. It'll take twenty minutes and we'll be home. Just follow the road to Gardenstown. I need a wee nap," said Danny with a yawn and stretching his arms.

"Thanks then…" said Marty in a certain tone.

Travelling through the bleak but beautiful scenery Marty noticed a buzzard hovering over some prey. The area was so wild and lacking signposts. After nearly forty minutes, Marty noticed a portly woman on a quad-bike herding sheep.

"Excuse me. How do I get to Gardenstown?" he asked once he had wound down the window.

"Oh dear… Yer must have driven right past it. Yer in Keith," she said with a smile. "Yer nearly thirty miles out of yer way," she said switching off the shuddering engine. "Yer need to get back onto the road to Banff and make yer way that way."

"Thank you," said Marty glancing into the back of the van. The couple were fast asleep.

Marty followed the signs to Banff but kept driving in a circle. For thirty minutes, he drove around the village of Keith. Eventually he parked Bertha, climbed out and stretched his legs. The 'Welcome to Keith' sign was a covered by grass. Marty glanced at a wall nearby and intuitively felt the urge to peer over. Numerous signs for Banff were in piles. With a shake of the head, he realised that some bugger had purposely been sending tourists in circles. "Twats!"

After another hour of driving, Marty negotiated his way down the windy road to Gardenstown. He glanced in the mirror; Shana and

Danny were in deep sleep with their mouths open. "You little blighters missed out on Keith... I hate that bloody place now!"

After a swift twelve-point turn, Marty parked Bertha beside the edge and switched off the engine. He turned in his seat and sighed. The couple looked so sweet together but any chance of a proper relationship had already been ruined. The man of the sea had connected with her, which meant he was going to call. As he understood it, there was no way to resist once there was a connection.

Marty quietly crept out of the van and left the couple sleeping. He strolled up Straight Lane to Crooked Cottage and noticed the net curtains twitching. He waved and smiled. He definitely deserved a nice afternoon nap!

CHAPTER 25
Woken by chocolate.

Shana sat bolt upright in the back of the camper. "Marty the little...!" She glanced over at Danny; he was fast asleep. "five o'clock, " she muttered glancing at her watch. With a tap to Danny's forehead, Shana waited. No response. She then tapped him on the end of the nose. Danny rolled onto his back. With his mouth open, he began to snore.

"Bloody hell Danny! It's like trying to wake the dead!" Shana smiled to herself and clambered over the front seat. She placed her key in the ignition. Brrr. Brr. Bang! Shana jumped, seagulls launched frantically into the air and in a nearby yard, an old woman was caught off guard as she hung her washing. She jumped, blew off and grabbed her chest. What the hell was that?

Back in the van, Danny rolled onto his side.

"You have to be kidding me Danny!" Shana said sharply. She climbed back over the seats and searched the cupboards for food. A bar of chocolate and a packet of salt-and-vinegar crisps was all she could find. She opened the bag loudly close to Danny's ear. Nothing! She rifled through the packet and wondered off into a daze. The day had been far too intense. Crunch! She glanced over at Danny. CRUNCH! She waved the salt and vinegar packet under his nose and then pulled out another crisp and examined it. CRUNCH!!!! Life was like a crisp: fragile and easily broken. In the last two days she had used up two of her potential nine cat lives. She had to be more careful! The group had been reckless but they had been lucky. Any of their escapades could have ended in disaster or even death.

"Aaah!" screamed Shana as she jolted. Danny's hand burst from beneath the blanket and extracted a crisp from the packet.

"Danny! Now I've tried everything to wake yer... And it took the smell of food to pull Sleeping Beauty from the dead. It did... didn't it eh? God, you're weird!"

Danny sat with puffy eyes and pillow creases entrenched into his face. With a smug grin, he attempted to smooth his gravity defying hair.

"I'm starving," he said with a crunch.

"Danny!"

"Ach, the way to a man's heart is through his stomach. The way to the rest of him takes that same route," he said gesturing to the packet.

Danny rummaged around the packet and selected the last remaining fully formed crisp.

"Danny... that there's the best one! Yer left me with the crumbs and the burnt bits. Give it back!" said Shana opening her mouth and pointing.

"Shana, you're going to have to learn to share if we're going to continue," said Danny waving the crisp by his mouth.

"What you mean is I'm going to have to learn to give! Danny this was a two way street – now you'll have to compromise too. Danny share that big crisp with me!"

Danny shoved the crisp in his mouth and watched Shana's reaction.

"So that's how it's going to be then Danny?" said Shana with a snarl. She wiped her finger about the packet and licked the salty remains.

Danny lay for a moment studying Shana. He admired her fire. Whatever happened there was always a fight, even if there was no real need for a fight.

"What you looking at Danny?" demanded Shana.

"Nothing," he replied.

"What do you mean nothing? I'm not nothing!" she said.

"Think I might go for a surf... Just over at the point, by the caves," said Danny.

"Will yer now?" said Shana sharply. "And it hasn't gone unnoticed that you ignored what I just said!"

"First I'll eat... Then leave it an hour. You want to come?" he replied.

"Danny you infuriate me! You know that don't you? Well I think I've had quite enough excitement today. I'll go and see what Marty's up to. He will answer me when I ask a question!"

"Right, as yer will," he said glancing out of the window.

"Danny will yer help me unload and put these boards in the shed?" asked Shana in best her 'little girl' voice and flickered her eyelashes.

"You want me to deal with the spiders Shana?" asked Danny.
Shana nodded and unwrapped the chocolate. Big mistake!
Danny opened his mouth and gestured, "the deal is half the bar in exchange for facing spiders."

Shana sighed, why did she have to make all the compromises? The ultimate compromise was chocolate!

CHAPTER 26

Life drawing or drawing on life.

From the cottage window, Shana watched Danny peddle hastily up the road.

Marty plodded down the stairs, his eyes looked bleary.

"He's a fit boy," said Shana admiring him.

"Shana I've been meaning to talk to you… Are you sure you're making the right choice?"

"I don't think choice is involved anymore. I will find a way to let him down easily," she replied. "I think I've found a way – the right way…"

"Good, because you're both my friends and I don't want to be stuck in the middle," he replied honestly. "The sooner you sort it out the better!"

"I know Marty… I just have to find the right moment," said Shana with a sigh. "So what are you up to this afternoon?"

"Painting… I came here to get better…"

"You want me to model?" asked Shana thoughtfully, as though she was doing him a massive favour.

"Well if you don't mind… But it will be clothed." Marty smiled to himself as he waited for Shana's reaction.

"I didn't suggest otherwise!" said Shana with a frown. "Marty as if I would offer to pose naked… That would be weird! I will wear a strappy t-shirt. You can then paint hair over the straps. But don't get carried away, I don't want to look like a yeti," she said arranging her hair.

Marty smirked. "I'd love to give you a moustache!"

"You dare Marty!" said Shana skipping to the studio.

"The bearded woman!" said Marty following.

Shana took her position. "Oh no Marty not the bearded woman. You and your life drawing – didn't you name one of your pictures the growler and the other the tripod?"

"The woman with a wide smile but not on her face," said Marty with a chuckle. "God, that was so embarrassing!"

"Tell me the story again Marty… I love that story!"

"You know - it still embarrasses me," he said with a slight blush. "The model was so attractive with her long curly hair and curvaceous figure," he said gesturing. "All the boys sat together in an unspoken camaraderie. We were all about to lose our visual virginity. Of course, the model sensed our discomfort, so she positioned herself in such a way that the boys had a view that not only shocked them but also revealed where babies emerged. Any who had aspirations of becoming gynaecologists soon changed their mind. And I reckoned she might have had been double-jointed too!"

"Oh Marty," said Shana shaking her head.

"That course should have been called an introduction to rug making," he said.

"So how did you deal with it again?"

Marty quivered as he remembered, "one of the guys leant over and asked 'are you going to draw the growler?' I shook my head because I had come up with a plan."

"And?"

"When the tutor came round to assess our imagery, the girls were praised and the boys well, they had all had very similar images."

"Marty come on…"

"We all had drawn the soles of her feet... The tutor asked me if I was shy. I said that I loved feet because they were so challenging to draw. The other guys had coincidentally developed the same passion."

"So why call it growler?"

"The soles of the feet were set against a dark scribbled background – the growler!"

"Oh Marty… I remember your teacher told yer ma who told my ma. Your mum was proud of the fact you handled the situation with such dignity. She said the model was a slut!"

"I forgot about that," said Marty.

"Yer mum told everyone she knew. You know I still find it amazing how our mums got to know each other. It was fate…" said Shana.

"Life Shana…People cross paths. That's it, I still don't understand why my mother went on holiday to Ireland when she was eight-and-a-half months pregnant," said Marty setting up the canvas.

"Hormones Marty… But Marie would never have had the same birthday as me older brother... It's amazing how different they are. He

129

likes the land and she likes her city…" said Shana arranging her hair over her shoulders.

"Shana you have enough hair there to cover your whole body," said Marty.

"What yer trying to say?"

"You're a mass of hair. Bald men would give their right arm to have hair and there you are a potential wig factory."

"I have a theory Marty… I reckon there is only a certain amount of hair in the world. As I grow hair, numerous men about the world gradually lose it. It's the same with fat people."

"What they get hairy?"

"There is a total body mass in ether. When one person loses fat it floats through the air and sticks to another."

"You have developed some rather 'interesting' theories!"

"Probably Danny's influence, he has provided me with a whole new world of random thoughts. Take for example my hair. You know one day it will be so long that I will be able to create hair bunches in the right places. All me parts will be covered and then I will go to a nudist beach."

"You actually thought that?"

"Yep, now I think you need to concentrate Marty. All this joviality isn't making a picture now is it?"

Marty glanced at the canvas. Where to begin?

CHAPTER 27
The Killer kiss.

Over at Hell's Lum hillside, Danny sat gazing at the sea chomping a cheese-and-pickle sandwich. It was breezy with the sun breaking through the clouds. Danny lay for a time digesting and noticing obscure cloud shapes. "I wonder why God made clouds look like sheep and cotton wool. They could have been any shape – doughnuts would have been good. Mmmm doughnuts," he muttered. He laid staring at the sky and thinking about Shana. Something in his solar plexus clenched. At the same time, the story his great-gran had told niggled him. Did she know what was going to happen? "The time will come Danny. The time will come and you will be ready." Was she some kind of witch? Whatever she was, she had always scared the dollop out of him!

Danny pulled out the anatomy of sea people book from his rucksack and rolled onto his stomach. He skimmed through the pages and rested on his head on his hand. The images began with the sea people's time in the womb and progressed through to adult. Their innards were bizarre!

"Rufff, Ruff!" A playful Scotch terrier, wearing a tartan coat, bounded up the hill. Danny shoved the book back into his rucksack, clambered to standing and headed down the old staircase to the cove.

The plucky little pup gave chase and barked again. Danny fidgeted; something was afoot, he could feel it. His great-gran's words played through his mind. How did she know so much about that room? Why was she associated with the manor-house? If there was a fire then how did his great-gran survive? Had his great-gran's mother been involved with the villagers who burned down the house? A bubble of thought burst – 'they' had viciously killed his great –great-gran. Was it connected? If that was the case then had the family lived in Crooked Cottage too? He had to allow his mind to digest…

Danny made a decisive decision and dashed over to a corner of the beach. Quickly he changed into his wet suit, and within a few minutes, he was sitting comfortably on his surfboard out the back, behind the waves. Calm settled the surface and a subtle humming approached. Amongst the resonation, a playful giggle echoed. Beneath the surface, a shadow darted past and shoved Danny's board. Splash! Danny submerged and a beautiful woman swam towards him. Danny attempted to swim to the surface but she grabbed his hand and dragged him towards the seabed.

Connection!

He struggled, broke free and swam frantically upwards. On the surface, the girl leapt over him and emerged beside him. Danny grabbed his board and climbed on. He lay facing the sky recovering his breath. The girl swam closer and peered at him. Danny purposely ignored her but she was persistent.

"Get away- yer almost killed me!" shouted Danny.

She retreated and stared with a sympathetic expression.

"Look I know what yer are…"

She resonated and gazed into Danny's eyes, into the depths of his soul. The resonation increased, Danny was spellbound, how could he resist? She was beautiful but controlling. The girl swam slowly closer and carefully looked him over. She gestured to her ear and then at his. She turned and pulled back her hair and revealed an ear of a completely different design. The girl took his hand and guided it to her lobe, which twitched and flapped.

"Are they gills?" he asked.

No answer.

Danny frowned, what had happened to her?

With a curious look, she edged closer and placed one hand on Danny's knee. A jolt of static shot through him. The girl glanced at the board, into Danny's eyes and then crunch! She bit the board.

"What are yer doing?" Danny stared incredulously at her.

She chewed a lump of wax and spat it out.

"Don't bite me board!" said Danny half smiling at the horrified look on her face.

She smiled innocently back.

"Geese - you're warm," said Danny noticing her distinct lack of clothing.

"Awas blwais, sper," she said pointing at her mouth.

"Is there something wrong yer her mouth?" he asked leaning closer.

She patted her mouth again.

"It seems all right. No gum disease or cuts… I'm no dentist so I do ney know about cavities."

He gazed into her eyes and then to her mouth. With a sudden motion, the girl grabbed him and kissed him.

Shit!

At first, he resisted, but finally he gave in. She was strong and certainly knew how to kiss! Danny couldn't help but just let go and be in the moment. There was a strange kind of chemistry between them, an electrical tingle. It was beautiful but quickly destroyed by the image of her eating raw fish and the question of how she cleaned her teeth popping to the forefront of his mind.

"Ruff, ruff," went the mischievous Scottie dog. With a flash of red tartan, the fluffy white mess darted across the beach and gave chase to a seagull. Splash! Danny submerged but by the time he climbed back onto the board, she was gone.

"Damn it! We're connected now!" he muttered glancing around. "Are yer there?"

Silence.

CHAPTER 28
Raw fish concerns

After surfing fifteen waves, Danny paddled in. When he was close to the shore, he flicked himself off the board and waded through the shallows. He glanced over his shoulder. Nothing.

The same naughty little dog appeared from behind some rocks dragging a massive stick. It ran past Danny and whacked his leg.

"You little shit!" said Danny rubbing his leg.

A portly man trudged across the beach holding a leash. The ball of white fluff ran towards him and diverted his course back to Danny. Danny bent over and removed the surf leash from his ankle. The terrier sniffed his behind.

"Would yer leave me alone?"

The terrier growled, cocked his leg and marked his territory on Danny's rubber surf boot.

"Now how would yer like it if I did that to you?" Danny asked with a shake of his foot.

The terrier panted with a mad look in its eye.

Donald, the dog's owner, chuckled and clicked Butch's lead to his collar.

"He owns yer now Danny," said Donald.

"Since when did a dog own a human?" asked Danny studying Donald, who he hadn't seen for a long while. He admired the deep lines engraved on his face. His life as a fisher had weathered him. With his split, greying beard and one gold, hooped earring, he looked robust like a typical fisherman.

"Always… Now when did yer return?" asked Donald.

"I've been back a few weeks now…" replied Danny.

"Called yer back did it?" asked Donald.

"Kind of… You can travel around the world looking for somewhere better, then discover where you were was best all the time," he said with a cheeky grin.

"So yer ran out of money then? You lasted three – that's good for someone so young!"

Danny nodded.

"So how's yer granny then?" asked Donald with a twinkle in his eye.

"Doing well… Baking shortbread and all that… We visited this morning," said Danny.

"She was always a good cook," Donald said patting his portly stomach. "Good to hear yer visit her now and again – family is deeply important."

Butch panted, the little bugger was planning his next course of attack. "Does that peeing routine all the time now. You would have thought he had drunk a lake the way he carries on," said Donald glancing at Butch. "Some people find it funny; others go quite red in the face. Depends how people take it and the cost of their shoes." With a deep sigh, Donald glanced out to sea. "Seems to be coming to mating season. Solstice is on its way."

"Mating season?" asked Danny curiously.

Donald watched the horizon for a moment, he then checked over his shoulder. "Between me and you I saw what happened with the girl. Similar incidents happen every year, but we keep it to ourselves. You know the stories in the family… Now imagine how difficult it is to keep a phenomenon like them from the outside world. We takes care of them, and they takes care of us. Be careful with them – they have needs beyond humans. Once they have contact they have no emotional defence and get broken hearts real easy… Then we get a disaster on our hands," whispered Donald.

After a silent pause, Donald studied Danny thoughtfully, "so where you living then?"

"Crooked Cottage," he replied.

"Oh," said Donald. "Were yer never warned enough not to live there Danny? I was sure that from the day you were born you were told not to live in that cottage."

Danny nodded.

"Why did yer do it then? Whatever possessed you?"

"It came up at a time when I needed it," he replied.

Donald shook his head remorsefully. "Danny it's in yer blood. Yer best ask yer gran, I'm not one to talk 'bout such things," he said gravely. "All I can say is it's funny how lines of fate comes up. Seems you can't avoid them."

Donald sighed, "be careful of the house and be careful of them.

One kiss can mean life or death. I mean it – be real careful. I'm a man who knows these things."

Danny attempted to fathom Donald's facial expression, what was he trying to say without actually saying it?

"Jealousy's such a useless emotion. Thems of the sea are not the same because their hearts rule them. From the moment they make 'contact', they will call yer and haunt yer until yer give in. Their drive for love is so strong that they will risk everything including their lives... Now I suggest yer warn yer friends. This is our biggest secret – a secret that could destroy the village if it gets out."

Danny stared at Donald in horror. Both Shana and Marty had had contact. Did that mean they were destined to be in love with the one they had contact with? A shudder ran down his spine... He had had contact too! He hadn't asked for it! It had come to him!

"Danny there are generations of secrets in this village. Look at the people, not all are what they seem. Notice how their ears and the eyes give them away. Now that is all I will say," he said with a tap to his podgy nose.

Butch wagged his tail and Donald laughed a hearty laugh, "Danny remember we keep this in the village because we do ney want the outsiders to know... Promise!" he said. "Oh and you never know what form love will come in. Love chooses you – not you it!"

Danny nodded and watched Donald turn. As he trudged along the beach, he gave a wave.

With an agitated fidget, Danny realised that one moment had changed his life and that change was not his conscious choice.

CHAPTER 29

Apparitions listening.

It was evening when Danny boldly shoved the back door open with a thud! He darted through the kitchen and up the stairs with his wetsuit hanging from his waist. On the landing, Danny awkwardly removed the urine-filled boot whilst hopping past the front room. He jerked to a halt and adjusted the stinking boot to capture any drips. "Bloody hell Butch!"

Mid-hop, Danny paused by the studio and peered in. Marty painted whilst Shana stared into space with her hair arranged over her shoulders.

Shana noticed the shape by the door and side-glanced Danny without moving her head. "Now Danny would yer stop staring?"

"Nope... Erm, you look very... Erm... Nice," said Danny with a naughty grin.

Marty wiped his paintbrush on a tissue and turned towards the door. Danny awkwardly hopped into the studio wearing one boot and carrying the other.

"Marty that's er... well- cool," said Danny peering at the painting.

"Thanks... Well cool eh?" he said trying to work out what Danny was up to.

"Yer... Really cool!"

"Well, if it is well cool now, imagine how cool it will be when I'm finished," said Marty thoughtfully. "Danny what are you doing?" he asked gesturing at the boot.

Danny followed his gaze and appeared awkward. "Erm... I think it's better that I go..."

"Danny have you peed in your wetsuit?" asked Marty noticing a certain aroma.

"Nope, I got peed on..." said Danny with a sigh and lifting the boot.

Marty quickly recognised the origin of the stink.

"Donald's dog used me foot to mark his territory."

"Oh Danny! What is it with you and dogs?" asked Shana.

"No idea Shana. Now I'm going to get a shower 'cause I canny bear the stink. You want me to leave the boot with the both of you?" asked Danny directing the boot towards Shana.

Marty shook his head as he picked up his palette. "No thanks. You could have left it outside..."

"I forgot I had been peed on until I took it off. Shana you want it?" asked Danny.

"What do you think?"

"By the way Marty, I need to ask your advice," said Danny pausing by the door.

"I thought you didn't take advice Danny," Marty replied.

"I can learn... That is if the advice is any good."

As Danny bounded up the stairs, Shana glanced at Marty with a certain look.

With a shift of position, Shana grimaced. "I think I'm going to get cramp Marty... I'm sorry I think that I am going to have to-" Shana fell into silence as she stared directly behind Marty. Marty waited... "Shana?"

Shana's gaze was fixed on a point behind him. Marty frowned as he watched the blood retreat from her skin. "What? What is it Shana?" asked Marty turning to search the area behind him.

"Marty... There was a woman standing in the corner for just a second..."

"Come on Shana..."

"She was looking at the painting... Then she was...well... she just disappeared..."

Marty frowned and glanced at the corner. "Are you sure?" A gust of wind rushed past and disappeared through the wall. "What the...?" he said taking a step backwards.

"Something's going on Marty..."

"Something has woken her up... She left us alone until now... So what has changed?"

Marty stepped away from the wall and sat down.

"There must have been a doorway there once," said Shana standing up.

"I think it's a sign to call it a day Shana. I won't be able to concentrate now..."

Shana limped over to where he was sitting, "I think she's

138

curious as to what you're doing," she said studying the painting. "It's going to be a woman of the sea isn't it? Maybe that's why she's in motion. Maybe she's something do with them."

"Shana are you scared by her?" asked Marty.

"I just find her a little disturbing. Essentially, we are living with a dead woman whose behaviour is erratic. We have no idea what her intentions are," she replied. "Admittedly I would like to know more about her because she fascinates me."

Some paper blew from the wall.

"She's listening to us!" whispered Marty retrieving the papers.

"What is it?" asked Shana.

"It seems to be a small painting of 'her'," said Marty glancing at the image and turning it over.

"Look, there's something written on the back..." said Shana.

"The day I died," read Marty flatly. The woman in the picture looked pained as she gazed into the distance.

"That's intense," said Shana softly. "It makes me feel quite sick actually," she said rubbing her solar plexus.

Marty thoughtfully propped the image on the white, florally embossed mantelpiece.

"Marty I'm going to make some food down stairs. Maybe she'll get the message and leave us alone," said Shana watching Marty's expression.

"I'll catch up with Danny," he said, his glance circumnavigating the room.

Shana paused by the door and checked the time on the grandfather clock on the landing. "Johnny Boy's late. He must be in the pub with all the other old farts," she said with a smile. "He's missed out on a lot today. I feel like I've lived ten years in a day Marty… What with the manor, the surf and everything else."

Marty stared at the painting on the mantelpiece, "I don't think Johnny's taking the ghost thing too well, is he?"

"He doesn't like anything out of the ordinary. If you can't box it – Johnny dislikes it!"

Marty readjusted the painting before turning towards the door.

"What's going on in that mind of yours Marty?"

"You have to admit that the whole situation is a little screwed up," he said.

139

"I know, but try and think of it as an adventure. There aren't many people who live lives like this. We're lucky!" she said enthusiastically.

Marty raised an eyebrow, patted her arm and made his way up to Danny's room.

CHAPTER 30

Confession

Danny was drying himself off in his room when Marty knocked on the door. Amongst the vast array of clutter, surf regalia and general mess, Danny stood with defined muscles, a tanned physique wearing his red floral board shorts. His hair was damp but intending to rebel.

"What's up then?" asked Marty.

Danny darted across the room and jumped on his bed. After crossing his legs, he gestured at the chair laden in dirty clothes for Marty to sit down.

'Where's Shana?' Danny mouthed.

Marty pointed down the stairs before he picked up the pile and dumped them on Danny's duvet.

Danny nodded and breathed a sigh of relief. "Well, I was surfing-"

"And?"

Danny took a breath, "well... er... this errr sea hotty... Well she almost drowned me. She grabbed me and dragged me under. I struggled n'- got to the surface but it was close," he said full gesture. Marty watched the show curiously.

"And.. Well she did ney know I could ney breathe beneath the sea. Then she pointed at her ears... I think they were gills – so weird! She made that bizarre sound, looked into my eyes and then I was like in another world... Everything on me just gave in..." Danny fidgeted and flicked his hair.

"Danny I have no clue what you're talking about..."

"Well... She erm... Well, she stared at me for a while then she er- put her hand on me leg and pointed at her mouth." Danny shook his head and sighed. "I'm so naïve sometimes. I thought she'd hurt her mouth... Really I did Marty. I thought she might need a filling or something."

Marty smirked and leant back in the chair.

"I was sure she was trying to tell me something. Then while I was close, looking to see if there was something wrong with her..." Danny cringed.

"Danny?"

"Well she grabbed me and kissed me. Not like a peck but a full on snog! At first I struggled... Well, then I gave in. She was strong... Marty I didn't mean it to happen. I feel bad but - I erm..."

Marty remained silent while Danny fought with himself.

"Have I betrayed Shana?" he asked.

"It was just a kiss, wasn't it?" asked Marty.

"Yeh," Danny replied.

"And you didn't initiate it, did you? What do you think?"

"Well..." Danny shook his head, "you know at first I thought she probably ate raw fish and that she might try and eat me. Pictures of sushi swam about me head and then I wondered how she cleaned her teeth."

Marty couldn't help but smile. "I didn't mean like that. I mean do you think you betrayed Shana?"

"I don't know..."

"Did you like it?"

Danny blushed, "it was like nothing else Marty. It was like my blood stopped flowing and I was in a... erm... different space. That kiss made me whole body tingle. I didn't want it to stop... Ever!"

"Then what happened?"

"The dog that peed on me shoe turned up. I turned to see what was going on and by the time I turned back, she had disappeared. I surfed for a bit and then paddled in. When I got to the beach, Butch whacked the back of me leg with a large stick and then peed on my boot! The little bugger!"

"Did anyone actually see you with her Danny?" Marty asked with a concerned expression.

"Only one of the old fishers - Donald. He's fine, there's a rumour about him saying he married a mermaid," said Danny. "The story goes that she killed herself when he innocently kissed a barmaid under some mistletoe in the tavern. The local gossips said that the jealousy poisoned her heart and killed her. How sad is that?"

"My question is how true is it? If what yer gran says is true then how come he's alive?"

Danny shrugged, "who knows? This village is full of myths, rumours and legends."

"Did he say anything else?"

"Donald told me to warn you all about the fact that the sea

people have a tendency to fall in love instantly. Plus as soon as you have contact they have you, they start calling yer."

Marty frowned, "what did he say about contact?"

"Nothing much Marty. Once they have contact 'they' have no emotional defence and get broken hearts real easy… Then we get a disaster on our hands."

Marty rubbed the back of his hand as he thought. What was myth and what was real?

"What are yer thinking Marty?"

"There's something funny going on. How could such a phenomenon be kept from the outside world? And why have 'they' come into our lives? What is it about us 'attracting' them in?"

Danny shrugged, "these things just happen to some people."

There was a creak on the stairs.

Danny and Marty glanced at each other.

"So was it a good surf?" asked Marty with a wink.

Shana lurked silently beside the door.

"It was okay…" Danny replied. "Oh, oh, and it's their mating season coming up… Like salmon."

"Mating season?" asked Shana walking past the door as though she was just passing.

"For the people of the sea," said Marty watching her expression. "So how long have you been there Shana?"

"Oh, no time," she replied. "So if they're a bit – you know randy then we're in trouble aren't we?"

"I think we just have to be a bit careful when we're out in the water." Marty slowly exhaled and glanced at the floor.

Danny and Shana gazed at each other; both had secrets.

Thud!

"Geese that must be Johnny Boy now," said Shana with a jolt.

The uncoordinated collisions of a weighty man rebounding off the walls came from downstairs.

"Woops!" Smash!

"It's a drunken elephant!" said Shana.

A loud raucous laugh evolved into a cough. Smash!

"Woooooopseeeey!"

Shana, Marty and Danny crept down the stairs to witness Johnny stumble sideways, collide with a wall and use his face to rest against it. A trail of sparkling saliva graced the walls whilst Johnny slid into slumber and began to snore.

"Is he asleep?" asked Shana incredulously.

"Not for long," whispered Marty.

Johnny gradually slipped down the wall leaving a skid of spit. The increased momentum jerked him awake. With the shock of the jolt, he stumbled one way, rebounded and landed against the opposite wall with his back arched. In his right hand, he maintained his open bottle of whisky.

"Good will ta the lotta yer!" he said with a salute. A moment later, he crumpled to the ground with a thud.

Shana clapped her approval. "Now would yer look at that? Not a single drip fell from the bottle onto the floor. That man's a drunken genius!"

"He really isn't dealing with the goings on well is he?" Marty tilted his head to the side and folded his arms.

"God, help anyone he resuscitates tomorrow. He'll give them alcohol poisoning for sure," said Shana, adjusting her hair.

"Johnny?" said Marty, kneeling beside him.

"God, the smell of it." Shana crouched beside him and used her jumper to cover her nose.

Danny sat on the stairs smiling. "What a complete dick! He's completely shit-faced!"

"Will he be able to work tomorrow?" asked Marty.

"I think tomorrow is his day off," said Danny.

"I hope for everyone's sake it is," said Shana.

"I think we should get him upstairs," said Shana attempting to remove the bottle from Johnny's hand. With one eye open, Johnny Boy fought back and clung to the bottle.

"Johnny, let go of the bottle please!" said Shana.

"Burp!"

"That was right in me bloody face there Johnny!" she scowled. Marty and Danny sniggered while Shana flashed fury. "Will yer look at that! I help a drunk and the bugger burps in me face. What kinda gratitude is that now eh? I wonder why I bother- really! We should leave him to sleep it off. If he dies in the process – well that's his own fault!"

"We can't just leave him here. We should take him to his room," said Marty.

Shana stood up and placed her hands on her hips, "nope! I'm not willing to shift the deadweight up two flights of stairs! Let's make him drink water so he can move himself!"

Shana went to the sink and filled a plastic beaker with water.

"I wonder why he got himself in such a state. He does ney normally drink," said Danny.

"I have no clue," said Marty. "He can normally handle quite a few of pints, but I've never seen him drink this much and end up in such a state."

"Surely there has to be more going on than has happened in the last couple of days," said Danny.

"We all cope with things in different ways Danny. I would say that Johnny is trying to avoid the situation by pickling himself."

Shana shook her head, "now Johnny is always going on about his body being a temple and one so grand that a king would be grateful for a peek inside..."

"Johnny can you hear me? Why are you so wasted?" Marty asked in a sympathetic tone. Johnny stirred, farted, smiled drunkenly and passed out again. Danny pulled a tissue from his pocket and Marty used his t-shirts to cover his nose. Unfortunately, Shana arrived the moment of absolute fruition.

"Christ, what the hell is that now?" Covering her mouth with one hand, she retched. "It'll turn me water cloudy!"

Danny and Marty giggled behind their nasal barricades.

"So what? He has no control of his bodily functions now?" she said studying Marty and Danny. "You could have warned me!"

"Wasn't the t-shirt over the nose a giveaway?" asked Marty.

"I'm sick of ghosts," muttered Johnny pathetically.

"Well, I'm sick of the smell of the interior of your intestines!" said Shana.

"But ghosts are dead... And I'm sick of them!" said Johnny again.

"Well, it's just as well that I have some water for yer. You won't be sick and then we just have the ghosts," said Shana with her own special logic.

Marty and Danny frowned while Johnny lifted his head towards

145

the glass. He was just about to take sip but drifted off again. Marty shook his head, "okay, this is annoying me now!" Johnny bolted upright knocking the glass of water everywhere.

"For goodness sake!" said Shana becoming increasingly infuriated.

"An fish people. Big ol' fish people with fishy legs and people heads. I jush.. Thing- it's no right, you understand me? Fish is fish in the sea an' people on the land..." Johnny announced. With a swing of his whisky bottle Johnny took a deep breath. "Next it will be fish-birds... Flying and flying and people will be mixed with octopus. All those tentacles... Oh God, the thought of eet. It all started with fish," he said reclining.

"You need to drink water Johnny," said Marty in a flat tone. Shana refilled the glass and passed it to Marty.

"Johnny open your eyes and drink the bloody water!" said Marty.

Johnny's one working eye glanced up and down the glass dubiously.

"Does it have fish?"

"No, it's water. Drink it Johnny!" said Marty sternly.

"Will there be fish near it- Marty? I hate fish. I told yer didn't I? I think I may go vegetarian and only eat meat so that I don't have to go near fish," said Johnny pushing the beaker away.

"Ah, yer i-diot you'd only eat vegetables if yer vegetarian Johnny," said Shana.

"I know Shana," said Johnny in irritation.

"Okay-okay Johnny. Just saying!" said Shana.

"Shana- you're so pretty," said Johnny in his sweetest tone accompanied by a loud burp. She turned her head to avoid to blast but Johnny reached out and pulled her close. "Come here Shana. Burp! I hate fish you see and I hate seeing dead people. Don't let me see them Shana okay?" he said wretchedly.

"Okay Johnny, drink the water now and then you won't see no ghosties no more okay?" said Shana manipulatively.

Johnny sipped from the cup looking confused. "You know what'll make me right?"

"No? - Go on," said Marty.

Johnny smiled a drunken smile, "more whisky." He nodded while his eyes took a tour of the surrounding area to arrive at destination whisky bottle.

"Let's get him up the stairs," said Marty. "Danny get the whisky bottle out of his hand."

Danny wrestled Johnny but he was too strong. Johnny clenched the bottle so tightly that no levering of fingers could extract it.

"Johnny look over there… Ten naked women doing the cancan!" cried Shana.

Johnny's reaction was slow, but it was enough to distract him from bottle extraction.

"Where Shana?" said Johnny searching.

"Sorry Johnny, I was mistaken. It was the mirror," she replied.

Danny and Marty glanced at her with questioning expressions. The girl's brilliance shone at some of the most crucial moments!

Danny took an arm, Marty took the other arm and Shana unhappily pushed from behind.

"Now why do I get the bum deal?"

"Shana wherever you go there will be something stench-worthy," said Marty.

"Let's just get him up the stairs," said Danny.

The group attempted to leaver the limp body to standing. Johnny's legs fold beneath him, forcing his full weight on Danny.

"Johnny pull yourself together and use your legs!" said Danny in a tone Marty and Shana had never heard before.

Stair by stair the group made a slow ascent.

"I'll bloody get him tomorrow morning," said Danny kicking open Johnny's bedroom door. When they drew parallel with his bed, they all let go. Johnny fell like a mighty oak tree onto the mattress and bounced.

"Do you think he's going to be all right?" Shana asked sympathetically.

"Shana- check me bed for fish- will yer?" said Johnny in a small boy's voice.

"Not this crap again Johnny!" said Shana sharply. She glanced at Marty and gave a mysterious smile. "Look Johnny, no fish here, it's safe. There are no fish anywhere, especially not in your bed," she said in her sweetest tone.

"Okay thank you... And there are no fish with legs or fish with people heads anywhere are there Shana? Check the wardrobe for me, and then I'll know I'm safe."

Shana stomped across to the wardrobe. "Would ya look Johnny. There's not a fish to be seen there," she said opening the door. "Now does that make you feel better?"

"Thank you," said Johnny in his cutest little boy's voice."Shana…"

"Yes Johnny," she replied.

"You're nort a fish are yer?" he asked.

"No I'm bloody not!" she scowled. "Now come on Johnny, sort yer self out!"

"Good. 'Cause you're me friend… If you were a fish now…" he said drifting into a snore.

Shana waited and glanced at the other two who were shaking their heads.

"So if I was a fish - what?"

Marty and Danny shrugged. Who knew?

CHAPTER 31
Tripping over stuffed cats!

"It's only eight o'clock," said Marty glancing at his watch.
"Shana you want to come for a walk with me?" asked Danny
closing Johnny's bedroom door.
"What you thinkin'? Just a stroll?" she asked studying him.
"Sounds romantic," said Marty with a wink.
"Ach, why not? Where to?" she replied.
"Thought we'd go to the cove. It's full moon tonight and it'll
look cool," said Danny.
"The water's edge at full moon? Okay that'll be grand but you
know what? I would describe the moon shimmering on water as
beautiful, esoteric or captivating... Not just cool!"
"Well cool then," Danny said with a cheeky grin.
Shana sighed and rolled her eyes. "Marty what are you up to then?"
she asked noticing he was subtly reversing out of the room.
"As boring as it may seem for a Saturday night, I think I'm
going to paint or even read – how terrible of me!" he said
sarcastically.
"Come on then, let's leave Marty to be boring!" said Danny
taking Shana's hand and leading her out of the cottage.
Marty wondered into the studio and picked up a paintbrush. He
glanced at the wall where the paper had blown out earlier and paused.
He grabbed his jacket, checked for his wallet and made his way out of
the cottage to the nearest tavern, the only tavern, which was strangely
named a hotel.
In the centre of the village, Marty peered through the tavern
window into a bar gratified with a warm orange glow. The bar
appeared inviting enough, even if it was small, cosy and filled with
locals. The decor was fifties bed-and-breakfast style and the dark roof
beams were so low they could graze the top of the average person's
head. It certainly had a distinctive interior.
Marty hesitated by the door, he had to fight himself not turn
and go home. He had to learn to do things alone and not dither! He
took a deep breath, bent down and stepped through over the threshold.

A bell rang and stirred the old men in their various booths. Each stopped what they were doing and stared. Without paying attention to his feet, Marty tripped over a stuffed cat and ran at the bar. Silence.

In his best attempt at 'styling out' the dash, Marty grabbed a stool. One of the old men unconsciously shook his head. They were rigged! One leg was shorter on each of them. Marty hovered awkwardly by the bar. He turned his attention to a framed photograph screwed to the shelf. A man in his late forties, who was portly with dark hair, held a huge salmon beside him. He wore a silver necklace and drank from a whisky bottle. Written on the plaque below was 'Landlord Sully's great day with his wife.'

The sensation of eyes burrowing into Marty's behind increased. The room held a stagnant silence and darts were paused mid-air. Over at one particular booth, near the jukebox, a number of old men whispered and nodded in his direction. Marty sighed there was one thing for it! With a look of determination and the finesse of a tightrope walker, Marty carefully climbed onto the least rickety seat. Silence.

A phenomenon had occurred; Marty was technically levitating with the aid of a wonky stool. He had defied the law of physics!

Over on the headland, the moon rose and clouds drifted past. Danny and Shana strolled towards Hell's Lum beach inhaling the sea air. At the top of the hill, they paused, nestled into each other and admired the illuminated arrangement of cottages against the harbour.

"It is so lovely here," said Shana, her shoulders dropping.

"It's me home and it's not ruined by the outside world," said Danny.

"You're so lucky to have your traditions, secrets and stories," she said thoughtfully.

Danny took her hand and led her back to the track. "Let's go to the cove."

To adjust to the darkness took a little time. The glow of the moon accompanied by a universe of stars framed the ocean as the pair navigated the path to the cove. Once on the beach, he gestured to an area near the water's edge. Smooth rocks formed the perfect viewing platforms. He laid his jumper down and the pair made themselves comfortable. With a gentle slide of his arm, Shana responded and nuzzled into his neck contentedly. He smelled of fruity aftershave. All her conflict subsided as she chose to enjoy the moment. As much as Danny was humorous, he was sensitive and something special.

With a loud sigh, the pair admired the view: the calm sea softly lapped against the stony shore. Shana lifted her head and admired the universe reflected in Danny's eyes. He smiled and kissed her gently. A subtle hum tinged the air. Danny purposely ignored the resonation intended to capture his attention. Instead, he gazed admiringly at Shana's strong features and grew increasingly passionate. The urgency in the tone of the resonation revealed its neediness. As much as he could hear 'her', there was no way Danny was going to stop.

Out to sea the girl Danny had met that day surfaced. Sensing Danny's presence on the beach, she swam closer to the cove and hid behind one of the many half-submerged rocks. In the moonlight, she recognised the figure of the man with whom she had connected. His heart had summoned her, yet there he was entwined with another woman.

Silence.

Shana and Danny were unaware of the watcher. Both were absorbed by the moment, in each other.

In silence, the girl of the sea trembled. Tears slid down her cheeks as her heart began to contort. She glanced down, took a deep breath and her heart ruptured. In silence, she submerged. Her strength was also her weakness. Her ability for feeling the world resulted in her destruction. Her heart carried no understanding of rejection and fractured when dishonoured. From beneath the surface, she held her heart and gazed through the water at the moon. It had happened to many of her kind before and it would happen again. The rejection forced her heart into convulsion and she released a terrifying reverberation from the pit of her existence. The power was immense and would be a catalyst for repercussions.

Shana covered her ears as Danny grabbed his heart and convulsed. His head swooned, he jolted and his eyes rolled back in his head.

"Danny?"

Danny did not move, his nose bled and his eyes stared into nowhere.

"Danny?" demanded Shana, searching the horizon for the

source of that god-awful scream.

Danny remained still - emotionally petrified. The severance of the heart connection had resulted in emotional solidification.

Out to sea a mortified figure floated elegantly on the moonlit surface. Her hair drifted like seaweed, while glistening tears trickled over her cheeks. The young woman clenched her chest as she sobbed. The sea churned as the transformation began. The waves around her increased in size as her emotions merged with the lucid field around her. "Ey Tine (I'm lost), Ey Toom (I'm empty), Ey Greet (I weep). Her body trembled and contorted as she clutched her heart. A deep resonation left her body, her eyes flickered and she moved into the second phase. The sad emanation rose from her heart, swirled about her and formed a mist on the surface of the sea.

The girl of the sea gazed at the moon, "Ey e bean im Toom, im Tine" (I'm a woman who's empty and lost)" she whispered. The moon was silent but sympathetic.

"Ey threap a speir per desert, sloch, Aye threap a speir per desert, sloch, Aye threap a speir per desert, sloch! (I assert to ask for hermitage at my grave).

She closed her eyes and began to tremble. Her physical form began to disintegrate. The moon's surface became blood crimson. The transformation would result in vengeance. It had to be that way.

On the shore Danny jolted, his heart raced as the melancholy song arrived on shore. Shana was fixated on how the moon had transformed from white to dark red in a matter of seconds. As the moon transformed, so did the ocean. With a sudden shift in mood, waves raged towards the rocks. At the same time, Danny's eyes rolled back in his head. "Come back Danny!"

On the surface of the ocean, the girl floated with her eyes closed. The waves pulsated from her and cyclically formed a storm. With a final sigh, her eyes rolled back into her head and the ocean opened to receive her. From the density of silence, a whirlpool began to spin. From the pool grew a red tinged mist. The morbid resonation rose from the depths. The sky grew into a ravenous storm and a wall of cloud formed out to sea. The resonation gained momentum and travelled towards the land. She was searching... There would be death!

CHAPTER 32
Battering windows

Marty sat by the window in the tavern with Donald who had taken pity on the 'outsider.'

Donald was kind enough to introduce Marty to two more of the local fishers. One had an incredible resemblance to Tom Jones. The other, with his two gold earrings, looked exactly like a fisherman should- with his blue cap and his greying beard. They all sipped large stout pints apart from Marty who had half of cider.

'Enjoy that woman's drink,' said the Tom Jones look-alike.

"You should try a Lochness Monster, one of Sully's special brews- blows your hat off!" said Donald proudly. "If yer do ney have a hat it'll blow someone else's off – mark my words!"

"So, where are all the young people?" asked Marty.

"Most are on the rigs," said the old fisherman. "Those that are left... It's Saturday, they go partying to the larger towns."

"This is no place for youngens if they want to party," said the Tom Jones look-alike. "They go to Aberdeen or Peterhead." With a glance out of the window, the Tom Jones look-alike grimaced, "the forecast is clear and looky here, there's a storm a-brewing."

"There weren't no indication within nature," said the fisherman "and me barometer says fine as does the seaweed hanging at me door. Something's ney right."

"That there's a big storm all right," said Donald as hail unexpectedly pelted the windows and roofs.

"We never have this weather at this time of year normally- strange it is," said Sully, emerging from the back room, polishing a glass. The men nodded in agreement. Sully returned to his usual position behind the bar.

"That's the largest hail I ever saw," said Marty glancing at the moon as it emerged from behind a cloud. "The moon is dark red too. Is that normal up here?"

The old men glanced at each other shiftily.

"There might not be much for the youngens but there is always pub games such as tiddlywinks or dominoes. I like that game- n' there's always darts. Best darts game we ever played was blind folded," Donald said with a loud chuckle as he remembered.

Marty studied Donald why had he deviated?

"Only joking," said Donald with a chortle.

Marty smiled but turned his attention back to the storm. It had an edge and was moving at speed towards them. With a squint, Marty frowned he had noticed a transparent form amongst the mist.

"Something feels out of sorts with that front," said Donald standing for a better look.

"I think we should move away from the window," said the Tom Jones look-alike.

"Move to the fire place, it's in the centre of the pub."

Picking up his half pint, Marty reversed towards the hearth and stood in silence with the other men. The mist turned in on itself and when it reached the pub window, it sounded like nails scratching metal.

Bang! The tavern door blew open and slammed against the wall. Glasses smashed in all directions as the translucent figure burst in. A shrill scream mixed with the resonance blasted through the room carrying a melancholy song. The noise entered and manoeuvred about the room blowing into each person's face. "Fey me fey," said Sully. Instantly the mist sucked backwards through the door. Instantly he launched at the door and closed it.

With his back to the fireplace, Marty watched the mist re-form on the path. 'She' changed direction and continued her search. With yet another shrill scream, the battering winds attacked the village and torrential rain struck. Lightening blasted in all directions. There was something super-natural taking place!

CHAPTER 33

Vengeance chasing.

Shana dragged Danny's limp body inside Crooked Cottage just in time. Huge chunks of hail pummelled the ground and bounced. Danny made a loud gasp, jolted and suddenly woke. "Where am I?" he croaked.

"Yer back at the cottage because I bloody dragged you from Hell's Lum," said Shana sitting him down on a kitchen chair. Shana plonked down and wiped her eye. "I thought you'd died Danny. Really I did now."

Danny covered his ears and winced.

"What is it?" asked Shana.

Danny couldn't respond; the drone inside his mind was too intense. After numerous dry retches, he laid on the floor. "Shana what's happening?"

Shana stood up, glanced out of the window and froze. A 'form' was gazing back from the darkness. The scratching sound of metal on glass accompanied the storm.

"Get away from the window Shana!" shouted Danny.

The mist noticed Danny, drew back and rushed at the glass. Shana swished the curtain closed and rotated to use the wall as a cover. She glanced at the door; the handle began to rattle. She dashed to the sink, wet some kitchen-roll and jammed it in the keyhole. Scratching, sobbing and crying filled the air. The handle shook violently; there was a twisting noise and creaking. Shana closed her eyes and searched her mind. "Fey me Fey yer ger away... then what?"

"She's going to kill us!" said Danny incredulously.

Shana studied Danny, why would 'she' kill them? "Danny we need to remember that poem."

"I canny remember," he replied.

Shana screwed her face up, "Danny you need to remember!"

"Something about a dark hollow grave," said Danny searching his mind.

The bung of kitchen-roll dropped to the floor and the beginning of red tinged mist began to travel through the keyhole.

Danny was silent. "She's going to kill us!"

Shana squinted, "Danny we have to remember, it's the only way this thing will leave us."

The mist gathered momentum and seeped through the cracks in the door. Once on the other side it began to re-form.

Danny was silent, watching.

Shana focused as she searched her brain. She took a deep breath.

The mist formed a figure.

Danny was transfixed, he recognised the features. The playful girl he met that day was forming in the blood red mist. *Be careful Danny, and then we have a disaster on our hands,* rang through his mind.

"Fey me Fey,Yey ger 'way o fash me lasho si dubh ochd," said Shana.

The mist stopped expanding.

"Fey me Fey,Yey ger 'way o fash me lasho si dubh ochd."

The figure within the mist turned to Shana and shook her head sorrowfully.

"Fey me Fey,Yey ger 'way o fash me lasho si dubh ochd!" said Shana.

The shape appeared like red ink in water, expanded and the sucked back through the key hole.

Shana studied Danny; he was guilty of something. There was no way such an entity would attempt to kill an innocent party. What had taken place?

CHAPTER 34
Trouble Brewing...

"What was all that about then?" Marty hoped to get a straight answer but the old men glanced at each other dubiously and shuffled back to their previous positions.

"It's a sign of trouble a-coming," said Donald with a loud sigh.

"Aye. There's trouble on the wind. And full moon too. Sign of death that... And change," said the old fisher.

"Ney been anything like that for a while. I feel there's trouble-a-brewing," said the Tom Jones look-alike.

Sully rung the bell for last orders.

The pub punters simultaneously glanced at their watches. There were numerous headshakes, frowns and grumbles.

"Come on Sully, there's a good half hour yet," said Donald.

"Sully we need to drink in times of crisis." The Tom Jones look-alike cut in. "We need to steady our nerves and there's a storm outside. Would yer really turf yer best punters out into that - now?"

"You remember the last time?" said Sully eyeing Donald. "You know as soon as such an entity enters here it's time to close. Now go on and return to yer families. Think of Dora sat alone in the cottage without you while you steady your nerves with a drink. She's probably scared half to death. She probably has a sense of what's coming," said Sully glancing at Donald.

He was right.

"So my friends there's ney another half-an-hour when me door is blown open and a pained call blows in," said Sully.

Marty gazed at Sully's irritated features.

"You know it foretells trouble. What with the-" said Sully losing himself.

"Enough of that Sully," said Donald. "You'll scare our new friend here!"

Marty studied the group, how much should he reveal he knew? "If you're talking about what I think you're talking about - I know something of it."

"Our Sully is a little untrusting of strangers Marty. He's been

158

lulled into a false sense of security by those journalists snooping around looking for their damned stories. Last time he was quoted speaking of cannibals in the area, cannibals I tell yer!"

"Were there?" asked Marty.

"So the papers say," said Sully folding his arms.

"They reckon they ate travellers who were passing. Gave them a bed n' a bath; then ate the buggers or so the papers say..." said Donald trailing off.

"I said nothing of that!" Sully slapped the counter defensively.

"The villagers taunted him for his trusting outsiders for years after that," said Donald.

"Learned my lesson then," said Sully counting the coins in the till.

"What happened to the cannibals?" Marty asked.

"Got eaten – by each other," said the Tom Jones look-a-like with a smirk.

Sully gave 'Tom' a look.

"Disappeared" said Donald. "The whole family, all at once."

"Look, we don't want strange sorts like that ruining our lifestyle," said Sully sternly.

"So, what do you know?" asked Sully curiously.

"I know about- you know..."

"About what?" asked Sully.

"Fish-" Marty paused 'n' people. People n' fish."

Donald glanced at Sully and back at Marty.

"Would yer care to elaborate?" asked Sully with a furrowed brow.

"I surf; I am out in the water. What else is out in the water?" said Marty cryptically.

Glances exchanged around the room. The slurping sound of Butch licking his balls penetrated the silence.

"Marty yer know what yer know. I say keep it to yerself. We do ney want more trouble... And gentlemen it is time for you to leave. I intend to lock up." Sully nodded towards Butch and raised an eyebrow. "Look at your dog Donald...I hope he didn't learn that from you! Now he needs his bed or a decent bitch!" said Sully.

Donald smirked and glanced at Butch, he always knew how to break an atmosphere, even if he was unaware of what he had done.

Marty watched Sully suck his lip in contemplation.

"Men, be aware of what's washed up." Sully navigated the tables and collected the glasses. "Scour the shore Donald when walking Butch there. If something comes ashore, we need to find it before anyone else does- you understand?"

There was a mass of nods.

"Marty you're implicated now," said Sully.

"What exactly am I looking for on the shore?"

"You'll know when you see her. The resonation came from a female," said Sully moving over to wipe down the table. "Jealousy kills them, but not like death – a movement to the world between."

Marty studied Sully and picked up his coat. "I was told that they don't have the same human emotional defence."

"They have no defence. Once they make contact that is for life. Whoever 'she' made contact with will have contact for life unless he seeks forgiveness."

"They never learned the human ways of suppressing their emotions and not feeling. They feel life completely; they are absolutely authentic, not like us and our fragmented selves. Not like our civilisation where we appear rather than be," said Sully thoughtfully.

"Now that was deep," said Donald.

Butch wiped his nose on Marty's trouser leg.

"Likes you then," said Donald.

Marty crouched down and patted him. Butch licked Marty's cheek.

"He always does that after licking his balls. I wonder what goes on in that doggy mind of his," said Sully.

"We think he's gay," said Donald. "He sniffs all the boy dogs' bums and ignores the bitches!"

Marty smirked.

"Although he does like to stick his head into women's crutches when they least expect it" said Donald in contemplation.

"Learnt from his owner too," said Sully waiting for the Tom Jones look-alike to down his drink.

Donald gave Sully a playful punch on the arm. The atmosphere had been broken.

"Well, I'll see you around then," said Marty opening the door and peering outside.

"I hear you're a bit of a painter Marty," said Sully.

"It's currently just a hobby," said Marty to avoid sounding too pretentious.

"Be careful what you paint. You know what I mean. We don't want any imagery going to the outside world," said Sully.

Marty studied him.

"Just be careful is what I'm saying. I know it is tempting to paint them or photograph them," said Sully. "We need to protect them and protect the village. Imagine the repercussions if something like this turned up in the outside world."

"I hear what you're saying," said Marty. "Good night," he said with a nod.

CHAPTER 35
A rude knicker awakening!

When Marty arrived at Crooked Cottage, he was wet and windblown. After removing his jacket, he crept up the stairs to discover Danny and Shana asleep on the sofa. He continued up the second flight of stairs to Johnny's room. The floor creaked. He stood in the doorway to Johnny's room and listened to the gigantic snores filling the room. Johnny had missed everything that had happened. Why was he avoiding it?

Making his way to his perfectly ordered, cream and grey room. Marty pulled his mobile from his jacket and dialled his mother. The phone was engaged. Beeeep. "Hi mum," he said awkwardly. "It's Marty... I er... Just wanted to let you know things are going well up here. There have been quite a few strange coincidences. Do we happen to have any ancestry up here? Talk soon... L-o-ve you. Marty, your son. Remember?"

Marty put down the phone and lay back on his bed. He felt so far removed from his remaining family. His mother's attention was with her new man and Marie's focus was on work, it was always work. With a loud sigh, he shuffled across the bed and hung up his coat. It felt heavier than he remembered. He riffled through the inner pocket. The book from the manor was inside. He opened it on a random page: Mermaid Myth and Symbol.

"Men are drawn to the water by the mermaids: representing a man's inate fear of women and lack of commitment," he read aloud. Marty switched on the side lamp, propped up his pillow and glanced down the page to the section on drowning. "Drowning represents a man's fear of emotional commitment and emotional expectation." He had never really considered women and their emotional needs. Emotion was an anomaly, society taught people to suppress it; yet the sea-people experience their life through it. What's more, living in the sea made their emotion so intense that it would drive them to kill or move to a realm beyond worlds. Marty had never experienced that kind of emotion or maybe he had - he just didn't know how to 'feel' it. Marty rubbed his heart; he had been numb since his father had passed. With a loud sigh, he wondered what the world 'felt' like from the sea people's perspective. He laid back and imagined an innocent world full of love where you connected with one person and that was it – done! People would not build distrust and bitterness generated from the feelings of rejection from numerous relationships that went wrong. He laid back with his hand on his heart; he had 'felt' something briefly when Iris connected with him. What did that mean?

Marty's alarm rang at six in the morning. He jolted, sighed and then flopped out of bed. With gravity-defying hair, he made his way over to the window and smiled. The wind had swung offshore. He dashed into the shower and gave a mischievous smirk at the thought of Johnny's face when he woke him up.

Once dressed, Marty stretched and then cracked his knuckles. He needed all his wits to extract the big man from his slumber. Marty crept across the landing and peered into Johnny's room of self-adoration. Shelves full of medals, photographs of himself and two full-length mirrors revealed how he wanted to appear. In addition, the mirrored wardrobe covered one wall and reflected Johnny's wall of achievement. The third wall had a window with dark red curtains while the final wall, with the huge black and white canvas of a naked woman draped over rocks, was where his bed was located.

As soon as Marty stepped over the threshold, the smell of alcohol violated his nostrils. Amongst the pong, Johnny laid flat on his back snoring like a lawnmower. Consumed in the depths of sleep, with a furry tongue and dried saliva encrusted around the side of his mouth – he was certainly an attractive sight – not!

The creak of the floorboard disturbed Johnny who rolled onto his side. Marty considered his options. How should he wake him? What if he got up and fought? He'd done that before with an ex-girlfriend. He silently studied Johnny; what kind of woman would settle with him or simply tolerate his weird and not so wonderful ways? No doubt she would have to be strong, stubborn and resilient - a female Johnny. Admittedly, he had changed lately; he'd started washing his underwear according to colour, which meant he had bought more than one pair in more than one colour. Was he nesting?

In the corner, Johnny's pool cue caught Marty's attention. It had recently been chalked and was the ideal tool for the monstrous awakening. Marty checked the weighting, aimed and prodded Johnny in the back. He shrugged it off but Marty was determined and poked his buttock once more. He did not respond.

Marty's shook with amusement as he took a deep breath, used the pool cue to pick up a pair of Johnny's dirty gym underpants and carefully navigated them across Johnny's body. Once the pair were in position, Marty refined the alignment of the crutch with Johnny's nose. And… One loud snore, a hearty cough and a gag, Johnny woke up. "Get those fish outta me eyes!" he shouted swiping the air. With a rapid swish, Marty propped the pool cue against the wall.

"What are you doing in here Marty?" Johnny asked huskily, swiping the underpants from his face.

"You asked me to wake you to go surfing," said Marty with a straight face.

"I did?" asked Johnny gruffly clutching the pants.

"We'll have the bacon down stairs… You mentioned it last night remember? Then we'll go okay?" Marty maintained his best straight face.

Johnny retched at the thought of bacon. "Are yer sure I said I would go surfing?"

"Who in their right mind would risk waking you Johnny unless you had asked?"

"If I said it then I have to go," said Johnny rubbing his eye, wiping his mouth and trying to work out how his underpants had landed on his face.

After a warm shower, Johnny stomped down the stairs looking queasy. On the way he noticed Shana and Danny entwined on the sofa. With a loud grumble, Johnny continued down the stairs to the kitchen.

"What's up Johnny?" asked Marty dropping the smoked rashers into some sizzling oil.

"Nothing," said Johnny unconvincingly. "Just feel a bit rough." Marty studied his friend and shook his head. "You're so transparent Johnny. You're jealous, aren't you?"

"You've got me with no resilience Marty. That's no fair!"

"You are…"

"Not so much jealous… It would just make a pleasant change

to meet a decent woman. With my reputation what hope do I have?" said Johnny pulling up a seat by the kitchen table and resting his head in his hands.

"It can happen at any time from the most unexpected place." Marty arranged two crunchy rashers on some wholemeal toast. "Eat up then," he said with a nod.

Johnny stared at the toast and retched. "I need some brown sauce."

Marty passed the bottle over and watched Johnny struggle. Eventually he focused and fought the urge to gag as he chewed.

Up in the front room the smell of bacon caused Danny to stir. He re-adjusted his numb arm and closed his eyes. A continual drone played through his mind. "She's torturing me."

After breakfast, Johnny and Marty left through the lower door. As they walked down the street, Marty noticed Johnny's skin revealed a tinge of green.

"You might need these," said Marty rifling through his rucksack and handing him a can of coke and a bottle of water.

"Thanks," Johnny replied with one eye closed.

"You want to get in then?" Marty opened Bertha's door and watched Johnny work up the energy to climb in.

With an amused smile Marty climbed in the other side, turned the key in the ignition and Bang!

Johnny jolted, grabbed his chest and his head simultaneously. "Why?" he muttered sadly. "I do ney deserve this torture!"

Marty glanced over at his friend while Bertha's engine rattled into warmth. "Right, we're going to move. Are you ready?"

Johnny shook his head so Marty pulled away slowly. With the curve of each corner, Johnny groaned. "Marty you're going to have to pull over! Now!"

Johnny bolted to a grass verge and bent over. The sound that came from the pit of his guts resembled a goat being murdered.

"Got any mints?" asked Johnny gruffly when he climbed back in the van.

"There are Fisherman's Friends there…" he said nodding at the compartment in the door.

"Thanks," said Johnny glumly.

Up on Hell's Lum, Marty parked the van and watched perfect green waves rolling in.

"Why couldn't you just leave me to sleep?" asked Johnny in a coarse voice.

"You were insistent - whatever happens wake me you said. You told me the best cure for a hangover was water, coke and surf," said Marty avoiding eye contact. "Plus… You burped and farted in Shana's face last night."

"Mmm," said Johnny suspiciously.

"As you said… Best cure for a hangover. Drink some water and we'll get that blood moving!"

"More like best chance of cramp and then drowning," muttered Johnny. "If I die my head won't hurt anymore…" he said optimistically.

"They're the best waves I've seen in ages," said Marty excitedly.

"At this moment Marty I hate you. You'll go to hell for this!" Marty smirked; Johnny was going in.

"You're so smug Marty!" said Johnny with a scowl.

"Well, what are you waiting for?" asked Marty grabbing his wetsuit.

"I'm going about this slowly. I'm not doing anything that will shake my brain," he said with exaggerated slow movements.

"An old woman would move faster than that!" Marty stood watching Johnny's gentle movements. He maintained his head in one position whilst carefully climbing into his wetsuit.

"Not if she felt the same way as I do!"

Once Johnny had changed in slow motion, the pair paddled over the waves to the calm beyond the break.

With plenty of bellyaching, Johnny lagged behind. "Bloody idiot!" he muttered.

The quick flick of the board enabled Marty to sit and gaze at the oncoming sets of waves. He rubbed his stomach, the atmosphere felt odd – empty.

Silence.

The ache in his solar plexus increased. Something in the

atmosphere felt all wrong.

When the first set neared, Marty paddled and launched onto a wave.

Johnny's attempt at paddling was pathetic. After a few waves, Johnny admitted defeat. Every wave he caught shook his brain and every wipe-out provided an ice/alcohol headache.

While the pair sat waiting for the next set, Johnny jolted with the first tremors of cramp.

"Shit! Cramp!" he said with the onslaught of full muscle seizure.

"Go in Johnny," said Marty paddling over. "Go and get some fluids into you."

Johnny gritted his teeth, "how pathetic!"

"You want me to come with you?" asked Marty.

"No, I'll be right. I'm going to go and nap in the van. Catch some waves for me, will yer?" Johnny lifted both legs, paddled to catch a wave and rode all the way in on his stomach.

Marty straddled his board and waited. A subtle resonation wound through the air but the song was melancholy. Beneath the surface, a shape rotated through the water and slowly emerged. Her presence revealed helplessness and sorrow. Marty reached towards Iris who took his hand and rested her chin on his knee.

"What's wrong?" whispered Marty.

"One among us pass. Is sad. When one chooses to go, hurts all. We different breed to you. We live different - we 'feel' life. She feel love connection but love broke her. All feel pain. She leave echo," said Iris gazing deep into Marty's eyes.

"What can I…"

She shrugged, "we just allow ourselves to feel pain until pass." She studied him curiously. "Is possible for you breathe in water?"

"It is not natural for us. We need special equipment," he replied.

"Can get?"

Marty nodded. "Why?"

"I feel I show you our world. Our timing. The pain. You will understand. Between me and you," she said.

Marty studied her, what was she intending to show him?

"Meet me half way between midday and sun set," she said.

167

"Ahhhhhh!" a loud, gruff scream came from the beach. Iris studied Marty, shook her head. "Danger," she said and submerged.

Marty turned and frantically paddled to shore. The scream had come from Johnny. Why was he still in the water? As Marty drew closer, he noticed Johnny revealed a hideous expression. He was holding something limp in his arms. Was Johnny sobbing? A jolt of realisation shot through him. "Johnny?"

Johnny shook his head and fought his emotion. A lifeless figure floated on the surface of the water. "I just found her," he croaked. Marty froze and held his heart.

"Marty… She's one of them… How did this… come about?" he stammered.

Marty stepped forwards, his solar plexus clenched. "We should get some help."

Johnny's lip trembled, "she was too late for resuscitation. She's been gone a while… We need to move her."

With a subtle gesture, Marty went to help carry her but as the pair moved she exhaled.

"The last breath," muttered Johnny.

Marty studied the girl. Her eyes were empty, her face was serene but she was now just a shell.

"I don't get it Johnny. How could she choose to do this to herself?"

The pair gazed at the girl's beautiful and innocent face.

"Loss of love Marty can destroy a person," he said trembling. With sadness filling his heart, Marty shook his head. Loss of love was the ultimate fear.

"What do we do Marty?" asked Johnny searching for guidance. "What if someone sees?"

"We need to get some locals. They'll know what to do," said Marty considering all possibilities.

"But we'll be blamed. I know what they're like…"

"They won't blame us…"

"Marty I know how they are. They're going to point fingers and there'll be trouble," said Johnny.

Marty frowned, would the village really react like that?

CHAPTER 36

Finding.

"Marty?" called Donald from the edge of the cove.
Johnny glanced at Marty; circumstance had dictated the outcome and they could not avoid what they had found.
Donald trudged over in trepidation. All the while Butch dug his hind legs into the shingle and resisted. "Come on you bugger!" For about five hundred metres, the pair struggled until Butch finally gave in. Donald reached the water's edge and crouched next to the body.
"Woof! Woof!" Butch began a barking frenzy.
"Quiet!" said Donald. "So you found her then. We need to get some of the others down. I'll get the bell sounded. Don't let anyone from outside see her." Donald made a loud sucking noise and sighed. He then pulled an oversized mobile out of his pocket. "I hope we get a signal," he said dialling.
"Sully, yer need to round up some men. She's been found over at Hell's Lum cove," said Donald scanning the area for potential unwanted witnesses.
"You need water Johnny?" Donald studied Johnny remembering his previous night's escapades. "I always like to be prepared for all eventualities," he said handing him a silver canister.
"How come you carry water with you?" asked Marty wiping his eyes.
"It's to water down me whisky," he said producing a second smaller canister. "You may need to be drinking this to calm yer nerves Johnny."
Johnny shook his head. "I canny do hair of the dog and we need to sort this lass out."
Over on the hill, a group of villagers carried a stretcher towards the cove.
Marty held the body while Johnny unhitched his leash.
"She's the one who caused last night's storm - remember? This is what happened to me before. This is the result of jealousy Marty. I tell yer someone's upset this lass. There is no other reason for this to happen. I pity the soul who is connected," said Donald.

"What's going to happen?" Marty waded ashore and attempted to manoeuvre the body.

"Different things to different people," replied Donald.

The men from the village reached the group. With stern faces, all of them reacted with sympathy.

"What a bloody waste!" said Sully with a frown.

"The resonance will begin the calling," said the Tom Jones look-alike. "Last night was just the beginning. "The culprit will rise to the surface or drown. Or there will be more deaths..."

"It wasn't me," said Johnny defensively.

"Do yer think she would have let you find her if it were you Johnny? Don't you remember the stories you were told as a kid?" asked Donald.

"I thought I was being fed crap – to scare yer," replied Johnny.

"Let's get her out of the water and away from here," said Marty.

The villagers nodded in agreement while Donald studied Johnny curiously. How could he purposely reject his whole family history?

"What's wrong with yer Johnny?" asked Sully.

"I've got cramp," replied Johnny rubbing his leg.

"Aye, yer were quite a performer last night. What with making me check the bar for fish. I did ney know what was going on in that head of yours... Now here we are... Sorrow."

"What do we do about this? Shouldn't we report it?" asked Marty.

"Not much we can do. Who do we report it to? Marty yer choices are limited now and you're part of this history whether you like it or not," said Donald.

"The one thing we must do is return her to her own before they begin to resonate too. Their revenge will result in mass death," said Sully.

"How come no one knows about this?"

"It's none of their business Marty and that's why we keep it amongst ourselves," said Donald. "We're protecting those outside and protecting those in the water. It isn't just the village; we do ney want any attention from these incidents. You understand why we're so cagey now?"

The men sombrely lifted the body onto the stretcher. Marty

170

noticed they all wore gloves. One villager produced some material, wrapped the entire stretcher and secured the body. Finally, he covered the girl's face. The men paused and glanced at the wrapped shape before them.

"Right lift," said Sully.

As they lifted her, the church bell rang. The men paused and turned in the direction of the church. The vicar was running towards them.

"Take her to St. John's and not the central church."

"Why the ruins?" asked Sully.

"The crypt will keep her cool," said the vicar studying Marty and Johnny.

"That's a long way to carry the corpse. It could draw attention," said Donald.

"It is the only option Donald," said the vicar with a certain look.

While discussions took place, Johnny stared at the lifeless shape.

"What do you think made her do it?"

"Johnny it has to do with jealousy. She's fallen in love and something went wrong with it," said Marty.

"I never thought girls were that - well, so affected by men. God the way I've treated them too.... Marty remind me of this when I'm being my normal self. I'll never be unfaithful again, the next woman I meet she'll be the one and I'll treat her like a goddess!" he said convincingly squeezing Marty's shoulder. "Remind me - okay mate?" Marty nodded.

"And mate, do me a favour do ney tell the others about this. I don't want them thinking that I am well - you know a bit of a wet fart," said Johnny honestly.

"It'll go no further Johnny," said Marty sincerely.

The villagers carried the stretcher up the hill over Hell's Lum, while Johnny limped with Marty at the back of the group. Ahead of them, the ruin of St John's church carried a peculiar presence. Its remote location didn't make sense. What was it hiding?

CHAPTER 37
Beginnings of guilt.

With a sudden jolt Shana woke up wrapped in a soft blanket on the sofa. There hearth was cold and Danny was slumped over her. With a sudden motion she shifted his bulk sideways and wriggled from beneath him. "Danny?"

No answer.

She checked his neck for a pulse - he was fine.

After a big stretch and a yawn she plodded down to the kitchen to prepare toast. Once the toast had popped, she returned to the front room and watched Danny mutter in his sleep. "I just need quiet..." he muttered. As soon as the aroma tickled his nostrils he stirred. He rubbed his eyes, beckoned Shana over alluringly and bit a sizeable chunk from her breakfast.

"Aarhh Danny!"

"I am only playing Shana?" said Danny mid-chew.

"Yer hear that Danny? That ringing - it sounds like a church bell."

"No, I just hear an endless drone. A constant hum... It won't go away either..."

"Now when did that begin?" she asked curiously.

"It started last night..." he replied.

Shana studied him, "I think you might need to see a doctor. It's probably water in the ear or something."

"I'll give it a day..."

"So what do you think the bell is? It sounds like there's something up. Aren't you curious?" she asked making her way to the window.

Danny curled up in the blanket. "Shana I'm not interested and I don't want to get involved."

"Well, you do what you like. I want to find out what's going on. I'm going to head towards the harbour. You can stay here alone with the ghost!"

Danny folded his arms. Which was the lesser of the two evils?

Shana quickly showered and changed. In that time, her second round of toast popped up.

Danny sat at the kitchen table preparing his next tasty ambush.

"Have you washed your credentials Danny? I'm not hanging out with a stinker!" she said buttering the toast.

"I dunked them in the washing up!" he replied with a smirk.

"Ah Danny really?"

"No, of course not, I had a wash Shana. And sprayed deodorant," he replied.

Shana studied Danny, "Are you better now? Is that weird stuff from last night over with?"

"I have no idea what that was about," he said.

With a thoughtful silence, Shana studied Danny. "Well are you ready to go then? I'm dying to find out what all the fuss is about," said Shana fidgeting. Shana reached out for Danny to take hold of her hand. Danny paused, "Shana…"

"Danny we can talk later, now let's go…"

There was no one around Straight Lane or on the High Street. Most of the shops had their closed signs hanging in the window. An American tourist, wearing a distinctive diamante visor, noticed the pair of them and lolloped towards them. Her family remained salivating in front of the bakery window display.

"Excuse me… You know what time the bakery will open again?" she asked in a casual southern drawl.

"It's normally open all day," Shana replied.

"It kinda seems a weird time to close. None of the villagers are about neither," she said.

"Sorry, we have no idea. We're not local to the area," said Shana prodding Danny.

"Well, you go and have a nice time and we'll wait. There must be other people who will be in need of candy," said the tourist tapping her watch.

Danny and Shana glanced at each other, where had all the people gone?

"Something's going on," whispered Danny.

"Maybe it's some kind of public holiday or something…Look…" Shana broke into a jog.

The villagers carried a stretcher down the hill leading to the harbour.

173

Trailing behind was Johnny and Marty.

"Who is it? What happened?" asked Shana when she reached Marty.

The drone in Danny's ear increased. He stayed back. The feeling in the pit of his stomach was wretched; something violently fought inside his gut.

The wind picked up over on the hill and tore across the top of the sheet of the stretcher. The innocent but vacant face peered out.

"I recognise her," Shana muttered. "She was the... storm..." In that moment, a few things added up and she peered over her shoulder at Danny. How was he involved?

The procession continued.

Danny was rigid and leant against the wall. The closer the figure moved towards him, the more intense the drone became. When the stretcher drew parallel, he glimpsed her face. His solar plexus spasmed and pain shot through his whole being. The playful creature he had kissed was lying motionless. Danny stumbled backwards and tumbled onto his behind.

Shana ran alongside the stretcher and covered the girl's face. She turned back to see Danny sitting motionless on the ground. What was he doing? The procession continued along the harbour and up the hill towards St. John's.

"Are you okay Danny?" she asked jogging over.

"I... I've... Just I-," he muttered.

"What?"

"Feel weird again... She's so young and... dead. It's terrible," he said shaking his head.

"Danny it's sad but it happens," she said in her most sympathetic tone.

"No it doesn't... Not to them.... They have to choose it - remember?" he replied.

How did Danny know the girl was 'one of them' and not a local simply by her face?

"Shana I need some space. I'm not good at dealing with this stuff," he said.

"Are you sure?" said Shana glancing at the stretcher plodding

174

up the hill.

"It's just such…"

"A terrible shock?" said Shana hurriedly.

Danny looked up and nodded unconvincingly. "Yeh… A terrible shock."

"Are you going to be okay?" asked Shana.

"I'll be fine," he said rearranging the grass.

Shana helped Danny up. "I'm curious as to where they're taking her. I'll see you later," she said with a quick embrace before she broke into a jog.

"I'll be on the beach," called Danny.

While Danny walked, his mind assembled the events. "Shit, the beach last night." His head swooned and he grabbed the nearest rock to stabilise himself. "I killed her…" Flashes of her giggling and splashing played through his mind. "They warned me…"

The drone increased. He leant against the rock for a moment and climbed onto the flat surface where he laid staring at the sky. Even the bloody clouds resembled her!

CHAPTER 38
Enter the crypt.

St. John's church stood on the east hill overlooking Gardenstown. It was a shell of a church, without a roof for more than a hundred years.

"Do you know what happened?" whispered Shana as soon as she caught up with Marty and Johnny.

"Johnny found her on the beach," said Marty glancing over at him.

"Is everything okay there Johnny?" Shana asked.

"What other than the dead body, the cramp and now the chaff on my thigh?" he replied solemnly.

"Okay Johnny, you were pissed last night and now yer pissed off!" she said.

"I should have stayed in bed," he muttered. "Then I would have missed all of this."

With a definite fold of her arms, Shana watched the stretcher procession wait for guidance when they reached the church. She glanced down at the picturesque village with all the tiny cottages huddled in the harbour. It was beautiful, remote and now marred by death.

The vicar opened the creaky gate, stood aside to enable the stretcher to pass. The stretcher party navigated the gravestones, past the walls of the church to the chapel. The interior had a grass floor with a few floorboards poking through. Angular gravestones protruded like crooked teeth.

"Gravestones inside the church?" Marty studied Shana's response. What did she make of it?

The body was carried carefully along the line where the aisle used to be, the group stopped not knowing where to go next.

"I bet there's some kind of secret door," whispered Shana peering through a hole where a window used to be. "Marty look here… More pirates," she said pointing to a line of graves against the wall of the church. Each grave carried the carving of a skull and crossbones.

"It must be something to do with the village, they must have all been involved in some way," said Marty suspiciously.

"Some have fresh flowers on them," whispered Shana.

"Ahh herm…" said the vicar at the far end of the church where the chancel was located, a place where only the holy could enter. The vicar pressed his back square against the ancient wall, where the apse would have once stood. From the apse, he aligned himself with the lower bell tower and counted a certain number of paces that only he knew.

"Now you keep this to yourselves?" said the vicar as he pawed at the grass to reveal a large metal hoop. He tugged at it with all his might, the grass had grown over the grooves. With help from one of the villagers, he pulled open the cover to reveal a set of stairs.

Marty watched curiously and side-glanced Shana. She knew what he was thinking.

"I am growing to hate this village and its bloody secrets," said Johnny.

"Do you think the tunnels might connect to Drichen?" wondered Shana glancing at the pirates' graves.

"That would be one vast warren," said Marty.

"Now I wonder whether Danny's granny knows anything."

"Probably-" Marty said nodding thoughtfully. There was a system and a pattern forming, but how did it all link up?

Johnny nursed his leg.

"Still hurtin'?" asked Shana watching Johnny rub his calf.

"I don't understand why such a small village needs two bloody churches," he said glancing over at Gardenstown. "If it was anything to do with it being new then why couldn't we store her at that one? Something doesn't add up now does it?"

"A separate church for the village and a second for the gentry?" suggested Marty. "Maybe they bury pirates here to keep them separate and secret."

No doubt, there had to be more to it!

The procession lifted the stretcher and followed the vicar down the worn, stone stairs. When they entered the corridor, the width wasn't large enough to accommodate the men two abreast, so they strategically formed a single file with just enough space to carry the stretcher above their heads. In Marty's opinion, the locals were a little too experienced at such a formation. A respectful silence prevailed as the group entered the sacred space.

The sound of dripping water echoed through the caves. The aroma of damp moss accompanied wafts of stagnant air.

"Marty I feel claustrophobic and I can't see a thing," said Shana.

The vicar ignited some ready prepared torches placed at regular intervals down the corridor.

"This doesn't add up," Marty whispered to Shana.

The red rock formations above Shana's head had caught her attention. The rocks were smooth and well worn. Some dripped water from small yellow crystal formations while others resembled mercury.

"I've not seen rock like this before," she said.

The procession continued. The three friends followed even though their instincts told them otherwise. The group continued to an area of catacombs where mummified bodies hung in the walls. Were they guarding the tunnel?

"You think they're here as a deterrent?" whispered Shana reading Marty's mind.

"They're bloody hideous!"

Johnny had been preoccupied with his calf muscle and looked up at the wrong moment. A semi-decayed corpse silently screamed into his face. "Shit! What the... Right, I've had enough of dead shit!" he said glancing about erratically. "Now what the hell is this? Bodies bloody everywhere," he said in absolute aggravation.

"Johnny... Show some respect!" said Marty whacking his arm.

"I need some respect! Everywhere I go there are dead people or fish. The two bloody things I hate! Here I am following a fish amongst dead people. Marty it's nort right! It's just weird and we all have to pretend it's okay. Well, it's not!" spat Johnny.

"Shhh! Get over it Johnny!" Shana whispered cuttingly.

The procession slowed and Shana stood on tiptoes. What was happening? The passage continued but a tinge of cool blue light illuminated the red rock walls.

"There's an odd light ahead," whispered Shana wrapping herself tightly in her cardigan.

The blue glow intensified and became increasingly cold the closer they got. The corridor widened to reveal a carved frozen arch. It shimmered with specks of moving light. Beyond the arch was a crypt with smooth walls made of luminous blocks. Those blocks fitted together perfectly.

Shana glanced at Marty. Neither knew what to make of it.

"Do you think it's ice?" asked Shana.

The material was so unusual - An iridescence pulsated with the motion of gold particles. What's more, the room carried a deep resonation but there was no source.

A luminous altar stood at the furthest end of the cavern covered with inscription and symbols. Those engravings resembled hieroglyphs but with a Celtic feel. Each radiated with the same golden luminescence that appeared on the walls. Johnny was silent and glanced at Marty. What could he say?

"When I was a wee nipper the other kids used to say witches and loons hid in the caves. They cursed yer and made a strange noise that would send you into a trance and imprison yer forever! They used to say if you ventured in, 'dead pirates would come alive and kill yer'. But that was just a story told at night to scare the shit out of small kids by older kids. What if it was true?" whispered Johnny behind his hand.

The vicar directed the villagers to place the body at the centre on the luminous platform. As soon as she made contact, the gold particles swarmed towards her and disappeared. It was as if the particles had been absorbed.

Shana tilted her head, the humming increased.

Marty was transfixed, what was it about that material and the noise? Johnny rubbed his leg; the situation was too weird. He leant against the wall to rub his calf again. As he did so, the golden particles rushed into his hand. This time when Johnny rubbed his leg, the muscle relaxed and the pain subsided. Marty nodded towards the wall; Johnny guessed what he was thinking.

The vicar was aware of the newcomers' reactions and watched them inquisitively. There was no reaction from Shana or Marty, the pair appeared to accept such exceptional circumstances so easily. The pair noticed the vicar's attention and gazed back at him. There was an unspoken understanding amongst them and the 'outsiders' accepted the privilege of entering an ancient burial chamber.

"Tonight there will be a burial, everyone must attend. Tell yer families. We will return her to her own. We will bless her and hope she rests in peace. We must ask her forgiveness," the vicar said signalling for the group to return along the corridor. Each person bowed, paid their respect and returned along the corridor.

"What is this place exactly father?" asked Shana purposely waiting for the right opportunity.

"It's our ancient crypt, child," said the vicar, motioning for the group to return down corridor.

"It's friggin' cold," blurted Johnny.

"What's it for?" Shana glared at Johnny. Why couldn't he say something sensible?

"It's been here since before the church was erected. This location has always been a sacred place," said the vicar. "Often churches are built over other sacred places as religion evolves." With an incredulous look, Marty attempted to understand what the vicar was really saying.

The vicar placed his hand on Marty's shoulder, "I hope to see you all here tonight at midnight. You may just learn something of the old ways and witness that which is sacred."

Johnny stared sadly at the vacant body of the woman. "So- Ach nothing-".

"What- now Johnny?"

"You'll think I'm sick…"

"You're going to ask me about reproduction aren't you?" the vicar replied.

"How did yer know?' asked Johnny astounded that vicars could read minds.

"Just a guess… The breeding season is due," said the vicar.

"They emerge from the sea and walk among us."

"Are they naked?" asked Johnny with a smile and a dazed look.

"Johnny!"

"Well why can't they bang their own kind?"

Marty cringed and Shana covered her eyes.

"They can, but their genetics would mutate," said the vicar with a nervous chuckle.

"But they are mutated. They're fish with human bodies. If that's not a mutant I don't know what is!"

"Johnny! Mate, I think you should stop." Marty shuffled awkwardly. How did Johnny always manage to say the worst thing at the most inconvenient moment?

"Well, if there are fish with people heads are there also fish heads with people legs floating around somewhere - it must be some rule of nature?"

The vicar studied Johnny, how could he be so ignorant?

"But-" said Johnny revealing complete puzzlement.

"Look, Johnny, no offence mate, but I think we need to change the subject," said Marty.

"But there are so many questions to ask…"

"Learning takes time and patience," said the vicar with a friendly pat that suggested the conversation was over.

"Sorry… Just trying to understand," he said guiltily.

"Johnny you know the village has always been connected. Remember the stories yer nana told yer? Remember the line - they're us and we them," said the vicar.

"I was just a kid and I thought me nana was nuts. What's a kid to think when his parents left him to live with his nutty nana until he reached sixteen?"

"I'm hungry," Marty blurted.

"How can yer be?" asked Johnny guessing Marty might be peckish but not hungry.

"Marty's trying to save yer bum before you say anything you might regret- or should I say any more you might regret now."

Johnny bowed his head; he had denied his family history all his life. Something shifted in Johnny – his history made him who he was. Before the group left the darkness, Johnny paused and looked back, a gust of wind rushed towards the light. Johnny had denied and ignored who he truly was. The myths and legends were all part of his genetic. Maybe if he paid attention he might find answers.

CHAPTER 39
A necessary lesson.

As soon as the group returned to Crooked Cottage, Shana dashed up the stairs to her room. "I'll be there in a sec…" Her pink room was still full of unopened boxes. A purple, satin duvet with matching pillows covered her bed. On the decorative, silver, wall hooks hung her fleece, wetsuits and mechanical overalls. Shoes were scattered about the floor with a few pairs of knickers flung randomly amongst them.

In the front room, Marty glanced out of the window. "Johnny sit down. Shana has some answers for you," he said somewhat smugly.

Johnny followed Marty's direction and suspiciously studied his friend. "What are you two up to?"

With the tap of the nose, Marty grinned mysteriously. "You'll see."

Once Shana had located 'the book,' she returned to the armchair beside the hearth. "Johnny I think it's about time you learned a bit about your heritage. Then you'll get to see how a sea-baby is made."

Johnny sat back in the chair and crossed his legs. Maybe it was time he took an interest in all that he had denied.

Shana opened the book on a random page - a myth about a mermaid who carried a mirror accompanied by comprehensive psychoanalysis.

"Look here Johnny," said Shana. "It says here men who fear women of the sea also fear commitment in relationships."

"Of course it does," said Johnny planning his escape.

"Actually… According to this Johnny - the sea is meant to represent emotion and attachment," said Shana with a purposeful pause.

"The sea's the sea. It's wet and that's what it is," replied Johnny, shifting in his seat.

"The men who drown can't deal with emotional relationships. They drown in the female sexuality," said Shana studying Johnny's reaction.

"What kinda tosh is that? I thought we were going to look at their bits!"

Shana rolled her eyes. "We will in a moment. I'm just trying to get you to understand something."

"I think you need to say it straight, so Johnny can understand what you mean Shana," said Marty.

"Okay! Johnny I think you have fear of commitment. You resist and deny it," she said honestly.

"What me? I've been out with loads a women," he said plumping a cushion and placing it on his lap.

"No… Johnny you don't usually have a 'relationship' for more than a day or a night," said Shana honestly.

"Why yer having a go at me for? What about Marty?"

"Classic displacement and denial Johnny," said Shana. "Just admit it. You're scared, aren't you?"

The contorted face revealed the truth of how Johnny felt. He brewed for a moment, struggled and unconsciously shook his head. "Oh God! I leave them before they leave me Shana. All right?"

Shana glanced triumphantly at Johnny.

"Can I see the parts now?"

Silence.

"Yer think I'm a wet fart, don't yer?" said Johnny.

"We all have to embrace our weaknesses Johnny. Now I think you are more of a man for doing so!" Shana replied. "Marty... does your 'new' friend carry a mirror?"

"I haven't seen one," said Marty. "Anyway how would they make one?"

"It seems to be something they are 'supposed' to have."

"Why?" asked Marty.

"It says here the mirror reveals a clear picture of the viewer's soul. I wonder what a soul looks like and how it would appear in their mirror," wondered Shana peering closely at the drawn image accompanying the text.

Marty sat back in the chair and considered the concept.

"If you look into the mirror you are supposed to see your true self - what you really are in comparison to what you have become."

Shana stared thoughtfully into space. "Now I don't think I could handle that. Imagine if you were a complete bitch…"

"My soul would look like a warrior wielding a sword..."
Johnny arranged his arms behind his head and gazed into space.
"More like a puppy wearing a muzzle," replied Shana curtly.
"Well yours Shana would look like erm... A small neep," said
Johnny.
"God, how gutted would yer be? To discover what you went
through your life for-all the ordeals and that was it... Your soul... A
tiny turnip?"
"I'd like to be a knight, brave courageous and free." Marty slid
from the sofa to sit cross-legged on the floor.
"I wouldn't mind being the lady of the lake - or a nymph- or the
queen of the fairies, or maybe Johnny could be the queen of the
fairies!" Shana watched Johnny's instant reaction.
"Come on Shana – let's have a look..." said Johnny gesturing
at the book.
"Okay, God-impatient!" Shana turned to the back of the book.
HOW TO SPOT A SEA PERSON was written in large letters. "A
tail... Well there we are." Johnny moved over to where Shana was
sitting and peered over her shoulder. Shana turned the pages to reveal
a series of images of sea babies in the womb, through puberty to adult.
Shana noticed the men didn't grow hair on their face or their bodies.
"What does it say about their bits?" asked Johnny.
"It doesn't say anything about their thingys... Oh, other than
tucked away," said Shana.
"You put me through all that admitting stuff and... you tell me
their bits are tucked away?' With an obvious shake of the head,
Johnny glanced incredulously at Marty.
"Sorry Johnny. I thought there maybe something more. Seems
you shot a blank this time," she said.
"I want me bed. I need a nap!"
"But it's so nice outside," said Shana.
"I'm going for a walk then. Wanna come Marty?" said Shana
searching for company.
"No, I have other plans," said Marty in a mysterious tone.
Shana glanced at Johnny. They both had their suspicions.

CHAPTER 40

Bits with no pieces!

Shana grabbed an apple on her way through the kitchen and out onto Straight Lane.

Johnny followed Marty down to the kitchen. He hung back until Shana was gone, "Marty do yer really think I have a problem with you know..."

"You can't even say the word Johnny," said Marty slipping on his shoes.

"Look at it like this Johnny - in five years you won't be able to attract the women you do now. Plus, you'll be tired of using them and you'll more than likely damage some decent ones. Your reputation will stick and then what happens? You end up on your own. Is that what you want?"

"I never thought of it like that," he replied with a shake of his head.

"Sometimes you have to realise that the only person stopping you is you. The only person sabotaging you is you. Then you realise you have to face you to become you." After straightening out the sleeves of his jacket, Marty put it on.

"Are you telling me or telling you?"

Marty was silent as he thought about what he just said.

"You do spout some bizarrely analytical shit Marty," said Johnny. "Too much over-thinking!"

"No, mate... When someone dies who is close to you it makes you re-evaluate and realise you need to be authentic and that means facing yourself!" He checked his pockets and placed his keys in the right-hand side.

"I guess that's why you've been spending so much time alone," said Johnny. "Well maybe I will take your advice and get me the ideal woman - a model."

Marty shook his head with dismay, "get the magazine image out of your head Johnny. You need to meet a real woman – not a fake. You need someone strong willed who will challenge you. You don't need a female puppet to display on your arm like meat. Imagine being with someone who you connect with on a 'deeper' level. Imagine being with someone who really gets you and has fire and passion."

"Do they actually exist?"

"If you exist then there is your female equivalent out there." Marty attempted to conceal his horror at the potential of a female Johnny. Would she wear a red swimming costume with long socks?

"Thanks Marty... And yer know I do ney like to talk about all this emotional crap; but you know I'm glad yer me mate. I'll always look out for yer," said Johnny with a solid back pat that would wind most people. With a loud yawn, Johnny headed towards the sink. "I'm going to get some water and sleep off me hangover."

"I hope you feel better," said Marty hovering by the front door.

"Thanks..."

Marty waited for Johnny to go upstairs, grabbed a secretly stashed bar of chocolate and trotted down to the harbour to hire some diving gear.

CHAPTER 41
Diving alarm bells

With tingle of anticipation, Marty strolled along the harbour gazing at the undulating sea. The sun shone brightly warming his face, the atmosphere was subdued and the harbour was devoid of locals – it was perfect! Marty ambled to the tiny dive shop beside the harbour wall. Outside, the fishing nets and diving gear were only a hint of the treasure trove beyond: shipwreck artefacts, a whale bone and even an original figurehead (circa 1760, read the plaque) – and of course, a selection of tacky brass souvenirs. The three-way interior division displayed fishing, diving and news n' snacks.

When Marty entered the dive shop a brass bell rang on the side of the door. The short, stocky man eyed him, then gave a kind, welcoming smile. He was among the villagers who had carried the stretcher over to St. John's.

"Hi," said Marty, folding his arms and walking to the counter. The diver folded a map of the local waters and placed it on a shelf behind him with the other maps.

"So…" he said.

"Erm," Marty shuffled, were the locals paying more attention to him now he knew their secret?

"So what will yer be needing?" asked the diver.

"I just need a full diving kit and a boat," said Marty.

"For how many?"

"For one."

"You're nort thinking about going diving alone in these waters are yer? They're dangerous you know."

"No I'm going with a friend of mine. She has her own gear." Marty sucked his lip through his teeth and picked up a paperweight with a shipwreck at the centre.

"Is she experienced? Will she know her way round properly?" asked the diver with genuine concern.

"She's a dive master." Marty flicked through a book of underwater photography and avoided eye contact.

"Can I see yer diving card? I don't want to be responsible for a death. We don't need no more round here," he said with a wink.

"I have two qualifications," said Marty flashing the cards in his wallet.

"Okay. So when was the last time you dived anyway?" asked the diver.

"Six weeks ago, in the Red Sea," said Marty.

The dive shop owner drew out the silence. "Be careful out there because there's some strange stuff going on. People get 'called' and there are cases of revenge."

"I'll be extra careful," he said adjusting his wallet and placing his card on the counter.

"Good. You have this equipment for a couple of days then. When you're finished leave the boat at its mooring, put the equipment inside and lock it. If there is any damage - I know where you live and have your card details. So do you need any assistance going over the workings?"

"No I'm fine," said Marty. "Oh actually…Do you have underwater cameras for hire?"

"What you planning on photographing?" asked the diver with a raised eyebrow.

"Whatever's there at the time I suppose." He held the photography book open on an underwater picture of a wreck encrusted in barnacles.

"I'll give you a camera but be careful what you capture…" said the diver in a certain tone that Marty clearly understood. "Now I will meet you outside with your equipment cart." The diver handed over the boat's key. "Please just sign here," he said pointing at the book.

With his cart of equipment, Marty made his way along the harbour and paused. At the far end of the beach, Danny sat alone on a rock. Staring into space, he threw stones at the water. Marty watched for a moment, he wasn't doing anything too strange so it was probably better to give him space.

Moored halfway along the quay, between two large yachts, was a little yellow boat. It was cute and did the job. After arranging his equipment in perfect order and spacing, Marty turned the key in the ignition. As he pulled away from the dock, he glanced over at Danny. Something about that 'picture' stuck in his mind.

Danny sat uncomfortably gazing out to sea. His mind played

repetitious images of the girl. Could he have changed what had happened? Surely he was innocent. Whose fault was it that she had connected with him? He had done nothing to lead her on either… So why did he feel so guilty? Danny sighed and shook his head. When the procession had passed he'd been aware of 'her' presence throughout, when she was near the resonation had intensified. Why was that? That familiar sense of dread filled his stomach. What should he do? It was only a matter of time before Shana guessed something.

"The guilty always rise to the surface in this village or drown," one of the villagers had said to another when he walked past earlier. Was that a coincidence or the response of a guilty mind? With clenched fists, Danny's mind looped the same repetitive thoughts. He had spent his whole life living amongst myths, illusions and secrets. It had to end! The conversation in his mind became a storm. The more he thought, the more his jaw tightened. It was not fair! "I've had enough of these stupid secrets... A secret shared is not a bloody stupid secret anymore!"

With a flash of motion, Danny launched himself off the rock and jogged along the harbour. He dashed up Straight Lane to Crooked Cottage. "Is anyone in?"
Silence.
He sneaked up the stairs to the digital darkroom and grabbed Marty's digital camera. He turned and froze. What had shifted? Why wasn't he scared anymore? What stood before him was an entity trapped between two planes.

"Yer will be cursed for what yer do... It's the blood… Child..." said the apparition.
"Leave me be!" he said.
"I am protecting yer. She will be calling yer… Then there will be death!"
Danny shook his head, "no! Times are changing and this is now a conflict of wills!" He darted down the stairs, slammed the door and rushed onto the lane. He launched into a light jog in the direction of St. John's church. It had to end once and for all!

CHAPTER 42

The undiscovered.

Marty steered the boat in small circles hoping that he would spot Iris. Unfortunately, a wall of mist blocked his view. Eventually he gave up, switched off the engine and reclined on some blue-striped cushions. The soft lapping of the ocean against the side of the boat filled the air with a relaxing rhythm. Every so often, a gull's squawk would jolt him from his daydreams.

Five minutes passed and the mist still had not settled. A patch cleared to reveal a circle of blue sky filled with sunshine. Silence tinged with a resonation in motion revealed someone was nearing.

"Iris?" Marty sat up.

A shape darted beneath the boat and surfaced on the other side.

"Ready?" she asked with a sideways blink and a blush.

"I just need to change…"

She rested her arms on the edge of the boat and watched Marty struggle with his wetsuit. She then placed her head to the side as watched him hoik on his diving tanks.

"Look heavy."

Marty paused and nodded, "all this to be able to breath under water. And you have it naturally."

Iris grinned excitedly.

Splosh! Marty slid backwards into the sea, cleared his mask and placed the breathing apparatus in his mouth. He then prepared his camera and glanced at Iris who had already submerged. He followed her beneath the surfaced to find her illuminated by rays of light. Her golden hair drifted like a halo.

As Marty adjusted his buoyancy, Iris swam elegantly about him. When she thought he was ready, she took his hand and jerked him towards the ocean bed. Marty resisted and freed his hand. Iris turned and paused with a confused expression.

"Too fast," he gestured.

Iris recognised his thoughts, smiled and resonated imagery into Marty's mind.

Marty covered his ears, what was she doing?

Iris watched Marty's reaction curiously. Why didn't he communicate back? Why was he resistant?

She took Marty's hand and guided him at a slower pace. She listened to his thoughts - his mind was full of swear words, inadequacy and struggle. How he 'appeared' was in absolute conflict with his interior. Many of those of the land were the same - they fought daily with their minds to suppress how they really felt. It seemed as if Marty lost control, he believed he would lose everything.

"Marty we hear thoughts through water and air," she said.

"Am I making this up in my head?" Marty closed his eyes, how could he hear what she said if she had not said it?

"I thought the humans knew of this. It is written and recorded. The church has our records. We agreed on them before the two tribes chose to separate – it is the book of water secrets."

Marty gazed at her through his mask, "I have never heard of anything like that. Can you hear me?"

"Yes. Humans look outside for everything. Truth inside. Inside not harnessed. Once harness mind power - universe open," she thought. "If people focus mind with heart feeling then civilization change for better. If mind connect and feel too then world become peace."

Marty was not convinced the thoughts were coming from Iris. Would his mind play tricks on him to distract from the situation? She paused and smiled, "I send you thought in images and feel. You translate them for you."

He gave Iris a gentle tug to slow down. She guided him to a shallow area where he checked his air. He had hardly used any. He glanced at Iris who moved with such ease and grace. Her hair wafted about her as she settled in a position for a short time and then darted off again. Who she was was beautiful. Something about her initiated deep longing in his heart, yet his mind was in conflict. The logic of the situation was all wrong yet he desired to kiss her.

A puddle formed at the base of his mask, the ocean had invaded the seal. There was a deeper pool beneath his right eye, which was slowly rising. Marty leant back and cleared them by breathing bubbles through his nose. He resealed the goggles then gazed forward to witness something monumental. On the ocean floor, a stone circle pulsated with absolute luminescence. Huge, carved stones carried ancient symbols. Each stone glowed with a different colour and stood in a circular formation with an upturned oak positioned at the centre.

"This special. This where we from," Iris thought as she gazed deep into his eyes.

"If you penetrate my mind I have no privacy," Marty unintentionally responded. With a squirm, he realised that he had no control over what he thought. He could not hide anything – he was now an open book and she had access to all parts of his mind – even the nasty thoughts. That was frightening!

"Forget about thought. Enjoy beauty," she said gazing at him. Marty reached out for Iris who obligingly took his hand and guided him closer. The circular formation of perfectly aligned and spaced stones felt magnetic. What's more, different tonal hums came from each of the stones – it was like a harmony. The pair swam above the circle to get a closer look at the upturned oak. It must have been there thousands of years. How could it survive so long in salt water? Actually how did it even get there?

With a gentle smile, she let go of his hand and left Marty to explore on his own. He was reluctant at first but soon gained confidence. After the incident at Drichen, he ventured into the stone circle with trepidation. How did he know the stones didn't carry strange creatures? How did he know anything? Everything he had known had collapsed in the previous days. He was now in unknown territory, beyond the illusion that he had spent his life living.

The ornate carvings became his distraction. They carried incredible detail, similar but not the same as monuments built by ancient civilisations. A few moments after entering the circle, Marty glanced at the surface and noticed the area was brighter within the stones than on the surface. There was a luminescence coming from the stones similar to the glow in the crypt. Marty went to touch the stone.

"No!!!! Do ney touch stone... Danger!"

Marty jerked away and rotated towards the upturned oak. As he drew closer, small bubbles of lustrous pollen-like substance swirled about him as if being freed by the tree. He quickly checked his air gauge - thirty minutes to go. Iris sensed she had 'time' and guided him into the oak's root complex. Contorted limbs, covered in silver-encased buds made up the system. The nodules captured the light and sparkled. As he watched, a shoal of silver fish swam towards the stones. When they noticed Iris, they erratically scattered. Marty had seen a natural rhythm but Iris has seen food. He would love to watch her hunt. In fact, he was pretty much enamoured by everything about her. Was it possible that their connection was right for him? A tingle filled his heart. He had never felt that before. His mind blocked the feeling – it was unrealistic!

Iris tugged at Marty's arm, pulling him toward the surface. Marty resisted, he hadn't had time to photograph so pulled back, adjusted his camera and took a shot. Iris watched inquisitively. An object pointing at the stones was very important to him. Iris gave him some time to do what he needed with the strange object in front of his face. While Marty photographed Iris moved to each individual stone and rubbed them. Motifs similar to the signs of the zodiac glowed then disappeared. What was she showing him? With a quick glance at the gauge he still had fifteen minutes; three of which he needed to spend three metres below the surface to allow his nitrogen levels to balance.

Iris mischievously burst one of the silver root buds. Golden particles glimmered, burst into light and then vanished. "Is fuel," she said in thought.

The mist above had lifted enabling beams of light to illuminate the whole circle. As he clicked away, he forgot himself. The thirteen stones in the circle including an altar-stone made a phenomenal picture. The altar was individual; it had an isosceles triangle cutting straight through it. Below the triangle there was an inscription accompanied by a cross section of a shell in perfect formation. Could it be the golden ratio? Beneath the shell was the symbol that Danny and Johnny wore on their necklaces. The symbol resembled a curved European seven with a dot just to the right side. His mind began to churn – how did it all link up. There was a silver path from the altar to the oak tree. It seemed that somehow upturned oak branches had formed a woven plinth. There was something unearthly about it. Why did the seaweed bed and cockles stop at a specific distance away? Was something protecting the circle? The light from above intensified and created a sharp beam that lit the Gemini stone. Were the stones a time dial?

Iris guided Marty closer to the surface. As he drifted, he

glanced back. The beam of light would soon reach the zodiac sign of Cancer. The carving on that stone resembled a beetle and not a crab. Wasn't the sign of the crab originally a scarab beetle showing transformation, death and regeneration? Iris let go of Marty once again, she swam in the direction of the stones and pointed out the sign of the crab and Virgo - the woman with legs. She gestured to where on the stones the time of change took place. Was the circle a clock for the people of the sea?

"Time for decision" she sent by thought and pointed at the woman with legs. Virgo was glancing back in the direction of the crab while she clung to her legs.

With a mind full of fuzz, Marty's breath became short. Iris waved and everything spun. His consciousness dwindled and his mind retracted into the path his life had previously followed. The canister was empty and he fell into unconsciousness. His small, limp body remained suspended in the vast ocean. Everything was blank...

CHAPTER 43
Drips, sobs and moans.

Danny arrived at the steep, worn steps leading up to St. John's church. He focused his intention and now planned to take action. He hung his head, scrunched his shoulders and scurried along the ground. "Shit!" he muttered when his trouser leg snagged on some thorns. The more he struggled the more tangled he became. Danny ripped his trousers and shredded his calf. The drone increased, "I won't give in!"

Impressions on the grass revealed where the villagers had carried the weight of the stretcher. He followed the track to an area where the men had waited for guidance. He knelt down, felt amongst the grass and discovered a metal hoop. With a definite tug, Danny heaved open the heavy metal to reveal a set of stairs. Of course, he didn't have any matches or a lighter. With apprehension, he peered into darkness, the resonation intensified. She knew he was searching for her.

After testing the metal door from beneath, he realised he could re-open it from inside. Just to be sure, he wedged a flint between the door and the rim. A hint of light illuminated the beginnings of the steps. Danny crept into the darkness. He clasped Marty's camera tight to his chest as he explored the stairs with his feet. When he reached even ground he paused and listened. Drip! Drip! It matched the speed of his heartbeat. The air smelt stagnant, damp and putrid. A shiver shook his spine. He was in the darkness with 'her' - the resonation.

Danny adjusted the camera and cradled it with his inner elbow. Flash! He must have hit a button but the explosion of light travelled the length of the corridor and set Danny on his path. The high-pitched sound of the re-charge resembled the resonation. Together it was enough to drive a person crazy – or crazier! Danny squared himself by touching both sides of the wall with the tip of his fingers. He pointed the camera down the tunnel and pressed the button. Click! Another blast of light raced down the tunnel. Coloured blobs obscured his vision but at least he could navigate.

Danny walked approximately a hundred metres, but felt disorientated and what was the stench? Danny lifted the camera and flashed it. "Ah!" An embalmed body screamed at him. Instinctively he stepped back, into a suspended corpse. The damp remains brushed the bare skin on his neck. Danny attempted to slow his breath and breath through his mouth but the rancid smell made him gag. He shuffled forwards and turned ninety degrees. How had he rotated? Was it the weight of the camera in his right hand?

Flash! The path ahead was straight and nothing appeared to be suspended. He would illuminate every thirty paces just in case.

A melancholy sobbing combined with the resonation made an echo. Sadness filled the tunnel and Danny felt it in the depths of his stomach. He paused and blasted the flash again. This time he noticed a speck of light in front of him. He had something to aim at! Near to the light an area of tunnel branched off, wind rushed this way and that not knowing its own course. Danny received a gust of cool air to the face, as it whistled past. The crying transformed into a sinister moan as he moved closer.

The bright light was intense at the opening of the tunnel,. Once his eyes adjusted, he stared at the lifeless creature on the altar. Danny leant against the wall, shook his head and sucked his lip. He had been the cause of that effect. He held his heart and sighed, "I'm so sorry. I did ney realise…" he muttered with a trembling lip.

"But I have to do what I have to do or we will all carry this burden. This village has to change or… Or this will happen again and again."

CHAPTER 44
Life and nothingness.

Suspended between life and nothingness Marty accepted the inevitable.

Silence.

A hand cut through the darkness and jolted him.

"Marty breath! It's ney yer time! " came an urgent voice.

In the darkness, a tingle of static energy radiated over his lips, through his mouth and into his lungs. The vital force ignited his neurons and revealed a vision of his whole existence. The second elongated and his life flashed through mind in reverse: his father's death, his college time, school and his years as an isolated child. A moment later, the illusion dissolved. The reality was that Iris was supplying him with air while suspended deep within the ocean. What's more, the passionate kiss of life revealed her desires and intentions. She only wanted him forever.

Iris gazed into Marty's flooded goggles. She smiled kindly and provided more oxygen. However, this time she took the opportunity during seconds between breaths to kiss him seductively. They were connected, he was alive and he could sense who she truly was. She was beautiful, authentic and pure. He had never 'felt' a person's presence before but now he did.

The surface was ten metres away when Iris slowed their ascent. He had experienced death and now he felt life. The pause provided a chance for Marty to rest and for his blood to settle. As she took another breath, she filled his lungs and kissed him with increasing passion. Marty turned rigid, he was powerless yet he needed her to survive. Iris sensed his resistance, returned to simply supplying him with air and continued the ascent.

The passion had been broken and Marty's mind fired with all his fear: why was he always in such conflict? Why did he constantly resist? Why did he always doubt? Why couldn't he trust that he had been connected to a beautiful soul – maybe there was no one better? How could he know? That was him all over – was there something better in the future? Why couldn't he enjoy the now?

Iris gave Marty a lung-full of air and pulled away. "I feel your doubt and it causes me pain. I know we're different but I only choose one and I chose you. Your heart call me. Ask yourself why yer canny have one connection in your life? Why do you have to have many when the one could be perfect? Stop thinking – heart is numb. When heart numb you live as dead... Now feel, do ney think! You only know what had when lost."

Marty's heart desired her, but his mind fought with all its might. He had been fed ideals his whole life - this did not fall into any boxes and was beyond his comprehension. How did he quieten his mind to allow his heart to speak? How did he learn to be like her and trust his instincts? In fact, how did he even learn to trust life after what he had been through?

CHAPTER 45
Guilt and the guilty.

After emerging from complete darkness, the brightness of the crypt was overwhelming. Where Danny stood was a pure, white altar with a corpse laid upon it. The sense of guilt shook him. The more he struggled, the louder and more intense the crying, singing, moaning-resonation became. Finally, he shuffled towards her and paused. What was he doing? He should leave. Yet he felt compelled to see her.

He took a deep breath and stepped forwards. The resonation intensified filling the crypt and reverberating. Her face was porcelain and her eyes empty but clear. The purity of her vacant eyes penetrated his heart. "I'm sorry," he said, his voice cracking. "I am so… sorry. I… I didn't know." He fought back a sob.

A whimpering resonation filled the crypt. She was crying too. Was her essence still there? Could he talk to her? Would she understand? Danny shook his head and his body caved in, he shouldn't leave her. Maybe he deserved to die too. Tears viciously stung his eyes; he crouched on the floor and rested his head against the altar. "Please forgive me."

A gust of wind rushed past him and circled the crypt. The motion snapped him out of the moment. He was there for a reason and he intended to complete his plan.

Another breath filled Marty's lungs; Iris pulled away and studied him. His emotional conflict revealed itself in the rigidity of his body. Of course, Marty did not realise that. He gazed at the beautiful creature before him. What was he doing? Iris was different, she was unaffected by civilisation - its fears, its suppressed emotions and its doubts. He had the opportunity to lead a completely different life with someone special. Yet he had to make the decision based on no comparative experience. The only life tools he had at his disposal were instinct and intuition. How could he trust himself? How could he make such a decision after such a short time? He didn't even know her properly.

"You must feel and not think," came the answer.

Marty gazed back at Iris who carried a twinkle in her eye. "Thinking hinder. You think yourself out of everything good and destroy joy

with logic. Ask heart what desire Marty. Your heart always reveal truth of soul. Now heart open for first time in life. Close eyes and ask.When you receive the answer you will 'know'."
The pair paused and Iris provided him with a final breath. He had the opportunity to kick to the surface alone or with her. "Marty I have a choice to remain in sea or transform. I make sacrifice when transform I walk on land. The stones change me. I will only do if feel connection in your heart and I know you be there for me after change. I made my decision on how feel and now I know - now this life decision yours."
Marty closed his eyes and listened to his heart. Was Iris really the one for him?
Why was he being forced into decisions so soon?
      "Stop mind. Feel!"
The sense of focusing on his heart was alien to Marty but in that second, his heart revealed the truth. He opened his eyes and gazed at Iris. The intense feeling of love filled his being. It only happened when he stopped fearing. With a kind smile, she gently filled his lungs with air. Something in him had shifted, he intended to stop struggling and allow life to take him where he needed to go. He trusted what his heart had revealed and for the first time in his life, he felt truly connected.

After pacing for a short while, Danny made his decision. He gazed into the girl's empty eyes and sighed. It was an accident; her death was not his fault. "What can I say... I'm so sorry? You were so sweet, so full of mischief and life. It's such a bloody waste! Why did yer have to do such a daft thing?" With a fold of the arms, he paced some more. The timing had been immaculate. He paused again and peered at her. With a shake of the head, he gently stroked her cheek, "forgive me but what I am about to do is necessary. There has to be an end to this secret. There has to be an end to this history."
He lifted and focused the camera. Click.

CHAPTER 46

Thinking about not thinking.

Marty kissed Iris passionately just below the surface of the ocean. In a matter of days she would now transform, she had chosen to make the sacrifice for the unison with a man she had only just met. Where was the logic in that? How did she know it would work out? It made no sense, yet it 'felt' right.

The pair broke the surface into brilliant sunshine. Iris placed her head contentedly on Marty's shoulder. For the first time in a long time, he felt at peace. Something had shifted in Marty's perspective, he could feel and his heart had answered when he had asked. Why had no one ever told him that was possible?

"Yer were close Marty. We almost lost yer?" whispered Iris. Marty nodded, it was too close.

"But made realise what important in life," she said watching his reaction.

"It made me realise what I had taken for granted and it made me realise that I am not who I really am," he replied honestly. "I am made up of everything I have been taught. I have lost my true self and being close to death showed me something. I know I haven't done anything worthwhile. I have always been selfish and now that has to change. I have to learn to commit, to feel and not be scared anymore."

A sideways blink and a soft smile revealed Iris's thoughts.

"Life will change now you are connected and feel with heart."

Marty could already feel change was due. He would start with himself and see how that affected his life.

"And Marty you saw stone circle. Big honour. Sun lights special time and then body transform. We break apart and reform. We die and then live," she said. "Like you... Death come to birth."

"Why would you do that to yourself? Surely you could meet a nice man of the sea. Why would you do that for me? You don't even know me."

"It is biological, nature and instinct. Why salmon swim to mating ground and man salmon die? We must make choice -

otherwise we die out. It always been this way," said Iris "and when ask for good man you arrive. That is how I know."

Marty studied Iris, could it be as simple as that? She asked for a man and he arrived. Her world was different to his and unintentionally she had revealed the village's secret.

"Marty they us and we them. We suffer to remind us we not natural to land. We chose sea yet we desire land," she said.

It made no sense.

"Only us who do ney have mates go through process," she said. "Biology is powerful!"

Something occurred to him, were the villagers and the people of the sea simply the same race? At some point in history, had there been a choice where some had chosen land and the others the sea?

"Did yer hear something?" asked Iris scanning the horizon.

"No nothing…"

"I have to go Marty…"

"One question – what does the woman holding legs mean?" asked Marty.

"Time of choice. We can return to the sea…" she said gazing at him sadly.

What did that facial expression mean? Why would they go back to the sea? Marty had so many questions.

"Sun set soon. Must go."

With a loud clunk, Marty removed the air canister and dropped them on the deck. Iris gazed at him with desire as he rolled down his wetsuit. He blushed when he felt her gazing at his broad shoulders and strong physique. She wasn't subtle in her gaze either.

When he was dressed, he sat on the edge of the boat and took her hand. "Thank you for saving my life."

Iris squeezed his hand and smiled, "I had to."

"No you didn't have to… You know Iris there were times underwater where you simply disappeared."

"When swim fastest yer canny see me but tires me," she replied glancing at the setting sun.

His curiosity ignited, her limitations were so different. If he could perceive the world through their eyes then maybe he could share.

"One more thing - can you hear my thoughts?"

She nodded, "our race talk in thought and your race become closed. We think to each other underwater. Thoughts work in waves. Every thought heard. You just learn how to hear. People on land think thought inside brain. Not true. No barrier - all can be heard. We need to survive. If shark attack we let each other know. We need tell formation to attack, to survive. The shark uses sonar so we use other way."

Marty studied Iris, what she said made sense.

"Your mind controls you. That why you no feel. Too many thoughts too much mess. Block heart with mind. No room for feeling. Makes people sick. Now time to go," said Iris gesturing.

"Any other advice?" he asked.

Iris looked at him intensely. "Mind is a tool. You rule it. Make space for no thought then feeling will come. Things will change when you know that."

After a gentle kiss Iris submerged and disappeared.

Marty tugged on the string of the motor to start the engine. He was already thinking about not thinking. How did that work?

CHAPTER 47
Who is whose responsibility?

The sense of guilt made Danny feel queasy. Yet he still circled and photographed the vacant body. Click-flash! Click-flash! With every click, a blast of light filled the room and a saddened echo responded. She sensed his intentions and did not agree.

After he had taken a series of pictures of the whole crypt, he photographed detailed images of the merged leg deformity. Once he had more than enough pictures, he paused and glanced at the screen. He still had space for hundreds more images but why did he need them? Although, he still needed flashes to navigate the dark tunnel back. How could he tell how many were left?

With a loud sigh, he leant over the body. "Yer understand why I have to do this, don't you?" A shrill resonation resembled a scream. Danny covered his ears and reversed into the darkness. "You do ney need to be like this. Yer can get out of me head. We only met once... Just once yer hear? Yer should ney have done this over someone you do ney know. I am not nice neither... And yer did ney give me any choice, now did yer? "

As soon as he stepped into the tunnel the endless childhood stories of people wondering through dark tunnels for eternity filled his mind. He glanced back into the crypt; a phantom hovered over the body. He stood silently watching her. She felt him watching, turned and reached for him. She did not enter the darkness but instead stood gazing longingly at the threshold.

"What do you expect me to do? You are not and never were my responsibility!" With that, he jogged into the tunnel and triggered the first flash. It was fainter than he expected, at least he had an impression of where he was going. After about two hundred meters, Danny paused. He felt unbalanced, lifted the camera to fire the flash and nothing. The pungent smell of rancid corpses surrounded him. He was amongst them but he could not see them. The intense sound of dripping aggravated him too. His adrenaline pumped as his heckles rose. For a moment, the only sound was panting and dripping. From the ceiling, a small, cold droplet of water formed and descended.

Splat! It hit the back of Danny's neck. He burst forward, arms flaying, trying to escape. He ran into the wall, rebounded and collided with a damp suspended figure. In the darkness, he stepped back and hesitantly reached out and felt about. The bodies were suspended either side of him. A creaking noise and a thud revealed some falling to the floor. There was now a body in his path. What more could go wrong?

CHAPTER 48
Concealing.

Marty watched the shoreline drawing closer. With a large exhalation his shoulders dropped. All the while, his mind kept tricking him into thinking. How did he break the habit? He took a deep breath, how did he actually feel? How did he know how he felt? Why had he learned to hide his feelings? He chewed his lips – he intended to live a very different way now – even if other people didn't like it!

After navigating his way through the bodies, Danny cracked his neck. Something didn't feel right. He brushed his shoulder, his hand found something solid and damp. In the semi-darkness, his mind constructed what it was: a severed finger. "Errrrgh!!!" he said throwing on the floor and swiping his shoulder. He glanced at the beam coming from the trap door above him. He wanted out!

In the setting sun Danny stood in the remains of the church gazing down at the village. That was an idyllic little fishing village filled with secrets! It was all going to change. He resealed the trap door and arranged the grass. He then lolloped into a wolf-like jog. After ten minutes, he scrambled amongst rotting seaweed and across the beach towards the harbour. Pieces of driftwood filled his path and were scattered like hurdles. Everything was an obstacle!

He fumbled awkwardly with his key outside the cottage. The others would be back soon. He had to be quick. Once inside the cottage, he kicked off his shoes and silently checked the rooms to see if anyone was around. No one!

He slid stealthily into the digital darkroom, rigged up the camera to Marty's computer and hit download. The egg-timer flashed up – three minutes. He glanced at the door and jogged the stairs to his room. He needed his memory stick.

With his USB in hand, he paused on the landing and glanced out of the window. Where were the others? Was there enough time to complete his plan?

The mooring was a welcome sight as Marty sailed into the comfort of the harbour. As he tied the boat to the berth, there was a rumble. "Fish and chips," he muttered with a pat to his stomach. The thought of salt and vinegar was enough to initiate salivation.

Calling on his last reserves of energy, he hoicked the diving canisters to the lower cabin, locked the door and glanced at the horizon. The clouds were purple with red trim. His life had shifted, his perspective had altered and now he was connected. He would never have noticed the colours in the sky six months previously. He had been blinkered and essentially staring at his feet.

Once he had double-checked the boat was secure, he climbed the walkway to the harbour and strolled with his hands in his pockets. Crimson light danced on the surface of the cool ocean and for the first time in Marty's life, he 'felt' it rather than simply observed. He was present in that moment. For a short period, he did not actually think.

"It's quiet in here." The inner voice cleverly broke his mental peace. It would do everything to keep him thinking. He intended to resist!

The photos were taking forever to download! The more Danny stared, the slower the process appeared to go. Danny shifted nervously and shallowly breathed. When would the others return? He said a silent prayer in his mind as he stared at the screen willing the download to go faster. Nothing changed.

On the edge of Straight Lane Marty crouched down to tie his shoe. With an empty mind he noticed the smell of freshly baked bread and wafts of barbeque mingling with the warm evening air. It felt magnificent. With a smile on his face he continued up straight lane admiring the tiny, stone cottages. It was amazing how when a person lived in their mind they missed the subtlety of life and the simple things that had always been there. Outside Crooked Cottage Marty's stomach growled once more. The sooner he ate his dinner the happier he would be!

Danny couldn't help but jiggle as the last four images downloaded and the computer's egg-timer was flipping. "Come on!"
He placed his memory stick in the USB port ready for transference. He paused and glanced at Marty's printer. He needed hard copies too.

While the last images were saving, he set up the printer with photographic print paper. The images arranged themselves on the screen. He urgently selected four images and hit print.

Marty turned his key in the lock, walked into the kitchen and switched on the kettle. With a loud jerk it began to heat. In the meantime, he leant against the kitchen counter. Something felt wrong. Since he had lived in crooked cottage there had never been a moment of silence. He cocked his head to the side, somewhere in the cottage there was a rhythmic rumble.

The ink cartridge skimmed back and forth with that rhythmic beat of the paper feed. Danny watched the printer gradually feed the images into the holding tray. The vacant features of the girl emerged. With a sad sigh, he rubbed his solar plexus. It didn't have to end like that. He scratched his cheek as he studied her. Her full body was visible including her mutation. The person who received the images would definitely question 'their' existence. She existed and the world should know!

A whistle of the kettle jerked Marty from his daydream. His back tingled - something was definitely wrong. He didn't understand this new language of feeling. Should he go upstairs and what was that rhythm he was hearing? Was it something to do with Iris?

There was a high-pitched whistling sound from downstairs, which could only mean one thing. Someone was down there. With only one print left to complete, he was nearly there!
"Come on," he muttered glancing at the door.

Marty picked up his tea and started walking up the stairs. He stopped and turned to go back down. After having a couple of shortbread, the tingle on the back of his neck got the better of him. Marty had to investigate. Creak! He stepped on the first stair. A moment later, there was silence. He carried on up the stairs, past the darkroom to the attic area. He paused for a moment by the digital darkroom and listened.

Silence.

Up on the landing Marty peeked into Johnny's room. He laid in the classic starfish position but on his back. Snoring away. The snoring made a rumbling sound but was it enough? With a shrug and a sigh, Marty trundled down the stairs to the front room. He carried a cup of tea with crispy shortbread. They would tide him over until salty fish and chips!

The depressed power button had paused the last print three quarters of the way through. Danny nervously stared at the door. He quietly attempted to extract the remaining image manually while listening for Marty's location. Once he had the prints, he urgently dragged the downloaded images to his memory stick and deleted them off Marty's desktop. How could he get out of the darkroom without being seen or having to explain? As he logged off, he grimaced. All that remained of Marty's allocated computer usage was twenty minutes. The count showed that the last session had spanned fifteen minutes. Would he notice? Of course he would – it was Marty!

By the darkroom door Danny dropped to his knees and peered out. Marty was sitting in the front room gazing at the fireplace eating a chocolate digestive. If he stayed low he was out of eyeshot. With stealth he crawled to the stairs and light-footedly climbed to his room.

    With precision, he silently opened his bedroom door and closed it behind him. Cast across Danny's bed were the last vestiges of evening light. He switched on his bedside lamp. When he was sure there was going to be no interruption, he pulled the images from beneath his t-shirt and froze. "The camera!"

Silently he opened his door and checked the landing. He used his upper body strength to keep his weight on the bannister and off the creaky stairs. With the agility of a gymnast, he made his way to the middle floor and crept back into the darkroom. Marty was lying on the sofa watching tennis on the television.

    Inside the darkroom Danny shook his head in dismay. The camera remained hooked up to the computer and nothing was back in its correct place. Order and control was Marty's way. Since moving to the cottage, the group had noticed some of his unusual habits. One of them was making sure that everything was in the right place and at the right angle. The camera would have given him away instantly. Without putting everything in the correct place, Danny was asking for trouble! Even the chair had a specific alignment.

"Fish and chips. Yum!" muttered Marty. With a jangle of his keys he made a decision. Fish and chips from the van in Banff. Who could resist the pickled onion vinegar? Marty stood up, stretched and made a loud yawn.

With a sudden jolt Danny leant against the wall. If he had stepped out a second earlier then the pair would have collided. In silence, he listened to Marty trample the stairs to the kitchen door. Slam! He had a small window of time. No doubt the others would be home soon. He had to complete what his task.

Night was falling and Marty watched the moon rise. Something was niggling him as he plodded down Straight Lane. With a loud BANG! Bertha rattled to life. Seagulls launched and people in nearby gardens glanced at each other as they jolted.

Danny glanced out of the window, his shoulders dropped as he exhaled. Bertha rumbled up the road, the same way as she always did. What a relief!

At the first junction after the harbour, Shana appeared, bounded down the hill with an ice-cream in hand. Beep! Shana was shaken from her dream and practically jammed the ice-cream up her nose.
    "Ah Marty!" she said with a scowl.
Marty smirked and wound the window down.
    "Where yer goin'?" she asked wiping ice-cream from a nostril.
    "To get some fish n' chips, you want to come?"
    "Is Danny home?" she asked studying him.
    "He wasn't just now," he replied.
    "I think I should go back, and Marty fish and chips make yer

210

fat," she said licking the ice-cream.

Marty raised an eyebrow, what could he say?

"You know Marty I t'ink Danny and I need to have a little chat. There's a few things to sort out if you know what I mean." With another lick of the ice-cream, she awaited his response.

"Okay… A depressing conversation or the smell of vinegar and the taste of batter?" he said licking his lips.

"Well there's some choice Marty, but I have stuff in the fridge to use up. But thanks all the same now," she said, nodding at the ice-cream.

With a hoot of the horn, he drove in the direction of Banff. He glanced in his rear-view, Shana skipped towards the harbour in her own special world whilst licking her ice-cream.

Danny arranged the images on the bed and considered his next steps. Did they look real enough? So many people could authentically manipulate most photos, so would they capture the attention he intended? The world had to find out!

Shana turned the key in the front door. With a loud slam and window vibration, she went straight to the fridge. What was actually for tea?

He still couldn't find the answer. If he sent digital files then they could be manipulated. If he sent digital prints how could they be proven to be real? Was he over-thinking? Surely the images would gain attention anyway. With a deep exhalation, he understood that all he could do was take an action and hope the result would be what he planned.

"Danny- you in?" called Shana shovelling a handful of cashew nuts in her mouth.

With a rapid motion, Danny gathered the images and shoved them under his pillow.

Scrambling two stairs at a time Shana arrived at Danny's room and listened.

"You in Danny?" she said knocking on the door.

"Yes, I'm in," he replied.

"Are you decent? Can I come in?"

"I'm never decent but you can come in," he said.

Shana opened the door and gazed at Danny who was lying on his front on the bed. He rolled over, yawned and stretched. "When did you get back?"

"Just got in," she replied.

"What time is it?" he asked.

"Late – coming up to nine," she said. "So have you been asleep," she said taking a seat on the edge of the bed.

"Yes. The last couple of days have been a bit intense. I think I might be coming down with something," he replied noticing a print poking from beneath the pillow.

"I've been reading the book from the ruin Danny it's really interesting. There's all this stuff about mirrors," she said pulling the book from her crotchet bag.

"What about them?" asked Danny curiously.

"Well, it says here that if you look into a sea-person's mirror you'll be able to see what your soul looks like Danny. Danny flicked his hair and shifted awkwardly. "I don't think that's something that I'd like to see. In fact I don't think anyone should see that."

"It's a weird thought though. At least you would have an idea of what your true essence was," said Shana thoughtfully. Unconsciously Danny shook his head and chewed his lip. Who really wanted to see their true essence? What good would it serve? "Would yer really want to witness that?"

For a moment Shana considered it. "If it actually happened I would probably turn away," she said studying Danny. Something was out of sorts. If he had been asleep then why had he woken so easily? Why was the light on when she arrived? "So… Are you feeling…"

"Better? I'm still a bit all over the place but garlic and broccoli will sort that." He waited for her reaction.

"Oh God help us with that?" she said. "So did you know there will be a burial tonight… We need to return the girl to her own. Apparently they start calling if she is not."

Danny studied Shana, "what happens if they start calling?"

"I think people drown," she said.

Danny scratched his nose and sighed, "an accidental death and innocent people die. It is ney right." "How do you know it's accidental?"

"Just a feeling I have," said Danny. "Those creatures fall in love so easily and jealousy kills them. It's not fair if someone accidentally has contact with them without knowing it… Then the next thing the girl is dead because she got jealous. It's not fair on anyone!" he said with a crack in his tone.

Studying his expression, Shana frowned. What was he trying to say without saying it?

"Come here," she said and placed her arm around him. "Death happens. It is a fact of life." Shana jolted, Danny was rigid in her arms. That wasn't like him.

"Is there something you need to tell me Danny? Your body gave you away."

With a flick of his fringe, he sat upright and gazed into her eyes.

"What's going on Danny? You're so transparent," she said studying him. "You knew her, didn't you? That's why you said it is unfair."

Danny picked the skin on his hands but remained silent.

"Oh Danny…" said Shana. "So... how long has it been going on?"

"Shana it didn't go on... You have to believe me. I am completely innocent! Yesterday I was surfing; she knocked me off my board and kissed me that's all. Shana I swear that's all that happened. I didn't ask for it… And now this."

"One kiss can't be enough for a girl to kill herself!" she said questioningly.

Danny shook his head. "No, but I think she saw us last night - on the rock. Remember how they get jealous? She connected to me and… well there we are snogging right in front of her!

The blood withdrew from Shana's face. "What I caused it too?"

Danny nodded, "we are both innocent. She just… Well she just did what she did. We couldn't have helped it."

"But I didn't know…"

"Nor did I!" said Danny.

"I don't believe it! She actually killed herself because of jealousy?" Shana folded her arms and huffed. "That is ridiculous! Bloody hell Danny. What if the villagers find out?"

Danny shrugged, "they will find out one way or another. They always do... This place is cursed!"

Shana stared at Danny, "Danny... The man of the sea connected to me when I was underwater. If this happened to the girl then I think we have to be careful. Two deaths because of you and me..."

"They have us then. We have no choice... we can't be together..."

Shana gazed sadly into Danny's eyes. "Neither of us have had any choice in this. It's not fair!"

Danny nodded, "that's why things have to change! It isn't fair! We should be able to choose."

"I'm going to make me tea," she said standing slowly. "If I'm going to be completely honest I feel gutted. If there had been no interference, you and I could have had a really nice time. I almost resent them for what they have done!"

With sadness in his eyes Danny sighed, "she's been calling me Shana. It is going to get stronger and I don't want to die!"

"There has to be away to break this curse," said Shana wrapping her arms around him.

He nestled his head into the curve of her neck, "Shana this is all part of my history. I have to break the pattern but I don't know how." There were no answers. Shana realised that and studied him. "Now Danny do you want me to stay?"

He shook his head, "I think I need to be alone to try and work out what to do."

"Okay..." She got up and stood by the door. "I am sure your gran will be able to offer advice."

As soon as Danny heard Shana go down the stairs, he pulled the prints out from under the duvet and chewed the dry skin on his lip. What was the best approach? A two-fold tactic would leave no room for error or images being overlooked. Hastily he logged onto the internet and searched 'newspapers uk'. A list of papers with the contact details for the different news/picture desks appeared. The question was how could he remain anonymous? With a loud puff, he sat back on the bed. He had to create an alias. Mid-profile construct he paused. Was the world ready for such a revelation? Did they have a choice? He didn't have a choice so why should they?

Once the profile was complete, he uploaded the images and

urgently shoved the prints into an envelope. He scribbled a note to the editor of the Times and sealed the envelope. As soon as the pictures uploaded, he hit send and squashed a few stamps onto the letter. As soon as he was sure he had everything, he left the cottage through the door on the middle floor, turned onto Straight Lane and jogged up the hill to the postbox. The plop of a letter landing on other letters was the finalisation. There was no turning back. The cause was bound to have an effect; it was just a matter of time.

CHAPTER 49

Involvement.

The aroma of fish and chips trailed Marty as he stepped into the kitchen. Johnny was sitting at the kitchen table swigging from a milk carton. Colour had returned to his cheeks.

"You look better," said Marty placing the grease-stained paper on the table.

"I can finally face food," he replied eyeing the pack.

"Oh no you don't!" said Marty noticing a certain mischievous look.

"Got your dinner then?" said Shana bounding down the stairs into the kitchen. "Mmm, smells lovely," she said licking her lips.

"You said you didn't want any," said Marty opening the pack. At that precise moment, Danny arrived, inhaled the aroma and licked his lips. Marty looked up, the sense of being circled by sharks was apparent.

"Look over there Marty!" said Johnny.

Three chips mysteriously disappeared from the packet.

"Come on you lot. Get your own food!"

"But you got an extra-large portion there," said Shana. "My guess is that you anticipated chip thievery."

Danny opened the fridge and peered in. A shrivelled tomato, some mouldy cheese and a couple of sausages sat on his shelf.

"Put the kettle on, will yer?" asked Johnny.

Danny glanced over his shoulder and raised a defiant eyebrow. "I am not yer skivvy Johnny."

"But yer right by the kettle. It'll take no effort at all…" he said. "There's pot-noodle in it for you if you do."

Danny eyed the mouldy cheese and shrivelled tomato, a pot-noodle was slightly more appealing.

Shana set up her dish and put her pre-made bolognese in the microwave.

"So how's the cramp?" asked Marty crunching the batter on his fish.

"The muscle is still tight but I drank plenty of liquid and ate some salt. It should be good by tomorrow."

Silence.

Marty swallowed his food and sat back in his chair. "So... I kind of need to get something off my chest."

The group turned to look at him.

"I actually almost drowned this afternoon," he said flatly.

"What?" Shana spun on her heel.

Johnny spat a mouthful of milk back into the carton. "Bloody hell Marty!"

"That's twice in a matter of days," said Shana.

"So what did yer do?" asked Johnny.

"I was scuba-diving when me air ran out. And yesterday we had a derelict manor collapse on us." Marty selected a rather vinegar sodden chip and bit it.

"That's where we found the books," said Shana. "The books about how the sea babies are made."

A blank expression revealed Johnny's alcohol imbued amnesia. "The book where you said that if I looked into a sea person's mirror I would look like a small turnip remember?"

Danny smirked at Johnny. "You really know how to flatter a woman Johnny."

"If you flatter them too much they take it for granted!" he replied.

"The book with their bits Johnny!" she said.

"Ah yeh. Their bits... See, I remember."

"You already remembered, didn't you?" she said accusingly.

Johnny gave a mysterious grin and swigged from his milk carton.

Marty chomped on another chip while Danny shook his head. Never get involved.

"Weird old day then," said Marty breaking the tension.

They all nodded in agreement.

"When has it been normal?" asked Johnny with drip of milk on the end of his nose.

"Normal is dull. Who wants normal and be bored to death?" said Shana checking her bolognese.

"What you making Shana?" asked Danny.

"I'm heating me bolognese" said Shana. "Now don't you think

217

you're getting any."

"You'll make a great house wife one day," said Johnny with a wink at Marty.

Splat! Warm bolognese sauce collided with Johnny's forehead. Shana licked the spoon and watched Johnny's slow reaction.

"Come on-" said Johnny.

"Why should I? Oh let's wind Shana up. Well, Johnny there will be repercussions," she said with a smirk.

Johnny wiped the sauce and tasted it. "I think you should at least share!"

"Go on; make your bloody own Johnny. Sitting there holding court and thinks dinner arrives just like that! We are not living in olden times where woman serves man…"

Marty chewed on a crispy chip and frowned. He could feel her rage brewing.

"Come on now Shana, we all know yer have penis envy, that's why yer always around men!" Johnny couldn't help himself - she always took the bait!

"You think I'm jealous of a bit of floppy skin that can get caught in a zip? 'Cause that's all the difference is Johnny!" Shana gritted her teeth and pointed her wooden spoon at him.

Johnny folded his arms. "That has only happened to me three times and I learned not to wear trousers with zips!"

"Oh Johnny. Imagine - evolution for the male with two brains and not enough blood!" Shana stirred her bolognese and plonked the dish down on the table. As she took her seat, she paused. The boys were salivating. "Sod off- will yer? What is it with you lot and food? Now I'm not sharing Danny. Just because the only thing that wakes yer up is food… I suggest yer get off yer arse and make your own!"

"So, tonight then," said Marty changing the subject.

"What about it?" asked Johnny watching Shana twirl her spaghetti.

"Well we are going, aren't we?" said Marty.

"I don't think we have any choice do we?" said Johnny flatly.

"I don't like the secrets here," said Danny.

"Danny…" Shana glanced at him mid-chew.

"I mean this place is based on a secret and I don't like it," said Danny.

"Most places have secrets," she said mid- spaghetti twirl.

"I just wish we weren't involved," said Danny.

"I think because we found her we have to go. Plus I'm curious," said Marty.

Danny studied Marty and sighed. "The more we know the more issues we will have and the more trapped we will become."

The group glanced at each other. How many more issues could they have?

CHAPTER 50
A Return.

Danny, Marty and Johnny Boy stood outside the cottage looking smart and wearing black. The three fidgeted as they anticipated what they were about to be involved in.

"Come on Shana!" said Johnny glancing at his watch.

"You know this road definitely isn't straight?" Marty tipped his head to the side as he studied the road.

"Who do you think named it Straight Lane? asked Danny.

"Some drunk," said Johnny.

"Maybe they meant it was a more direct route. All the other roads round here wind about the place" suggested Marty.

"What on earth is she doing?" asked Johnny.

"Remember she is female. The fairer species," said Marty.

"She might be fairer but she's taking bloody ages!" said Johnny.

"She should hurry up or she'll miss it...If you want, I'll stay behind and wait for her," said Danny.

"Maybe she's intending to miss it," said Marty suspiciously.

"If none of us turn up then we can blame it on Shana," said Johnny optimistically.

"They can't do anything to her because she's Irish," said Danny.

Marty glanced at Danny and frowned. What difference did her nationality make?

"You're scared of the people here aren't you Danny?" asked Marty.

"Marty, strange things go on here and there are endless whispered stories. I don't want to get involved. That's all I'm going to say." He stood with his hands in his pockets and shuffled.

With a slam of the door, Shana appeared wearing black jeans and a black polo-neck top. Her hair was down and she looked remarkably feminine. Johnny and Danny glanced at each other as

Shana placed her keys in her handbag.

"You look pretty... ready for a funeral. You look more-," said Johnny trailing off.

"Girl like-" said Danny.

"Thank you – I think... Well, maybe I'm exploring my feminine side," said Shana. "Right, let's get going!" Reluctantly, the grouped walked to the harbour and across the shady beach. No one said a word; instead, they all glanced at the ocean and the stars. Danny shifted nervously; he really shouldn't be there! The moon shone brightly and revealed other dark figures walking in the direction of the church.

Once inside St. John's chapel, the villagers gathered and waited for the vicar to initiate the prayer. The moonlight illuminated shapes and shadows in the stone while fire torches lit the congregation. Shana glanced up at the starry sky as the prayers were read in the old language, Doric. Marty followed Shana's gaze and sighed. The atmosphere was sorrowful, beautiful but intense.

When the prayer was complete, the villagers lined up for identification to pass to the far end of the church. Speculative whispering filled the air. Who knew what response they were about to receive?

With a loud clunk, the church gates closed and then locked. The vicar waited for the area to fall silent.

"As you know one of them has chosen to pass over," he said in a serious but sullen tone. "You know what this means?"

The congregation nodded.

"We must return her before they begin to call," said the vicar. Shana and Marty glanced at each other and frowned. The vicar noticed.

"We all know that when the person of the sea is not returned the others will mournfully resonate and no one can resist that song. We never want to witness mass drowning again," said the vicar with a sigh. "For those who are new to the village, St. Johns is the burial place for those who have been taken by the sea. To stop it happening again we need to demonstrate our remorse and show our respect," said the vicar gesturing at the trapdoor. "We will have our way lit by fire as we walk the path to make our peace."

"They take their revenge by calling the villagers to the sea?" said Johnny incredulously. "I never knew that!"

There was a pained silence. All the while, Danny chewed his lip: his unintentional mistake could kill numerous innocent people. It wasn't fair!

Marty was having his own thoughts... were there answers in the cottage?

"Let fire light our way and may peace preside amongst our two tribes. God let them be forgiving," said the vicar. "Light a torch and follow me. We must carry her to their sacred place." Before the vicar stepped into the darkness, he tied some items onto his belt and carried some metallic adornments around his neck. He picked up a red satin satchel and descended into darkness. The villagers followed one at a time down into the dark tunnel system. Danny stayed back, had anyone noticed anything odd about the trap door?

Undulating shadows and firelight filled the dim passages. Marty, Danny, Shana and Johnny were enthralled but followed uncertainly. The constant drip from the ceiling bothered Danny but not as much as the sorrowful resonation penetrating his skull. The vicar paused and glanced at the group, the sound was external too. Had he sensed that the culprit was amongst them?

The vicar paused by the body on the path and frowned. He remained silent, brooding. He glanced ahead and gestured for the villages to be aware of the body. Something was not quite right. Who had visited? The blue light of the crypt filled the cavern and the girl remained on the altar.

"You, my dear, are yet another tragic victim of innocent love," he said with a sad sigh. "Our world does not have the same rules as yours. Love is not pure anymore. Instead, it is conditional and destructive." From the satin bag, he pulled out some silver silk and red rosebuds. Carefully he wrapped her and arranged the flowers.

"Let these flowers remind us of your bleeding heart and let the silver silk reveal your connection to the moon, femininity and emotion." Placing his hands together, he bowed and stepped back. Four of the male villagers lifted the stretcher and looked for guidance.

The caverns beyond the crypt were vast and complex. Each could travel in a multitude of directions or reach a dead end. The vicar took the lead and paused at a crossroads. He took his necklace in his hand; the silver embossed symbol matched an engraving on the wall of the cave. Marty, Shana, Johnny and Danny glanced at each other, where were they going?

After walking for twenty minutes, the group entered a cavern full of stalactites and stalagmites. Beyond that was a bay. The moon illuminated the turquoise water, which carried an iridescent glow. With a gentle pat to Shana's elbow Marty gestured to a large rocky outcrop concealing the bay from the ocean. "No one would know it was here?"

"What is that glow?" whispered Shana.

With a shrug, Marty sucked his lip in contemplation. The glow was similar to the stone circle.

"Do you think we are going to see where they live?" asked Shana.

"Surely they live underwater - on the ocean bed," said Johnny.

"And why's that Johnny?" said Shana.

"Well they canny build anything because they've ney got proper legs. How would they climb a ladder?"

A stagnant silence prevailed.

Marty watched the vicar illuminate a hidden door with his torch. Ancient inscriptions surrounded the outer arch. He carefully aligned one of the ornaments around his neck with the central sign on the door. There was a click and a rotation, which caused the door to roll back. The villagers surged towards the steps. Once everyone was inside, the vicar used another ornament from his necklace to close off the outside world.

A winding staircase led down into the cavern. Marty nudged Shana and gestured - the worn stairs revealed a history of visits. As the group reached the bottom of the steps, they arrived in a second cavern with a turquoise pool glowing at the centre. It radiated with that same iridescence found over at the stone circle. In fact, the whole cavern was luminous. What's more, there were fully grown oak trees inside the cavern. How was it possible?

"The pool's beautiful, it makes you want to swim," whispered Shana to Marty.

Johnny peered into the pool. "Holy shit, they're all down there," he said pointing.

Marty crouched down, the metallic rock forming the stalagmites and stalactites coated the pool walls. Something about that material and the clarity of the turquoise water was captivating.

"It's reflective," muttered Marty. "You can see reflections." Shana watched the people of the sea swimming amongst the depths.

"What a strange way to live."

The vicar tapped a stalactite with one of the tools from his belt. A high-pitched reverberation echoed through the cavern and informed the people of the sea that the villagers were present. Numerous 'creatures,' surfaced and studied the visitors. Finally, the leader swam forward. Shana and Marty studied her; she appeared youthful with her long, wavy, dark hair. In fact, none of them appeared to be older than twenty-five.

The vicar gestured for the group to place the body before the leader. The leader gently caressed the silk and gazed sadly at the villagers. Eventually she bowed her head in gratitude.

"Het me fein," she said gratefully (thanks for bringing her). The vicar responded "Wey hest di." (we had to).

The leader nodded, "Quye o' Quye? Premi ens sederchi."(Why oh why, first in ten solstice).

The expression in the vicar's eyes revealed his thoughts. The leader understood and glanced at every individual present. One particular person amongst the group captured her attention.

"Ke."(Thanks) she said guiding the body into the water. A melancholy resonation amongst the sea people grew in intensity. The villagers covered their ears but the resonation was beyond sound. Whatever it was the melancholy chorus created physical side-effects on the human body. Marty now understood why people were lured to the water. The sound was both tormenting and controlling. Death would be better than suffering such a tormenting sound for eternity.

"If we hadn't returned her the resonation would be more intense than you can possibly imagine," said one of the old local women. "The sea would grow stormy and the heavens would open. The only way you could end it would be death. I feel sorry for the wrongdoer, for he will rise to the surface."

Shana gazed at the old woman, how did she know a man had caused her demise?

"Through denial and avoidance we made that mistake many

times before in our history. We must always face our wrongdoings, take responsibility and ask forgiveness. It's the only way or trouble will brew – we have endlessly repeated this pattern! It is time for it to end! It always turns up in one form or another," said the old lady patting Shana kindly.

The vicar acknowledged the end of the ceremony by ringing a different tuning fork. "Everyone please touch the altar, it's tradition," said the vicar.

How could it be tradition unless there was a repeat cycle? Marty watched the villagers touch the stone. When they touched the stone their necklaces glowed for just a second. Marty gestured to Danny, Shana and Johnny to avoid touching the stone. Something about it bothered him. Johnny and Danny shook their heads and connected with the stone. However, he and Shana were not local; they did not have to follow their tradition.

"What you thinking Marty?" whispered Shana curiously.

"I think the stone has something to do with their transformation. I'm just not touching it just in case. Now I think we should go," he said. The group hastily caught up with the villagers who chose an alternative exit route through a neighbouring warren of caves. Those tunnels emerged onto the headland, which was marked by a mound of stones. It was all so well set up. He watched how the villagers gave their torches to two designated collectors before they scattered into the darkness.

The vicar strolled over to Marty, Shana, Johnny and Danny who hung back. "Now you will keep this confidential and only talk behind closed doors to each other and no one else. As a matter of respect…"

The group remained silent but nodded. They had so many questions but that was not the time.

CHAPTER 51

Going public.

The editor of the Times battled through the swarms of commuters to reach his office. From the moment he entered the office, phones continued to ring and endless e-mails piled into the inbox. He hung up his jacket, glanced out of the glass window and focused. The news market had been sparse lately and there had been nothing 'special' to spark controversy or scandal. With the gentle poof of the chair, he prepared to start the day. 'Assume the greeting position,' was why his chair faced the door. If he faced the away did that then mean 'sod off?' How was that bad chi? What did wind chimes actually do anyway?

The editor sat down and fell into his usual routine. On the in-tray laid a large pile of pre-sorted post. He opened it gradually and unenthusiastically. Danny's dishevelled envelope sat on the top, it had survived the secretary's sift. The editor's jaw tightened when he noticed a scribbled note, which was barely legible and did not warrant any time. If a person couldn't be bothered to present well then why waste time with the contents? Admittedly, it had made it past his secretary and she generally knew a nutter at ten paces.

'LOOK UP THE HISTORY OF SEA PEOPLE IN GARDENSTOWN NEAR BANFF- HERE IS EVIDENCE - LOCAL'.

The editor checked the back of the paper. There was nothing else written. With a loud sigh, he sat back in his large leather chair. What was it with people? Why did they think he had time for cryptic clues? The editor screwed up the note and tossed the envelope into the waste-paper basket. Just as he did, his editorial assistant walked in and glanced at the bin.

"What's that?" she said noticing photographs poking out.

"Some kind of cryptic clue which I don't have time for," he replied flatly.

The assistant gave a glimmer of a smile to appease the man.

She picked up the photos and shook her head, "these are why I came into see you. If the net gets hold of these they will go berserk!" She handed back the images to his outstretched hand.

"How authentic are they?" he asked.

"We can't detect any compression, file history or layers. As far as we can tell they are real!"

"Have you heard any whispers from the other news agencies?"

"From what I can gather, they have been sent exclusively to us. It is a very flat market at the moment," she said with a sigh. "She could sell some papers… Especially if no one else…"

The editor paced, "where's Banff anyway?"

"Scotland," replied the editorial assistant.

The editor's expression changed. The assistant read him instantly; she knew what she had to do.

"We need to take an academic angle to maintain authenticity. Get some specialists involved. I want someone credible, none of those airy-fairy sorts who wear purple velvet. We need a professor!" he said definitely. "Let's hope this shifts some papers, oh and see if you can find out who this fruit loop is and get the rights to the images."

The editorial assistant nodded and departed the office. Her job was thankless!

Early the following morning Waterloo Station was almost silent during rush hour. The only real sound was the rustling of newspapers. The images fascinated and raised numerous unanswerable questions.

CHAPTER 52
High heels, wellies and leaks!

News travelled fast. Inside one of the most notorious television news departments in the country, the Controller flushed red. "How can you be sure it's not a hoax?" he demanded. His back was hunched and his jaw tight. "Why the hell didn't they inform anyone?" He shouted, covered the mouthpiece of his phone and turned to his male assistant.

"Get the remaining teams in now. We need to find our own angle!"

The Controller was completely bald with squared glasses and a squidgy figure crammed into his well-cut suit. His solid shoulders almost touched his ears. He was a man of order, structure and control. When he didn't get what he wanted, well, someone had to pay!

"Get Marie here. Call her off the financial scandals and send her a brief," barked the Controller.

Within the hour, three news teams sat in the meeting rooms awaiting their brief. Some sipped coffee; others drank caffeine-filled drinks while they speculated about what they were about to report. The Controller stood at the front of the room searching the group. With a glance at his expensive watch, he gritted his teeth. She had thirty seconds… With five seconds to spare, a five foot five redhead sauntered in wearing red high-heels. She flicked her hair and smiled sweetly at the Controller who instantly melted.

"Ladies and gentlemen, I assume you have read the treatment and are aware of the imagery that has been published by the Times. As of yet we have not heard of any news agency capturing this 'phenomenon' on film. We will be the first! Get your arses up to Banff and do the research to get this on film! If we are the first we can sell it on. You want to make a bonus – then this is what you have to do! The first team who sends me the film will be adequately rewarded."

Some of the producers glanced around the room. Marie examined her chipped red nail varnish; she needed a manicure.

"Do you know where Banff is?" asked one of the new producers.

Marie smirked; you never revealed how little you knew amongst the others. That was like revealing you were meat to piranha. Marie gestured for her team to follow her. Her allocated cameraman and sound engineer had heard about her antics but accepted her ruthless nature would get them the bonus.

"So, darlings, let's get ourselves up there this afternoon. I'll give my bro a call. He happens to be in Gardenstown, it's near enough to Banff- I hear." Marie stepped into the lift with her team. Mark was in his early forties with dark receding hair. He had the features of a wolf and the paunch of beer belly. Matt, on the other hand, was early thirties, lithe, sharp featured with spikey blonde hair. He looked warn, as if he had been avoiding nutrition for the last five years. She produced her mobile and scrolled through the numbers. She couldn't find Marty's number. After rummaging about her handbag, she produced her Filofax. She flicked through that and still couldn't find his number. She was always so organised!

As they departed the lift Marie strutted into the foyer while her crew assembled their kit.

'Hello mum can you text Marty's number to me. Thank you. See you soon. Say hi to Ron. Will catch up over lunch when I'm back. Kiss, kiss."

"Ready?" asked Marie brightly. She glanced at her list and muttered. "Right, we can buy clothes when we get there. Oh and we're booked on the next flight to Aberdeen. Let's get straight to the airport then..." Marie eyed their stack of equipment. "I have someone calling the airline about that." With a quick tap of the screen, Marie called Marty's number and waited for a response. "You want to load up the van while I find out what my brother knows?"
The crew did what they always did and just got on with it.

Marty was painting in his studio when the phone rang.

"Hi Marty, it's your big sister-" said Marie brightly on the other end of the line.
Since when had she ever contacted him unless she wanted something?

"Marie? I haven't heard from you for ages- since the- funeral."

"Always busy – that's city life darling! Plus, I don't waste time getting all-emotional. What happened is over – you have to move on," she replied.

"So…. I guess you want something then…"

"Don't be like that darling," she said.

"Well?" asked Marty.

"Darling, big news has broken here. Apparently, someone found a mutation close to where you live. It's causing quite a stir. So much so, they are sending my crew and me up there… I know that the news market has been sparse lately but to send me… Imagine! I thought I would kill two birds with one stone. What a coincidence!" Silence. *Shit!*

"Marty are you there-?" asked Marie with concerned.

"Sorry… The line is rubbish."

"Maybe it's a bad connection. I have a news team coming up. There are three of us. Can you get us some rooms somewhere nice?" she asked hopefully.

Marty smirked; his sister luxuriated in style and class. What would she make of the local tavern and Sully? "Just do the best you can do… If it's not too much trouble darling... If you could do it as quick as poss… I am sure you can anticipate at least ten teams coming up and I don't want to camp. Have to go. We'll be up there in four hours or so... maybe five. Depends on the traffic - darling. We'll be driving from Aberdeen."

"We'll see you in a bit. Bring some wellington boots. You really are going to hate it here!"

"It can't be that bad! You have lasted and it will be lovely to see your new lifestyle. Is there any shopping?"

"Nope… Just the bakery."

"Oh... do they have any cakes without carbs?"

Marty smirked, "no and there isn't a gym."

Marie was silent, something about the place made her stomach fold.

"Got to fly Marty- look forward to catching up. Byeeee."

Silence.

Gardenstown had no clue what was about to descend on them. "Shit. SHIT. SHIT!" How did it get out?

CHAPTER 53
Scattering Dominoes!

With a slam of the cottage door, Marty ran up Straight Lane to the tavern. He was breathless when he arrived and recovered by leaning against the wall. Slam! Dominoes scattered as the old locals jolted and turned to see a red-faced Marty burst in. Sully jammed the cigar he was chewing in his mouth, regained himself and frowned.

"Sully I need to book three rooms now," shouted Marty across the bar.

"Who for?" Sully opened the dusty leather-bound guest book placed next to the phone.

"My sister and two others. They'll be arriving this evening," said Marty with a relieved exhalation.

"That'll be nice," he said with a raised eyebrow. "So we'll get to meet yer sister. Will any more of your family be emigrating this way?" he asked resuming his cigar chewing.

"No, she's the only one. Be prepared, she's pretty feisty."

"Don't you worry Marty, we're used to all manner of pre-Madonna," said Sully writing Marty's names in block capitals across three rooms.

"Funny… We've been quiet for ages and now that's the last of me rooms. Ney room at the Inn," he said with a chuckle.

Marty studied Sully, what was the best way to break the news? The phone rang again and Sully rolled his eyes. "Sorry, we have ney rooms left. I would ney care if you were the bloody Prime Minister. We're full!" he shouted down the phone. "I do ney care about customer service!"

"That there's the tenth call in the last hour," said Donald placing his last domino and turning to Marty. "Sully, if he's lucky, gets that a year and most of them are from my missus." Donald studied Marty and paused, "Has something taken place Marty?" Sully slammed down the phone down but it rung instantaneously. With an exasperated look on his face, he picked up. "What's going on?" he said covering the mouthpiece. "Sorry, no… We don't have any rooms for the next week. No…. No camping pitches either."

"I spend all year trying to get business and it all comes in a week…"

"The world knows…" said Marty.

The room was silent and filled with frowns. Accusing glances darted about the room.

"Bugger!" said Sully slamming his palm on the counter.

"Marie is a news producer. She won't leave London unless there's a decent story."

"How did it get out?"

"I have no idea," said Marty with a shrug.

The diver ran into the pub carrying the Times. "Look! Someone has betrayed us!" he said glancing accusingly at Marty.

The domino players stood up and peered at the paper. The front cover displayed the image of the dead 'girl.'

"Oh no… troubles brewing," said Donald with a shake of the head. "How we going to hide them from the world? It will become a hunt and they will become just another media spectacle. Then we will have greater trouble." He returned to his seat and took a large gulp of bitter.

"I told you," said Marty.

"We need a village gathering," said Sully. "Donald will you do the honours?"

Donald gulped the remains of his pint and lurched towards the door. With a loud yelp Butch was unexpectedly dragged across the floor.

"That'll teach him to lick his balls!" muttered Donald.

"We need to make sure it's only villagers. We should return to the old language," said Sully.

The chime of the church bell summoned the villagers to the central church. A number of tourists became curious and followed.

"This is a village meeting. Yer need ney concern yerself lassie," said one of the village elders.

The tourist frowned at the old woman and turned to go into the bakery. "Closed?"

Inside the church the vicar stood in the pulpit waiting. Marty noticed his housemates standing awkwardly towards the back.

"Marty, do you know what's going on?" asked Shana.

"Someone has let out the secret. There are pictures of the girl all over the papers," he said taking a seat.

"Now who would do such a thing?" said Shana with a sigh. Silence prevailed when the vicar cleared his throat. He glanced at the congregation and signalled to close the church doors. "Everyone please check those around you, any faces you do not know should be asked to leave," he said in Doric, the local language. The elders glanced at each other; at least the language was still alive and useful. The few outsiders were politely escorted to the door. "Yer would ney understand anyway because we talk the old language in these congregations for the villagers," said Sully in his politest voice. He returned to the row where Marty was sitting and gestured for him to move over. "Johnny are you still able to speak the language?" Sully asked in Doric. "A bit rusty but I will do my best to translate," he replied.

"You may wonder why you have all been summoned to the central church but our secret's out. News of the girl that we returned last night has reached the press. As a result, numerous news teams are on their way and they are hunting for a story. We need to warn 'them' and tell them to keep out of sight. Remember this secret is the foundation of who we are. This 'hunt' will result in death if any are hurt or injured. We must protect them to protect ourselves," said the vicar in Doric.

The congregation nodded in agreement. "Aye."

"Now what concerns me most is that someone has maliciously betrayed us and them. There is a Judas amongst us. As before, our Judas will rise to the surface. I sense that same individual is responsible for her death. Pay attention to the shores because the calling will begin. It has happened before and it will happen again. There is no resistance to her revenge," said the vicar.

The diver glanced at Marty accusingly. "You hear that Marty? The Judas will rise to the surface," he said studying him. "There is no resistance to the call."

Marty frowned, "I thought that it only affected the culprit."

The diver studied him, "true and the culprit could be closer than we think."

Marty studied the diver's accusing eyes, what were these cryptic clues?

After a glance that circumnavigated the room, Marty jolted. "You think it was me, don't you?"

The diver was silent.

"I suggest before you make accusations you find evidence," he said.

"Well, if it's ney you then who is it? The timing ties in with you and the boat. Isn't it strange that your sister is on that news team? A coincidence like that makes people point fingers Marty. Plus you found her," said the diver maintaining eye contact.

He was right. It looked bad!

"Well whoever it was will reveal themselves in good time. Mark my words, they are going to suffer and that serves them right! The resonance will drive them insane and often suicide is the only escape."

Marty glanced across at Johnny. Would he betray the village he had grown up in?

"There's no use hiding guilt, it will eat away at a person's soul until the truth is revealed. The truth will be revealed in one form or another," said Sully standing. "You can leave, the vicar has finished."

CHAPTER 54

Extreme zip-ism!

Four hours after Marie's phone call news teams arrived in Gardenstown. Down by the cove, cars and vans with antenna clustered together. Numerous people in combat-coloured tops with far too many zips assembled complex electrical equipment. Tourists huddled watching the spectacle.

Marie had already parked her van away from the mass. She studied the competition and shook her head. "Sheep," she said so the soundman could hear. "Sheep are just clouds with spindly legs!" With her definite hippy walk, she wiggled up to the village high street and noticed the pub. With a loud sigh, she shook her head. "The Old Inn," she read. Marie peered through the window, surely there had to be somewhere better to stay than that?

After taking a deep breath she flung open the tavern door and paused. Instantly she noticed the stuffed cat, stepped over and made her way to the bar. There she stood with her hand on her hip. The old men of the village glanced at each other but continued their domino games with certain looks that revealed a man's thoughts. Sully finished clearing his glasses, spat on one, polished it with a cloth and then plodded back to the bar. He picked up a cigar bit the end off and lit it. Thick bluish smoke rose as he turned to greet Marie.

"Aren't bars in Scotland smoke free?" she asked waving the smoke away.

Silence.

Numerous domino games were momentarily suspended. Sully was up to something; it would definitely provide a spectacle.

The sensation of eyes upon Marie made her glance in the mirror on the shelf. What was the barman planning? What was her contingency?

"Can I help you miss?" said Sully in his politest voice.

The old men around the bar smirked. Miss?

Marie placed her red handbag on the bar.

"Apparently this is where I'm staying," she replied.

"You Marty's sis?" asked Sully.

"Yes, and my news team are just outside" she said pointing.

The camera crew extinguished their rolled cigarettes and stepped over the stuffed cat into the tavern.

Sully took a large puff of the cigar and studied Marie. "Now let me tell you how it is here... That is if I let you stay. Marty, being my friend, got you and your 'crew' a room here. Nowhere in the near vicinity has any space, so peering down the nose thing you're doing had better stop!"

Marie's mouth fell open.

"The way I see it lassie, is there's numerous people who would appreciate staying here, so be grateful!" said Sully opening the dusty reservations book and wiping the dust onto her handbag.

Marie folded her arms. She needed the room but... "You know who I am and who I work for don't you?"

"Do I care? And just so yer know... Many a drunk uses that very same line. I suggest originality in the future! It might help yer progress yer career," he replied tracing his finger down the page.

A flush of red rose up Marie's neck.

Noticing the reaction, Sully took a pair of glasses with no lenses and put them on. The old men around the room subtly shook their heads and smirked at each other.

"What you have to remember young lady... Is that this village is far removed from that city of yours. What they care about does ney concern us one iota. Their rules are not our rules. Now I will let you have the room if you promise to be well behaved."

Well behaved?

With a loud ring, the phone beside Sully vibrated. "That there's more customers for your rooms... Well?"

"Yes, of course we do... erm... thank... you," she replied through taught lips. She attempted her sweetest smile but a grimace revealing murderous eyes was the reality.

"Good, I've given you the haunted ones so your crew have something to film at night. I'll show you the way," he said gesturing for the group to follow him.

With a loud sigh, Marie glanced at her crew. Her face revealed what she was thinking and the flush contained what she was suppressing.

"Now your brother's a nice lad. Are you adopted?"

The crew hid their smirks.

"I've known women like you before – all strong on the outside but strength hides weakness. Things change up here, you'll see. You just need a good man to sort you out!" said Sully waving the cigar at her.

Marie rolled her eyes; she would not chase the bait!

"You may not realise it yet but there is reason for you to be here. Or else you would ney be connected. You've all been called for a reason. Now I will watch fate do her best. This time next year I sense you'll still be here. I can feel it in me water and now that water has to be passed," said Sully gesturing to the three rooms and handing them the keys.

"I can assure you that this time next year I will be in the city doing the job I love, but thank you," said Marie. "Oh and it is possible that your 'water' could be wrong."

"Never been wrong yet," said Sully with a wink.

Marie offered Sully a pound tip. Sully frowned at the coin and handed it back.

"Thank you all the same but I am not your skivvy! Get your own luggage. What do you think we are? A hotel?" said Sully walking away.

With her arms folded, Marie glanced at the other members of her crew and shook her head. What was going on in that man's head?

"I'll be at the bar after the can," said Sully. "Oh the bath and toilet are at the end of the corridor. I do ney want any ablutions in the wardrobes."

"What? There's no en-suite?" asked Marie.

Sully stopped abruptly and turned, "this tavern is nearly seven hundred years old. When it was built, people used wooden tubs to bathe in; so you're bloody lucky I had that convenience fitted. Otherwise you'd be bathing in the yard and warming the water on a stove. Maybe you would like your bare body on view to the locals!" Sully watched her reaction. Looking pleased with himself, he turned and marched down the wooden stairs.

Marie unconsciously shook her head. Did the man have no concept of service? After a short pause Marie gathered herself. "Right, we have work to do! Unload what you don't need then we'll go hunting."

"Marie I think you need to be a bit careful around here. They don't want us here and they could make things difficult. I lived in a village, I know how they are!" said Mark.

"Well, the sooner we get the story then the sooner we can leave and collect our bonus," she said. "Plus, I can't bear that man! The sooner we are out of here the better!"

"Doesn't your brother live here?" asked the soundman.

"Yes, unfortunately. We'll see him later, when it gets dark when we've made inroads into this stupid bloody story," said Marie in calculation.

CHAPTER 55
Rock-pool diversity!

Down in the cove, on the farthest edge of Gardenstown, Johnny was engaged in watch duty at the lifeguard station. There were a few tourists splashing around or colliding with each other as they were washed up on the beach and the rest were no doubt concocting ridiculous questions that made no sense: 'is there an equivalent to the Lochness Monster in the sea?'

At the same time, Shana followed her usual route during her late afternoon jog. On the way, she made it a habit to stop off at the lifeguard station and use their free weights. In addition, the large open windows and watchtower provided an incredible view.

Johnny swung on his chair and fidgeted as he stared out of the huge glass windows. Behind him, hooks filled with yellow t-shirts, red shorts and all manner of wetsuits were in the periphery of his vision. The neat arrangement was a rare sight. The room was usually a mess of wetsuit items slung all over the place. Of course, news of the Gardenstown invasion at headquarters meant that Johnny and his colleagues had to tidy. Further into the hut was a kitchen area, changing area and shower – it had been cleaned (just in case). Everything was whitish now including the shelves filled with dark technical equipment and keys for the jet-skis

After tidying for an hour, Johnny made another definite jiggle. The need for mischief was welling up - he just needed a playmate. Scanning the beach through his binoculars, he noticed that amongst the 'greater flabby' tourist appeared another entirely new breed of person. 'The greater spotted television tit.' Markings included camouflage gear, a multitude of useless zips and a rolled cigarette. Cliché? That was an understatement. Was it possible to have permanent combat trousers pasted onto people? Maybe the combaters had a special trouser genetic. He surveyed the area once more with his binoculars.

Shana jogged the last stretch and climbed the tower to find Johnny scanning the area.

"Hi," she said.

"Have you seen how many film crews are here?" asked Johnny. "You should see the main village. It has been invaded! Now I reckon this is just the beginning too."

"They look like they're in a war zone or something. So much camouflage makes them stand out!"

Shana sighed and picked up a pair of three-kilogram dumbbells. "I think if one of them so much as finds one of 'them' it will all be over!"

Marie found a bench overlooking the harbour and sat down. She peered at a local map and the newspaper article. The soundman and cameraman sat on the harbour wall and examined their GPS. "I think that Macduff to Banff should be our first check, we will skim the area. Can one of you look up mermaid sightings in Scotland on your phones?"

The pair waved their phones around, "the signal is odd here," said the Mark.

"Can you shift network to roam?"

The pair played with their phones, "the signal is really odd," said the soundman.

"Typical!" said Marie. "We will just have to work the old fashioned way!"

Over in the watch tower Johnny and Shana sat with binoculars watching hoards of camera teams set up.

"This is ridiculous – you would have thought something major had happened! Idiots!" she said without removing the binoculars from her eyes.

"I'm bored now," said Johnny in a certain tone.
Shana glanced at him; he had a certain look, which meant Johnny trouble!

"One totty spot and then we will have some fun!" Johnny said scanning the area. "I think some of the women need to shave, either that or the men need to cut off their pony tails. I canny tell which is which because of the man boobs!"

"Oh God, they all have moobs!" said Shana making her own motty spot.

"Watch this-" said Johnny with a mysterious giggle.

At that precise moment, Marie arrived. "Mark, keep this camera hand-held for the moment. But keep the tripod just in case and Matt be ready." Marie wiggled onto the beach and found the perfect spot to stand with her hand on her hip.

"There's one. There is actually a nice bit of totty there!" said Johnny excitedly.

"No Johnny! You can't get distracted now! You have to finish what you began!" said Shana folding her arms. "Johnny!"

"Look, over there." He said pointing in the opposite direction. Shana frowned, "now what is it Johnny?"

"There's a duck over by the rock pool," he said keeping his binoculars poised on the feminine form.

"So-?" asked Shana, not understanding the relevance. Johnny removed the binoculars from his eyes and shook his head. With a loud hoot of the lifeguard Tannoy, Johnny cleared his throat.

"Can all swimmers leave the water please?" The two remaining swimmers obliged and glanced at the waters behind them. Was there something out there? Was that why all the film crews were there?

Johnny grinned mischievously at Shana. "There... There, there-look. There is definitely something," he said as if he had forgotten to switch off the microphone. "To the right of the bay at three o'clock. Don't say anything too much. We don't want people to panic." The film crews rotated their cameras and scanned the area. Producers and reporters urgently prepared and...

Shana grinned with her arms folded, "yer wicked Johnny!" she laughed. "This is actually good fun though!"

Some of the crews glanced back at the hut looking for some kind of direction. Johnny contained his amusement and pointed his largest binoculars at three o'clock. "I've never seen anything like it before..." he said over the Tannoy.

Shana grinned while the film crews searched.

"It is a rare day you get to witness such a phenomenon in Gardenstown..."

"Oh Johnny, now yer milking it!" said Shana giggling.

"This is ney a great day but a special day that should be remembered by the world. That there duck by the rock pool is special... Ducks like fresh water! So it must be on its holidays! Do yer feel priviledged? I do... To witness such a rare sighting is a no less than a blessing. And that is the rear end of the naturist update today."

"Did you mean naturalist?" asked Shana.

Johnny shrugged as he collapsed onto his seat chuckling. "Oh that feels good. I feel like the real Johnny is back!"

"Halfwit!" said Marie half-stomping and half-wiggling over to the lifeguard hut.

With a raised eyebrow she noticed the pair cracking up.

"Savages! Lads, we'll never find a bloody creature like this. We need to try other tactics. I need a helicopter and some heat-seeking equipment…" she said glancing up at the tower.

Johnny had resumed scanning the area for other natural spectacles to share with the media when Marie stomped up to the lifeguard station. The motion drew his attention and he followed her struttatious trajectory towards him.

The jolt of recognition shot through Shana when she recognised 'the walk.' She glanced around the hut - where could she hide? The wave of panic shot up Shana's spine, she couldn't talk to the woman… Too late!

Marie stomped up the steps and Johnny Boy followed her through the binoculars until he was gazing into her eyes through the lenses.

"Er… Johnny Boy, she's standing in front of you," said Shana hiding behind her hair.

Johnny surveyed the woman through the binoculars and Shana slapped him when he arrived at a particular area of woman.

"Hello there. Do you have a number for air rescue in the area?" asked Marie in her most seductive tone.

Shana frowned and noticed Johnny was hypnotised by her snake-charming tones.

In a dazed state Johnny stood up and a pen flicked over his shoulder. A cup of water crashed to the floor breaking his trance.

"Whoops. Er… Boobs…Yeh…Hello. I'm Johnny.. Nice to…" muttered Johnny with a full blush.

With a tilt of her head Marie took her time to allow her gaze to travel over Johnny's masculine physique.

In the meantime, Shana was horrified. What was going on? Marie had enticed Johnny - the wind up merchant and now Shana wanted him back!

"So can you help me with that number?" she said with a swish

242

of her hair.

"I'll just..." Johnny paused and grinned to himself as he jotted down a number. "Actually, this is my number just in case."

"Thank you. And the helicopter?" asked Marie gazing into his eyes.

With a definite fold of her arms, Shana stepped forwards. "What do you want the number for?"

Marie studied the woman before her and paused. Why did she recognise her? "I just want some aerials of the area," she said innocently. "Johnny, I'm sure you use heat-detecting equipment. A man like you must have access to that sort of equipment."

"Why?" asked Shana.

"I was talking to Johnny," she replied snottily.

"Excuse me, I need to talk to you in private- now," said Shana leading the gawking Johnny away. "Will yer be thinking with yer dick there Johnny?"

"I'm a man I always think with my dick. Two brains not enough blood – you said it!" Johnny remained with his eyes fixed on Marie.

"Johnny we don't want to give anything away. She's the enemy! Think of the village, think of your home and imagine the blood rising from your dick back into yer brain now," Shana said forcefully.

Johnny frowned as he attempted it. "Not possible – me dick is the more powerful brain and gravity is working!"

"Johnny I know you want to get into her knickers but tell her you don't have the number," said Shana.

With a penetrative stare Marie sensed the pair were not intimate by their body language.

"Okay!" said Johnny, appearing to search through piles of paper. "Sorry, but we lost the number."

"So if there's a disaster, how do you get in contact?" asked Marie.

"Pigeon?" said Johnny.

"We radio?" said Shana glancing at Johnny with horror.

"The radio is prohibited. For lifeguard and emergency use only," said Johnny watching Shana mouth the words.

"So what you're actually saying is you won't help me?"

"No he won't! Now I think it's time for you to leave because you could be distracting Johnny from saving someone's life," said Shana turning Marie round and guiding her out of the hut.

"You just made a huge mistake!" said Marie venomously and out of Johnny's earshot.

As soon as Marie began her strut, Shana stuck her fingers up behind her back. Marie turned back to witness the offensive two finger salute. That was it!

Shana stomped back into the hut to find Johnny swinging on his chair.

"I'm in love…" he said honestly.

"No you're not. Johnny, she's a bitch! She's always been a bitch! Now snap out of it!"

"Boys, let's get a boat and then we'll be able to see what's going on," said Marie when she reached her crew.

They remained silent. They knew Marie, her moods and when definitely not to say a single thing.

"They're hiding something. That behaviour made it obvious," she muttered.

That mental churn was building. It would become a storm of anger and that anger would drive her. That famous temper made her successful but through being ruthless. Silence was always the answer on such occasions.

"Let's try the diving shop first," said Marie.

Accompanied by the ring of a bell, Marie and her crew arrived in the diving shop. The clutter of bits and bobs made her fists clench.

"Good afternoon, I would like to hire a power boat. Do you have any of those RIB's?"

"Nope," said the diver shaking his head.

"Any boats?" she asked

"Nope."

"Anything at all?"

The diver shook his head. "Nothing, not even a pink Lilo."

The soundman and cameraman glanced at each other. The locals were resistant! Marie paced for a while before she crossed her arms. With a loud huff, she studied the man. "You must have something. I'll give you a thousand pounds for five days…Cash!"

"You don't get it do you? We're not hiring boats for this blessed hunt! And that is that!" said the diver glancing at his dumpy wife who smiled her approval.

That famous red flush crept up Marie's neck. "I sense you're hiding something…" she said leaning forwards. "I will find them…" she growled with a slam of the fist. "Oh, and the hunt makes this job a pleasure. Why do you think this is my profession?"

The diver glanced at his wife who was frowning in the doorway. The woman's determination was fearful. She was not the type to give in!

CHAPTER 56

Sisterly manipulation!

Marie stormed along the harbour oblivious to the soundman and cameraman trying to keep up. The wind picked up and blew her hair in all directions as her mind churned her options. There was no way she would give in. When Marie found Crooked Cottage, she noticed the door was on the latch. She glanced at her crew, as if advising them of her intentions, and simply walked in and up the stairs.

The trance music played while Marty was absorbed in filling in Iris's details. In the doorway, Marie silently watched him paint. She had always found his concentration fascinating. She waited for Marty to remove the paintbrush from the canvas and took a deep breath.

"Marty darling!" she said.

With a sudden jolt Marty grabbed his chest. "Bloody hell Marie!" he said taking a sheet and covering the painting.

He picked up a towel, wiped his hands and walked towards the door.

"Marie… You look… A bit flushed!"

She shook her head, held her neck and smirked, "I'm having trouble getting a boat. The locals are purposely creating obstacles."

"Come into the lounge," said Marty to the group. "We can have some tea."

"Marty you avoided responding to that darling… What's going on?" she asked curiously.

What was it with sisters? "It's how the village works. They don't like the world invading them so they will be as awkward as possible," he replied thoughtfully. "So…"

"Coffee… Three please…" she said automatically. "Oh, this is Mark on camera and this is Matt on sound."

Mark and Matt smiled gratefully and took a seat in the armchairs. Marty headed to the kitchen with Marie trailing behind. "Marty, I need to ask you a favour."

Marty filled the kettle and switched it on. "No. Marie you're in producer mode to get what you want," he said turning to her. "Remember I'm your brother and I live in this village. I know what you want but I am not willing to give any kind of interview."

"Come on Marty, we can adjust your voice and put you in silhouette," she said.

"Marie I said no. I am not going to get involved! This is where I live…" he said.

Marie lent against the counter and had a face like a slapped behind.

"Well, how am I supposed to get this story?"

"Maybe you're not supposed to. What are you doing Marie anyway? This is nothing like the work you usually do… This is almost a joke. How do you know it isn't a set up?"

Marie shrugged, "I was sent to get a story and that is what I do. Do you think I want to come to a place like this where women drive quad bikes and don't wax under their noses?"

Marty smirked, "Marie…"

"Well come on Marty… The women here wouldn't know a piece of art from a cow-pat!"

"Marie it doesn't concern them! It means nothing… They still have to survive. Life is real here, not the endless chasing an invisible golden carrot that just gets further away. This village is full of real people with amazing life stories. Imagine friendly, authentic people who are kind and talkative! This place is about who they are and not what they have or appear to have…"

There was a heavy atmosphere as the kettle boiled. Marie stared at her shoes as she considered what Marty had said. Something in her gut was niggling her.

The sound of pouring coffee filled the silence. He handed Marie two cups and gestured with his head for her to follow him up the stairs.

"Marty I can't go back with nothing, I have to win!" she said.

Marty paused on the landing, "Marie this is all about your ego. Find another angle. Don't get consumed by the mermaid story. It will only lead to death."

With that, he turned and walked into the lounge. Marie hung back and glanced around the landing. Her neck was tingling with static. Something triggered in her gut. There was a story and she sensed it. "It will only lead to death," she muttered and smiled to herself.

Matt and Mark sipped their coffee and watched Marie brooding.

Marty watched them watching and sighed, "have you been on any interesting assignments lately?"

"We've been in Egypt for the last few months – it's so hot and sandy. It makes a nice change to come somewhere like this," said Mark.

There was a loud slam of the door and chatter downstairs. Marty glanced at the door and heard a stocky figure stomp up to the landing.

"Evening," Johnny said and paused.

"Johnny this is my sister Marie," said Marty. "And this is the film crew Mark and Matt."

"That's yer sisty Marty? Why did yer never say?" said Johnny. Shana bounded into the doorway beside him, "even… ing…" she said, trailing off.

Marie glanced at Shana and had a jolt of recognition, "my God, I didn't recognise you."

"I noticed earlier but I wasn't going to say a t'ing," said Shana with a smirk.

"You knew that was Marty's sis? And yer did ney tell me?" Shana shrugged, "you didn't ask now did you?"

With an incredulous stare, Johnny shook his head.

"Is there something going on here?"

"Johnny was directing the film crews to a freshwater duck in a rock-pool this afternoon," said Marie studying his strong physique like an eagle.

A subtle blush filled the patches of his tattoo. Marie noticed and found it endearing. "Right, I need to get a boat," she said standing up.

A third figure appeared in the doorway. "Oh, and that would be Danny, the last of my housemates," said Marty. "My sister Marie, Mark and Matt."

He gave a wave and then bounded down the stairs.

"Right, Marty I have to get on. Time is money and I have people to contact to get the transport I need. If I can't get it here I will simply go higher…" Marie paused and nodded to herself. With an optimistic look, she glanced at her phone. Of course, there was no signal!

Marty gazed at his sister, she had figured something out and that something sent a shiver down his spine. "Marie I am warning you… This story is not worth it. Please just listen to me… Do not annoy the locals. Keep away from this story… It will mean death if you get involved."

There was a silence in the room as Marie glanced at each of them. There was no way that she would leave without a story!

CHAPTER 57
Bursts of light.

News teams and photographers were poised for something 'out of the ordinary' to take place. Climbing across the seaweed-clad rocks, Marty and Shana paddled out beyond the break. Once they were clear, the pair scanned the water. A subtle resonation echoed about them accompanied by a ripple. A moment later Iris gently broke the surface between their boards.

"Marty I had to see you," she said gazing into his eyes.

"Iris you and the others have to keep out of sight," he said reaching into the water and taking her hand.

A mechanical hum filled the air and helicopter blades whirred.

"I don't believe it!" said Marty.

Shana shook her head, "that woman is unbelievable! She actually got one! She's probably got heat-seeking equipment too!" The urgency in Shana's tone caught Iris's attention.

"Iris hide! Please hide directly under my board. Lay so it completely covers you. When I tap the board swim your fastest to the caves."

"What is?" asked Iris.

"A flying machine," said Shana. "Iris tell the others to stay deep in the water. The machine above us can find you by detecting your body heat. If you need to swim, swim in groups with porpoises, dolphins or seals."

"Who's hunting us Marty?"

With a loud sigh Marty shook his head. "There are many but one of them is my sister."

"Yer sister? Difficult. Blood and water," said Iris before she submerged.

The pair watched the helicopter fly towards the horizon. With the tap of the board they watched Iris dart below the surface towards the caves.

The helicopter was a five-seater - two seats in the front and three in the back. The back windows had been removed so Mark could film. Nothing special other than a pair of surfers had caught Marie's attention on the heat-seeking device. That was until a flash of heat like a shooting star burst across the screen and evaporated. Marie peered closer. There was not enough time to determine a shape. "I think we should call it a day boys." The air of pessimism coming from Marie was infectious.

CHAPTER 58
Chinks in the armour

The tavern was full of television crews devouring the 'specials' menu: Henrietta Burgers with tattys and nips, Ophelia Sausage and Mash and Iona steak pie. Sully stood looking smug and a damned sight wealthier when Marty stepped over the stuffed cat and took a seat by the bar. "How's it going Sully?"

"Busy as yer like," he said with a sigh and polishing a glass. "Marty me friend, they have a rhythm. Like animals. You can predict their movements... Regular like... They move in herds as if they are following a biological clock."

Marty studied Sully curiously. "Then why do you look so fed up?"

"I miss me old mates. They've evacuated for the crews and there's ney one single domino or tiddly-wink to be seen. I wanted them to see the Lochness Monster rear its ugly head. Over the years that drink's provided many a spectacle. Johnny was our most recent!"

"What's going to happen to them then?" Marty asked glancing around the room.

"Locals got livers like lead. They built their resistance. Now these people are the monster virgins!" he said with a twinkle in his eye. "To say it'll knock them sideways is an understatement!" With a tilt of the head Sully anticipated the outcome. With a cheeky smile he continued to observe the media creatures like prey. "Now back to that media routine: breakfast six forty five to seven forty five, then lunch at one, dinner at seven. Then back out for the night until ten then they'll drink 'til their stupid then stumble to bed... If they'll make it that far."

"So why is that relevant?" asked Marty watching the crews. Sully glared at Marty, was he an imbecile? "They don't seem to be doing shifts Marty. They are working like a herd. It means something..."

With a frown, Marty glanced at the crews, why was their timing so important? What had Sully anticipated?

"It gives us a doorway if we have to step in, if you know what I mean." Sully stared Marty in the eye and waited. With a jolt of

252

realisation the proverbial penny dropped.

"I miss me boys," said Sully. "You know last week I thought I couldn't look at another domino... Then..."

Smack! The door of the tavern swung open, crashing against the wall. There, in the door way, stood a radiant redhead. She looked relatively pleased with herself as she strutted in. Heads turned and an inebriated crew recognised true beauty with the influence of beer goggles.

With a definite strut, Marie made her way to the bar.

"Any luck?" Marty asked.

The room fell silent, even those who were half-conscious listened.

"We have a few rushes darling, but they are for the network only. I think you may have even made the footage with Shana... It was you surfing, wasn't it? We will have an edit tonight."

"I thought that was you in the helicopter," Marty said glancing at Sully who was selecting a pub snack.

"You remember how strong willed I am darling. If I want something I get it! In this case, I had the 'copter sent from Aberdeen. We have it again tomorrow..."

"That will be fun," said Marty vacantly. "Erm by the way will you be visiting my house at all?"

"Darling, there's not really time... We have had our 'us' time today." She rummaged through her handbag and frowned. Where was her phone?

Marty studied his sister, how was that time for them? "But you were there for only a few minutes... I would have thought you might have at least... "

"You don't understand darling. I'm against deadlines, this is my job, my life and I have to get a bloody mermaid and that's it!" she barked.

Marty and Sully leant back, the unexpected viciousness in her voice was astounding.

"I reckon your biological clock is ticking quite loudly missy. Makes women go a bit mad. What are yer thirty five?" said Sully, digging through a bag of pork scratchings.

"No, thirty two..." she replied. "Anyway, I use the best moisturiser!"

"Angry ovaries make a woman go loopy! That's why you feel the need to prove yerself – yer want to be loved," Sully said crunching

253

a pork scratching. "Yer need yerself a man to look after; that'll sort yer out."

"The answer to all things is not a man! A woman can be independent and powerful without a man!"

"A woman needs a man…"

Marie shook her head, "these are modern times - vibrators!"

The bar, which was mainly filled with men, fell silent. There was a buzz in her handbag and everyone stared curiously. "For goodness sake it's my phone!" She pulled out her phone and lifted it in the air. As soon as she stepped to the side it stopped buzzing. Marie glanced at Sully with a bemused frown.

"Signal round here's a bit messed up," he said. "Lucky you waved that phone while it was… you know…"

Marie smiled coyly and put her phone away.

"Fiery one that, and I didn't think women did that sort of thing," whispered Sully.

Marie slapped the bar to get attention "I want room service."

"You'll have to serve yourself," said Sully thoughtfully.

"This bloody place is a battle of wits!" said Marie storming to her room.

Sully admired her stomp and then resumed studying the human animals, "I think she's a lesson brewing - I can feel it in me water and me water's rife. She can't last like that for long without those bricks 'n barriers a-falling down."

"You read people well Sully," said Marty.

"Confined spaces filled with endless life stories. You link up all the pieces and come out with a mess!" he replied. "Now separate to that - time is drawing closer Marty. Those amongst us are feeling it. Longest day is near. Only two days now…" said Sully with concern.

"What are you thinking?"

"We're going to have to do something. Why do you think I'm studying this lot? I do ney like looking at them, do I?"

Marty smiled. No.

"Just so you're ready for it," said Sully turning to Marty. "Some are saying in the village that you sent those pictures. They say you sent them to your sister so you could both become rich and famous. You need to be warned Marty. People turn when this kind of thing happens – they're looking for their goats, the scapegoats."

A look of absolute shock washed over Marty's face.

"I thought so," said Sully. "Look lad, I know it was ney you. You're nort that kind of person. Plus, I watch your sister and there ain't no way you'd be giving stuff to her. Yer innocent – I know it. So that means the culprit is in the village and has access to a decent camera. Who knows what'll turn up next!"

Scraping his fingers through his hair, Marty sighed, "I completely get what they're thinking. It makes sense... How do I prove it wasn't me?"

"You wait for the person who did it rise to the surface!" said Sully studying his young friend.

A series of thoughts stampeded through Marty's mind; did he know who it was? With a chew of the lip, Marty jolted, could Johnny hate them that much that he would betray his own village? He did hate everything to do with them and... The series of events ran through Marty's mind, he couldn't believe it. The evidence was pointing right at him!

While Marty's mind churned Sully poured him a beer. Marty eyed the pint suspiciously.

"No, it's not a Lochness Monster," said Sully with a wink. "It's on the house..."

There was a moment of silence between the pair of them. Sully knew what was going on. "Have yer drink, then go and do what yer need to do! When yer done there'll be a Lochness Monster waiting for yer! It'll blow out any cobwebs and guilt!" he said with a glint of mischief.

CHAPTER 59
Solstice looming.
June 20th

As the sun ventured onto the horizon the film crews followed their schedule perfectly. The teams had set up by eight o'clock and waited for something, anything to happen. Marie's cameraman and soundman watched the other crews. "There ain't no creatures 'ere," said Mark searching the sky for their helicopter.

"I think we all know that, we just need some decent news to break." Matt checked his settings on the sound equipment while Mark rolled himself a cigarette. "We need to find another angle and then get out of here."

With an exaggerated wave, Marie wiggled towards the beach.

"Morning chaps… Now I can see you both look despondent so it's time to shift our thoughts and be positive! We will find a mermaid today and that is it!" she announced. "Oh, and the 'copter will be ready at nine, some Sheikh hired it and they considered him more important... How rude!"

Matt noticed Mark squinting as he licked the paper of his roly. The way that he watched revealed his thoughts. Shana plodded sleepily towards the beach to check the surf, her hair floated elegantly about her shoulders.

Continuing his glance, Mark lit his roly and took a drag. Marie noticed Mark was distracted and followed his gaze. "I know what you're thinking and the answer is no!"

"What about we film her swimming? She would fit the part. We only need a ten-second rush." Mark paused; Marie had already fathomed his plan.

"Never! Mark you know me, and think of our reputation. Imagine faking a bloody mermaid - we would never live it down." She paced with definite arm fold.

"We don't say that she is a mermaid. We report the story and have her swimming as the imagery. That way we cover the story and are able to add footage. The viewer will make assumptions. 'Cause the way we're heading Marie, we'll end up with nothing and that won't help your reputation neither."

Marie sucked her lip through her teeth and glanced at Shana. "We take the helicopter, if nothing comes from that then we will reconsider the idea."

Up on the headland the helicopter landed and Marie and her crew climbed in. "God if they exist let me find them! Amen," she muttered as the helicopter took off.

Mark glanced questioningly at Marie. Something had changed in her; she seemed lighter – more feminine. Had the fresh air enlivened her?

"I feel like something wonderful is going to happen!" she purred.

With a raised eyebrow, Mark caught Matt's eye. He had also noticed something had shifted. Marie was not the usual bitch!

After flying for ten minutes, some colours flashed over the heat sensor. "Look, there's something in a mass and it's got body heat!" said Marie bouncing up and down on her seat. "John can you take us down. Boys get your stuff ready… We have to get this on record!" As the helicopter swooped down, Marie stared at the surface of the ocean and jiggled excitedly.

"Look here... They look the right shape on the sensor. Look – a head, body and weird tail-like thing. It is… Film, film, film!" screeched Marie.

Mark focused on the point shown on the sensor. According to the heat seeker a massive group of creatures swam just below the surface. "RECORD!"

He urgently positioned the camera. There was a sudden flash and a ripple. A moment later, there was nothing. With a shake of the head, he glanced at Marie who also appeared confused. "Whatever that was just simply disappeared," she said, incredulously. She glanced at her crew; they glanced silently at the screen.

"I reckon it's dolphins or porpoises," the pilot said flatly.

"Bugger!" said Marie.

Underwater, Iris glanced towards the surface. The sky hunter was hovering. She had actively cooled her body temperature but that could only work for a short time. Was it enough time for the hunter to give up chasing its prey? The others with her were awaiting her direction.

It was the day before transformation and the group had to take on extra reserves to enable complete metamorphosis.

Up in the helicopter Marie deflated, "that's it! I give up! We tried our best... Do what you have to do to get imagery. I have a headache and I'm going to have a lie down."
With a twinkle in his eye Mark glanced at Matt, he had a 'plan'. That plan might have been Irish but she certainly looked the part. As long as Shana did not speak they were fine!

CHAPTER 60
Fake?

There wasn't any surf so Shana was at a bit of a loss. She had taken an early lunch hour and Johnny was apparently busy with statistics. Out of the corner of her eye, she noticed Marie's film crew walking towards her with a certain walk. What did they want?

"Hi... What would you say to five hundred quid to allow me to film you swimming?" Mark chewed his short nails as he asked.

"Five hundred?" said Shana.

"Yes." Mark studied the girl's poker face.

"What's expected then?"

"A natural looking shot of you swimming... Erm you can cover yourself with your hair," he said awkwardly biting another nail.

"Now, be away with yer. I'm Catholic for goodness sake! What'd me Ma say to seeing her religious daughter all over the news with her bits hanging out?" said Shana with a smirk.

"Seven hundred and fifty then... That's my last offer," he replied.

"I want it in writing and a cheque now. Then I'll put on me tanned tankini," said Shana triumphantly.

He had been taken for a ride! Mark glanced at Matt who shrugged his response.

"I'll give you half now and the other half when we have completed the filming," he said putting his hand out for Shana to shake.

With a definite nod Shana shook his hand. "When shall we film?" she said glancing at her watch. "I need to go back to work for one, but I can ask to finish an hour early and make it up tomorrow," she said thoughtfully, as she watched her cheque being written.

She glanced at the beach. The lunchtime exodus was taking place.

"How long do you think it will take?"

"All I need is film of you swimming. A maximum of ten to fifteen minutes," he replied as he handed her the cheque.

"Right, I'll be back at four, I need to get me swimming cosi on, go to work and then I'll be back," she replied. With that, she broke into a sprint across the beach.

As Shana darted up Straight Lane to the garage, she passed Donald chatting to one of their neighbours. "Innocent until proven guilty! Anyway, you all know the guilty one will be called. Then we'll know who the culprit is. Then see if I'm right about the man-you can buy me my beers for a year…" said Donald trailing off.

At four o'clock Shana sprinted back to the cove wearing her tanned tankini under her hoody and jogging bottoms. Ahead of her, Marie strolled down to the beach. The way she walked was less urgent and her posture less rigid. Shana frowned; Marie was different.

"You're paying her far too much!" said Marie folding her arms.

"It'll be worth it just to get out of here and collect our bonuses!" said Mark looking for support from Matt. He did not respond; he was testing his gun microphone by pointing it at locals and listening to their conversations.

"And how are you going to justify the additional cost? We paid someone to fake?" said Marie pacing.

"No, we will say that the girl provided local knowledge and whereabouts," said Matt, pointing his microphone at Marie. Marie studied him and made a loud exhalation. "Let's just get it done! Then at least I can return to my protein diet and gym."

As Marie considered what to do she paused, she still had that niggling feeling. It was as if she was supposed to be there. Her head kept tingling and her body felt relaxed for the first time in years. She glanced along the harbour; that place did something to her.

"Seems we're crossing paths again Marie," said Shana darting past.

Marie propped herself down on a rock, "mmm. Seems like it-," she said vacantly. She watched Shana curiously; something was bothering her about Shana too. Shana was a very different person now, yet that gut feeling came about when Shana was around. What did she know?

"So show me the second cheque and I will do me swim," said Shana.

Mark opened the chequebook. A pre-written and signed cheque was prepared.

"Let me give it to Johnny," she said. "Oh and we should go

around the corner – away from prying eyes."

"If she doesn't do it we cancel the cheques," said Marie with a shrug.

"I'll go get me-self ready in the lifeguard hut, I'll see you here in a few minutes," she said bouncing excitedly along the beach.
A moment later, Shana burst in to the hut to find Johnny watching Marie through his binoculars. "So much for the statistics- you bloody stalker!"

"I'm on me break and I'm watching a rather beautiful creature," said Johnny.
Since when had Johnny said anything so nice?

CHAPTER 61
Lessons due...

Marty sat in his studio studying his new painting. The image was of Marie underwater peering at the caves behind her. Directly behind her three distorted figures hid beyond her visual periphery.

He sat back in the seat and crossed his legs. Something was bothering him about what Sully had said about Marie. Did she really have a lesson coming?

He took the paintbrush, added in some additional detail and paused. How was he going to approach Johnny about betraying the village? Could he really do such a thing? All the while that the culprit was not found Marty was going to receive the blame. How could he prove them wrong? He wandered into the digital darkroom and switched on his camera. A horrid realisation shot through him. "What on earth?" He really was in trouble now!

"Now Johnny would yer look after me things and stop staring at Marie?"

"Yes and no," answered Johnny, turning to Shana with the binoculars still firmly attached to his eyes.

"Johnny!"

"What?"

"Can't you share in my excitement? A film crew are going to film me... And I am going to be on the television," said Shana, jiggling excitedly.

"Very exciting!" said Johnny, sarcastically. He turned back to admire the female view.

Shana put her hands on her hips, "Johnny!"

"What Shana? You're wearing a tankini in the sea – whoop! The world gets to see something astounding. Why are you doing it anyway?"

"I was offered money to swim. Who wouldn't?" said Shana. "Anyway, once they get the film they will leave."

Johnny sighed, put down the binoculars and gazed at Marie with a look of longing.

"You really fancy her, don't you?" Shana noticed and frowned.

"Leave it Shana!"

"But she's ten years older than you!" said Shana, noticing that Johnny had been reading a dictionary and highlighting words.

"So? She's soooo hot!"

"Well, get some balls and ask her out!" said Shana. "Men just spend all their time dithering and being ball-less. What's the worst that can happen now? Rejection? If she blows you out then at least you got it over and done with!"

Johnny studied Shana. Would a television producer even consider giving a lifeguard the time of day, let alone the time of his life?

"Why don't you come out now and keep a lifeguard's eye on the proceedings? Health and safety and all that... There's no one in the water and if we pop over there none of the crews will see," said Shana watching Johnny blush.

"I like your style," he replied, hiding a book about philosophy and a second about being in touch with emotions.

When Johnny and Shana joined the crew Marie purposely sauntered down to the shoreline. She glanced over her shoulder at Johnny and revealed a slight blush rise up her neck. Quickly she turned her head and recovered. What was going on?

In a small cove, concealed by an outcrop of rocks, Shana placed her towel on the beach. When she was ready she gracefully dived into the water. Once she had arranged her hair she turned to the crew. "What do you want me to do?"

"Just swim but do just do butterfly legs. Oh, and every now and again do a large dive. Do what a mermaid would do."

"I thought they combed their hair," said Shana with a cheeky grin.

With a flick of her hair Marie wiggled over to where Johnny was standing. "Can you sing Shana?"

"You know I can... It's in me blood!" she replied.

"So we have and Irish mermaid singing Celtic songs in Scotland. Marvellous! A tap-dancing leper would be more likely!" said Marie, sharply and folding her arms.

Johnny frowned and glanced curiously at Marie. She could be rather course. He liked it!

"Monomania's a good word," said Johnny, quite randomly in his poshest voice. "It means madness confined to one person you know."

What was he trying to say?

"Right, let's get this done. The sooner we do this the sooner we can all get out of here!" said Mark.

Shana, in the meantime, splashed about quite happily but paused when she realised everyone was waiting. "What do you want me to sing then?"

"Something Celtic," shouted Marie.

"When Irish Eyes Are Smiling," sang Shana at the top of her lungs.

"Funny- very bloody funny!" With an obvious shake of the head, Marie's features soured. "Shana we are running out of time... So please just hum something...."

With a deep breath Shana hummed and then swam. As she hummed she recognised a resonation making its reply. Her heart pulsed; he was nearby. "I'm going to swim now. I'm getting cold," she called. "Oh, and Johnny... you can go back to the tower... I AM GOING to practice my 'FREE-DIVING' now."

Since when had Shana free-dived? He attempted to read Shana's expression for answers but he never had been able to read her.

With that, Shana swam, and after a few beats of her legs she launched into a deep dive. Underwater, her man was waiting. Upon her arrival he instantly wrapped her in his arms and provided her with air as he whisked her away.

There was a ripple on the surface of the water and Shana was gone. Johnny recognised a subtle resonation. With a jolt, he realised Shana's free-dive involved one of 'them.'

"Right, Shana is free-diving so that is it," said Johnny deciding that avoidance was the best tactic. He turned towards the tower and avoided eye contact with any of the crew.

"What is free-diving?" asked Marie watching the water.

"It is where you train yourself to hold your breath for a really long time under water," said Johnny glancing at her.

"Something isn't right," said Marie running beside him. She took hold of his arm and gazed into his eyes. Johnny melted and felt a twitch in his nether regions. There was a silence between them; Marie blushed in response. Neither said a thing.

Mark and Matt watched, was that what had happened to Marie? Was that why she was in a better mood?

"Don't worry, she'll be fine, she's an excellent swimmer. I think she might even have a pony canister on her. She's more than likely doing this free-diving to wind you up!"

"How can you be so sure?" Marie asked suspiciously, but finding herself tracing her fingers along the soft skin of Johnny's inner arm.

"When Shana says she's free-diving, it means leave me alone," said Johnny, crossing his legs. "Now she will be fine. Marie I need to go and sit down." Johnny thought about all manner of disgusting things. Cockroaches, mashed sprouts and toenail fungus. Anything to stop stiffy-publicus humiliation!

Alarm bells mixed with butterflies were in conflict in every part of Marie's being. Her intuition was at odds with her level of desire.

"Look, over there... She just surfaced... There is really nothing to worry about!" he said pointing. While Marie followed the direction Johnny pointed in, he conveniently arranged the towel to hide any potential groin-raising embarrassments.

"I can't see her," said Marie.

Johnny bent down, put his arm around Marie's shoulder and pointed. "Come on Marie, you're ney looking hard enough." He gently adjusted the hair from the side of her neck and pulled her close.

"Is that her? At that distance?" she asked incredulously.

"There's a lot you don't know about Shana," he replied.

"It still isn't reading right, can I borrow a board?" asked Marie. "I want to have a bit of a paddle."

"You ever been on a board before?" asked Johnny, returning to his full manly stance.

"Of course I have," she said avoiding eye contact. "Anyway, it can't be that difficult!"

"The paddling isn't difficult but the sea constantly changes... Now I really think it's better you don't," he said glancing at his watch. It was gone five and he had to clear the remaining flags. The other guards were now off duty.

Placing her hand on her hip, Marie gazed seductively into his eyes, "but if you keep an eye on me I will be safe won't I?" She dropped

265

her chin and spoke in a little girl's tone.
He couldn't help it, he melted.

In the lifeguard hut Johnny hid the dictionary he had been making notes in, and against his better judgement gestured at one of his old boards. "You can take Pearl, but be careful with her. She has been the love of my life!"

"And do you happen to have a spare wetsuit?" she said with a flick of the hair.

"Shana's spare wetsuit is hanging up over there," he said, pointing at a hook. "You can change behind that curtain. Marie I really think you should reconsider… You're putting yourself in unnecessary danger for the sake of a stupid myth!"

"The world is a myth Johnny, I work generating myths… How else would society survive if it didn't have a story to follow?" There was a drawn silence, not only was the woman beautiful but did he fancy her brain too? Was it possible to be attracted to a mind?

"You know if there is something out there I will find it," she said peering from behind the curtain. Johnny noticed her bare shoulder and bra strap. He took a deep breath and concentrated on the image of giant tortoises eating bananas.

"So… Erm.. Is there room for a man in that busy London life of yours?"
Marie was silent for a while, "I keep my private life private," she finally replied.

"So that would be a no then. You just work…" said Johnny listening to Marie struggling with the wetsuit.

"I have plenty of choice…but…"

"Do you want some help?"

"No… I can manage by myself."
Johnny shook his head and smiled to himself. "Everyone can do things by themselves but the fun is sharing it with someone else." Marie poked her head from behind the curtain and studied him.

"Okay… I give in…" She stood in front of him. With her back revealed Johnny concentrated on old people eating porridge. "Look Marie, there's a swell coming in," he said directing her to look at the ocean. As he tugged at the back of the wetsuit, Marie remained silent with her eyes closed. The chemistry filled the silence.

"If you're going to play this game, be careful," he said tucking in the remaining flaps. "There really is a storm due and I do ney want you getting hurt," he said turning her towards him. Marie gazed into his eyes and sighed, "Johnny my intuition tells me these creatures exist. I have to find them. That is my job. It is your job to save people. That is our nature. Now I will find them. Thank you for your concern." She bit her lip as she gazed at his solid arms. She followed the Celtic tattoo up his arm to his neck and onto his face. The desire to touch it was overwhelming.

"Why do you have a tattoo on your face Johnny?"
He smiled, "I'll tell you over a drink when you get back."
She studied him and smirked, "I would like that."
With a sudden jolt, Johnny attempted to conceal his shock. She had agreed to have a drink with him!!!! Was there a mutual attraction?

Back on the beach, Mark and Matt re-watched their film clip. Marie wiggled in her wetsuit whilst Johnny carried the board. There was a moment when Matt and Mark glanced at each other. There was an unspoken understanding and a pair of subtle smirks. Nothing was said aloud but both had 'clocked' the same thing.

"I reckon we have what we need for our bonus," said Mark.
"I think we should get it sent through as soon as possible," Matt replied. "Before any of the other teams."
"Have a break 'n have a beer once it's sent," said Mark. "I'll wait for the girl and keep an eye on Marie. Although, I think she might be in some rather safe hands." With a wink, he watched Matt pack up his equipment and leave for them.

CHAPTER 62
Heart connection.

In the depths the man of the sea guided Shana to the caves. Using his body heat he kept her warm. After providing her with a lung-full of air, he leant back so she could glimpse their location. A luminous oak at the centre of a circle of ancient stones was below. Just beyond the stone circle was a series of entrances belonging to underwater caves. Each entrance was marked by the luminous material. Particles of light shimmered and shoals of fish undulated amongst them. It was divine. In that moment her heart pulsated, she felt so connected with life yet she could very easily be on the edge of death.

Her eyes revealed her feeling. Her man gazed at her, returned to kissing and providing her with air. Passion and life was all that Shana could feel. She had opened to an entirely different existence, one that she had never perceived before.

An immense carving with luminous pattern decorated the entrance to the cave. Shana studied the stone. From what she could gather, there was no easy way to shift it. Shana shared a breath and then watched as her man resonated in a certain tone. That tone initiated the luminous material of the stone to retract and reveal an entrance.

With another breath of life in her lungs, the man of the sea whisked her through the silvery warren filled with light particles. After another life-giving breath, Shana glanced over her man's shoulder to watch the gateway re-seal itself. The speed at which they travelled and his agility through the numerous rock structures was specific but powerful. Finally, they slowed down to arrive in the blue pool where the burial had taken place previously.

Once inside, he lifted Shana to sit on edge of the pool. "It's colder out of the water than in, though of course I don't have your body heat to heat me," she said with a shiver. The man of the sea smiled blankly at her.

"A man who doesn't talk and has to listen - perfect!" said Shana, pulling her knees into her chest and gazing at the beautiful creature before her.

He smiled and caressed her goose-pimples. "I know I'm cold, I need your body heat," she said gesturing. With a smile he welcomed her into a cosy embrace. "A living, beautiful hot-water bottle!" she whispered, as he infused her with his body heat.

For a moment he gazed into her eyes and she could sense a passion within him that she felt in herself. With a coy smile she leant forward and surrendered to passion. A tingle ran up her spine and through her whole body. In that moment she was absolutely connected.

CHAPTER 63
Resistance and pride.

Stubborn was an understatement when it came to Marie. Johnny was learning that more by the moment. The more he said not to go out in the storm, the more she rebelled.

"Mark can I have the small digital underwater camera please?" she said.

"We have enough footage. Matt is sending it off now," he replied. "I wouldn't bother putting yourself in danger when we probably have already sealed the bonus."

"Mark you know how my intuition is always right. I sense that these creatures exist and I intend to capture them on film! You know me – it has to be that way." She studied the digital camera in Mark's hand; it was small, compact and ideal for what she needed.

"I just think it's pointless," he said, folding his arms. "And what does the lifeguard say?"

"I think she is about to paddle into a storm without any experience of surfing. No offence, but that is sheer stupidity!"

"You won't stop me! Now Mark, the Camera," she said open-palmed.

With a loud sigh, he shook his head and handed her a digital underwater camera.

For a short while she fiddled with the settings. "It will be ready when I need it."

"Look, as much as I think yer being a dick, I'll keep an eye out for yer. Is there nothing I can say that will stop yer?" Johnny watched Marie; her stubbornness must have been one of her weaknesses. At least she had a weakness!

With a shake of the head, Marie gazed into Johnny's eyes. The pair were slightly more rouge than a pair should be out on a windy beach. Mark watched with amusement, he had never seen Marie behave in such a way around a man before. It was actually quite sweet.

A wave washed over Marie's feet and broke the moment. She took the camera and attached it by a strap to her wrist. "Can you help me get the board in the water," she said with a girlish pout. Johnny took the board to the water's edge and waded with her. "Marie be careful. I mean it. These waters can be treacherous."

"Darling, I have spent the last ten years surviving war zones. This is easier than that!"

"Never be arrogant with the ocean. She can be the biggest bitch when she chooses," he said shaking his head. "Now tie the leash to your ankle, lay on the board and paddle," said Johnny, noticing that Marie was at a loss. "Marie you really are wasting your time and you're putting yourself in danger. Even if they did exist they would know where you were and keep away."

"Well, I'm going and that's it!"

"God, you're a stubborn little shyte!" he said.

"A shyte?"

Johnny nodded, "now go for a little paddle and then come back. Then we can have that drink!"

"Wait for me then," she said with a certain look.

"I'm not going anywhere. Now if there are any problems please swallow your pride and come back in."

With a deep breath she launched onto the board and attempted to paddle erratically. Using a pretty front-crawl motion she didn't move very far.

"It's all about rhythm Marie. Now displace more water like this," he said demonstrating his paddling motion. "Paddle evenly otherwise you'll go in circles," he called noticing Marie wasn't moving in a straight line.

Her red face revealed her effort level and frustration. Marie had always been naturally good at everything and for the first time she revealed another weakness but, of course, she would not give in!

Mark stood next to Johnny with his arms folded, "you know this is the first time she has not been naturally good at something. I have been searching for a weakness for years. Then you come along," he said with a wink.

"Me gran always said the people who had the strongest exterior are the weakest inside. Why else would they build such armour?"

Mark turned and studied Johnny, "there's more to you than meets the eye isn't there?"

"People do ney look into the depths when the surface shines," said Johnny smugly.

Just beyond the break Marie aligned herself with the board; she had it! Her arms co-ordinated and she began to cut through the water. Unfortunately, paddling was exhausting. With her last remaining strength she navigated an approaching set and uneasily sat on the board. When she glanced over her shoulder she realised the beach was an eternity away and she didn't have the reserves to paddle back. What was she doing? What was she trying to prove? Once steady, she glanced at the horizon, the storm clouds were brewing and filled with lightning. She was in trouble and her ego had taken her there! Why couldn't she have listened?

With his binoculars raised, Johnny stood watching Marie from the shore. "It's getting late. She looks like she's had enough. It's nearing six thirty. She's been out there for over an hour."

"Stubborn blighter," said Mark.

"I'll give her ten more minutes and then I'll go get her," said Johnny with a sigh.

"Leave her. You need to teach her a lesson. You shouldn't have to rescue her. She needs to come in alone otherwise you'll go after her and she'll refuse you. She has to relent in all senses of the word," said Mark with a certain knowing smile.

"I'm not trying to break a wild horse!" said Johnny with a frown.

"You are trying to break something far tougher than that!"

"As much as I would like her to swallow her pride, that bolshiness is also what makes her attractive," Johnny replied honestly.

"You obviously like the fire and the hunt," said Mark with a grin. "The alpha female and all that."

"I like her fight and determination. Why be with someone who's not a challenge?"

"You know what's funny is when Marie first started in news she was a lovely girl. Something happened to her that made become power hungry and competitive. She soon became the construct," said Mark folding his arms.

"The nice girl must still be in there somewhere," said Johnny thoughtfully.

"Are you really willing to take all that on? It will be like taming a tiger!" said Mark.

"It's ney my place to tame her, but I am willing to peel back the layers of the onion," replied Johnny.

"Even if it makes you cry?" Thoughtfully, Mark studied the horizon. "Let's face it, we're not going to find any of those sea creatures. Even if they actually exist the locals are doing a fine job of hiding them." He carefully watched Johnny's reaction.

"What about Shana's clip?" asked Johnny curiously.

"It's already been sent. That's where the youngen went. The sooner we get it to the newsroom the sooner we can get on with a decent story - one that has meaning!"

"So when'll it be on?"

"It will probably be played tonight and tomorrow. That's as long as no one else comes up with anything better. Fingers crossed - eh?" Mark said with a hand gesture.

"What's the date tomorrow?"

"21st of June."

"Solstice?" asked Johnny Boy with a look of concern. Why was that relevant?

CHAPTER 64
Mesmerisation

A deeply disturbed sleep tossed Danny around his bed. Amongst the dream he shook, trembled and muttered. The dead girl was resonating and summoning him. Her deathly, penetrating eyes peered into the depths of his soul. She reached out, calling and coaxed him to the ocean. He would come to her!

"Stop plaguing me will yer?" he screamed. He covered his ears and buried his head in the pillows.

"Fey o' fey yer go away…" he repeated desperately as he curled into foetal position.

The sound did not cease but penetrated his mind. The curtains billowed with a draft as the shadow of a woman travelled across the room. The baby hairs on Danny's neck bristled.

"Danny wake… Yer made an innocent mistake... Yer canny die because of the blood. Danny let go - I beg yer," whispered the transparent figure as she reached for him.
Danny curled tighter into a ball but the calling grew more intense. His resistance waned; there was only a matter of time before he would break.

"I've been trying to warn yer Danny but yer did ney listen, now wake!"
Nothing.

The dead girl called more urgently and seized Danny's mind, he had to give in and go to her! Throwing the covers aside, he stood barefoot wearing only his board shorts. The constant summoning tugged at his core. It was as if an invisible rope was pulling him to the ocean, to her. Once united, the calling would cease but that meant death.

The sun touched the edges of the rolling, black clouds. With a constant fidget Johnny fought with himself. At that moment Marie was fine, Mark was right, she had to choose to return. It was her choice and one he should not force. Yes, he desperately wanted to save her.

"Mate, I'm sorry but I haven't eaten since seven, that's over twelve hours. I gonna have to get some food," said Mark.

Johnny felt awkward and hatched a plan: he was going to give her a maximum of thirty minutes. After that he had to give in and go to the rescue! In the meantime, there was no way Johnny was leaving that spot. He checked his jacket pocket for snacks: a packet of scampi-flavoured crisps and a chocolate bar.

"She'll come in eventually," said Mark, patting his back.

Would she? She was the most stubborn woman he had ever met! He lifted the binoculars - nothing had changed. Marie was still floating on the surface of the water with flush and a look of aggravation.

"Give me a call when she emerges. Here's my number." Mark handed him his phone number before heading up the beach.

With a glance at the handwritten paper, Johnny watched Mark walk towards the harbour. If he rescued Marie, at least he could have some tea. Johnny noticed a familiar figure approaching from the harbour. He peered through the binoculars, what was Danny doing now? It was late evening and he was walking vacantly towards the ocean wearing only board shorts in a storm.

"What goes on in that mind of his?" muttered Johnny.

With a quick glance over his shoulder, he realised he needed to keep an eye on Marie. Yet there was something very odd about Danny. His gut had revealed it.

The sea spray rose and formed the deathly figure of the girl. Every step closer Danny made, the more the resonation intensified. With her arms wide open, she beckoned him further into the ocean. He was going to drown!

"Oh God Danny!" muttered Johnny with a jolt.

The swell of the storm lifted the peaks of the waves and the water grew murky. The ocean had shifted mood; her anger filled the sky with lightning and vicious rumblings.

"Shit!" Johnny cursed, scanning the area. Now where was Marie?

A tavern filled with chatter and the smell of beef stew greeted Mark when he stepped through the door. He stepped over the stuffed cat and noticed Matt balanced precariously on a barstool. He rested his chin on his hand as he listened to an epic tale about a witch. Sully was enacting the poor woman's fourth round of dunking. His hands flayed as he screamed and then made gurgling noises using a glass of dark brown stout.

"Evening," said Mark, testing a stool before he sat on it. A moment later, his top pocket began to vibrate. "I thought there was no signal here," he said in surprise.

"And then she drowned, so she was innocent..." said Sully.

"On the right side of the pub there is ney signal but on the left there is. We call it the dividing phenomenon. No one can figure it out but that's the fun of it," replied Sully. "Dead but innocent... that poor witch – shame eh?" he reiterated.

Mark glanced at Matt who wore a fool's grin.

"Is that a Lochness Monster?" Mark eyed Matt's beer with suspicion.

"I sent off the clip. We don't have to get up early tomorrow because we've done our jobs. Sully here told me that the monster would warm me cockles up and me cockles are a raging inferno," he said with a slur.

"Want your cockles warmed Mark?" asked Sully with a smirk. "It's happy hour and that monster will make you euphoric during this happy time!"

Mark nodded, re-dialled the number and stepped into the area with a signal. While Sully poured the drink, he listened intently.

"Hello, you just called Marie's mobile," said Mark.

"Who is this? Where's Marie?" replied the rather cutting tone of the network Controller, Jonathon.

"Marie is otherwise engaged," he said flatly, watching Sully pretending to mind his own business. "The signal's terrible here. We could cut out at any time," whispered Mark.

"Well? Speak up..." said Jonathan.

Mark shifted his stool slightly to the left. "She's on a surf board looking for erm 'more' creatures..." said Mark trailing off. It sounded ridiculous!

"Of course she is," said Jonathan. "Why the hell aren't you out there with her?"

"She wanted to go alone. She was determined... Plus we have been busy sending you what we already have..." he replied with a wink at Matt.

"Well, when you see her tell I'll be arriving tomorrow… The rushes have sparked an international response. It has gone viral on the net and I want to oversee the proceedings!"

With a slight gulp Mark glanced at Matt and covered the mouthpiece. "It's gone viral!"

The Lochness Monster exploded from Matt's nostrils. "Since when does angry Johnny get involved? He doesn't usually leave the station!"

"So the bonus is yours… So how did you get one on film when they don't actually exist?" asked Jonathon.

Sully studied the pair; they needed a few more monsters before they would confess everything!

With a jiggle of the stool to the right, the connection began to crackle.

"You're breaking up," said Mark.

Sully watched curiously.

"You sound like you're in the distance." Mark raised the phone at arm's length and continued to speak as though he was in a cave.

"Okay, I'll see you tomorrow bright and…" The line went dead.

Mark shifted awkwardly, he sat with his head bowed and his arms crossed.

Matt gazed at him, "I hate that man. He's a control bloody freak!"

"Anything exciting?" Sully asked curiously.

"The story just went international and viral…" said Mark.

"But there is nothing to film… They do ney exist!" said Sully slapping his hand on the bar.

There was an uncomfortable shifting as Sully studied the pair. "Oh dear…" he said when he realised what had happened. "Gentlemen, we want this village to remain peaceful. We do ney want it ruined by a theme park to some non - existent creature. We like to keep ourselves to ourselves."

"We thought we would send a clip, get it over and done with and then leave you to it," said Mark with a sigh. "We really didn't mean it to happen. We just wanted to get back to London. I am so sorry!"

"Will it be scampi with chips then?" asked Sully, accepting that whatever happened next simply had to unfold.

"Scampi and chips would be lovely," Mark replied guility, whilst attempting to find a comfortable position on the wonky stool and scraping his fingers through his hair. On the way to the kitchen Sully peered out of the window, the second phase of storm was moving in. The calling had begun.

On the beach the wind howled and whipped up the waves. In a state of absolute mesmerisation Danny took his first steps into the ocean. The water was freezing but he was numb. With a tug at the core of his soul he trudged forwards. She had him. He had surrendered!

If Johnny went to Danny then Marie would be lost. If he stayed where he was, his friend would drown. In that moment, he was torn; either way someone was going to suffer. Which was the most likely option to enable him to save both?

Out to sea Marie clung to the board as the waves tossed her about like drift wood. For the first time in many years she felt sick, weak and vulnerable. She had actively placed herself in a powerless situation where she could die. What was the point?

Danny being entranced and closest to death was how Johnny finalised his decision. With a glance up the beach, Johnny aligned his position with two rocks jutting from the sand. The question was: would Marie be lucky enough to avoid being caught in a rip tide?

The apparition of the girl kept calling. Danny reached out but the ocean was resistant. The more he attempted to drive forwards, the more the waves pushed him back. The mesmerisation had possessed him because now he absolutely desired to be with her! He fought to move forwards and wrestled to reach her but she was just beyond his reach! Just a few steps deeper and they would be united!

Breaking into a sprint Johnny darted across the beach. The ocean, as it ebbed, was level with Danny's throat. One wave and he would be gone. The apparition glanced towards Johnny; she was close and Johnny would not stop her! With a flash of lightning, the wind tore across the sand and shingle pelted him. A second blast of wind forced

Johnny backwards. At the same time he felt a sudden pang - Marie was in trouble too!

Gathering all his strength and will, Johnny threw off his jacket, put his head down and drove his body against the wind. He was determined! As he glanced ahead he saw the apparition rising and gathering power. The girl's hurt and rage was her fuel. A wave rose up behind her; she grinned victoriously as waves swirled around Danny and consumed him. He was hers!

"Shit!" screamed Johnny as Danny vanished. With a distinctive dive, Johnny submerged. Nothing! Frantically he scoured the depths. He had a matter of minutes… Where was he?

Marie sobbed with the feeling of absolute helplessness. She was alone, out of control and couldn't see a way out of the situation. Was it the end? Why hadn't she listened when she was warned? Why hadn't she demonstrated her attraction to him? What was she trying to prove? No one really cared! It was helpless and pathetic! The first shiver ran down her spine, her body temperature was in decline. It was just a matter of time before hyperthermia set in.

"Help!" she screamed.

Silence.

Gathering all her strength, she attempted to paddle ashore. She was too weak.

In the end she simply clung to the board, closed her eyes and accepted her fate. As she slipped into unconsciousness, a subtle hum filled the air. Death was singing to her.

Was there any point trying one more time? As Johnny caught his breath, he made a decision. If he didn't find Danny this time - that was it! Danny's family curse would have been resolved. With his eyes closed, Johnny took a series of deep breaths and concentrated on the image of finding Danny. In that moment, a picture of Danny stuck in the depths and held by the apparition filled his mind. The girl was preparing to persuade Danny to breath in the ocean. His body was resistant – he wanted to survive!

"No," Johnny muttered. She would not have her revenge with Danny's life. Johnny would not allow it. It was now his will over hers!

Yet another powerful wave broke over the limp figure clinging to the board. In a state of unconsciousness, a wave picked Marie up and hurled into the bitter ocean. A second wave ripped the leash from her foot. For a while the ocean toyed with her like lion cubs with prey. Finally, there was no resistance left; it was then that the ocean devoured her and left only the yellow board behind. She was gone.

The resonation cut through the water. The hypnotising sound penetrated his mind; she had set her intent on drowning Johnny too. He would not tolerate it! With a definite motion, Johnny swam towards the origin of the sound.

The last vestiges of breath evacuated Danny's lungs as he reached for the girl. The spark of connection travelled through the water as he reached for her extended hand. He was about to step into the realm 'in between'. She gazed triumphantly into the depths of his soul.

Smack!

Rage flushed through Danny's whole body – he had relented and now his forced removal had destroyed his unison! In that moment, the apparition transformed from the image of innocence into her polarity. She exploded into rage and clutched at Danny's throat. The current became turbulent and dragged Johnny backwards. He clung to his friend as he kicked towards the surface. His will was not wavering. He intended to save his friend and survive!

The constant wriggling from Danny made the ascent difficult. The resistance drove Johnny to kick harder to the surface. His lungs were already empty and in a matter of seconds, his reflex would force him to inhale the ocean. If Danny continued to struggle they would both drown. Danny had to let go but he fought. The more he battled, the more she restricted his throat. Johnny's lungs ached with exertion as he kicked his hardest. As if that wasn't enough, a 'glimpse' of Marie entered his mind - a limp figure, suspended in the dark depths of the ocean. Death was ready to seize her.

CHAPTER 65
Truth of the soul.

In the depths of darkness there was a sound. Time was elongated and no sense of direction could be determined. Only the sensations of rushing through a black void accompanied by a few random oscillations were impressed on Marie's unconscious mind. Her body felt light, like there was no gravity; all that remained was a piercing coldness.

Bursting from depths Johnny broke through and gasped for breath. He urgently dragged Danny to the surface but a wave pummelled his limp body. His airway was constricted and his heartbeat lost. With numerous arm pulls, Johnny hauled Danny towards the shore. Once out of the ocean maybe they would stand a chance.

With gritted teeth, Johnny lugged the weighty figure and plonked him down on the sand. He checked again for a pulse – nothing! With sheer determination, he attempted to resuscitate him - he was dead!

Behind Johnny, the ocean morphed into a figure. A scream of euphoria resonated from the girl as she rose victoriously into the air. With her arms outstretched and her back arched, she grinned triumphantly at the moon. The water droplets constructing her translucent body dispersed and then dissolved. The storm became the vessel for her final release of rage. It had gained power and would soon reach its peak.

Danny's dead shell remained in a heap with his friend frantically attempting to resuscitate him.

"Breathe yer git!" shouted Johnny, filling Danny's lung's with air. "Yer ney going to die for this airy fairy crap!"

With a jolt Danny inhaled but began to struggle.

Slap!

"Pull it together Danny. Come out of it!"

His eyes remained glazed and focused in the distance.

"Come on, Danny wake up!" How could Johnny tell if the calling had stopped? It was all in Danny's mind and the last thing he wanted was for Danny to wander back into the ocean! The storm calmed briefly, but that was the illusion. Her power was growing and the atmospheric static revealed that she intended to release her full wrath!

"You are not going to take him! I won't let yer leave him like this!" he muttered. Hastily, he hoisted Danny onto his shoulder and lumbered towards the harbour. He had to break the trance. If it was broken then maybe he stood a chance.

The rhythm of his feet pounding on sand freed up Johnny's mental space. A series of images of Shana at the kitchen table travelled through his mind. The Bolognese, how Danny licked his lips and something that Shana had said gave him an inkling of hope. He laid Danny on the harbour, darted across the beach to retrieve his jacket and rummaged through his pocket for the scampi snacks. Once he was back with Danny, he opened the packet and sniffed. "If these don't bring yer back then nothing will!"

Chewing his lip in concern, he wafted the packet beneath Danny's nose and waited. For a few seconds Danny's eyes remained glazed and fixed longingly on the ocean. In desperation, Johnny jammed the whole packet over his nose.

With a loud cough, Danny jolted. "What the?"

Johnny smiled and hugged his friend.

"Johnny what yer doing and where am I?" Danny asked glancing at the ocean.

"Danny can yer hear her?"

"It's stopped," he said tipping his head to the side.

"Keep that packet of crisps under yer nose. It has woken yer up and stopped the calling. All the while that bag of crisps is under yer nose yer safe – yer hear?"

The smell was making Danny's eyes water, but at least he did not hear her anymore.

"I need you to stay where I can see yer but yer need to contact yer gran and find out what to do. I now have to find Marty's sister - she's disappeared too. I have to call Marty so do not move!"

Danny held his face with one hand; it throbbed. With the other, he kept the crisps positioned below his nostrils. He didn't say anything; instead, he sat watching the ocean growing in fury. She was out there somewhere and her rage was apparent. He needed his gran, he needed to know how to make things right!

"I'll get you some fresh clothes from the hut, in the meantime wear my jacket - there's chocolate inside. Oh and Danny I worked out what you did… You bloody idiot!" said Johnny launching into a jog.

"I don't understand. I don't get why this is happening. I didn't do anything wrong…" he replied.

"You rejected her - plain and simple! Rejection hurts Danny. She exchanged the pain she felt from that rejection with your life. They are not human – they do ney have resistance!" With that, he turned and ran across the sand.

Danny gazed at the ocean and kept the scampi crisps under his nose. There had to be a way to make his peace and find his resolution. He didn't mean to reject her, he wasn't even aware that he had!

In the lifeguard hut Johnny changed into his survival suit and quickly warmed up. After calling the other lifeguards he realised the unexpected storm was now occupying their time. What's more, the storm was gaining momentum. When it released its full power, the village would suffer. In that moment Johnny had a revelation: rejection had the power to motivate destruction. He had never considered it before. The winds picked up and the waves battered anything in their path. All of this was because Danny had really messed up!

With a chew of the lip, Johnny glanced at the phone and dialled. "Marty you might want to get down here. Marie's in the ocean and I can't see where she is. The other lifeguard crews are out picking up yachts and ships… And… "

The clench of the fist and the grit of teeth revealed Marty's feelings. Slamming down his phone, he grabbed his coat and sprinted down Straight Lane. "My sister's in the ocean. Can you get Sully down to the beach please," he called, running past Donald.

Butch watched Marty and cocked his leg on a pair of shoes on a front step.

There had to be answer! With a constant pace Johnny walked back and forth from one end of the hut to the other.

"There are no available men or vessels," said the voice at

headquarters at the end of the line.

"There has to be someone or something…" said Johnny.

"This storm came from nowhere. There was no indication on the forecast, so it caught all the vessels off-guard. Johnny you are going to have to solve this one alone," was the final response.

Since when had Johnny been in such a situation with no support?

After an urgent power walk up Straight Lane, Donald burst into the tavern. Sully glanced at his old friend; Donald's furrowed brow said it all!

Clang! Sully rang the bell for last orders.

"It ain't time yet," said one of the crew glancing at his watch.

"It's time when I say it's time lads, and there's a storm with people drowning. We need to save lives!"

The crews downed their drinks and took their leave.

The expression of concern revealed Sully's thoughts as he gazed at the storm through the window. With a shake of the head, Donald glanced at his old friend. That was just the beginning.

The torrential rain wouldn't stop Marty. He ran as swiftly as he could to the life guard hut and found Johnny preparing his jet ski.

"Where is she?" he panted.

"Marty I did everything to stop her but she wouldn't have any of it!" he said, leading Marty to the markers. "She was level with this when I last saw her. There was no one around to help and… well someone else was in trouble too…"

Sully drove his hulky Land Rover onto the beach. The headlights illuminated Danny who sat silently in the torrential rain with a packet of crisps under his nose.

Sully glanced at Donald; something about the scene was out of sorts.

With a slam of the Land Rover door, Sully, Butch and Donald put their heads down and battled the wind to the shoreline.

"What's happening?" asked Sully. He battled against the wind to get to Johnny and Marty.

"Marie took me board. She was determined to find them- fish people," said Johnny.

"I can't believe you let her out of your sight. What kind of lifeguard are you?" said Marty scathingly.

"An off duty lifeguard trying to stop the most determined woman he ever met! Standing in front of an avalanche would have been easier! Have you ever been in that situation Marty?" replied Johnny.

From the harbour wall Danny watched the conflict brewing. He didn't want any part of it. With the packet of crisps under his nose he headed back to the cottage. His mind churned the previous events, he felt sick. He needed to sleep but how did he know she wouldn't call him again? He was stuck!

"Look there is no use being angry with me! I'm not to blame!" said Johnny.

"You left my sister to drown Johnny! What am I supposed to think?" shouted Marty.

"That and the fact you brought this on the village!" said Marty, pointing accusingly.

Johnny shook his head and studied his friend. After all that had happened how could he possibly think he was the culprit?

There were frowns and glances between Sully and Donald. Could Johnny really be the betrayer? One thing was for certain, the feeling of rage filled the air. Something was about to kick off.

With a shove, Johnny barged past Marty.

"You're abandoning again Johnny. Whenever anything big happens, you run the other way. Coward!" said Marty, viciously. There was definite silence and a clap of thunder. Johnny turned slowly. No one called him a coward! Smack! Marty grabbed his jaw. The throbbing pain took him by surprise. As Johnny walked away Marty ran and jumped on his back, dragging him to the ground. Butch barked excitedly as the two men rolled about the floor, encrusting themselves in wet sand.

"What's going on?" whispered Donald.

"I think Marty thinks that Johnny left Marie to drown and caused this situation. As a kind of guess I think our Marty's unresolved anger has finally broken through!" replied Sully.

"Do you think Johnny was the one?" asked Donald curiously.

285

"Nope, because she would ney have allowed him to find her," he said.

"Don't you think we should break this up then?"

"No. It's their dispute. They need to resolve it," he replied.

"Over there," Donald pointed to a solitary, yellow board. "Look, the leash has been torn off too. Sully, she came up here to find 'them'. I hope to God they've found her, it's her only chance."

The pair left the pair rolling in the sand and dragged the lone board up the beach. The fighting ceased when the pair noticed the shape out of the corner of their eyes.

As Marty stood up, he wiped the blood from his mouth and glanced at Johnny. He traced his finger over the cut on his own brow as the blood mingled with rain.

"Was that what she was on Johnny?" Marty asked as he walked over and crouched beside it.

"Yeh," said Johnny. "And whatever you might think of me I would never go behind a mate's back, nor would I go against the village. I am not the one who caused this," said Johnny. "There are others who are less obvious close by!"

"I couldn't give a shit! I just want my sister to be alive. I can't deal with another death," he said with tears merging with the rain. Marty stared out to sea for a moment, then wiped the snot from his nose and turned towards Donald and Sully. "Tell me honestly. Does she stand a chance?"

CHAPTER 66
Facing shadows

With the flush of the cheek and the power of passion, Shana glowed with love. She had never experienced anything like it – the connection between her and her man had ignited something deep within her. The unison was innocent, pure and so very respectful. The feeling filled her heart with joy and an absolute connection with life. She actually felt love.

Beneath the surface of the turquoise pool, two souls had united their thoughts, senses and emotions. The connection was beyond anything Shana could have possibly imagined. As soon as she surrendered he recognised her authentic self and accepted it. What's more, he did not hide or run away; he gave it back. It was not like humanity, instead the innocence and lack of boundary was refreshing but daunting. Shana understood why the 'creatures' broke so easily. With such pure and open hearts they had no defences. Rejection literally killed them. Rejection made their existence pointless, and in that state they chose to remove themselves from this 'plane.' It was a strange phenomenon but Shana had discovered the answers as soon as her heart had opened and fully revealed its truth. The love in that moment was eternal! She did not want that 'now' to end.

In the glow of passion a dark shape snagged the periphery of Shana's vision. The figure laid on the edge of the pool. The distraction made her 'man' follow her gaze to the surface. He smiled into Shana's eyes and illuminated her soul. Their perfect moment was at an end because someone else demanded attention.

Cautiously, Shana climbed up on to the white surface and tested the pulse on Marie's jugular. It was weak and her skin cold. At least she was breathing. Shana glanced at her man who rested his chin on the edge of the pool. Her mischievous expression revealed her plan as she searched the area for a loose piece of shinny stalagmite. She found one and gestured for permission from her 'man'. He raised an eyebrow and smiled, he knew her intention. She picked up one of the protrusions and avoided peering into it. She wasn't ready to see what she truly was. During the motion, a second 'creature' rose in the pool and watched Shana's antics curiously.

Marie had drifted off when Shana pressed her hand flat into Marie's wetsuit clad stomach. "She's unconscious," she said to the onlookers.

They did not understand. It seemed that mental images did not travel through air so well.

"Here we go." Shana pointed at Marie. "Limmer (Rogue), Tinne" (lost).

In response to the bemused expressions, Shana attempted her best mime. The two men smiled at her efforts. The man who brought Marie in made an attempt at a reply. "Sonsie," he said (meaning -Jolly good looking).

Shana studied him as he gestured at Marie's face. She shook her head in response. "Ney" said Shana. "Stravaig!" (wonders aimlessly).

The man maintained a sympathetic expression as he looked at Shana, gestured to Marie's heart and covered his own. Shana didn't know what he meant and frowned. He then gestured again at the heart and demonstrated that Marie's heart had been broken.

Shana peered at Marie, something made sense. Had she become such a bitch because heart had been broken? Was that her way to cover her hurt?

The man then gestured again. He could not connect to a heart that was broken or unavailable. Shana chewed her lip, in that moment she had a revelation.

"My heart called you didn't it?" she said aloud. The series of events flashed through her mind. Her heart had called her man. Marty's heart had called Iris and Danny... Oh God, Danny had called but was not ready for the connection. Instead, he had broken it by mistake. He hadn't listened to his heart; instead, he had been in his mind. Shana had been lucky, her man could have seen her with Danny too, and it would have destroyed him. She sat for a moment in contemplation; the timing was immaculate. Suddenly it all made sense. It was no accident, the resonance had known they all existed. It had called them to that specific place at that specific time. Marie had also been called; she had to see what she had become for her to be able to love again. "Mus ploy" - (must do something), "El daft" - (she is mentally deranged), said Shana, waving the mirror. The men of the sea gazed at the woman sympathetically. The woman was about to witness the truth of her own bitterness.

"Am I dead? Am I in heaven?" said Marie, her eyelashes flickering. She lifted herself, rested on her elbows and gazed at the bright white area. "Beautiful!" She squinted at the figure before her and jolted with recognition. "Shana?"

"Marie you're not in heaven but you are about to witness your soul," she said, placing the metallic stone in front of her face. Marie stared into the clear surface at something she could barely comprehend. For a moment she was silent. Her body began to shake and convulse until she was on all fours dry retching and sobbing. She had just witnessed and recognised her own internal darkness. With recognition and acceptance, all the bitterness and sadness rose to the surface. The suppressed emotion fought to escape through every pore, but once it was gone she would be free to love again.

Once the retching was complete, Marie curled into foetal position and sobbed. "That was me wasn't... it? I'm a mon..ster."

"That was the mirror to reveal your soul," she said gently but with a distinct tinge of guilt.

"Shana I need to go home... I need space... I..."

"You need to rest and process Marie. You have a chance to start again, what you have become is an accumulation of your life's rejection. They told me that," she said gesturing.

"They are real?"

Shana nodded, "and you are privileged to be here. They saved your life. They are the catalyst for your heart to heal. Don't turn them over to the world. You will kill them if you do."

Marie sat crossed legged and held her heart. Tears cascaded down her cheeks. She never got emotional! "They're... So pure..." she whispered.

"They haven't been ruined by the human condition and they are surrounded by this material which reveals the soul. What do you expect?" she replied.

"Shana I feel... awful..." she sobbed. "But I understand that you have done something for me. I don't know what it is yet but I know that I was a bitch to you when we were kids. In truth, I was always jealous of you and your family. You were always loved..."

Shana gazed sympathetically at Marie and thought about how close her family had always been. In truth, a family who were not affectionate had abandoned Marie and Marty. That family was obsessed with wealth, success and status. Marie had chased endless, meaningless goals to feel loved. It had never worked. They were just trophy children.

"Between you and me Shana… I have always felt so alienated. So much so, I needed to prove myself. To win I became ruthless, but winning did nothing. I just chased the next goal. That mirror just showed all of that. In truth, all I want to be is me - the authentic version. That is what I asked and now I received the answer... Can we keep this to ourselves?" She wiped her eye and sniffed.

Shana studied Marie and opened her arms. Like a small child, Marie accepted the affection and burst into tears. "I don't even know how to give affection Shana. I never had it. If a person spends their life rejected, they reject everyone Shana. The mirror revealed that…" she said with tears trickling down her cheeks. "What a sad world we live in… We need to make it right!"

"Marie, you have the chance to start again. You have the potential of love with Johnny. Give him a chance…" said Shana kindly. "He might not tick all the social boxes but his will give everything to you. In that moment Shana had a revelation: if the soul mirror surrounded the sea people then they could self-correct. They would never be ugly from the inside.

"Ey mus neh hope dar," (we must go to the bay now) said Shana, turning to two people of the sea who both carried twinkles in their eyes.

CHAPTER 67

Saved by Scampi

On the beach Johnny sat glaring at the water with his arms folded. He was helpless.

Marty perched on the surfboard with his head in his hands. What if Marie was dead?

"I didn't betray the village Marty. Whatever it is that you think of me – this is my home."

"If it wasn't you then who was it?"

Johnny shrugged; it was not up to him to point the finger. With a wipe of his nose, Johnny stood up. "We have to do something!"

"Like what?"

Johnny paced; what could he do?

"Why didn't you stay with her Johnny?" Marty asked his with a crack in his voice.

"I had to save Danny, he was in the water too," he replied flatly.

Sully glanced suspiciously at Donald.

"The packet of crisps under his nose," Sully muttered.

Donald gave his friend a certain look; he knew his meaning.

"Look," said Donald pointing.

Two weary figures trudged through the shallows.

"They're alive!" said Marty, breaking into a jog.

Johnny swiftly followed.

"She looks changed," said Sully, with a wink as he returned to the Land Rover and opened the door for Donald.

"You think she's seen into the mirror?" Donald replied as he took his seat and Butch jumped on his lap.

Sully nodded as he turned the key in the ignition. "I knew she was here for a reason. She was called. There is ney such thing as coincidence, my old friend."

"And what of our culprit?" asked Donald as Butch licked his face and wagged his tail excitedly.

"Donald can yer get Butch's arse out of my face? And our culprit has a curse within the family that seems to repeat through the generations," he replied.

"Aye…" replied Donald, who was wrestling with Butch and his doggy breath in the front seat.

Both Shana and Marie were shivering when Marty and Johnny reached them. Marty wrapped Shana in his jacket and watched Johnny remove a jumper from beneath his survival suit for Marie. "What happened?" Marty asked, sensing something was 'different.'

"Would yer mind taking us back to the cottage Marty? We can tell you everything once we've warmed up. There's no use standing around in the storm," Shana replied.

"Marie?" said Marty studying her.

With a sad look in her eyes she gazed guiltily at her brother and reached out for him, "I am so sorry."

Marty was confused. She had never shown him affection. "I have never been there for you Marty, and you are my little brother. I have been such a selfish bitch!"

With his eyes closed, Marty shook with emotion.

"Johnny let's start walking," said Shana, pulling him across the beach.

"What's going on?" asked Johnny.

"Marie has just had an intense wake-up call," said Shana.

"What happened to you Marie?" asked Marty, studying her.

"I have seen them and I saw into something that revealed what I had become. It was hideous! I need to change everything. I have spent my life chasing an illusion to feel better about me. I ignored what's important and that is family and friends. The armour I have built to protect myself is ridiculous and I didn't even realise," she said honestly. "How could I have been such an unaware idiot?"

Marty studied his sister; she would never normally say anything like that. She had been broken and softened.

The subtle resonation filled the air. Marie and Marty glanced at each other. "I have a few things that I need to tell you that you don't know about them," said Marty.

A female form that Marty recognised, surfaced in the shallows. Marie noticed his reaction and noticed her brother carried an awkward expression.

"You…are…" she muttered as the full implications sunk in.

"I… am connected," said Marty wading up to his knees. "What are you doing here?"

Sully and Donald climbed out of the Land Rover and trudged to the shoreline.

"Evening Iris," said Sully.

Donald waved whilst Butch wagged his tail at his sea residing friend.

"I talk with others. We need help for those who make transform. We are hunted and fear transform time be destroyed. If process break, we break. If we caught from hunt - we all call and everyone drown. We do not choose. Is instinct," said Iris with concern.

"Everyone is called?" asked Marie curiously.

"This is my sister," said Marty.

Iris scanned her posture and smiled sympathetically. She could read what Marie had just experienced. "Marty it instinct. We cannot help - we survive by drowning enemy," said Iris.

Sully folded his arms. "We don't want to see that happen again."

Marie glanced at Sully inquisitively; mass drowning had taken place in the past?

"We need to allow them the space to follow their rhythm uninterrupted," said Donald.

"What can we do?" asked Marty.

"We need to find them a safe place to transform," said Donald.

"We need to call a meeting," said Sully.

Iris studied Marty, "from tomorrow we together on land."

Marie watched her brother closely, what was going on? As far as she knew, Marty had only been in the village a short time. At what point had he made a commitment to the creature?

"Have those who intend to transform ready at sunrise and we'll get you ashore before the crews are active," said Sully calculating timings.

"How are we going to manage to get them ashore without anyone noticing?" asked Marty.

"We'll take them to the old war hospital up in the hills by St. John's. We can use one of the secluded bays and our four-wheel drives to ferry them."

"There's an old war hospital in the hills?" asked Marie.

"We used to keep the pilots up there when we got bombed,"

said Donald watching Butch have a scratch.

"Why would you get bombed here?" asked Marty.

"We had all the transmitters up here. We listened to them Gerry's," said Donald watching Butch sniff a piece of driftwood and nudge it with his nose.

Sully deliberate over Marie, "you know you are technically the enemy. How do we know we can trust you?"

"You don't, but I am sure that you will understand what I have just experienced with that 'mirror' can change a person in an instant," said Marie with a shrug. "Suddenly everything I have been chasing is meaningless."

Iris watched Marty's sister curiously; something about her could obstruct her unison with Marty.

CHAPTER 68
Warm eyeballs.

In the front room of Crooked Cottage, Danny sat gazing into the log fire with the packet of scampi crisps jammed beneath his nostrils. He heard the slam of the door and voices downstairs. He didn't move because he was absorbed in the sensation of heat on his eyeballs again. As long as he remained awake and had a packet of scampi crisps under his nose he did not hear her.

In the kitchen, Shana grabbed a towel and wrapped herself in it.

"So Danny was actually called to the water?" asked Shana curiously.

"He had gone under when I reached him," replied Johnny unzipping his survival suit.

"I think we need to have a chat to him. In the meantime, I think we need to call Danny's granny. She'll know what to do."

"We need to sort this out," said Johnny. "I am not taking any more blame for things that I haven't done."

"Well, I'm going to have a shower," said Shana. "Then I think we should talk to Danny and find out what really took place."

Shana darted up the stairs just as Marty and Marie arrived. Johnny stood awkwardly admiring Marie. Marty noticed and frowned. She gazed at him in a way that he had never seen her look at anyone before. "Okay, what's going on here?" he demanded.

The pair remained silent.

"Nothing has gone on Marty... Look mate, you seem to be accusing me of everything lately... I'm not willing to constantly be blamed!"

"What am I supposed to think? And Johnny, she is ten years older than you..."

Marie stood between them and turned to Marty. "Marty I need a moment with Johnny. I need to apologise. He did everything to stop me going into the ocean and I ignored him."

The tension in the air was extreme. Marty didn't want to leave.

"I will be back in a moment. I need to talk to Danny. Oh and give Marie some of Shana's clothes – her washing is hung over there…" said Marty studying the pair dubiously.

Danny broke his stare from the fire when he noticed Marty standing in the doorway with his arms folded.

"What happened? asked Danny, noticing Marty's contorted expression.

"Johnny- and I- well- we had a fight," he replied flatly.

"About ?"

"I assumed he betrayed the village. What's worse is the locals think it's me," he said sitting down. "Danny why have you got scampi crisps under your nose."

With a shake of the head, Danny sighed. "Marty I am being bothered by the sound of the girl."

"The one you kissed?" asked Marty. "I hear Iris but it doesn't bother me…"

"Iris isn't dead is she?" replied Danny.

Marty studied his friend, "the girl you kissed is the dead girl?"

He nodded, "but…"

"I didn't do anything wrong Marty. I think she saw Shana and I…"

There was a moment of silence as Marty digested the information. "Danny I don't understand…"

"Marty think about it. Think about what happened. You and I have made connections with the women from the water. It all happened instantly. We didn't have any choice. Now you are connected to this Iris creature. What do you actually know about her? She wants to come to land and it is assumed that you are going to spend the rest of your life with her or she will willingly choose to die like the girl I connected with. Marty what is that about? That is a forced decision. I did not choose it! It just happened and now she's trying to kill me. Don't make the same mistake. Break the connection because you're too young to make a commitment to 'a creature' you barely know. She is your distraction Marty. She is you avoiding your grief and dealing with your feelings about your father!"

"No Danny, this is your issue and not my distraction. My situation is different. I want this and I am connected for a reason."

"What if it goes wrong Marty? Are you willing to be drowned

296

for this choice?"

Marty was silent. That was the truth of the situation. How did he know it would work out?

The seed of doubt had been sown. Tomorrow Iris would transform to be with him. She intended to sacrifice her life in the sea for unison and now doubt combined with logic was his poisoning his mind. The situation was ridiculous. How did he actually feel?

"Think we need to get your granny here. She'll know what to do," said Marty avoiding the truth of what Danny had said.

"She can advise you, but Marty you need to get this clear in your mind by tomorrow," said Danny studying his friend.

"Danny I'll be back in a minute. I need to make sure Marie has clothing and it is very quiet down there."

Descending the stairs to the kitchen, Marty froze on the stairs. He couldn't believe it. Johnny and Marie were full on snogging!

"Hrrp hmmm," said Marty with a look of horror.

The pair broke apart and Marie wiped her mouth guiltily. She looked like a naughty girl but one who was glowing.

"I don't know what to say…" said Marty shaking his head.

"You're my sister… and Johnny you're supposed to be one of my best mates. 'this' makes me feel sick!" he said gesturing.

"Marty stop! From the moment Johnny and I met, there's been something between us. It started with the duck in a rock pool crap!" said Marie calmly and glancing at Johnny who shifted like a naughty boy. "Now come on Marty, at least Johnny is human!"

"That's not funny!" said Marty.

"Marty I just called Danny's granny. I need the keys to the camper. I'm going to go and pick her up," she said thundering down the stairs. "They make a lovely couple!" She caught the keys that Marty threw and ran out of the door with a grin. "Oh and Marie dungarees suit you!" she said, popping her head round the door before she slammed it.

A pin could have dropped; Marty certainly wasn't pleased!

"Well I will leave you two to it then!" he said, trooping to his digital dark room.

"I think you're what I've been missing," said Marie gazing into Johnny's eyes. "But don't you dare tell anyone that... I have a reputation to keep!"

"I can't guarantee that," he replied with a wink.

Marie studied him intensely; he was going to be a challenge!

Once inside the darkroom, Marty switched on his camera and went to erase the memory card. He paused, the pictures of the dead girl stared back at him. His camera was the tool that had caused all the fuss! What's more, that camera implicated him. Marty switched on the computer and opened up the digital darkroom. "Recent documents," he muttered. Listed were all the uploaded pictures with the photograph time. He skimmed through them searching for evidence and there it was. "Danny!" he said when he recognised an image of a certain pair of deck shoes. Shoving his chair backwards Marty stormed into the front room. "Danny what else have you got to tell me?"

Danny glanced up from the fire and noticed his friend's accusing posture. "I don't know what you mean?"

"The pictures are on my computer and your shoes are amongst the images Danny!" He spat.

Busted!

"Look, I didn't expect all this. I just wanted people to know so that it stopped being a secret. It's not right that innocent people are drowned for making contact with a creature. I thought if people knew then it would end it!"

"You know that I had a physical fight with Johnny over this and he's bloody innocent! Danny you really are a sneaky little bastard! If any of the villagers had accessed my computer - they would have blamed me! I have had enough of this shit Danny!"

"Anyway, your granny is on her way. I suggest you get your explanation straight before she arrives. Now I'm going to take a shower!" he said stomping away. "And Danny... How can I trust you anymore?"

A lip tremble accompanied by a throat contraction made Danny cough. Tears fell down his cheek. A woman wanted revenge and intended to drown him. His best mate didn't trust him and a ghost was harassing him. If the villagers found out about the betrayal then they would ask him to leave the village. Could it go any more wrong? In the corner of the room a breeze lifted the curtain. The small hairs on the back of his neck bristled. He followed the phantom to the bookshelf where a book fell to reveal another behind it. "There will be yer answers Danny," whispered Megan.

The temperature dropped as soon as Marty entered the room. The light bulb crackled and flickered. Where should he go? "Yer answers are in a box in the attic Marty. And do ney be too angry with Danny. His bloodline has cursed him," said a transparent figure sadly.

"I suggest yer go and learn the truth," she said and then disappeared. Marty frowned, a ghost had talked to him but he hadn't felt fear. Something had shifted!

The attic smelt woody, dusty and damp. He switched on the light and noticed cobwebs decorated the majority of the space including an old rocking-horse and some wooden toys. The light-bulb flickered and buzzed. The hairs on Marty's arm rose, she was there again. "Over here," whispered Megan, flickering beside a carved, wooden box. The light dimmed and she was gone.

Crouching beside the box Marty wiped away the dust. With a click of a button, he opened the ornate catch to discover a series of letters with pictures of a circus mermaid. For a moment he pondered, why did Megan want them to read the letters? Was everything inter-linked? Marty skimmed through and shook his head. He would be better going through it all in his room; at least he could lock the door.

Opening the old wooden box in his perfectly ordered room made Marty rigid. The dust was a collection of hundreds of years of dead skin cells. He fought with the thoughts as he sifted through the contents of the box. Wrap! Wrap! There was a knock on the door. Marty jolted but hid the box under the bed and sat cross-legged.

"Can I come in?" asked Johnny.

He nodded and folded his arms.

"Can we get this sorted?" asked Johnny taking a seat on the armchair in the corner.

"Of all the women in the whole world Johnny… Why my sister?" he asked.

Johnny shrugged, "it just happened. She's hot and we have chemistry. These things happen, and Marty, mate… Yer hardly one to talk… Yer connected to a bloody creature of the sea. You wouldn't have chosen that would you?"

299

"Johnny you dare treat her like shit and…"

"She is different Marty. She has a real fight in her and to be honest she wouldn't allow it would she?" he replied.

Johnny was right. "But I don't get why you left her to drown Johnny."

"Marty mate, imagine there are two people in the water. One you are watching, the other is in the water about to drown and you can't get to them both- so what do you do?" asked Johnny. "I had no one there to help and I had to make a logical decision. Marty you know what you are like at making decisions – what would you do?"

"Probably dither and run back and forth," he replied honestly.

"Well, I went to the nearest and that was Danny. I hoped to have enough time to get to Marie as well. Unfortunately, the storm was forming and I lost Marie when the storm hit," said Johnny with a sigh.

"So what are we going to do about Danny?" asked Marty.

"Keep scampi crisps under his nose. We can construct some kind of nose bag," he replied thoughtfully.

"You know that's not the answer... I think we need to figure out what has happened in the past and use it to solve this situation," he replied.

"What do you have there?" asked Johnny, noting the box poking from beneath his bed.

"It was in the attic," he said, showing Johnny the pictures.

"You think it has the answers?" asked Johnny.

Marty shrugged, Danny's gran probably had the actual answers.

300

CHAPTER 69
Granny's waiting.

The wind battered the old camper as Shana clung to Bertha's steering wheel. "Now would yer make this easy for me?" she muttered. The headlights illuminated trees ripped from their roots and dumped on nearby verges. Rain pounded the windscreen and the wind screamed. In the distance a lone stone cottage carried the glow of a lamp in the downstairs window. Nelly was waiting for her.

With the slam of the front door Nelly scampered across to the camper wearing a beige Mack and a pink shower cap. Shana studied the old lady as she climbed in.

"I see yer admiring me innovation Shana," she said watching Shana's reaction. "Well, a shower can be in a bathroom or a rainstorm," she said, making herself comfortable with her bag on her lap.

"What's in the bag?" Shana noticed a collection of small bottles wrapped in paper labels and elastic bands.

"Herbal remedies. We may need them for purification. We can use others to block mesmerisation. Now before yer get excited I would ney want to burn at the stake. This is all part of me lineage and our passed on learnings," she said with a wink.

"Now you knew this was coming didn't you?" asked Shana.

"When a connection is made it is likely to come in threes and that means someone somewhere will be hurt. Unless yer know the rules how do yer play the game?

A slam of the brakes jerked the pair forwards. An unaware pheasant strutted and then darted in the opposite direction. "Run 'em over next time and I'll pick it up. We could have it for supper," said Nelly brightly.

"Erm, Nelly, you know that Danny's having some problems," said Shana keeping her eyes on the treacherous road.

"Aye, I know. I sensed it, that's not all I sensed though..." she said glancing at Shana. "Tomorrow is the day of transformation. It means to change from the old and accept the new. There are always big implications when changes take place. It means that yer have to let go of yer old ways and adapt to an entirely new life. Dramatic changes can happen in a day!" she said.

What was Nelly really saying?

"So how do you want to play this?" asked Shana.

"Aye, we need a plan. I say we call in at the church and arrange a meeting. We need to have a strategy to bring those who have made the choice ashore. Er... Shana dear... There's something I need to tell yer about. It's between me and you as it's a sort of warning," said Nelly.

"Okay," said Shana side-glancing Nelly dubiously.

"After me husband died. I felt lost and alone-" said Nelly seriously. "It happens when you're in grief... Sometimes the rebound can be more painful than the loss..."

Where was this going? Shana glanced at Nelly. She appeared to be planning how best to say what she needed to say. "Now rules were drawn up in ancient times between the villagers and the 'creatures.' It seems that those in my family have a tendency to ignore the rules."

"I don't understand," said Shana.

"Now how blatant do I need to be?" asked Nelly. "Shana I attracted a man from the sea."

"Yer what?" asked Shana swerving.

"I told yer that we all have stains on our doorstep and that was mine!"

How was it possible?

"The problem is he liked the sea and I liked the land. I spent a year in the sea with him. I chose to give it a go nonetheless. Living a life in the ocean was more difficult that you could ever imagine. Eventually we agreed to sever our tie and break our connection. So, we amicably went our separate ways. Although the heart never truly lets go and I still have an attachment to him and can hear him sometimes. Now do you understand what I'm saying?"

Shana shook her head. "Hang on... You went to the sea?"

"Transformation can go in two directions and there is the time of choice in the autumn equinox. Some will choose the sea while others choose the land," said Nelly.

Shana focused on the road as the implications swam around her mind. How was it all possible? Shana frowned, Nelly did not die.

"I know what yer thinking...I did ney go with anyone else but the rejection was an issue. Their connection is for life and they cannot break away unless the heart dies. Every time I tried to keep away, he pined for me and called me to the sea. I had returned to being human and became hypnotised by his calls. In doing so, I went to the water and... well you can guess what happened. Luckily Donald saved me."

It was too much, yet it did not make sense.

"Shana I chose to stop my heart to sever the connection. It is like how they choose to pass. However, there is a tipping point where a connection can be broken but you have to have someone bring you back to life within moments... Donald did that for me... Now I assume you've seen the stones," asked Nelly.

Shana shook her head, "not properly."

"Shana you're not going to like this... But the man you have connected with is the very same one I was connected to."

Shana slammed on the brakes. The downpour intensified as she stared at Nelly's wrinkle-free face and clear eyes. "It can't be.... You are so much older than me!"

Gazing into Shana's eyes, Nelly smiled as she re-adjusted her seatbelt.

"I still hear him Shana. His tune has changed since he met you. Now I need to warn you. If you choose to go to the sea, you'll change your DNA and end up with a non-ending life. That is unless you make the choice to pass. And that, my dear Shana, is why I remain youthful. The curse of that is that I will have to choose me time..." said Nelly.

Shana scanned Nelly's face, her hair was all that revealed her age. "So why did you move from the sea?"

"I have me reasons but when yer have died once in the ocean yer would generally choose ney to be reminded on a daily basis eh? Anyway, enough of this discussion - it's too serious. Let's be a bit brighter," said Nelly. "Oh and Shana I saw you on the news tonight my dear. The world thinks you are a mermaid. Of course, it could be an omen or a coincidence."

"It's on already?" asked Shana in surprise.

"Aye and it was nice n' all..."

"But we only recorded that at lunch time," said Shana putting Bertha into first gear.

"The digital world... Shana me wee pipe-cleaner, there'll be even more attention now I dare say. Aye, there will," said Nelly with a shake of the head.

"I thought that film would end it," said Shana chewing her lip.

"Ach nooo, they did ney say yer were acting. So it has international interest now... No doubt the world's press will descend upon us. I should have baked some more shortbread," she said thoughtfully.

"If that's the case then how are we going to get 'them' through the change?"

"Where there's a Scottish will there'll be a kilt in the way," said Nelly.

CHAPTER 70
Community amongst the chaos

Marty and Johnny stood in the doorway watching Danny. He was asleep with his eyes open and the scampi crisp packet arranged under his nose.

"He can't spend the rest of his life like that," said Marty seriously.

"I can hear you... I haven't heard her since I smelled these crisps," said Danny remaining in the same position.

The pair pulled up armchairs close to him. "Danny…"

"Oh look, I have something here," said Danny trailing off. "It tells her story from the son's point of view," Danny continued hopefully, knowing the pair had purpose in their visit.

"Whose story?" asked Marty, irritated but interested, Johnny nudged him to be quiet.

"Megan's," said Danny. "They buried her in the wall."

"That's all very well but Johnny and I have a few questions before the others arrive," said Marty.

With a guilty look Danny sighed, he had to confess.

Shana pulled up as close as she could to the central church. It was solid, definite and rose above the tiny cottages with an air of dominance. The ornate, stained glass windows glowed from inside and made her feel welcome. Between the church and the van, the rain pounded the road but that did not deter the gathering congregation. Helping the creatures was their duty and tradition.

Once Shana and Nelly stepped through the door, the vicar greeted them. "Good evening Nell… It's been a while but we can always rely on you in a disaster," he said with a kindly glint in his eye.

"Aye, disasters are us and I am always up for a challenge!"

"May I guide yer over here," he said gesturing.

Both Shana and Nelly followed him to a quiet corner decorated with cream coloured candles.

"We came to call a meeting," said Shana.

The vicar nodded, "Aye, young Shana… It is in process."

"Look father I am really sorry but this is entirely my fault. I thought that if I swam about a bit then the media would get their film and leave. Now I was completely wrong and have caused an international reaction," said Shana folding her arms and shifting awkwardly.

"Shana it's very rare for a young person to take responsibility for their actions. Well done! Now your intention was good, but yer did ney consider the consequences did yer? We have had many an incident in the past and yer ney to blame, but we now have a greater problem to solve," he said patting her shoulder.

"There's an awful lot going on. I say we get on with it… All talk and no action does ney get to the bottom of anything!" said Nelly.

"Well Nell, we have already arranged for beds to be set up. So there is space for transformation," he replied.

"Are we using the old war hospital in the hill?" asked Nelly.

"Aye… Remember those years Nell?"

"How could I forget now? The best years of me life," replied Nelly thoughtfully.

"You were the very essence of Florence Nightingale with all those wounded soldiers," said the vicar in a tone of praise.

Shana watched the pair reminisce, there was such a history in the village. She had never considered how the locals had all relied on each other for so long.

"I brought me herbal compressions father - just in case…" Nelly tapped her nose. "The family secret. Now talking of secrets, I need to see me grandson before the meeting. When are we going to have a full congregation?"

The vicar glanced at his watch. "If you could be back in about half an hour then we will hold the meeting then."

Once inside the camper Shana drove Bertha back to the harbour and parked away from the edge. Nell watched her curiously, "now what is going on there young Shana?"

"I hate that edge," she replied.

"Yer fearing the edge there Shana. Face the fear and then there is no need for it any more. Fear and love canny exist simultaneously!"

306

said Nelly rather randomly.

Shana had no idea where that had come from.

Nelly reached over the seat and grabbed one of the blankets. "Now are yer ready for a mad dash Shana?"

The pair arranged the blanket over their heads and hurried up straight lane. Nelly didn't even lose her breath. Maybe she was telling the truth about her mortality.

As soon as the pair burst into the kitchen they paused. "They're all in the front room," whispered Shana.

"Well, we best break the fog then," said Nelly.

What did that mean?

"Oh Shana, it means to break the tension in the room," said Nelly noticing Shana's bemused expression.

With a definite presence, Nelly stepped into the front room. "Well good evening to yer all. Now I know that something is going on but I am going to tell yer what yer need to hear before any of yer mutter a word! When yer comfy give me a nod... Now Danny come on! Resorting to jamming scampi flavour crisps up yer nose is nort a long-term solution!"

Johnny gave up his armchair and gestured for Nelly to sit by the fire. She sat down, removed the shower cap and made herself comfortable.

"So I sense yer hearing the song of the dead girl aren't yer now Danny? She's haunting you."

"But I did ney do anything wrong? I did ney even ask to make a connection with her gran. I promise." Danny sat up in the armchair and crossed his legs.

"Aye, that may well be true but these creatures are fragile. Now think of it from her point of view. She fell in love in an instant. She had all those feelings in her heart and the next thing she is rejected. All that hope of love destroyed. The truth is it breaks them Danny – actually all of yer little scribbins... They are not human, they are not taught to close their hearts. When they love, they love completely. In truth you unintentionally rejected her but the disappointment broke her and she had to seek her revenge." Nelly studied Danny's expression. He was doing his best to understand the girl's perspective.

"Well, what can I do? She's trying to kill me - actually she did kill me..." he said.

"You need resolution, child. The first step is to release the attachment, so here's a special mixture to rub on your chest. It will start to heal yer heart. And Danny, the first step to resolution is forgiveness. Accept your responsibility and ask for forgiveness. It will begin the healing process. Then yer need to let her go. There are two sides to every quarrel and both fuel each other in the drama."

"Will it stop? Will she stop calling me?" asked Danny desperately.

"Aye, that she will. Ask for forgiveness, apologise and ask her to be laid to rest. When she feels completion, she will gradually cease the calling. Although Danny yer said she already killed yer. Did yer heart stop?"

Danny nodded, "it did didn't it Johnny?"

"Yep, and I had to resuscitate him." Johnny grimaced at the thought.

"Well, then she achieved resolution through taking her revenge. Yer died Danny – you are now new… We will know true resolution is complete when the storm of white light comes." Nelly turned to Johnny, her eyes skimmed over him. "Now Johnny, when Danny was unconscious did yer 'see' anything?"

"The transparent girl looked pleased, rose into the air and smiled at the moon. I sound like a loop." His shoulders rose and he crossed his arms. He hated that weirdness!

"Danny get the crisp packet from beneath yer nose. Let me guess it has been there all the time and yer think yer canny hear her because of the smell. Ney, it's the fact that yer died and she has been resolved. Yer daft wee neep Danny!"

"How would I know that?"

"Yer wouldn't Danny, and yer fear clouded yer!"

"I really didn't mean to hurt her." With a shake of the head, he remembered her twinkling eyes and cheeky giggle just the day before.

"Danny yer fear and frustration is making it worse. She can feel it and it unsettles her," said Nelly kindly.

With a gulp Danny took a few deep breaths, "I feel so awful."

"Feel the feelings Danny. It is good to feel because then they pass through. If yer hold them in, they will turn up in a different way at a different time. Then yer just repeat the same patterns with someone else."

308

Marty and Shana glanced at each other; they had never met anyone as wise as Nelly.

"Megan come forth," she said turning her attention to the wall.

"Now Megan, I think we need to share yer secret and why you chose them all-"

"What do you mean chose?" asked Marty.

"Aye, there are strange forces in this world and a ghost can call people to a place and time... Megan wanted yer here for a reason," said Nelly.

With her face shrouded in a dark veil, Megan wore a black dress with black shoes. Silently she lifted the veil to reveal a kind, open and ruddy face. She was barely older than they were! The group shifted awkwardly. She was more solid than before – she was real! What's more, they were in a room with a ghost and they actually accepted that?

"How is it you came to end in Crooked Cottage of all places?" Nelly asked the group.

The group glanced at each other and shrugged.

"Actually, we need yer sister here too, she's involved," said Nelly.

"I'll get her," said Johnny running to the door.

"Yer won't need to go far," said Nelly.

Marie was standing against the wall listening.

"Erm... Marie..."

"Hi... I was... erm," said Marie awkwardly. With a sudden jolt she noticed Megan, "Ahhhhhhhhhhhh!" she screamed.

"It's only a dead person – it's you without yer body now. Calm yerself and stop playing the bloody drama queen! It really is dull and not the real you!" said Nelly rolling her eyes. "Now I notice yer have Ross's dairy, Danny. He was Megan's son and that diary was hidden years ago."

"We also have a box of the clippings from the freak circus," said Marty.

Megan charged across the room and burst through the wall beside Marty.

"What did I say?" asked Marty clutching his chest.

"Megan they do ney know yet. Now settle yerself woman! They have no idea what they are talking of."

Megan re-entered the room and sat in an illusionary rocking chair. Marie shuffled across to Johnny and wrapped herself in his arms.

"I hate this crap too!" he whispered in her ear.

Nelly studied the group and sighed. "Well, this is what yer need to know. There's been a curse on this cottage for years. It runs through the family. Meg's from my family - a decedent. She gave birth to Ross who had a daughter - Margaret burned for witchery. She was the mother of Gail, who was drawn to the water and killed by Drichen manor. Megan's eight generations from Danny. This week he has unintentionally repeated the bloodline's history. Marty and Marie had a grandfather who lived for a time in Banff; he moved over here from Keith and married one of the Gardenstown villagers. He was present at a time when all hell broke loose with the mass drowning. So that's why you're here," said Nelly.

A flush of red rose up Marty's neck as he glanced at Marie.

"What's wrong with that Marty? At least you're not cursed," said Danny.

"Danny I got lost in Keith and now you tell me that's my ancestry- typical!"

"Why would I be here?" asked Johnny.

"Well, you lived here all your life. Your ancestors are buried up by St. John's church. Your family is part of the pirating line. It is in your blood to be close to the water. Look at your name, for goodness sake Johnny – St. John's," said Nelly as though it was the most obvious thing.

"Pirates are sexy," whispered Marie so no one else could hear. Johnny grinned to himself and pulled her closer. There was a certain amount of twitching going on in his underwear. Only the pair of them were aware of it and gazed at each other with a certain look.

"Shana genealogy stems from here. Her grandparents were of a woman of the sea who chose legs. The family moved to Ireland to start a new life. So it is interesting that you, of all the people in the village, emulated the girl of the sea," said Nelly.

"If that's true then that's probably why I love the sea." Shana smiled to herself.

"So why is Megan trapped here?" asked Marty.

"Aye, a sad story," said Nelly shaking her head. "I hear yer read some of Mermaids at Dawn eh Marty?"

"Did she write it?" asked Marty.

"She started but the tragedy stopped her from finishing," said Nelly with a sigh. "The day that she refers to in the story wasn't the first time she'd encountered the sea people. She kept her interactions quiet because she was frightened that implication would cause her the same trouble as her mother. She wasn't willing to be classed as insane or burned for witchery."

"Okay, if she had seen them before then why was a sea-woman searching out Megan?" asked Marie. "The girl in the story was seeking Megan because she had made a connection to Megan's husband. The girl was completely in love but intended to rid Cameron of Megan to free him to be with her. It was against everything that the creatures of the sea had ever done before. Usually they can sense when someone is with someone else through the heart connection. A closed or half-hearted attachment confuses them. It makes it difficult to sense whether someone is actually available. In their innocence, they assume the other person is free. That was the case with Cameron; he didn't love Megan so the girl assumed he was available to her. When she worked it out the jealousy eventually drove the girl insane. Her rage fuelled a storm when she worked out that she had made an attachment to a man who she could never have. As an act of revenge, she willed herself to pass and began the calling. Megan was innocent; however, when she gazed into the eyes of the dead creature she witnessed her tortured future. The girl blamed Megan for her unrequited love. In the creature's mind, if Megan died Cameron would be free for her. That is never the truth; the person who strays is at fault, not the partner! However, there is usually reason for the other to stray – but that is their drama! Everyone knows on a subconscious level, but just never admit it! All this genetic history has made the family sensitive – it our way of survival – that and knowledge of herbs and their uses. It's passed down to us."

"Anyway, Cameron had connected to the girl of the sea. He had had liaisons with her too. Megan witnessed it in the vision but how could she leave him? She was stuck with the issue. That night, when she took the picture to the printing press, it was her way of ending the secrets. Admittedly, her motivation was money, but things had to change! I assume that was precisely how Danny felt too."

While Danny sat forward in his chair, he glanced at Megan.

They had both been wronged.

"The girl of the sea also decided that Cameron had to suffer for misleading her and took her revenge. She swam into his net and willed herself to die there and then. Forced to face the problem and knowing of the Resonance's revenge, Cameron brought the body ashore in hope to avoid the wrath. It didn't work. The calling began and Cameron attempted to use alcohol to block his senses. In the end his liver failed because he drowned his sorrow."

"So did he die quickly?" asked Marie.

"No… You'll see. Megan was distraught by her vision and took to walking the beach at night. She tried to throw herself in the water but a male from the sea people saved her. From that moment they were connected. Megan, so sorrowful, relished the attention. So much so, she fell in love. Megan fell pregnant soon after. There was scandal in the village. The gossips named the pair the drunk and the whore. The locals had noticed that Cameron slept on the streets at night, so there was no chance of liaison. Cameron's sons received the brunt of the comments but her own son suffered endless teasing. The relentless torment resulted in them leaving the village when they were old enough."

The fire crackled and the group glanced at each other. The young woman had suffered.

"In 1837, Megan's deepest desire came true and she gave birth to a baby girl. The midwife's face was appalled at the deformed creature. The child was born with its legs bound in a bizarre skin. Cameron heard of the creature, abducted her and sold her to the circus. The child lasted only a matter of days because she instinctively willed herself to the next world. The story arrived in a newspaper and the daughter Megan had so wanted was lost. The child's revenge fell on her mother. She believed Megan had rejected her and began calling her to the water but the man of the sea kept saving her. The grief drove Meg mad. Finally, she couldn't take it anymore and in an attempt to sleep, she took too much of a sleeping remedy and did not wake up. When Cameron returned home drunk one night to confront her he found her body."

"That's so bloody awful!" Shana's eyes glistened and she shook her head.

"What a tragedy," said Marty.

"The shock of it all led Cameron to drown his many sorrows and that night he passed too. What was worse was the sons were not able to bury the mother in the graveyard, so they created a tomb behind the wall there. It was once a bedroom,' said Nelly pointing at the position Megan emerged from.

"So that is why I keep seeing her there," said Danny, studying the wall.

"She has been trying to help yer," said Nelly.

"So what happened to her children?" asked Shana, watching Megan rock on her chair.

"They kept fishing and looking after each other. Then when they were old enough, they went out into the world, to escape their family curse. Two of the village spinsters took on Megan's son. He took endless flack throughout his childhood, but when he was old enough he opened the tavern but never drank. He was Danny's great-grandfather."

"Now I understand why the curse stands in our blood and history repeats itself," said Danny gazing at Megan who nodded kindly at him.

"She was trying to tell yer Danny, but yer would ney listen. She was doing her best to protect yer." Nelly gazed at Megan.

"And the woman who saved the people from the sea... Where does she fit in?" asked Marty curiously.

"Aye, she's me mother's mother. They burned her for love and for being a witch. It was a shame that happened in the manor. That's why Danny's great-gran, my mother would tell the story repeatedly. It was her way of getting it out of her system. She could ney let it go. Such a good woman to save people, but burnt for what others did not understand," she said shaking her head solemnly.

"So when did the village and the sea people go their separate ways?"

"A short time after Megan's article was when the 'hunt' began. When the sea people are in danger they resonate in mass to protect themselves," said Nelly.

"That results in mass drowning," said Shana thoughtfully.

"The villagers were pre-advised. As we always say - they are us and we them. So they went inland for three days. Upon return, hundreds of bodies washed ashore. From that day, the people of the sea and the villagers had to disassociate themselves. Liaisons were frowned upon and connections ceased. It worked for years, albeit a few strays, but they were kept quiet. Unfortunately, over the last forty years the two races have once again been attracted to one another. Maybe it is because 'their' numbers are dwindling," she said as an afterthought.

"We should go," said Shana glancing at the clock.

"Aye, we should…"

CHAPTER 71

Best decoys are us!

The heavy tone of the central church's bell called the remaining villagers for the meeting. The quaint cottages emptied themselves of their resident contents. Once locked up, the villagers funnelled down the streets. The downpour beat them.

"What's going on?" asked Mark propping up the bar.

"Nothing that concerns you. It's a mass for us," said Sully closing the bar. "Gentleman and any ladies… I am going to have to close the tavern for a short time. I hope you will be respectful and leave accordingly."

"But… You can't close the bar," said one of the punters.

"Yer can when it's your bar," replied Sully. "Now I will re-open in an hour. Go give your livers a detox before the next Lochness Monster swims down yer gullet!"

With a guttural instinct Mark glanced at Matt, there were no locals in the pub and the mass must have meant something had taken place.

"Okay, if yer all go now there will be a special price on the Lochness Monster- all yer can drink for a fiver! Then if yer all ready for it yer can try me 'angry monster' for a fiver," he said brightly.

"But can't most people only handle a pint?" asked Mark.

"Shhh! They don't know that!"

A cheer and the grazing of chair legs on wooden floors filled the room as the crews showed their respect and left. Sully and Donald watched Matt and Mark head in the direction of their rooms. Something was wrong!

When they were out of earshot the frown revealed Donald's thought, "surely we should be keeping the crews in one place."

"I think we need to be at that meeting and they won't get past our filtering system," he said with a wink.

While Sully locked up, Donald waited outside the door and watched a torrent of water run down the street. "Why does it always rain when there's a disaster?"

"It rains when it rains," said Sully wisely. "I see Butch is doing his special sitting hover so his bum does ney get cold or wet. That dog has more brains than we give him credit for!"

Once Donald and Sully had begun walking down the street, Matt and Mark slipped out of the side door wearing dark raincoats with their hoods up.

"Do you have your recording equipment?" Mark asked.
With a nod Matt gazed back at Mark, "I think I already have a hangover! That monster is one powerful drink!"

The large wooden doors of the church closed with a thud once the remaining stray locals had sat down.

"Right, we are gathered here today to sing hymn number... And as is tradition we will continue the service in Doric," said the vicar. As the congregation sang, he surveyed for outsiders. The vicar whispered to the nearest members of the local congregation to ask the outsiders politely to leave.

"For those of you that aren't local to the village, I do apologise, but this is the only time that our villagers have the opportunity for private worship in our own dialect. It will not be beneficial for you. We will be open for general worship on Sunday at ten," said the vicar kindly. The locals smiled apologetically at the tourists and crew who took their leave.

Mark glanced at Matt who had strategically placed the black digital sound recorder under a pew. Both had earpieces and once outside Matt triggered the record button.

Once the vicar was convinced that the room was clear of outsiders, he continued the discussion in Doric. "As yer all know, tomorrow is the day of change."

Marty, Shana, Nelly and rest of the group slipped in through the church doors and took a pew at the back. The vicar eyed Marie curiously. "Nell, now should that outsider be included?" he asked in Doric. "Aye, she has seen into the mirror and has been transformed... You know the depths the mirror reveals."

Marie realised the room had turned their attention to her and blushed.

"Now I can vet her, and she knows any betrayal will result in death," said Nelly in Doric.

"What did you just say?" whispered Marie.

"That you'll die if you betray the village," replied Nelly matter

316

of factly.

"Oh," Marie replied with a confused expression.

The whispering among the congregation settled; Marie had been privy to one of the many secrets. If 'they' trusted her, then the village should trust her.

"Now we are all here today for a common reason. We need to come together as a community to help those in need during the 'time of change," he said in Doric.

"What do you need us to do?" asked the wife of one of the farmers.

"We are about to be inundated by international media who are set on a 'mermaid' hunt. First we have to conceal their existence and then we must honour the agreement to help those who wish to transform and come to land. The agreement stated that even though the tribe split there will always be choice. We know that those of the sea follow their hearts and when love comes, they may actively choose to transform to be with their beloved. So in honour of love, we will provide the space for those who wish to transform safely. If we do not allow this then as you know there will be death," he said with an unconscious shake of the head.

"What is the original agreement?" whispered Marie curiously.

"Those of the sea and most of the villagers are from one origin. Back in times gone by, we made an agreement between the 'tribe'. Since we were from the same origin, we could choose land or sea, but there would always be opportunity to experience the 'other side'. We have honoured that agreement throughout our village's history," Nelly whispered.

"Curious," said Marie with a glint in her eye.

"What do yer need us to do?" asked a dumpy mother wearing a heavy woollen shawl.

"We will need to transport them to the old war ward. We need people available for transport and care. You know the pain is worse than childbirth!" The vicar paused and glanced about. "Me gut is telling me to be weary. I canny be sure but I feel as though we're being heard. Now you know what to do but we also need a distraction. I am sure you can be creative and make a remarkable Scottish spectacle!" he said in Doric with a particularly mischievous grin.

"What time should we be ready father?" asked a smart local in a tweed jacket, a peak cap and wellington boots.

"Dawn," said the vicar, "we'll meet to the left of Moore head and follow the track down. We can take them from the cove and through the caves." The vicar glanced about the congregation; there was still a great sense of community – a rare thing in modern times.

"How many we movin'?" asked a heavyset farmer in a black Mackintosh, jeans and wellington boots.

"We canny be sure," the vicar replied. "Be prepared for at least ten," he said as an afterthought.

"We'll see you all tomorrow and any discussions are to be held in Doric. Now nort a word to any of the outsiders. Keep the shops open and consider the best way to distract. Decoys could be quite a creative challenge." The vicar smiled to himself – the locals loved a creative challenge. No doubt they would come up with something special.

In the front row one of the portly grannies chuckled as she knitted, "what about old naked swimmers? Or crochet bikinis."

"You offering Mo?" asked Nell.

"Ach why nort? Only if some others will join me though. I am ney have me saggy bum gyrating alone," she said. "Or we can knit some rather fetching trunks…" she said, glancing around the room for support.

"Aye, that'll be fun. We'll join yer Mo. Let's create a Scottish spectacle that'll make their eyes water!" A group of eight middle-aged fishers gathered. "Porridge n' podge can be the theme," said one, rubbing his portly belly.

"We can jig and jiggle at the same time," said another.

"Yer do ney want to jiggle so hard it falls off Fraser!" said one of the others.

"Do what yer need to do and remember this could be yer fifteen minutes of fame!" said the vicar with a grin. "Now make yer plans among you and be ready for a big day tomorrow."

The congregation dispersed full of Doric chatter and amusing suggestions. They had a night to create an international decoy, a Scottish monster creation that the world will never forget!

Lochness Monster attack!

The trudge back to the tavern through torrential rain did not impress
Sully at all. What's more, crews were lined up waiting for their
Lochness Monsters. "Give me a minute to get me self organised
behind the bar, and Donald, I might need yer to do yer best barmaid
impersonation and give me a hand."
"What do you want me to do with Butch?"
"Give him a treat or something. He'll be fine - he always has
his own balls to lick if he gets bored!"
"Wish I could do that," muttered Donald as he took his place
behind the bar.
"Right are yer ready Donald? You know the price and yer know
the quantity. I suggest yer wear the busty apron to protect yer
clothes," he said handing him an apron decorated with the cartoon
torso of a woman wearing lacy underwear.
Donald nodded and tied the string of his apron.
"You take that pump and I will take this one. Go!" said Sully.
The line went out of the door as the crews got as many rounds in as
they could.
After an hour Sully took a break when the queue calmed. He
went to join Mark who sat at the end of the bar with Matt.
"That is me whole summer season's profits in one evening,"
Sully said, rubbing his arm and wiping his brow.
"Are you alright?"
"Aye, just not used to pulling the monster at that rate," he said
watching Donald who was looking weary.
"So how was the church service? It was rather short by general
standards," asked Mark, carefully watching Sully's reaction.
"Short and sweet," he said. "Those few prayers and hymns is
enough to keeps us in the 'good' books," said Sully watching Matt sip
his pint. Matt was watching Butch chase his tail.
"Daft bugger," said Sully with a grin.
Butch stopped what he was doing, turned towards the door and
growled.

"That's not like him," said Sully following where Butch was staring.

The room quietened. Butch's growl and a few monster slurps filled the atmosphere. An ominous shape of bald man in a well-cut suit filled the doorway. Kicking the stuffed cat aside, he marched towards the bar. Sully watched his motion and folded his arms. Donald paused and glanced at Sully just as the 'Controller' reached the bar. Donald stood tall with his breasty apron on full display. The Controller eyed Donald, glanced about the bar and sucked his lip through his teeth.

"Someone's got the smell of a rancid fart under their nose!" whispered Sully to Mark.

"That's our boss," Mark responded.

"Evening, are yer here for the Lochness Monster?" asked Donald politely.

"No the mermaids," replied the Controller.

"We don't have a beer under that name," replied Donald. "What other local beers do we have Sully?"

"The Lochness Monster, Soggy Bottom, Stinky Sporran, Piddley Porridge and Witch's Winkle," recited Sully without breathing.

"I wasn't after a beer. Who's in charge?" he demanded, studying the 'imbeciles.'

"Can I help yer?" asked Sully who stepped back behind the bar. He studied the Controller, what sort of man didn't even acknowledge his workers?

"I need a room," demanded the Controller.

"So does half the world. We only have tent pitches left," said Sully with a straight face.

"Is there a producer called Marie here?" said the Controller glancing about the room.

"Hmm, an aggressive red head?" asked Sully.

"That's her," replied the Controller with a glimmer of hope.

"Lots of those in Scotland!" Sully replied thoughtfully.

The Controller brewed in an angered silence.

"In truth there's been no one like around for days," said Sully glancing at Donald who was tapping.

"Okay," said the Controller, clicking his mobile to reveal

Marie's number. He stood on the left side of the bar. Sully shot a glance at Mark and gestured for him to shift his stool. Mark shuffled his stool sideways just as Marie's mobile vibrated in his front pocket. He slid off his stool and shuffled sideways until the phone ceased ringing. The Controller's phone stopped and switched to answerphone. Sully gestured for Mark to go. Matt picked up his beer and subtly swaggered towards the corridor leading to their rooms. The Controller paused, there was something wrong in the way Sully was watching and glancing across the bar.

"Wait!" he called to Mark and Matt.

Sully gave a small stamp of his foot and glanced at Donald who gritted his teeth.

"Aren't you part of her team?" asked the Controller.

"Yes Jonathan," said Mark, unable to lie to his boss.

"Oh good… And you… You're the other part," the Controller asked Matt who clutched onto the doorframe to keep himself upright.

"I'm just going to the toilet," said Matt, drunkenly bolting towards the door.

"Outside loos," said Sully helpfully as Matt legged it into the street towards the church.

Jonathon frowned; their behaviour didn't make sense. A few moments later Matt returned completely drenched.

"A mighty flush!" said Sully opening a packet of pork scratchings.

The Controller turned his attention back to Mark. Matt waved something at Mark and gestured to go upstairs. Mark nodded and turned his attention back to Jonathan.

"Do you two have your own rooms?" he asked.

Where was the question leading? Mark grimaced.

"Right, you two can share then and that will solve our problem," said the Controller.

"That's ney right! Two hairy men canny share a room in my hotel! It's against the law!" said Sully.

"I am paying for the rooms and it is a feasible option! If you have any objections - provide me with your procedures and I will pass them onto my lawyers. Now show me to my room!" he demanded.

"Give him the haunted one," said Sully staring at the man. No one outwitted him! Not in his tavern!

With a smirk Mark noted the Controller's response. Sully's wicked ways were endearing.

When everything settled, Matt and Mark sat on their twin beds and listened to the recording. It wasn't very clear but they heard something. "They're bloody talking in their own dialect. Clever... They have to be hiding something," said Mark with a sigh.

"We could be lucky," Matt said glancing at the books in the room. One of them was a book on Scotland, which carried snippets of the Doric language.

"Let's play it again," he said plonking himself on the bed. Also get Google translator up.

The pair used both methods of translation and came up with something similar.

"Something about dawn and changing," said Matt.

"Sounds like they're transporting something," said Mark, reading his translation.

"Well, we'll be ready then won't we?" said Matt, rubbing his temple.

"You'll be ready with one monster of a hangover." Mark studied his colleague; he was going to suffer in the morning. "The clever bugger! He's purposely knocking the crews out with the monster! If they all have hangovers..."

"Shrewd and respect to him," said Matt rubbing his gut. "Do you think Marie is okay?"

"That girl always comes up smelling of roses and the lifeguard is on her case. Don't you worry yourself. We'll be up early to get this story," said Mark.

"What about Jonathan?"

"What about him? I couldn't give a flying fart what he does," replied Mark arranging his equipment. "I'm not arse-licking or nut-nuzzling him. He's overlooked me for years so bollocks to him!"

CHAPTER 73
Bagpipers and hangovers...

In Gamrae Bay, bleary-eyed crew questioned their sanity after a heavy night with the Lochness Monster. To make matters worse, a number of rather plumptious local men and women danced the jig in tartan themed body paint. Purposely placed sporran and long wigs covered anything that may wobble, flap or cause a blush. For the finale, the group followed a bagpiper into the shallows and pretended to comb their hair like mermaids.

Those international crews who had just arrived watched in wonder. Was that what they had flown at least eight hours for?

"What's going on?" asked a producer from the United States.

"They are mocking the fact that we are here for sightings," said one of the hung-over camera crew.

"The villagers have quite a humour about them. They have a beer called the Lochness Monster which will provide the most monstrous hangover imaginable!" said his soundman rubbing his head.

"You should try it tonight. It's good stuff," he said, only managing to keep one eye open at a time. "Half a pint and you'll be everyone's not just anyone's!"

Mark and Matt sat in their four-wheeled drive and watched the heavens open like a cracked egg. All the while, the Japanese crews, wearing their yellow, plastic rainproof sheeting, filmed every spectacle. The wind blasted them about the beach but they enjoyed every moment in an impeccably mannered way.

"Are you thinking what I'm thinking?" asked Mark.

"I can't really think, the monster has eaten my brain," he replied looking queasy.

"This has to be a diversion," said Mark rolling a cigarette. The pair jumped when Jonathan, wearing his suit, climbed in the van and slammed the door.

"Where's Marie?" he demanded.

"She kind of went off last night," said Mark glancing in the rear-view mirror.

"Went off?" he asked with concern.

"She wanted to do her own thing… To get more pictures," said Matt huskily.

"Have you heard from her?" he asked.

"We have her phone," replied Mark.

With a suspicious look, Jonathan studied them, what weren't they saying?

Just beyond Gardenstown, at Moore Head, Land Rovers gathered in a sheltered bay. The waterlogged track down to the bay received the torrential rain cascading down the hills. Sully watched the beat of the windscreen wipers and smacked his lips together. "Donald this could become treacherous. We only have a limited time before the hill starts to slide and there are ten to transport. It seems that nature is against us this time."

Inside the old war hospital, the ward was prepared. The dark russet walls had numerous orb-like lights with black wires dangling amongst them. Glass lanterns filled with candles sat in carved alcoves. Faded black tiles divided by chunks of russet dirt that had fallen from the ceiling covered the floor. The metal-framed beds with thin mattresses were prepared with crisp white sheets. Trays of disinfectant and cotton wool were regularly spaced throughout the ward. The air was cool and smelled like clay. Nell stood with her hands on her hips beside Shana. "We have ten beds ready. I hope that will be enough."

"Not being funny now, but how are we going to carry them?"

"Ach, they'll use the wheeled stretchers and brute force." Nelly plumped the nearby pillows. She glanced at Shana who appeared to be attempting to figure things out. "Shana, I know what yer are thinking and the decision is what initiates the transformation. Their physiology will begin adapting, the pain will begin and they will be weakened until they emerge from their metamorphosis."

"I guess unless you have experienced it, you can never comprehend it," said Shana humbly.

"The first ones are on their way," called someone at the other end of the cave.

"You will be able to witness nature's true power to transform

Shana," said Nell with a wink.

Excessive Scottish dancing, trays of shortbread and cups of tea could only work for a certain amount of time before the crews became suspicious. The locals glanced at their watches; they had to give more!

"This is a decoy," muttered one of the crews.

"Their keeping us distracted," said another.

The sound of bagpipes filled the air as pipers marched through the torrential downpour.

"You've got it wrong," said one of the locals. "We're giving yer a show so that you haven't come all the way here for nothing," she said, handing out more shortbread with tea. "No one knows about our small village and this is good advertising for our tourism," she said with a smile. "And how else are we going to get on the television?" The crews glanced at each other; it was true. How often did a remote Scottish village make the international news?

"Keep them occupied with tea and shortbread," said one of the swimmers in Doric as she wrapped herself in a towel. "If the biscuits stop working then bring out our reserves - the monster!"

"They are putting on quite a show," said Jonathan, with his arms folded. "It doesn't feel right."

With a shake of the head Mark reversed up the beach and glanced at Matt.

"I never noticed that before," said Matt gazing up at St. John's.

"Nor did I," said Mark, nibbling a gum from the packet and offering it to the others. "This all started last night with the bell ringing for mass. Notice that the remaining locals are not in shops or houses. There is no smoke either... So where are they all?"

"They're all in on it aren't they? Marie was right, her gut is always right," replied Matt.

"They can't be far... They must be close... I bet it's right under our noses," Mark said with a flash of remembrance. "The screen in the helicopter ... When the girl went under water which direction did she swim in?" he muttered.

"I don't know," said Matt closing his eyes.

"I'm sure it was that way..." Mark nodded towards the church.

325

"Get the map out Matt and look for things like caves and coves that are close by. Look for a sign which might suggest a monument – we are looking for a hospital," said Mark.

Matt studied his GPS. "There are loads of caves around here and numerous monuments. There are also burial mounds everywhere. I don't know where to start? Oh God, something is going on and we have to find it!"

Jonathan unfolded the local map he found on the back shelf and shuffled forwards. "What are you thinking?"

"What is at the centre of the burial mounds?" Mark asked reflecting on the conversations he'd had with Johnny and Sully.

"The church," Matt replied.

"What else?"

"Caves," he said.

"That's our answer," he said, pressing his foot on the accelerator and driving out of Gardenstown. He had a plan.

The storm raged over on Moore Head. A deluge of water dragged a sizeable chunk of cliff-face towards the beach.

"Bloody hell! We need to go faster," Marty said, glancing at Iris who waited patiently with the three remaining sea people. One of the men was Shana's man.

"If we no move from water we stay this form," Iris said, concentrating on the motion of the storm. At the centre of the gale, the clouds parted and bright sunlight generated a beam that aligned with the location of the underwater stones. The shafts of light linked up to form a laser, which ignited the stones' energy. A burst of light radiated through the ocean – the time of transformation was imminent.

The rusty coloured, stone walls made the crisp white sheets look bright while the waft of ocean filled the air. Villagers paced the hospital ward whilst watching for the first signs of transformation to arrive. Sully stood with his hands on his hips watching the proceedings. "Doctor, we have four more left, do we have enough beds?"

"I'm sure we do but if the worst comes to the worst we still have stretchers," the doctor said nodding towards the corridor.

"We're cutting it fine and time is running out. Only thirty

minutes before all that dead skin ruptures," said Sully.

"Let's get these stretchers down to the beach and pick up the last of them," said the vicar pacing towards the ward's entrance.

"I fear the vehicles have created too much mud for us to get back to the cove. We should consider the caves," said Sully with concern.

"You can't transport as many," said the doctor glancing at his watch.

"Two teams and two stretchers," said Sully waving the others over.

A blast of static filled the room, the villagers paused and watched the people of the sea convulse.

"What's going to happen," asked Johnny.

"Their skin will come loose and will bubble and crack. Then we will see them suffer the first round of transformation. This is the first phase of the restructuring of their nervous systems," replied Nelly.

The hillside was sodden where Mark, Matt and Jonathan trampled across the waterlogged earth. Behind them St John's church marked the boundaries of the quaint village they had grown so fond of. With an aggravated action Jonathan studied his ridiculously expensive shoes. The mud caking his shoes had spattered his silver suit trousers; they were ruined!

Matt eyed the soaked suit Jonathan was wearing.

"You need outdoor clothes."

"I am aware of that," he replied sharply.

Mark climbed down from a rock, a huge crevice and some precarious rocks blocked their path. "There's nothing this way. Let's go around the headland."

"I think we'll have to climb," said Matt lethargically.

"Are you going to be able to make it in those shoes?" Mark noticed there were no grips.

"I am here for the hunt, so let me hunt! My shoes can be replaced at any time," he replied.

The pair side-glanced each other, since when had a 'Controller' wanted to be so involved?

The two groups congregated at the mouth of the red-stone caves. Heckles rose on their necks in response to the constant sound of dripping water.

"I don't know whether this is such a good idea," said the diver.

"We're wasting time! Now let's bring 'em in one at a time and then turn back for the final two," said Sully.

"As long as they are out of the sea they can change," said Donald glancing at Butch wagging his tail. He had just marked three areas of the cave. Donald studied Butch and frowned, how the dog managed to keep marking when he certainly hadn't drunk enough water was a phenomenon. Since they had been in the warren Donald had noticed Butch's hind leg was constantly in the air. This time he was directing his aim at Sully's shoe.

In the cave's hospital ward Nell and the doctor lifted a sheet to see what was taking place with one of the people of the sea.

"Their skin has started to bubble and shed. Metamorphosis is imminent!" said the doctor urgently.

"What's taking them so long?" said Shana gripping her man's hand as he convulsed on the sand.

Marty glanced up the track, "it's too dangerous to risk bringing the four-wheelers down that hill. There could be a landslide. They must be finding an alternative route."

Up on the hill three figures made their decent.

"Look, someone is coming," Marty said with rain in his eyes.

"So they really do exist," said the Jonathan in a devious tone. "And look, they have no escape."

A pang of guilt filled Mark's gut. The man beside him was famed for his ruthlessness and now something dark was brewing.

In the shallows one of the women of the sea convulsed with a whimper. Danny knelt helplessly beside her.

"Get her out of water or she canny change," said Iris urgently as she began to tremble.

"I don't understand," said Marty.

"We canny be in sea if we want legs. Marty you can lift her because you are not free for her and she canny make a connection unless your heart is available," replied Iris clutching her hips as she convulsed.

In the caves Marie and Johnny helped the vicar navigate the stretcher through the warren with Donald and Sully. The vicar kept glancing at the symbols engraved in the walls. The system was complex and he needed more time to work it out.

"Look, there's light in that direction," said Marie pointing. The vicar shook his head. "Don't be easily fooled Marie. It's tricky down here, there's a system of symbols to follow. The reflection is designed to deceive you. The only way we can emerge is by reaching the darkest point to recognise the light."

With a frown, Marie kept her opinions to herself. The vicar was going to get them lost!

Underwater, the first alignment took place and a shard of light cut through the ocean from the eye of the storm. The Cancerian stone column ignited with light. The upturned oak in the centre of the circle instantly sprouted luminous pink flowers on its roots. Yellow pollen erupted into the water and swirled about the stones. The water gathered momentum and pulsated with radiance until each particle, full of potential energy reached its full power. In that moment a mercury-like material flowed from the stones to the tree creating a web of connections. The energy for the transformation was ready.

At the end of the darkest cave was a pinprick of light. The depths of the cave revealed the way out onto the beach. Progressing into a jog Marie followed Johnny who sprinted to the beach and quickly lifted one of the men from the water onto his shoulder and carried him to the first stretcher. The sound of the bubbling and popping of skin penetrated Johnny's ear. Johnny set the man on the stretcher and turned hastily back to Iris who directed them towards the girl Danny was looking after. The pair lifted and carried her to the second stretcher group who waited at the entrance to the caves. "Right, let's get them up the slope and you can guide them from there," said Johnny driving the stretcher up to the first part of the cave where the others could steer from.

As soon as he was done he ran back down to the beach. Time was running out!

"They've seen us," said Mark.

"Well film then," demanded Jonathan. "There are only two left - now hurry! Actually, isn't that..." he said trailing off when he noticed Shana.

Matt and Mark remained silent and glanced at each other guiltily.

"That is 'the' woman from the film," he said incredulously. "She's got..."

Marie dashed across the beach, "hang on…Marie's already in there… You knew this, didn't you?" he pressed.

"We have no idea what's going on," said Matt attempting to work out how Marie was already involved.

"Right, let's get them," said Jonathan dashing down the hill.

Marie was the first to notice the film crew. "Cover them!" Danny, Marie, Shana and Marty formed a wall covering Iris and her friend.

"What are you doing here?" Marie ran over to Jonathan, she intended to keep him talking.

"I think that I should be asking you the same thing," he said studying her.

"I went to find them and they saved my life," said Marie honestly. "Don't film them. Leave them alone."

"Marie this is business not ethics! The world needs to know about their existence. Imagine how it changes the world's perspective. All this time creatures exist that no one had any clue about. How can that happen in the modern world? Think about it… We found them and we have evidence! We are making history!"

The inner struggle Mark was experiencing was like nothing else. He wanted to leave them to it but the Controller was right. The

330

world should know.

"Film," shouted Jonathan.

With the camera switched on, Mark shifted awkwardly. All he had to do was hit 'record'.

A flush of red rose up Marie's neck, unexpectedly she lunged towards the camera.

CHAPTER 74
Particles

The second pulse of energy burst from the stone circle.

"If I don't make it out…" Iris said urgently. "You will have the choice to come to the sea in September," she said caressing Marty's face. "You then make body sacrifice for me." She glanced towards Marie; she may have to swim at any moment.

"No, let's get you out of the water," he said, crouching to lift her.

"Marty the hunters are here…" she said, fearfully pointing. "They'll torture us like before..."

"They won't, they can't," said Marty pulling Iris towards him. As Marty lifted Iris she glanced over his shoulder. Jonathon revealed a vicious look in his eyes – he intended to hunt at whatever cost! "He does ney see us as human, he sees us as animals."

Marty turned to see the man Iris was talking about. His curved over posture and jutting chin revealed his intention.

"He is a cruel man," she said again. "I can see him for what he truly is… He will try and kill me or capture me."

Once Johnny knew the group could push the stretchers to the ward, he turned and launched into a sprint. He darted back through the caves, he noticed a situation had developed on the beach.

Sully and his crew pushed the stretcher into the ward, grabbed a fresh stretcher and rushed back through the caves. As a matter of urgency, Donald dragged Butch who appeared to be running on three legs with his hind leg cocked.

"Bloody sprinkler system," muttered Donald.

With a sudden grind to a halt, Sully gritted his teeth and paused. Smack! Completely absorbed by Butch's three-legged run, Donald collided with him.

"Donald! Now we've taken a wrong turn. I reckon we're close to the crypt under St. John's. That ruddy light. Look, it's best we go up by the church. Up and over," said Sully to the group.

"We don't have time," said the diver.

"We'll ney get there quick enough. It's best we go back to the hospital and start over," said Donald glancing at Butch who could have watered the lawn of a stately home.

"Face it, we're lost. It's best we go outside and navigate from there," said Sully.

"Sully, we may have an alternative. I think Butch has marked his way. I'm sure he can lead us the right way." Donald peered at his rebellious pooch – they had an understanding. Butch scratched his ear and continued sniffing.

Sully eyed Butch, he sniffed a rock with his right, hind leg cocked. Could Butch lead them? Butch noticed the silence and all the attention. In response he wagged his tail - *doggy chocs?*

"Find the hospital," said Donald.

Butch wagged his tail and tilted his head.

"Does Butch know the word hospital?" asked Sully dubiously.

"Find!" said Donald. Snap! - the leash cracked in torsion and Butch dragged Donald back into the warren.

At eleven forty five:

"Help us," Marie pleaded.

Unconsciously the Controller sneered. Matt and Mark glanced at each other, they had always observed and never been involved. Mark went to put the camera down.

"No," said Jonathan reaching over. He gripped the camera and stared into Mark's eyes. "Give me the camera and you keep your job!"

Mark clung to the camera, "you can stuff the job up your arse!"

Smack! Johnny barged the Controller out of the way. "There's ney time for this crap!"

On the floor - Jonathan's face contorted and his fists clenched. Marie had never seen him like it. He rose in blind fury and launched himself at Johnny. Marty noticed the scene and dived across to cover Johnny. Smack! The Controller gritted his teeth, put his head down and punched repetitively.

"We need to get them out of the water now!" shouted Shana urgently.

With a massive shove, Johnny barged Jonathan to the floor and ran over to Shana's man. Marty, Mark and Matt restrained the

Controller.

"You'll regret this!" he spat as he writhed. The man was full of rage; that gave him power and it would be hard to contain him.

The vicar motioned for the stretchers to continue. "We need more hands," he said glancing hopefully at Matt and Mark.

"Can you hold him while we get the others out?" asked Mark. With his knee on Jonathan's chest, Marty held him down. "I can hold him but please just get Iris out of the water."

"Marty I'll be back, we just need to get this stretcher up the slope," Johnny said glancing at Marty dubiously. There was no way he had the strength to hold the Controller all of that time.

"We should get back and help Marty," said Shana guiltily.

"There's something spiteful about that man."

"Leave him. I think you need to believe in Marty. As nice as he is, he has plenty of suppressed grief and anger to release if it comes down to it!" said Marie.

Underwater, the stones began to pulsate with the energy generated by the beam of light from the heavens. Golden pollen illuminated and combined with mercurial material flowing to the upturned oak. The root blossoms burst open and released a purple elixir into the ocean. The symbol of the crab turned luminous and pulsated. From the centre of the upturned oak, a vortex rose towards the surface of the ocean and gathered momentum. Emerging from the water a glowing waterspout took form and connected with the clouds. Outside the eye of the storm, lightning charged the waterspout as it travelled towards the land. Metamorphosis was imminent.

Up in the hospital ward, mass convulsions, skin cracking and whimpering filled the air. In that moment, chaos had arrived and expectation dissolved. Transformation was a particularly painful process that involved a complete physical shift.

At eleven fifty:
With an almighty burst of energy and a roar, the Controller kicked Marty off him.
Marty flew backwards and urgently scrambled to stand.

"How dare you! You arsehole!" hollered Jonathan. Stomping

forwards he grabbed Marty's hoody and pulled it tight round his neck... "You know who I am and I do not tolerate pathetic, pond life people!"

Marty gazed into the pair of venomous eyes. A fire raged in his stomach and he gritted his teeth. Smack! The head-butt cracked the Controller's nose across his face. Stumbling backwards, Jonathan shielded his nose with both hands. The blood merged with rain and flowed between his fingers, onto his white shirt and silver suit. While Jonathan stumbled about in shock, Marty took his chance and attempted to drag Iris ashore. Her hand was limp; she had given up.

"Marty," screamed Iris.

There was a dull thud as Marty's limp body slumped to the floor. The Controller stood over him brandishing a large rock. He glanced at the helpless creature in the water and smiled. "You speak, don't you? He said, shuffling closer and peering at her. And you want to be human, don't you?"

Iris gazed into the Jonathan's dead eyes and saw a heart filled with darkness.

"I could make a fortune from you." Jonathan crouched and contemplated how he would seal her in a tank and make her perform.

"We have to stop you changing. Actually, what if you half change – you would be even more of a freak! The world needs a spectacle like you…" He glanced at her position. "You are too shallow to swim away aren't you? And you are too weak to escape. Essentially you are helpless – the perfect victim!"

Shana's team, bearing the stretcher, burst into the hospital ward. The villagers gently lifted and transferred the man of the sea. He was rigid with convulsion.

"There's one missing," said Nelly noticing an empty bed.

"It's Iris." Shana affectionately stroked 'her' man's hair as he grimaced with pain.

"Iris connected to Marty?" asked Nelly glancing at the vicar.

"Yes," said Shana. "Why?"

The pounding of Johnny sprinting through the darkness filled the caves. Heavy breathing, echoes and the sense of urgency filled the atmosphere. He fought his limits to reach the beach in time. When he burst through the opening, a horrifying sight greeted him: Jonathan stood over Iris. She was collapsed in the shallow and was too weak to swim away.

With a calculating grin, the Controller figured out his plan. "So if I keep you in the water while all this metamorphosis takes place and then extract you – I have the perfect situation to transport you for the world to see."

Her whole body trembled. Yes, she was weak but the water carried particles filled with potential energy. With her eyes closed, she scanned the evil man's mind and saw his intentions. A life transported all over the world in a tank. People would come to see her and pay money. He would starve her to keep her under control and then make her perform. It was a life of slavery and imprisonment to generate him wealth.

"There is only one way we can do this. I don't want a struggle. This should be effortless and easy." Jonathan smiled triumphantly to himself. "Shame your boyfriend isn't here to save you now. You know in modern times men have stopped saving women. Quite a concern isn't it?" he said rising to standing and surveying his target.

"Your cruel, bitter heart make you very sad man. Your soul is blackened," she said.

"Who needs a beautiful soul in a world like this?" he spat, lifted his arm and lashed out.

Drawing on all the energy in the water, a sound that shook the depths of the soul resonated through Jonathan's being. Paralysis ensued and he collapsed on Iris who lay helpless beneath him. Johnny was frozen; he had felt something in the air and had watched a towering man crumble and collapse. What had she done? What should he do? Was he dead? Tentatively, he stepped forwards and dragged the limp figure off Iris.

"Is he dead?" he asked.

She shook her head weakly. "His dark side consumed him. He now goes through soul change."

"I don't know what that is but please don't do it to me." Johnny crouched beside Iris and gazed into her captivating eyes. "Look, I really don't get your kind or what you do, but Marty is my mate and I do not want you to control him. He is a decent man and you have made a connection to him without his choice."

Iris gazed into Johnny's eyes. "That is your belief but what you do ney know is heart makes call and Marty call me. That is why I found him. Whether you know or not we all connected and when a heart is ready it call the beloved into their life. Why you think all this happen with you? Why you think you found love at this time? Think about it. Think about what you experience and what you learn. Your heart call Marie Johnny. Your heart was ready. You face you. Your heart resonate like us.... Love resonate and you resonate. So I no lull Marty into anything. I am what he chose."

"But you hardly know each other," said Johnny.

"The truth is love can happen instantly. The connection broke by fear and too much think. When you feel love – it is true. Johnny you just have to learn to feel and trust."

"You want me to bring you ashore?" Johnny whispered. Iris nodded, "we are different to your society – we taught feel and love. You taught to hide, reject and suppress. Is it any wonder your world selfish?"

Jonathan came around with a sudden jolt. He felt different but rose and ran in the direction of the caves. He intended to complete what he had started. "The world will know you exist. It is their right!"

Eleven fifty five:
Underwater, the vortex of energy gathered momentum and erupted like a volcano. A cloud of static energy filled the air and connected with those who had made the decision to change.

In the hospital, the sound of ripping, tearing and skin shedding accompanied screams of pain. Metamorphosis had begun.

On the beach, Iris slumped in the shallows and wept when she saw the eruption. "I'm ney out of water. I too late."
With an awkward shuffle, Johnny considered how to comfort her.

"Come on..." he said crouching and glancing at Marty who was still unconscious. "You really want this don't you?"
Iris nodded as tears trickled over her face. "I feel it Johnny. No want."

"Well, if I have learned anything about will then it's never too late," said Johnny hauling Iris onto his shoulder. "If what you say about love is true, then you will transform." With a definite stride, he carried her to a sheltered overhang. "You're not coming this far and not committing!" Johnny set her down and covered her with his jacket while he went to retrieve Marty. With his hands under both of Marty's arms, he lugged Marty's limp body alongside Iris. He could never have anticipated what was about to take place.

The screaming pain of transformation echoed through the caves. It clearly revealed the location of the hospital ward. Jonathan stood for a moment in the darkness of the caves and listened. He knew where he had to go.

In the ward, Mark and Matt assisted the villagers as the sea people entered metamorphosis. Numerous convulsions and spasms made their backs arch. Roaring, screaming and crying filled the air. The onlookers stood with concerned looks on their faces. That was just the beginning.

A bolt of blue light penetrated the cave walls and encapsulated each of the sea people. A lattice of energy cocooned each of them in a transparent bubble. When the protective barrier fully formed, a silver mercury-like material flowed over the creatures' bodies. It was then that that the first division took place with a burst of light. In the flash there was a loud crack, which resulted in the formation of legs.

The locals silently watched the miracle of metamorphosis. They were unable to ease the pain of those who had made the choice. Marie paused and glanced at her watch, the first big ben chime filled the ward. How long would the pain and suffering last?

In a cave by the beach, Marty remained unconscious. Johnny watched Iris convulsing and a web of light surround her. A moment later, she was consumed in a transparent bubble.

"What is this weird shit?" he muttered.

In the distance a subtle sound of the church bell sounded. Iris jerked; a weave of silver, mercury-like liquid encapsulated her legs. Something made a sound like skin ripping. Johnny covered his eyes and turned away; he couldn't watch. With a frown and a gasp, the realisation plopped into his consciousness: Iris was going to be a woman. Even though she was trembling and shaking, he arranged his jacket over her, "yer need to cover yer dignity there, miss."

In the hospital, Mark's camera sat in an open case on the floor by the door. The Controller instantly noticed it from the corridor,. He crawled on his hands and knees to its location, switched the camera to automatic and checked the sound levels were correct. Using his phone as a transmitter, he prepared to make a broadcast.

The villagers stood silently with their arms folded by the beds of those transforming. All they could do was watch the phenomenon and offer support during the change. They couldn't provide painkillers because it might kill or physically damage the 'creatures'. The event absorbed the room, so much so, they didn't notice the Controller's presence until it was too late.

The Controller took off his jacket and picked up the camera. While kneeling down to the side of cave entrance he made an explanation into the camera. "This is Jonathan Calumny with MRT news. I am broadcasting the discovery of the people who live in the sea. What you are about to see will not only shock you but it is real. For the first time on television you will witness something that has never been broadcast before."

The bell tower of the central church sounded its eighth chime simultaneously with Marie's watch.

After advising his network that he was about to make a live broadcast, Johnathan prepared. When he was ready, with a deep breath, Jonathan focused, picked up the camera and pointed it into the ward.

The tenth chime sounded.
Sully and Donald were the first to notice the Controller charge into the ward with the camera.

"Cover them!" called Sully driving forwards and attempting to block the Controller's view. It wasn't enough. With sheer power, Jonathan was determined and shoved everyone in his path out of the way.

The eleventh chime sounded. Butch jumped with all his small-dog strength and bit into the Controller's free arm. It was the same arm required to rip back the sheet. With the dog hanging from his arm, the Controller directed his camera at the nearest sea-person. As he attempted to pull back the sheet, the small dog filled the camera lens. He was broadcast to millions of screens internationally. With a shake of the arm Butch was not budging, he intended to have his full fifteen minutes of doggy fame.

All over the country, people paused what they were doing and watched an adamant dog cling to a shaking arm in a hospital ward where people were screaming. What was going on?
The Controller reached for the sheet and struggled to rip it back.

The twelfth chime.
The ward turned quiet simultaneously.
    "Live on TV for the first time," said the Controller, as he ripped back the covers. The whole room turned their heads and averted their eyes. The camera focused on a certain newly developed appendage. There were sniggers and blushes around the room.
    "Daytime television too," said Donald with a smirk.
    "I did it!" he said. "The truth about the people of the sea," he said glancing over his shoulder and frowning.
The man of the sea had transformed. The broadcast demonstrated that the change was complete and he was definitely a man! In silence, he switched off the camera and dropped his head. Butch let go, elegantly plopped to the floor and scratched his ear.
    The silence in the ward revealed the general opinion of the man. The truth was Jonathan had just broadcast the close up of a male appendage on daytime television. There was silence around the ward and numerous folded arms. In silence, the Controller walked from the room into the cave. His mobile rang but became fainter until he lost signal.

Marty grabbed his head as he sat up. Pain thundered through his skull. Tentatively, he tested an area of dried blood. He didn't remember a thing. One moment he was gazing at Iris and the next it was pitch black. As he sat up slowly, he felt a pair of eyes watching him. To his right, Iris laid with her eyes closed, resting. Johnny's large coat covered her. Sitting against the overhang wall, Johnny grinned smugly with his hands wrapped around his knees. The last sheets of rain fell and a double rainbow filled the sky.

With a wince, Marty shuffled over to Iris and stroked her hair.

"Did you transform?"

"It's a girl," said Johnny brightly.

Marty and Iris gazed into each other's eyes and kissed passionately.

"Get a room!" said Johnny standing and turning towards the caves. "Oh, and there's a clean pair of speedos there to honour her arrival at womanhood." Johnny grinned to himself, if he had his way then the world would be wearing red trunks. With a saunter mixed with a skip Johnny made his way into the caves. What Iris had said had affected him. As he allowed himself to digest, he noticed a statuesque figure walk into the depths of the warren. The question was – how would the Controller deal with being out of control?

Evolving into a jog, Johnny returned to the ward. He glanced across at Marie who turned, ran and jumped onto him. She was full of life and her defences had shattered. She had made a 'decision' about him and he felt it. In that moment they gazed into each other's eyes and had that 'knowing' feeling.

Danny in the meantime was confused. Was he now connected to the woman lying in front of him? On the other hand, was he simply becoming a relationship butterfly?

"Remember you need to let go of the other before starting this a-new. You always have to let go completely, forgive them and yourself before you move on," said Nelly wisely. "It could be time to ask for the final forgiveness from the girl you scorned. Then she will have her peace."

Danny sat at the edge of the girl's bed. Could he manage to connect to one person for the rest of his life and for that to be it? Surely he should sow his seed and plant some oats.

"Danny I know what yer thinking but the best way to love is to grow with another person. Many loves does not necessarily mean better love. Too much emotional trauma will close off yer heart. Now feel what yer need in yer heart. Yer heart has the answers and yer mind delivers the necessary actions."

Nelly watched Danny; he needed time to mentally digest. Once he understood the relevance of what he had just experienced, he would know what to do.

Nelly turned her attention to Shana and patted the man who smiled kindly at her. "He obviously likes yer. Especially when he has taken such a risk. It is good to see that he has finally moved on. Resolution has taken place finally. Our attachment has been released and I am now freed, so thank you Shana."

Out to sea, the beam of light passed the sign of the crab and in a matter of seconds the storm spun in reverse. Underwater, the buds covering the upturned oak sucked the storm's energy into them. When each bud was full it closed and protected itself with a silver veneer. Those buds would lay dormant until the next period of change. The luminous stones stopped pulsating. The mercury-like material withdrew to its source, waiting for the time of choice.

CHAPTER 75
Time of choice.

For those of you who are interested: Late September (Virgo). The time of choice.

'They're us and we them- there will never be a time when the two tribes will not be drawn to one another.'

The sun was lower in the sky and the leaves had started to brown. The sea was calm as celebrations took place on the shore. Underwater, the stones accepted an orange tinted beam from the autumn sun. A group of villagers stood on the beach gazing at the sea, many people cuddled, looking relieved while others looked sorrowful knowing what was due. The locals knew that the important choices made resulted in no turning back for at least six months.

The Marimermamenhirs stones received the catalytic beam of light, which initiated the entrance to Virgo. The engraved image of legged people started to glow brightly. It hinted at the sacrifice due: stay on land or move back to the sea. At dusk, those who had chosen to stay and keep legs stood with their partners holding them tightly. The sea was calling them back but they had to restrain and go against the instinct. Iris stared at the water, feeling her calling.

Shana stood with her man and waved at those who were leaving. "If we went to the sea, how would we live?"

"We live as though wild." He watched Shana's expression intensely and squeezed her hand. "Would you want that?" Unconsciously, Shana shook her head, but maybe she hadn't really thought about it.

Johnny stood with his arm around Marie's shoulder. He grinned cheekily, "you are still in Gardenstown darling!"

Marie rolled her eyes in response, "what have I said to you about being smug?"

"But yer are still here," he said with a squeeze of her bottom. With a look of telling off, Marie cracked a smile. He was always on the wind-up!

With the crisp smell of autumn in the air, Danny stood amongst those who intended to go to the sea. He shifted nervously back and forth – he had chosen the opportunity to experience a life few would have the opportunity to live. Before him was the vast unknown of the ocean and the basic need to survive.

Nelly patted his shoulder, "now are you sure?"

"Who has an opportunity like this?" he replied, with a definite nod.

Nelly propped herself up by the harbour wall knowing what Danny was about to experience was one of the most beautiful free lives a person could live. It was beautiful but treacherous. Not only did you have to live and survive, but also a sea person had to face sharks and other predators.

"Are you sure about this?" asked Marty.

"Surely life is about living and experiencing," he said, stepping into the water and holding the hand of his woman. Danny had accepted transformation was necessary for the new life to be truly experienced.

"For him to survive his entire body is going to have to re-structure," said Marty in wonder.

"Every little detail will be transformed." Iris made a subtle smile and squeezed Marty's hand.

When the group was ready, they waded into the ocean. Those who originated from the ocean instantly changed and escorted those who wished to live in the ocean to the stones. There was a ritual where each human touched the stones causing their physiological transformation. With contact with the stone, a silver bubble sealed each person to enable space for metamorphosis.

"What are yer thinking?" asked Marie.

"I wonder what will happen to Danny's knob in the cold water," Johnny replied honestly.

She couldn't help but smirk. "So Johnny, in this emotional time, when your friend is about to experience absolute metamorphosis – you wonder what is going to happen to his bits?"

With a shrug, Johnny studied Marie. "It's natural – I'm a bloke. Other blokes get it."

With an affectionate nudge, Marie whispered her opinion in his ear. As always, she had impressed him and provided another point of view. "You know at least he doesn't have to work… And here we are - you've taken time out for me and no doubt you're going to need to do something have to bring some money in."

"Don't worry, I have that worked out Johnny. Being a journalist, I always look for stories, and my love, I think that I may have one just good enough for a book."

"If it's about this place - remember to say its fiction. We don't want any more trouble up here!"

Marie nodded. "Don't you worry, I have asked permission and I will explain that on the opening page."

Letting go of Iris's hand, Marty walked with his arms folded over to Nelly. There were a few things necessary to get his head round. He could not get his head round a few things. "Nelly, I just need to ask you something, do you mind? So…"

"It's ney all adding up, is it now? After Megan gave the article to the paper, trouble descended on the village. The villagers called a meeting to make a plan of action. They considered exorcising Megan but the priest could ney do it. He felt responsible for her actions. After the newspaper hit Aberdeen, a sorry situation developed where the hunting started. Men came up with guns and spears to hunt the 'demons' and put them on show. Marty it was cruel what those men intended to do... Men intended to torture the sea people because they didn't understand them or bother asking what they were... As yer know the people of the sea canny die unless they will it to be, so most endured the pain, viciousness and torture..."

"That is terrible," Marty sighed.

"So the people of the sea used their natural defence and mass drowning ensued. We could not take responsibility for such actions, so an agreement between their leader, the local churches and the village elders decided to separate the tribes. The church set a pact that the tribe of the sea stayed in the ocean and the locals remained with the land. The time of choice and transformation was no more. Nature rebelled against logic and some of the younger sea people went against the rules. Secret liaisons continued with selected villagers whose hearts called. As a result, a meeting was called. It was argued that people could not go against nature and if mixing was going to continue, the locals had to wear special necklaces with a sign. Attached to each necklace there was a piece of stone from the stone circle. That is why we are them and they us."

"When a document was found relating to the sea people by some of the higher people in the church, they decided that St. John's was being swayed by demons. In response, they promptly had the place made to ruin. They built a new church in the centre of town to keep the inhabitants central and away from the coves. However, they did ney know that the old church allowed entry to the caves below and that was where the ancient burial grounds were. The burial grounds contain the signs, Marty; the signs of transformation in the oldest language as well as the book of secrets. Their secrets."

It was a lot for Marty to take in, but it made sense.

"They're us and we them- there will never be a time when the two tribes will not be drawn to each other- that is our curse, our burden and our secret. Aye, it is written on the entrance to the crypt in old Doric." Nelly looked sorry for a moment. "Look what happened to the world... It is almost lost because we do ney connect with nature no more... Our hearts are closed and love is consumed. We need to change and to choose to change. We all actively need to transform to be the best we can be. We need to learn to give rather than take and then the world will change."

Marty gazed at Nelly with an expression of shock. "You mean transformation is something we choose?"

Nelly nodded, "now bring it into yer art and share it with the world!" Nelly fished in her pocket and handed Marty three small packages.

"These are a thank you from the village... one for Shana, Marie and yer self. The local children are given them at their christening. It marks a respect to nature and a connection to the tree of life."

Marty stared at the box.

"Well open it then, yer daft neep!"

Marty smiled and carefully peered into his box. Inside was a silver necklace with a sign-

"Yer an honorary villager Marty... And the stone... it's part of the mirror it will keep yer pure." There was a mysterious smile on Nelly's face. There was more to it than that.

"What does the sign mean?" Nelly grinned and patted Marty

"Ah, young man, it is the sign of transformation, transmogrify and metamorphosis. It means different levels of change Marty- and yer have been through transformation, aye yer have. One thing is certain... life shifts and yer have the opportunity to change. The lesson is to adapt to metamorphosis within all the moments you live. Do ney become stagnant or the same. Take every opportunity and follow your heart because it is resonating and calling the unexpected to you!" Holding the necklace in the palm of his hand, Marty turned to the ocean. For the first time in his life, he felt absolutely connected. Anything was possible. If that was the case then it could happen to anyone.

"I think it is time to celebrate the end of a cycle and prepare to welcome the new," said Nelly, waving the group in the direction of the tavern. "Oh and we need to celebrate that Iris found her right man. She was adamant to be alone for eternity rather than with the wrong one…"

"Well, I brewed a new beer in her honour," said Sully proudly. "Mermaid's Bladder Wrack!"

THE END

Printed in Great Britain
by Amazon.co.uk, Ltd.,
Marston Gate.